WARRIOR LORD

NANCY J. COHEN

OGP
ORANGE
GROVE
PRESS

Chapter One

Where else but Las Vegas could a bearded man wearing a cape and sword swagger inside a casino without drawing attention?

Erika Sherwood stared at the man who peered around, a bewildered look on his face until his gaze slammed into hers.

Her heart slowed, as though the world had frozen in that moment. Despite the bells ringing and people chattering and roulette wheels spinning, her awareness narrowed. She couldn't drag her eyes away from his searing glance.

Her pulse jumped when the man strode purposefully in her direction, his cape flapping behind him. With his powerful physique and resolute jawline, he looked like a superhero come to life. She supposed he'd bought that fabulous costume at a store along the Strip.

He claimed the empty seat beside her, exchanged a few words with the blackjack dealer, and set out a pile of chips. Tension charged the air around him. Her sideways glance absorbed his longish black hair and trim beard and the wide breadth of his shoulders. She pulled her skirt down, aware it had hiked up indecently, but his gaze didn't go there. Instead, his dark eyes fixated on her wristwatch.

"Miss?" The dealer's questioning glance fell on her.

"Oh. Hit me, please." She grimaced at the eight of spades she'd drawn. Drat, now she was over the limit.

"Not having any luck?" The newcomer nodded at her diminishing pile of chips. "Maybe this isn't your game."

"Excuse me, mister…?"

"My name is Magnor." He quirked an eyebrow when the waitress came by with another round of free drinks.

Erika lifted her third Viking Volcano from the tray. Who could resist? The fruity drinks were on the house, a popular ploy to keep gamblers in their casino.

She raised her glass in a friendly gesture before taking a sip. "Is Magnor your first name or your last name?"

"It's my only name." His mouth curved as he watched her reaction.

"O-kay." She wasn't in the mood to challenge him. Those drinks had already gone to her head, making her happy to accept his remark along with his blatant stare. Probably half the people in Vegas used false names anyway.

"Do you work here?" she asked, realizing his outfit matched the resort's Nordic theme.

He stiffened. "I should say not. I am a guest, like you."

"Sorry to have asked, but you fit the part."

"It is my customary attire as a warrior of the Tsuran."

"I see," she said in a noncommittal tone. Maybe he was an actor deep into his role. He could be taking a break from a movie set. Were they filming a sequel to *Thor* in the area?

"Nice timepiece you're wearing." He nodded at the object of his scrutiny.

Erika slid her hand under the table. "It was a gift."

Her parents had given her the watch for her sixteenth birthday with the caveat that she ask no questions about its unusual properties. It ran with no visible mechanism and no battery and had a peculiar symbol engraved on its face.

Her forehead wrinkled. Why had Magnor chosen to comment on her watch when most men would offer a line about her flaming red hair or her flashy clothes?

Come on, Erika, why do you care what he thinks? You came here for the art show, remember, and not to meet men?

It must be the alcohol causing that low buzzing sound in her ears and not his imposing presence.

"This announcement is for all of our engaged couples out there," blared a loudspeaker voice. "It's the last call if you want to enter our exciting contest. The lucky winners will be married on live television, after which they'll receive a complimentary stay in our honeymoon suite, fifty thousand dollars, and a new car. Entries are being accepted in the Green Room all day Friday until four o'clock."

"Fifty thousand dollars," Erika muttered. "Man, could I use that money!"

Magnor nudged her, a grin on his face. "Why don't we enter the contest together?"

The smile transformed his features, making her want to study the craggy lines and furrows that made his visage so interesting.

"What?" she said when his words finally registered.

"I need a room, and the hotel is full. If we win, that will solve my problem. You can keep the car and the cash."

"B-But the winners have to get married. On live television."

He waved a hand. "Oh, that. Las Vegas is all about fantasy, is it not?"

Her eyes widened. "You mean, the wedding will be filmed like a reality show, but it isn't real?"

He winked at her. "All of the contestants get bonus credits on their club cards. What have we got to lose?"

Erika stared at her diminished pile of chips. She'd lost two hundred dollars in less than an hour.

She scooped the remaining credits into her purse while considering the man's outrageous suggestion.

In her earlier days, she'd have accepted his proposal without a second thought. Back then nothing had mattered except her plants, her pottery, and her own pleasure.

Eventually, she'd erected an armor of self-discipline around herself so she could accomplish her goals. However, this resolve had evaporated under the influence of the drinks and the man's piercing gaze. Who wouldn't want a hunk like him as her fake fiancé?

Her head spinning, she wondered how a few cocktails could affect her so strongly. She'd been better able to hold her liquor in the past. Was there something else in those fruity drinks that made her so amenable?

Ignoring the warning bells in her mind, she scraped back her chair. Her knees wobbled when she stood. Magnor rose and steadied her with a firm grasp on her elbow.

"I accept your offer," she told him with bravado. "If we lose, at least we'll be ahead by several credits. And it might be fun."

"We should seal the deal if we are to play an engaged couple," Magnor said, closing the distance between them.

His head descended before she could protest, and his lips met hers. The pressure of his mouth electrified her and left her breathless. When he stepped away, she staggered.

He gripped her arm and guided her along. "This way, my lady. I believe the Green Room is just past that shiny black Jaguar on the rotating platform."

She let him steer her, berating herself for not heading toward the exhibit hall instead.

Then again, she'd already set up her booth for the art show on Saturday, so there wasn't much else for her to do the rest of today. She deserved a break, especially since this was the only getaway she could afford for the year.

When she'd wandered into the casino earlier, she'd quickly forgotten her purpose. The free drinks and enticing games had tempted her to relax and enjoy the resort amenities. Tomorrow would be time enough to get back to business.

People jostled them as they hurried along. Allowing the caped man to hustle her past the flashing lights and dinging sounds of the slot machines, she breathed in a deep breath of cooled air. Thankfully, this was a non-smoking casino. She hated the places where clouds of smoke pervaded the atmosphere.

Viking-garbed attendants stood at attention at various entrances, most of the men having deformed features like they all went to the same makeup artist. Mythological lore being the theme of the resort, she didn't find it odd. Instead, tipsy from the cocktails, she gauged their appearance to be appropriately troll-like. Their beady eyes watched her as she moved through the throng.

In the Green Room, an elevated dais held an arched canopy decorated with white tulle and tiny white lights. A pair of contestants sat in chairs on stage while their interview was filmed for broadcast. Wearing a portable microphone, an official questioned them. He had on an emerald robe more suitable to the Wizard of Oz. Why not? In Vegas, all was flash and little was substance. People expected weirdness.

Grabbing her hand, Magnor rushed forward as a clerk behind a corner desk called for final entries.

"Picture IDs and sixty dollars cash, please," the clerk said as their turn came in line. He had them fill out and sign several forms each. "There, you're all set if you win. Take this number and wait over there." His gesture indicated a queue of other hopefuls.

Erika's stomach turned cartwheels as they advanced. How would she answer those questions the official was asking? *How long have you known your fiancé? Where did you two meet? What made you know you were right for each other?*

Her frightened glance met Magnor's laser-beam gaze. He touched her lips with a gentle forefinger.

"Do not worry. Say whatever comes to mind. It'll be the right thing."

As she gazed into his mesmerizing eyes, she felt an irresistible compulsion to learn more about him. His slate gray irises glinted under her observation. She glanced away, discomfited by the reaction he aroused in her. They were strangers, and yet something sizzled between them.

Whoever this man was and for whatever reason he showed interest in her, she acted like putty in his hands. Since clay was her medium for sculpting, that said a lot.

It said more than she wanted, truth be told.

She approached the steps to the dais with trepidation after

the official, Dennis Slate, called their names. Was it her imagination, or was the crowd of observers thickening around them? More of the hefty attendants moved to strategic locations at the perimeter of the room, their abnormally large ears and long noses making her wonder if they were related.

Her pulse leapt when a pretty blonde grasped her forearm. The buzzing sound in her ears increased to painful decibels.

"Be sure to stop by the Longhouse Restaurant for a complimentary breakfast buffet in the morning," the lady said in a sugary tone. Her cold blue eyes sent a chill skittering along Erika's spine.

She withdrew her arm, her skin tingling where the woman had touched her. "Sure, I'll do that."

The blonde turned to Magnor at her side and made him the same offer. He snatched his arm away as though he'd been burned. His face flushed, and his mouth tightened. With a slight shove at Erika's back, he hastened her along, but not before she'd caught the flash of alarm in his eyes.

****

Sweat popped out on Magnor's brow. Great Cosmos, that had been close. If he hadn't kissed the fiery-haired Earth woman, he might have been confounded by now. Once spellbound to the Trolleks, he'd have been forced to join their sleeper army of mind slaves.

Hopefully, they didn't recognize him as one of the Drift Lords. He considered himself a team member even though his status was provisional. And while he lacked the unique genetic trait that his fellow warriors possessed, this difference might be what kept him off the enemy's radar. At least, Magnor hoped the Trolleks regarded him as another weak human.

Unfortunately, he'd run out of the elixir from his home world that had protected him from the Trollek mind spell, and since he'd been banished from his land, chances of getting any more were nil. Either he had to resort to the painful means used by the other Drift Lords for immunity, or he'd have to taste his lady's lips on a regular basis. Erika Sherwood had no idea of the power she held or of her role in the ancient prophecy.

Magnor didn't realize she'd be in the casino when he had stepped inside. His mission was to obtain the sacred Book of Odin. Supposedly, the ancient text mentioned a weapon that could defeat the Trolleks. He'd received a tip that a clue to the text's location was hidden at the resort.

The beasts roamed everywhere in the casino. Their alluring females passed around free drinks while their disguised troops made sure none of the humans strayed to forbidden areas.

He wondered where their recruitment center was situated. Doubtless this resort had one, like other tourist attractions commandeered by the invaders. He could explore later, once he and Erika had won this game and settled into the newlywed suite.

Her wristwatch had identified her as one of the six Earth women in the prophecy. Instinct must have drawn him to her. Now she'd become a target for the enemy, since his arrival may have activated her dormant power. Once they went upstairs, he could set up a protective perimeter in their room.

It was imperative she marry him for her own safety. Magnor regretted the trick he was playing on her, but she'd understand the necessity for it later. If not, he'd risk her ire.

She could divorce him after the threat to their worlds had been resolved. In the meantime, she'd have to rely on him to keep her safe, at least until she learned her role. Her participation was crucial to the success of his team's mission.

With an insistent pressure on her spine, he urged her onto the dais where their fate together would be sealed.

****

"Tell me, Miss Sherwood, how did you meet your fiancé? Oh, and where's your ring, dear one?"

Dennis Slate, the justice of the peace, peered at her with a kindly expression. He sported a white goatee that matched his sparse hair. The years had etched fine lines onto his tanned visage and around his firm mouth. He had a mole on one upper cheek and wispy eyebrows.

"I-I left my ring in our room safe," she said in a hesitant tone. "I didn't know we'd be entering the contest."

"I see." His eyes twinkled while the cameraman aimed his portable lens at them. "And your first meet?"

She cast a frantic glance at Magnor, seated reassuringly at her side. He grasped her hand in his large palm and gave her an encouraging smile. For an instant, it looked as though his eyes glowed, but it must have been a reflection of light from the overhead chandelier.

Now where would she meet a hunk like him in real life? A logical answer popped into her mind.

"We met at an art gallery. I have an exhibit in the show starting here tomorrow. I run a pottery studio in my hometown."

Dennis's brows twitched upward. "How did you get his attention? Was he interested in your work?"

Magnor leaned over to address the man. "Actually, I was there on behalf of my sister. I'm not into art myself, you see. But Sis couldn't go, so she asked me to, er—"

Erika caught his fumble. "To pick up a brochure on my classes for children," she finished, offering the camera a beaming smile. "I love working with kids. If we win today, I'll use my portion of the money to get an education degree so I can teach arts and crafts to special needs children."

"That's an admirable goal." Dennis tilted his head. "But tell us more about you and your fiancé."

Her pulse raced under his keen glance. "We liked each other on first sight. He asked me out, and we went to dinner at a Mexican place."

"Very good." Dennis signaled to an assistant, who handed Magnor a placard and a black marker. "Sir, please write your answers to those questions on the other side of the card. We'll see how well your fiancé knows your tastes."

Erika's gut twisted. Now surely, they'd be unmasked as frauds.

When Magnor was done, he handed the card over to the emcee.

"Miss, give us your responses, please. We'll start with the easy ones. Your fiancé's favorite ice cream flavor?"

Oh, gosh. Her preference was chocolate, but what would he like? Squinting at his costume, she compared him to Robin Hood, a nobleman turned woodsman out of necessity. Was Magnor's background similar in any way?

"Strawberry," she blurted on a whim.

The emerald-robed official beamed at her. "Score one! Next, briefs or boxers?"

Her gaze widened. "Uh, briefs." She didn't dare look Magnor in the eye. Heat suffused her cheeks as the erotic image of him in the aforementioned undergarment came to mind.

"Right, again. Where was he born?"

How would she answer that question without any clue as to his origins? Wait, another place where a costumed character might go unnoticed popped into her head.

"Orlando, Florida."

Dennis's startled gaze met hers. Clearly, he hadn't expected her to get that right.

"Location of a birthmark?"

Color warmed her skin. "His butt."

How did she know that? Was he beaming the answers directly into her brain? A tantalizing fantasy distracted her from that thought. Without his voluminous cape, linen shirt, and dark trousers, what would he look like? All rippled muscles and lean, hard body? Man, she'd bet he looked good in the buff.

Dennis didn't reveal her score. "Thing he most hates about his job?"

She squirmed in her chair, conscious of the hot stage lights aimed at them and the surrounding throng. A cacophony of background noise from the nearby casino competed with the low buzzing in her head. Her upper lip beaded with sweat. She shouldn't have consumed all those drinks.

"Can you repeat the question?" she asked.

Agreeing to this farce had been a bad idea. They'd never win. And—oh, God—what if someone from home saw her on television? This would totally confirm her family's opinion that she was too flighty to ever settle down.

Her mind absorbed what Dennis had said. "He dislikes having to depend on others," she replied with an assertion she didn't feel. She supposed a man like Magnor would take pride in his accomplishments, although she didn't have the slightest idea what he did for a living.

A depressing thought crossed her mind. The man could be a boring accountant from New Jersey or a farmer from Nebraska, for all she knew. She'd never suit him in either case. But then, he'd have to be a bodybuilder as well. No one could fake the way his chest stretched the fabric of his clothes, or the way his hand hovered over his sword as though he knew how to use it.

"Let me in!" a portly fellow shouted from the doorway. He barged his way inside past the attendants. "Listen to me! This is all a ruse. You're in grave danger. Don't let these monsters take you downstairs!"

As the bouncers approached him, he dodged them and sped toward the dais. A blond woman carrying a tray of drinks stuck out her foot and tripped him. As he toppled over, costumed male employees grabbed him and hauled him away. The gaping crowd parted to allow them passage.

What had that been about? Erika's thoughts scattered as Dennis grinned into the camera.

"Don't mind him, folks. He's merely another zealous fan. Let's finish this contest. Erika, here's the next question."

She stumbled through the rest of her responses, then stood aside with Magnor and the other contestants until the last couples had their turn. The robed official rambled on about the resort into the camera until another woman brought him an envelope with the tally from online viewers.

Erika frowned. She hadn't noticed before, but all of the female servers were blonde and beautiful. Why was that? To counter the ugly faces of their male co-workers?

Dennis flourished the opened envelope, diverting her attention. "And the winners are, Erika Sherwood and her partner, Mr. Magnor!"

Erika spun around as wild applause sounded in her ears. What? They had won?

Magnor pounded her on the back. "I knew we would do it. Congratulations!" He turned her toward him and planted a triumphant kiss on her lips. The crowd cheered louder.

"Miss, we have to get you ready for the wedding," Dennis said with an indulgent smile. "Please follow Sylvia to the alcove where we have a stylist ready to dress you."

A young teen showed up at her elbow. "This way, lady." When Magnor stepped forward to accompany her, Sylvia held up a hand to stop him. "You're not allowed to see the bride again until the ceremony. Wait here."

"What about the rest of our prizes?" Magnor said to Dennis as she strode away.

Erika's temples throbbed, and her gut churned. She needed food to settle her stomach, although she suspected it was upset more from nerves than from hunger. The nuptials might be a show for the broadcast audience, but the idea made her quake. Or maybe it was the after-effect of those cocktails she'd consumed.

She tottered after the girl, who wore a long blond braid down her back. They went behind a partition, and Erika gasped. A rack of wedding dresses stood by the wall, along with a dressing table stocked with hair implements and cosmetics.

The stylist introduced herself before instructing Erika to select a gown in her size.

"Have a seat," the woman said after she'd made her selection. "I'll fix your hair and makeup."

Once she was prepped, Erika donned the strapless white satiny gown she'd chosen. Her eyes misted as she regarded herself in the mirror. The sleek design complemented her figure, but it wasn't her appearance that made her teary-eyed.

She'd been a bridesmaid so many times that it seemed as though her own chances of wearing a wedding dress someday were nil. Adam, her latest boyfriend, had validated that belief when he'd left her in the dust. Her ambitions seemed to chase men away, but she wasn't about to give up her dreams in exchange for a wedding ring.

At least, not until now, but this marriage wasn't real.

"You look beautiful," Sylvia said after the stylist settled a short gauzy veil on her head. The teenaged girl drew Erika aside. "Here, take this." She held out a shiny gold-colored ring. "Put it on your man. Make sure he wears it all the time."

"Thank you." Erika took the ring, puzzled to feel its weight in her palm. Was it real gold?

Sylvia gripped her arm. "Tell him this talisman will protect him against the coming darkness."

The stylist approached, and Sylvia vanished around a corner before Erika could ask her what she'd meant.

"Miss, here's your bouquet. It's time to go." The woman thrust a flower arrangement into Erika's hands.

As Erika followed the woman, she noted a red carpet had been rolled down the aisle toward the dais. Cameras aimed at her, and a wedding march blasted from the speaker system. She resisted the urge to press a hand to her aching temples. Man, those drinks must have been strong.

Magnor waited for her under the canopy where myriads of tiny lights twinkled. He looked proud and tall, an unreadable expression on his face as he watched her step forward. His cape swung behind him, making him look like an avenging god with his impressive height and sword.

She took her place at his side and together they faced Dennis. The official had exchanged his emerald robe for a somber black garment. He held an open book in his hands. Dennis began the brief ceremony, his words bypassing her brain as she stood rooted in place, immobilized by the rapid pace of events.

"With the power invested in me by the State of Nevada and the city of Las Vegas, I now pronounce you man and wife. You may kiss the bride."

Erika's head whirled. Not even fifteen minutes must have gone by. Was this what passed for a Las Vegas wedding?

What a sham. She supposed that every minute they were on the air, it cost money.

Magnor's head descended, and he pressed his mouth to hers. As far as the TV viewers were concerned, they'd been married. The exchange of rings had felt real. She wondered who'd given him the one he'd slid onto her finger. Dennis, most likely.

The ruddy-faced official shook their hands, gave Magnor the key to the honeymoon suite, and said their car would be available for pickup from the valet. As for the cash, it was theirs for the taking. He handed them a large-sized signed check made out to Mr. and Mrs. Magnor.

"Oh, and one more thing," Dennis said. "I'll need your signatures on these documents, please. It's simply a formality, but we do need permission for the resort to use your likenesses for publicity. These papers also include transfer of title to the car, tax forms and such."

Erika signed with a shaky hand. In her frazzled state, she couldn't be bothered to read the details.

Magnor followed suit, then grasped her hand in his and raised it in the air. The watching throng cheered loudly.

"That's it then, wife." His low, rumbly voice broke through the haze in her head. "You're mine now."

Chapter Two

The next few hours sucked Erika into a whirlwind of activity. Foremost on her mind was depositing the money they had won. After arranging for the parking valet to transfer their new Toyota Highlander—or rather, her vehicle since she'd taken title—to the parking garage, she set up a wire transfer for the funds. It would take a couple of days to settle, but that was to be expected. She just hoped the casino made good on their word.

"You can use the honeymoon suite." She faced Magnor in the busy hotel lobby. "I already have a room here."

"Oh, no." His brows drew together like a line of thunderclouds. "We stay together, my bride. Otherwise, the resort might revoke our privileges."

From the firm set of his mouth, Erika gathered he wouldn't accept a negative response. Besides, he had a point.

"All right. I suppose we should play the part for a few more days. I'll have my luggage transferred." She made the arrangements at the front desk, pushing aside her unease.

What did she know about the man, anyway? He could be a sociopathic murderer for all she knew. They'd been perfect strangers up until a few hours ago.

He gripped her elbow as though realizing she needed convincing. "Look, we may be in danger. I'm concerned about protecting you, not bringing you harm."

It was true that people who recognized them as the winning couple might try to take advantage. And didn't the honeymoon suite come with room service credit?

She glared at him. "Fine, I'll go along with you, but don't expect me to share the bedroom. Our marriage is a farce."

He stiffened and stepped back, releasing her. "You needn't worry about my intentions. Let's go upstairs."

"Wait, I should check on my exhibit first to make sure I haven't forgotten anything."

Lines creased between his eyes. "What do you mean?"

"Remember I said I'm in town for an art show? It starts tomorrow, and I have a booth there."

She strode toward the exit that led toward the conference center. Her scalp prickled. Were they being watched? Why had he said they might be in danger?

People stood about in clusters, chatting with drinks in hand. As she and Magnor passed through the casino, heads turned their way. No doubt their notoriety had spread quickly, and that's what he'd meant. Or maybe it was Magnor's costume that drew unwanted attention. He should change into street clothes.

Come to think of it, where was *his* luggage?

Ding, ding, ding went the slot machines. Roulette wheels whirred. Dice hit the soft padding on the craps tables. A pleasant citrus scent pervaded the air while attendants with trays full of free cocktails roamed among the patrons.

She heaved a sigh of relief when they left the casino and entered the conference wing. The exhibit hall was down a long corridor past a number of breakout rooms. Magnor gestured to hasten her along. Impatience stamped his features.

Inside the show confines, exhibitors schmoozed as they set about fixing their wares. On the way to her booth, she passed by displays of wind chimes, beaded jewelry, pottery, and paintings of desert landscapes. She rushed forward toward her space, glad to find all as she'd left it.

"You make these creations?" Magnor examined the goods arranged on her tables, peering at the hand-painted sculptures of fantasy subjects with blatant curiosity.

"Yes, I've always been drawn to modeling in clay. Oh, I can

do the usual bowls and vases, and my studio offers them, but these forms call to me."

"You portray the Trolleks."

"Who?"

He pointed to her collection of trolls, short ugly figures with large bellies, long noses, and bad teeth. They were a sharp contrast to her winged fairies, dainty creatures with tiny pointed ears and sari-colored clothes.

"These ugly beasts that you create are similar to the Trolleks you met inside the casino, except real ones don't have an ounce of fat on them. They are muscled warriors and a lot taller."

"I don't know what you're talking about." Hmm, her products did bear an uncanny resemblance to some of those ugly bouncers. It must be coincidence.

She adjusted the line-up a bit and straightened her banner before chatting briefly with her neighbors. When she glanced up, Magnor was gone.

She found him further along the aisle, speaking to a wood carver. She'd never seen his face so animated.

"But how do you inlay these different colors?" he asked the artist.

"The coloring is due to certain stains I use. You have to apply them very carefully."

"So I see. Remarkable work."

"Thanks, fella. What do you do?"

"Oh, I've whittled away at figures like these, but my efforts are amateurish. I wish you luck with your sales."

"You make wood carvings?" As they headed out, Erika couldn't help pursuing the subject.

Magnor shrugged his broad shoulders. "I used to pass the time carving animals as a hobby, but it's nothing."

"Where are you from?" Did he live near the woods or in a rural setting?

"Let's not talk about it right now." His lips compressed as though she'd hit upon a touchy subject.

Silence weighed heavily between them as they took the elevator to Erika's floor so she could pack her bag. En route, she reminded herself how this awkward situation had landed her a new car and cash.

"Give me your key," Magnor said at her door. "I'll check inside to make sure it's safe before you enter."

She bristled. "Listen, mister. That costume must be affecting your brain. You need to change into something less conspicuous. Where did you leave your suitcase?"

"Downstairs. I'll get my equipment once you're secure."

"It's silly to wait for the bellhop to transfer my stuff. We can do it, and then you can turn in the key while you're in the lobby."

Twenty minutes later, they entered the honeymoon suite. While Magnor lifted her bag into the bedroom, she surveyed the accommodations. Her jaw dropped. Never mind the palatial marble, the silk-lined walls, and the gold-trimmed ceiling panels. They had a freaking whole apartment.

"Omigod, look at this view." She stepped over to the wide picture window and peered at the city. The sun had set, and lights glittered like jewels scattered against dark velvet.

Turning, she noted the fully equipped bar. A frosty pitcher stood on its glossy granite top. Was that the Viking Volcano mixture? She strode over, took a sniff of the pink liquid inside, and then poured herself a glassful. Imagine that, they had their own supply of free drinks.

Magnor explored the bedroom and bath. She heard banging noises, as though he were opening and closing interior doors.

"What are you doing?" she called, licking her lips after downing a drink. Man, she'd been thirsty. These concoctions tasted so good. She should have another. It wouldn't do to get dehydrated.

"I'm performing a routine search," Magnor hollered. "Make yourself comfortable. I'll be out in a minute."

"Sure. I can order dinner. What do you want?" Where was the room service menu? Her stomach growled, reminding her she'd been running on empty except for the drinks.

"Doesn't matter. You can choose."

Soon after she'd called in a meal order, a knock sounded on the door. She hurried over to respond, expecting the bellboy wanting to know if she'd retrieved her belongings.

Instead, the justice of the peace stood grinning at her. He wore a navy blazer, looking like an ordinary businessman.

"I'm so sorry to disturb you, Mrs. Magnor, but I need your mailing address."

"I thought I'd filled out the papers for the taxing authorities."

"Yes, you did, and I forgot to copy your address from there before we sent it off. This one is so we can mail you the original marriage certificate and instructions on obtaining certified copies."

Erika nearly swallowed her tongue. "What?"

He gave her a kindly look as though he expected newlyweds to act confused. "The marriage is duly recorded in our city registers, but you'll need documentation to change your name in your home state. Your address, please?" He poised a pen over a notepad.

Erika supplied an automatic answer while her mind reeled. After thanking the man, she shut the door with a bang.

"Magnor, we need to talk." She strode purposefully toward the bedroom.

He didn't respond, not to her at least. As she approached, she heard him speaking in a low rumble. He stood with his back toward her, facing a wide window where he'd drawn the drapes.

"I believe she is one of the six," he said aloud.

Was he on speakerphone? Erika didn't see him holding a cell. And was he talking about her?

"That is good news, but do not allow yourself to be distracted from your mission," another man's voice said.

"Aye, sire. I intend to conduct my search tonight. Winning that contest gave me the perfect cover, although I fear my presence may have endangered the lady. It's possible her vector device has been activated."

"If so, make haste."

"What news do you have about Kaj? Was your rescue mission successful?"

The other man gave a low chuckle. "Kaj didn't need our help escaping from the Trolleks. He'll tell you about his adventures later, but be reassured that he's safe."

Erika coughed, and Magnor spun around. "I have to go. I'll check in again later." He pressed something on his wrist and then stood mute, glaring at her.

"Would you care to explain that conversation?"

His lips tightened, his gaze not leaving hers. "I was speaking to a colleague on my comm unit."

"Oh, right, like on freaking *Star Trek*. Tell me, why did the justice of the peace knock on our door and ask for my home address to send us our marriage certificate?" Her voice rose along with a twinge of hysteria.

"I imagine he'll need to send us the proper documents." Magnor strode forward, put his arm around her waist and led her toward the living area. His gaze lifted to the bar and the half-empty pitcher. "You did not ingest more of that drink, did you?"

"I might have had a glassful. I'm hungry. Our meal is on the way." She pinched her nose while her thoughts tumbled and rolled. What had she asked him?

"Sit down." He guided her to the couch. "I need to go retrieve my bag. If the waiter arrives, do not open the door. Have him leave the food outside."

Erika laid her head on the throw pillow and closed her eyes. That drink had done a number on her. It must have been stronger than the ones they offered downstairs.

She dozed briefly. When she awoke, Magnor was setting up some poles around the perimeter of their suite. Their food had arrived, and he had already prepared the dining table with napkins and utensils.

Seeing she was awake, he reheated their meals in the microwave while she used the bathroom. Man, she looked a mess. Staring into the mirror, she noted her bleary green eyes and curly shoulder-length hair. The stage makeup gave her face an unnatural pallor and a greasy sheen.

And why was she still wearing her borrowed wedding gown? Heat flushed her face as she remembered the visit from the justice of the peace. She'd have to return the dress tomorrow.

Meanwhile, a change of clothes would boost her confidence and make her feel more in control. She veered into the bedroom to retrieve her cosmetics kit.

It felt good to scrub her skin clean. She went easy on the makeup, applying a light smattering of neutral powder that barely hid her freckles, a smidgen of blush, and a swipe of lip gloss. Then she donned the little black dress she'd brought for the artists' reception tomorrow night. It seemed appropriate to wear this evening, although she didn't want to give Magnor the wrong idea.

Then again, maybe she could use her feminine wiles to distract him while asking questions about his background.

In the dining room, Magnor sat at the table buttering a roll. When he spied her approach, he dropped the bread on his plate and leapt to his feet. He held out her chair while she smiled inwardly. And here she'd thought chivalry no longer existed.

She had ordered grilled salmon, broccoli, and rice pilaf, preferring to keep things simple even though lobster had tempted her on the menu. Magnor politely offered her the breadbasket.

"No, thanks. I have to watch my weight, and I'm sure there are enough calories in those sweet drinks to exceed my carb allowance for the week."

"As you wish."

"Listen, I don't believe our wedding was a sham."

****

Magnor watched her with narrowed eyes, wondering if she'd succumb to hysterics once she learned the truth. He could always feed her more of that blasted drink. It made people compliant, so the Trolleks could confound them. His bride knew nothing of the dangers here.

"Will you seek an annulment?" he asked, aware of the legalities.

Her gaze clouded, as though that possibility hadn't entered her mind. "Having a husband wasn't in my game plan, but now that I have you, you might prove useful."

"Useful?"

"Uh, huh." She gave him a sly smile that stole his reason. Impish dimples creased her cheeks, and a look of wicked delight entered her eyes.

His passion ignited as he imagined bedding his bride. That dress exposed her cleavage, and his gaze inadvertently strayed to the valley between her breasts. Her lush figure had already been evident in the scandalous outfit she'd worn earlier that exposed her midriff.

His glance rose to her face where she wore a knowing smirk. He'd like to kiss it right off her ripe, tempting lips.

When she moistened her mouth with her tongue, sliding it from one end of her lower lip to the other, his loins surged in response. Great Cosmos, he'd be hard pressed to resist her charms while in such close quarters.

But why was she changing her tune? She'd made it clear he was to sleep on the couch. Had she accepted their marriage as real? What had she meant by saying he could be useful?

As soon as he finished his meal, he shoved to his feet and paced the room. If he didn't know better, he'd suspect her of being a Trollek female sent to seduce him. But that was impossible. She wore the wristwatch and knew nothing of his mission.

She patted her mouth with a napkin and then rose. Her hips swaying, she sauntered toward him.

"I'd like to get to know you better, husband." Standing in front of him, she splayed her hands on his shoulders.

Now that he'd put up their defensive perimeter, he had

doffed his cape and sword. He stood before her in his black shirt and belted pants.

"Is that so?"

"Where are you from? Why are you in Vegas?"

"I have work to do."

"What sort of work?"

He liked how her pert little nose had a stubborn tilt. "I suppose you could say I'm in security."

"How so?"

"Protective services." Let her assume what she wished.

"So why are you here? To meet with a prospective client?"

"No, I need to find something."

"Oh, you search for missing items, or people?"

"Depends on the case. And you ask too many questions."

He gazed down at her, fascinated by her arresting green eyes. His hands fixed themselves in her hair, a wild mass of flame-colored tresses. A creature like her was totally foreign to him. The women in his tribe had brown hair and eyes. None of them would behave so willfully.

Or so he'd thought. His jaw clenched as he remembered the reason why he'd joined the Drift Lords in their mission to save Earth. Cast out of his home in disgrace, he could never return. And it was all because he'd been betrayed.

Women aren't to be trusted, remember?

He wanted to push away from his bride, but something compelled him to remain. His fingers ruffled her silken hair, and he leaned forward to sniff her fragrance. She smelled like lavender and soap. He hadn't realized he'd drawn her closer.

The softness of her body and her uplifted face broke his resolve.

He lowered his head and kissed her. He'd expected her to resist, but instead she wrapped her arms around his neck. His tongue flicked out, demanding entrance, and she opened to him. He thrust inside, claiming her for his own. His palm cupped her head for support, as he lost himself in a web of desire.

He drank from her sweetness like a man dying from thirst.

A doubt niggled in his brain. If she shared Nira Larsen's traits, she wasn't so far removed genetically from the Trolleks as he wanted to believe. If so, how much of her allure was due to that inherent influence, and how much was due to free will?

Then again, if she truly was one of the Earth women in the prophecy, she had a destined mate. Was he that man? Were they meant to be together?

It was too soon to know. And regardless of why she appealed to him, he had a mission to accomplish.

With a growl of self-disgust, he thrust her away. "I'm sorry. I didn't mean to—"

"Don't apologize. We *are* married."

He drew himself upright. "You made it quite clear that our married state is in name only. Or have you changed your mind?"

"Certainly not. Don't let this lapse fool you. It won't happen again."

She must realize she'd need him for protection. Perhaps that's what she meant by his usefulness. And so she would, until this land was safe from the invading horde.

Or maybe she was afraid to lose the cash prize if she cast him aside too quickly.

She poked him in the chest. "I thought we were playacting for the TV cameras, but you knew our ceremony was real. Why did you trick me?"

"I needed a room for the night, remember? And you wanted the money and the car."

"Oh, right. And you expect me to believe that's your only reason? What's really in this for you?" She stared him down, while he compressed his mouth.

"We'll discuss it later. I have to find the object I'd mentioned." Magnor turned his back on her and strode into the bedroom where he'd tossed his cape and sword. He made swift work of putting them back on.

Erika trailed after him, a pout on her impish face. "Where are you going?"

He suppressed a grimace of annoyance. "There's a historical exhibit upstairs I want to visit."

"Aren't the attractions closed by now?"

His gaze drifted to a curl of hair that licked her face. "That won't be a problem."

"I'll come with you. You are not leaving me alone in here on our wedding night." She grabbed her handbag, slung the strap over her shoulder, and stood her ground.

"You are safe in this room. No one can vector in to harm you. It's dangerous where I'm going."

"I have no idea what you mean, but you're the one who's in danger if you think you can desert me, buddy." She jabbed a finger in the air. "You're stuck with me, for better or for worse. Get used to it."

Chapter Three

"This is amazing." Erika surveyed the replica of an early Nordic village on the fourteenth floor of the Viking Vegas Resort. It looked incredibly realistic, from the thatched roof structures to the wax figures inhabiting the town.

Magnor had easily bypassed the locked doors and security measures to gain them entrance. The museum was closed at nine o'clock in the evening, although the casino, shops, and restaurants were going full blast downstairs.

Vegas was a city that never slept except perhaps in the early morning hours when people passed out drunk in their hotel rooms. Or else they quit gambling by then because they'd lost too much money at the gaming tables.

Like so many others before her, she'd come to Las Vegas to make her dreams come true. If she took home a prize from the art show, it would validate her work.

As the youngest of three sisters, Erika had to constantly strive to earn her family's regard. That need often took her down a path that made her parents despair for her future. After years of flitting from one job to another, she finally knew what she wanted. Coming here had been one step in that direction. She didn't intend to let Magnor, or anyone else, distract her.

Yet her gaze kept being drawn to his tall figure and noble profile, to his caped presence and lethal sword. He hadn't taken kindly to her suggestion to ditch the costume. And now her response to his kiss had probably given him the wrong impression. Damn, she'd meant to keep her distance. But why had he pulled away?

Maybe it was just her bad luck with men. Her last boyfriend had gotten skittish when she'd mentioned her plans. Adam didn't understand why she wanted to earn a college degree when she already had a business in the pottery studio. She'd thought he would be happy about her new goals, but apparently not. He'd liked her better as a free spirit. Her family wasn't used to her being a responsible adult, either. That's why Granddaddy had put those strings on her trust fund.

She raked her fingers through her corkscrew hair, hoping Magnor didn't have a low opinion of her.

"What are you looking for?" she asked in a soft tone, leery of surveillance equipment that might detect their presence.

He regarded the replicated street ahead of them. "I seek a document with lettering like the symbols on your watch."

"My watch? What does that have to do with anything?"

"The engraving is a runic inscription." He took a rectangular device from his pocket and panned it around. "We haven't deactivated all of the security measures. Laser beams are dead ahead."

"What is that thing?" She pointed to his hand-held gizmo.

"It's a PIP. Portable Intel Platform. The embedded sensors have an array of functions."

He pocketed the unit and withdrew a pouch. From inside the small bag, he scooped a fine powder and blew it outward from his open palm. A cloud of particles sprayed forward, revealing a maze of green lines crisscrossing the main street.

"Oh, great." She felt like a burglar in a movie. "Now what? I suppose you have a way to circumvent those beams?"

His skills were quite varied, she was beginning to realize. Who did he work for? Was he part of an art recovery unit? And how did he know her watch held runic writing?

He eyed the facades of houses lining both sides of the wood-planked village street. Braziers on posts burned faux fires along the route. In the absence of overhead lighting, the illumination not only was necessary for visitors, but it also lent a touch of authenticity in its design. How odd that the staff kept the lighting on at night after the exhibit closed, though.

At any other time, she might have liked to explore the full-scale structures and the merchant stands. The smell of peat smoke permeated the air, immersing her in the scene. So did the life-like recreations of its inhabitants. She studied the wax figures with fascination, wondering how she could use this resource as an inspiration for her clay models.

The men wore linen shirts and wool trousers fastened by a drawstring. Over this went a long-sleeved tunic with a leather belt. Some of the guys wore cloaks pinned over one shoulder, leaving their sword arms free. Leather boots covered their feet.

Her gaze slid to Magnor, whose shoulder-length ebony hair had two fine braids framing each side of his face, presumably to keep his vision clear, like many of these residents. Magnor's trim beard was black while theirs were fair. Aside from that major difference, with his cape and powerful figure, he could easily pass for a Viking warrior.

The women wore linen or wool dresses, over which they had on a tunic tied with straps at their shoulders. Chains hung from brooches that helped secure the straps in place. These chains held tools such as tweezers, combs, and scissors. Shawls or cloaks completed their attire. They all had long flaxen hair, either braided or flowing from a top knot on their heads.

"This way." Magnor pushed open the nearest door, which led into one of the replicated homes. He stood aside so she could pass through first. His white teeth looked brilliant in the dim lighting as he grinned at her.

Her heart soared at the warmth in his eyes. She'd done the right thing in coming with him, even though he had protested.

He used his device to scan the interior of the simple dwelling. A stone-lined hearth shielded fire for cooking, while a hole in the roof provided an escape route for smoke. Straw covered the earthen floor. One tiny window in the opposite wall was shuttered against gales that might rage outside.

Oil lamps and candles stood ready to be lit as though the family had just stepped outside. Beds consisted of wooden platforms along each side wall, furs and blankets tossed on top. In one corner, a loom stood for making cloth. A long table sat in the center, doubtless serving multiple purposes.

Magnor gestured to her. "I suspect the lasers are positioned along the main street. If we go out the window and keep to the rear of the structures, we might avoid the beams."

The window lacked glass when he unlatched the shutter. Speaking of back ends, she got a nice view of his tight butt as he slung his cape over one arm and hoisted himself toward the narrow space. He squeezed through the aperture with a grunt.

At her turn, Erika grabbed a nearby crate and used it to access the height. Hoping her makeshift footstool wouldn't slide out from under her, she wriggled her head and shoulders past the threshold. Maneuvering her hips past the window's edges was more of a challenge.

Reversing direction, she gripped the frame and dangled in mid-air. Her arm muscles strained from the burden of supporting her weight.

"Drop down," Magnor urged. "It's not far. I'll catch you."

A whoosh of air escaped her lungs as she let go. His muscular arms caught her and eased her to the ground. Erika stepped away and dusted herself off, while considering that her yoga workouts and Zumba dance classes didn't do enough to keep her in shape. She'd better add more muscle toning to her fitness routine.

"This way." Magnor turned on his heel and assumed a steady pace weaving through the narrow alley.

Less than five minutes later, they halted at the far end of the village street and at the entrance to a traveling exhibit.

Magnor's scanner showed a clear path ahead in terms of lasers. They proceeded with caution into a section that held glass-cased displays like in a museum. Explanatory plaques described each relic. Scrolled along the walls were lengthy history lessons.

She pointed to a camera mounted on the ceiling at the next bend. "The security staff will see us on their surveillance video."

He gave her an oblique glance. "No, they won't. Come and hold my hand." He twisted something on his belt buckle.

Her eyes narrowing, she complied. Wondering what his action had accomplished, she matched his stride. His cape flapped in the air-cooled hall as they ranged from one display to another.

Erika barely had time to absorb the items under glass cases: swords and axes, cooking implements, pottery, jewelry, and hair ornaments. At the end of the hall, which opened into another, was a full-length replica of a Viking ship.

"Awesome!" She let go of his hand, meaning to study the vessel, but he yanked her back.

"Stay with me. My invisibility belt only works for you if we maintain contact."

Erika stared at him. "Your *what*?"

His grip tightened. "The technology transmits visual information about our surroundings through the fibers of my clothing, so it seems as though we're not here. We disappear into the background. Please tell no one about this device. It's proprietary to my, uh, company."

She felt privileged that he'd shared something confidential with her. "Whatever you say, husband."

His nostrils flared. "Do not believe our status gives you the right to plunder my secrets. If you even think about betraying me, I'll hand you over to the Trolleks myself."

"Oh, and who are they?"

"Red-headed witch." He dragged her past more displays.

Man, she'd really like to examine those full-sized replicas of Viking kings in their glorious regalia. They were some hunks, not unlike her seething companion.

He skidded to a halt in front of a case holding an ancient parchment scroll. "This has to be it."

Magnor fiddled with his handheld device before releasing

her. "I've set the cameras in this room on a continuous loop. They won't show anything different than from a few moments ago."

"Good. I'm glad you've found what you wanted. What now?" She rubbed her forehead, wondering at her unusual fatigue. It could be due to the strain of the afternoon and all those cocktails. Their effects must be lingering in her system.

He retrieved another tool from a hidden pocket. It made a humming noise as he aimed the thing at the display. "There, I've deactivated the alarm." He put the tool away. "The next step is to lift this glass."

"Huh?" She gaped at him.

"You heard me. I need to borrow this scroll."

"Borrow, or steal? Do you mean to tell me you're a common thief? Is that what this is all about?"

Good God, is that why he'd suggested she enter the contest with him? He'd planned all along to snatch an artifact and meant to use her as cover?

The magnitude of her mistake made her want to sink through the floor. *You idiot. You've messed up again. Who would marry a perfect stranger without knowing anything about him?*

Her stomach threatened upheaval. All those drinks she'd consumed turned into a roiling, churning wave. She clapped a hand to her mouth, stemming the tide of bile in her throat.

His eyes darkened. "I need to copy the text and email it to a friend, Nira Larsen. This resort has a business center. I'll use their machines."

"Why can't you scan the material with your handheld device?"

"It would take too long as I'd have to go line by line."

"Won't the heat from the scanner damage the scroll? It's got to be fragile."

"I'll take the chance. After I'm finished, I'll replace it here. I've no wish to desecrate such a sacred object. Now stand back while I remove the case."

She stared open-mouthed as he twisted a dial on his PIP. The case shifted as though loosened from its moorings.

"Where did you get those tools?" She squinted at him. "You've stolen things before, haven't you?"

His reply was a sardonic curve of his mouth. "I'm going to lift the case with my levitator beam and float it over to you. See that it makes a soft landing on the carpet."

"Yes, sir," she said in a facetious tone.

"It's *My Lord.*"

"What?"

He cast an exasperated glance her way. "The proper form of address for a warrior of my status would be my lord, not sir." He grimaced as though afflicted by an unpleasant memory. "Then again, I no longer bear that title on my home world, nor do I possess the lands that accompany it."

My *home world*? This guy belonged in the loony bin.

He glowered at her, his eyes two chunks of charcoal. "I owe the Drift Lords everything, and I must not fail. Assist me in this maneuver, wife."

She could only stare in astonishment as a bluish beam shot out from his PIP device, surrounded the glass case, and lifted it with ease. He glided the case toward her until it hovered in front of her. Then he gently lowered the case to the ground while she made sure it wouldn't hit any rough spots on the carpeted floor.

"There, that was easy." His eyes glittering, he reached for the scroll.

"Wait." She held up a hand. "That parchment looks ancient. The oils on your skin might damage it."

"Good point." He wrestled his cape forward. Grasping a corner of the forest green fabric, he removed the scroll gingerly from its post. Then he wrapped the folds of his cape around the document for protection before tucking it under his arm.

He glanced toward the entrance. "Stay here and wait for me. I'll try to be quick."

Did he mean to leave her alone? "No way. I'm coming with you."

He shook his head, his thin braids swinging against his stern visage. "Listen, the shields in this place will prevent the Trolleks from vectoring in and taking you. You'll be safer if you stay behind."

Her resolve faltered in the face of his sincere concern. "What happens if a guard shows up?"

"Use your spell on him."

"My what?" Something must be wrong with her hearing. Invisibility belts, home world, spells—as in magic? She shook her head to clear her mental fog.

"You'll figure it out. In your hour of desperation, your power will appear. So it was with Nira and Jen."

"You keep mentioning Nira. Who is she?"

"I'll explain later," he said in a familiar refrain. "Do not move from this room. I will be as swift as possible."

Watching his broad back as he departed, Erika swallowed past a lump in her throat. This whole afternoon had been a disaster from the moment he'd stepped inside the casino and spotted her.

Then again, she had a husband, a new car, and fifty thousand dollars in cash. This made it within the realm of possibility to have her cake and eat it, too.

She found a cozy corner and sank onto the carpet, leaning her head against the wall. The money could fund her education while her inheritance—if she gained control of the trust fund—would allow her to build the gift shop she'd dreamed about next door to her pottery studio.

Her ultimate goal was to teach arts and crafts to special needs kids in the mornings and to offer classes for adults in the afternoons. She'd have to hire staff for the shop, but that wouldn't be a problem. She knew friends who were eager for jobs. Then she'd have a place to sell her own creations other than her crowded studio.

Her eyelids drifted shut as she happily imagined her future. She fell into slumber, dreams crossing her mind and turning into a nightmare when she got arrested for theft.

A dull tapping noise woke her. She snapped her eyes open,

realizing she had a crick in her neck. With a soft moan, she scrambled to her feet. One quick glance at the empty hall told her Magnor wasn't back yet. How long had he been gone? Alarm shot through her. What if he never intended to return?

Footsteps approached from the next room. It had to be him!

Low laughter sounded along with male voices. Oh, no. It must be a security detail patrolling the museum.

Her gaze swung to the glass case on the floor and the empty display. Despite the continuity loop on the video monitors, they'd know immediately that something was amiss once they entered the room.

She should put the case back in place. But wasn't it too heavy for her to lift? Presumably, that's why Magnor had used his levitation device.

A nervous giggle escaped her throat. Assuming he came back for her, she'd have to ask him about his spy tools.

Examining the glass cover resting on the carpet, she decided to give it a try. She bent from the knees and grasped it on two sides. To her surprise, the case lifted easily and didn't weigh so much. Instead, it was thin and lightweight, although she suspected it wasn't as fragile as it appeared. Tempered glass, perhaps?

She placed it back on the carpet and scoured the room. Her frantic gaze fell upon a poster on the wall. That would have to do.

Several quick strides brought her in front of the item. She pried it from the concrete, grimacing at the scrap of paper left behind despite the temporary glue. With trembling fingers, she rolled the poster and then propped it in the scroll's place on the display. Another instant and she had the glass case on top.

She stood back to examine her handiwork, aware the noises were growing louder along with the stomp of boots on tile flooring. Were those guards coming from a different direction than the main entrance?

She'd just noticed the visible fingerprints on the glass case she had replaced when the two male voices became more distinctive. Clapping a hand to her mouth, she wondered what to do. That must be why Magnor hadn't attempted to lift the glass himself. He'd wanted to avoid leaving his prints on it.

Her hands smoothed down her slinky black dress. She didn't have an ounce of fabric free to rub off those marks. Applying slight pressure with the fleshy part of her palm instead, she only succeeded in smearing the greasy imprints.

She suddenly realized the voices were coming from the next room and the footsteps were muted, likely by the carpet. Without a minute to spare, she scuttled into the shadows. Where was Magnor's invisibility belt when she needed it?

Questions hovered in her mind about how he'd acquired such futuristic technology. Perhaps he really was some kind of spy instead of a common thief. The nerve of him to leave her behind to get caught!

Her blood chilled at the notion that perhaps this had been his plan all along. She'd get arrested while he got away with the goods.

Gritting her teeth, she merged into a shadowed corner and crouched down, covering her face with her arms.

Good Lord, her hair would give her away. That flaming mass of tresses would be her downfall yet. She'd have to hope the guards wouldn't look in her direction.

She peeked at them as they strolled into view, two beefy guys with the same distorted features as the other staff members they'd encountered. The men spoke in gravelly voices. One fellow was bald except for a few tufts of hair sticking up from his head. The other one swung some sort of rod in his hand.

"The Grand Marshal himself put out the alert. Our monitors picked up her locator signal earlier," Baldie said, his beady gaze darting around as they weaved among the displays.

"We'll find the *maug* female. She has to be in the resort somewhere." His companion halted beside the glass case she'd replaced.

Erika held her breath as he glanced at the rolled poster.

"The woman isn't alone. One of the Drift Lords accompanies her. We've reinforced security around the portal."

The fellow with the long stick uttered several words in a guttural tongue. "I hear the queen wants the female alive. There's a generous price on her head."

"She's dangerous, if she has powers like her sisters. Don't underestimate her."

"Now that her beacon is active, she won't escape us. And the Drift Lord?"

Baldie snickered. "Queen Algie has some unique tortures planned for him." He wrinkled his nose. "Do you smell that? I detect a human scent."

Erika retreated farther into the shadows, an old fairy tale coming to mind. *Fee fie foe fum, I smell the blood of an Englishman.* Was that how it went from "Jack and the Beanstalk"?

Baldie's companion stooped to pick up a discarded gum wrapper. "Of course, you smell humans! They crowd in here all day, studying their meaningless remnants of history. At least the visitors become our *sloggs* by the end of their tour." His nasty chuckle trailed him out of the room.

Erika stayed glued to her spot, barely breathing as she counted the minutes of their absence. Glancing at her watch, she quirked her eyebrows. Magnor had been gone for almost two hours!

Her throat clogged with fear that he'd abandoned her.

Seconds ticked by as silence prevailed. Was it safe for her to move out now?

Shortly after she'd risen to her feet and decided to risk departing on her own, Magnor swept into the room.

"What happened here?" He charged to the glass case and whipped the scroll out from beneath his voluminous cape.

"I had to put the case back on its perch. Two guards showed up. They'd have noticed the empty space, so I substituted a rolled poster from the wall."

He grinned, his face transforming. "Good work, wife."

"Thanks." A warm glow lit her at his obvious approval.

"Stand aside." He lifted the glass and placed it carefully on the carpet. Then he replaced the poster with the original artifact.

After fitting the case back onto its proper mount, Magnor took out his scanner. He made an adjustment on a dial and then panned the device around the case, which settled into its grooves. As Erika disposed of the poster in a trash receptacle, he used another setting to clear the glass of fingerprints.

"Let's go." He pocketed his PIP and gestured for her to follow him out.

Her blood seethed at the presumptive way he took command. "Don't we have to get through those lasers at the village again? Because I think the staff uses a different entrance."

"Don't worry; I've already bypassed the defense grid twice."

They kept moving as they spoke, keeping their voices low. Erika thought to ask if the feedback loop he'd arranged for the cameras in the document room had been reset.

He didn't answer for a moment. "I'd set a timer. It had already finished its cycle when I returned."

"You mean the video went live?"

"Affirmative." He drew his sword, sliding it from its scabbard.

"Oh, great." She detoured around the replica of the Viking ship in the great hall. Their footsteps echoed in the pregnant silence. "I overheard the two guards talking. One of them mentioned looking for a female and picking up her signal."

He whirled to face her, his nostrils flaring. "Tell me exactly what you heard the beast say."

"I'll tell you myself, Drift Lord." A throaty chuckle sounded from the next chamber. Baldie marched inside their room, a troop of armed men behind him. "Drop your weapon and raise your arms."

Chapter Four

Ignoring the command to lay down his weapon, Magnor grabbed Erika, yanked her close, and kissed her on the lips.

"For protection," he said before thrusting her behind him. With a warlike whoop, he launched himself at their foe.

His sword flashed in the air. The balding Trollek barely realized Magnor's goal before his hand went flying along with his disruptor. The beast howled with pain and rage, his intent to murder evident in his eyes. A sweeping backslash from Magnor was all it took for his head to follow.

The quartet behind him snarled in unison. They may have been told to apprehend a Drift Lord, but they didn't know about his special skills. Magnor was a tribesman of the Tsuran, and that meant he'd trained as an expert swordsman.

Trolleks had their own innate abilities of extra speed and strength. From experience, Magnor had learned how to counter them. Wielding his sword, he blocked his opponents' offensive actions.

He cut through the Trollek who veered left, aware out of the corner of his eye that one had slipped behind him. Erika screamed, but he knew they couldn't confound her. However, they could drag her away while he was otherwise occupied.

He whirled around to see her being hauled off by her hair. His plan to aid her derailed when the nearest Trollek lunged forward. Magnor dodged sideways while slicing at the beast's ankles. With a grunt of surprise, the *riff* collapsed to his knees. Magnor finished him with one thrust. He must have hit an artery, because blood sprayed everywhere.

Erika's shrieks tore through the chamber, and he cast a concerned glance her way.

"Don't worry, these beasts are no match for a warrior of the Tsuran," he called to offer reassurance. Two more guards remained for him to subdue, but that was child's play for the men of his tribe.

His loss of attention cost him a steep price. As he turned to the Trollek approaching from behind, a blue disruptor beam hit his sword arm. His fingers loosened, and the blade slid from his grasp to clatter onto the floor.

White hot pain seared his flesh, but he gritted his teeth against it. With a roundhouse kick, he knocked the weapon from the beast's hand. The movement threw him off balance, and he stumbled as though the ground had shifted beneath his feet.

Regaining his sense of equilibrium, he aimed his next blow at the nerve center in the Trollek's meaty arm, but it was like hitting a wall.

The thug grabbed him by the neck and lifted him off his feet. His hand closed around Magnor's windpipe.

Magnor struggled to break free. His cape tangled between his legs, working against his efforts. His heart pounding, he clutched at the beast's fingers, attempting to pry them loose. They wouldn't budge.

The guard's grip tightened, squeezing the life from him.

A whistle of air made it past his tight throat, but it wasn't enough. His lungs burned, and blood suffused his face.

His vision receded as the beast's hot breath wafted into his nostrils. Maybe he could still do damage.

He aimed the palm of his hand at the beast's long nose, attempting to bash it up into his brain, but the Trollek merely leaned his head back with a bark of laughter. It ended abruptly in a choking gurgle.

The hand holding him slackened, and Magnor dropped to the ground. He landed upright, gasping in a needed lungful of air even as he reached for his fallen sword.

It wasn't there.

And then he saw her, standing behind the Trollek with a horrified expression on her lovely face, her hand on the hilt of his weapon. She'd buried the sword in the Trollek's broad back.

The beast whirled on her with a howl of fury. Magnor took advantage to retrieve his blade from the sinew and flesh of his enemy. Ignoring the pain in his right arm, he swung the steel with such force that the Trollek's head went flying.

Erika crumpled toward the floor. He threw down his weapon and caught her, gently lowering her to the ground. A quick check of her pulse told him she'd fainted.

How had she eluded capture by the Trollek who'd had her in his grasp?

He glanced yonder and noticed broken pottery scattered on the carpet along with shattered glass. In her struggles, Erika must have dislodged one of the displays. But how did that shard of glazed clay get stuck in the beast's throat?

The creature must have fallen on it, Magnor surmised. And then his woman had leapt to his aid without hesitation.

His woman. She'd been brave this night. Having assessed his plight, she had picked up the sword and thrust it into the Trollek. His chest swelled with pride. She was a worthy mate.

Good thing she was unconscious so she couldn't see what he would do next. He reached down and withdrew the Monix T-6 phase pistol tucked inside his boot. The laser weapon was standard issue for the Drift Lords. Its energy pack was fully charged since Magnor preferred his sword as weapon of choice.

He changed the setting to vaporize. One by one, he fired at each Trollek. They vanished in the sizzling beam in a burst of radiance. The blood spatter took more effort to erase.

Erika stirred with a moan. Her eyes open, she glanced around. "Magnor, are you alright? Where did everyone go?"

"They ran off." He ignored the way his body responded to her lustrous eyes and full, ripe lips. Even with her luxurious coils of hair disheveled and her dress twisted, she looked ravishing.

Focusing on business, he tucked the phase weapon back into his boot. He used a nearby drape to wipe down his sword before replacing it in its scabbard.

"Hold onto me," he said once Erika had risen to her feet. "We'll use my invisibility shield to escape this place."

Her mouth tightened into a stubborn moue. "I'm not going anywhere until you explain what's happening."

"Later. We don't want to be here when more patrols show up."

Erika's sharp glance observed how he cradled his sword arm. "You've been wounded!"

He shrugged. "It's nothing. I've had worse." Fortunately, the beam had cauterized the wound so he hadn't lost any blood.

Color returned to her pale skin. "You need medical attention. And we should report these thugs to the authorities."

"Do you jest, woman? What would we say, that we broke into their museum and borrowed one of their sacred scrolls, but just as we were returning it, they sent a security squad after us?"

She grimaced. "You have a point." Resolve turned her green eyes the color of deep malachite. "But I won't go anywhere with you until we treat your arm. Let's go back to our suite. I'll clean and dress the wound for now."

Did she have training as a medic? He'd gotten the impression that she worked as an artist. Nonetheless, the look on her face said she'd give it a try even if she were squeamish.

"Fine." He would comply, but only so he could leave her there while he continued his explorations. Also, he had a tissue regenerator in his bag that would initiate the healing process. Doubtless this wouldn't be his last battle, so he should use it.

He snatched her hand and pressed the dial on his belt to turn on his shield.

They made it to the boundary of the village, their presence unseen. Hearing booted footsteps, he halted behind a wall and held up a hand for silence. Erika huddled next to him as a troop of Trolleks rushed by.

It appeared they'd deactivated the laser array, certain of capturing their prey. However, a number of armed guards patrolled the corridor in front of the elevator, as he saw upon their arrival.

"We'll have to take the stairs," he whispered to Erika. "This way." When he was certain the beasts were otherwise occupied, he cracked open the exit door.

They slipped through without incident. Once alone, he let go of Erika's hand, missing the contact as soon as he did so.

What was the matter with him? This bold female, now his bride, was unlike any woman he might have considered for a mate. She continually defied him and surprised him by her actions. Instead of obeying him like a tribeswoman would do, she challenged his commands at every junction.

As he descended the stairs behind her, he couldn't help his gaze from feasting on her fiery mane of hair, her well-defined curves, and her long legs. He moistened his lips, remembering the taste of her. Ah, if only she didn't tempt him so mightily.

****

Erika trotted down the steps, aware of Magnor's hot gaze on her back. It felt as though he undressed her with his eyes, and that notion oddly pleased her.

How absurd. The man was wounded. She'd seen the ugly scorch mark on his arm.

What manner of weapon had hit him? Who were these creatures who'd attacked them? And why was that scroll so important?

Once she'd fixed his injury, she would get some answers.

Magnor took the lead on the way to their suite. He moved as gracefully as a panther, wearing the sword as though it were an extension of his body. Noting his broad back and powerful form reminded her that this was their wedding night. She'd have to remove his upper clothes to care for his wound.

She moistened her lips, eager to see her warrior shirtless. Various methods to divest him of his clothing drifted into her mind.

By the time they rounded the corner near their suite, her already rattled senses had alerted other parts of her body to awaken. Those feelings quickly got doused, however, when he stopped short. She almost bumped into him.

"Trolleks," he muttered, skittering backwards and dragging her with him.

Her heart pounded. "What? How did security target us so quickly?" The resort must have image recognition software. How else would they know where to find the two of them?

Perhaps they'd compared the video from the historical exhibit upstairs to surveillance footage from the casino.

Or maybe it was the fact that she and Magnor had been the stars in their televised production that had tipped them off.

"We must flee the premises." Magnor tugged on her arm.

From the reluctance in his voice, she surmised he was none too happy about that decision.

"But my luggage is in there."

"So is my equipment. Sometimes retreat is the wiser choice." His cape swirled as he hurried down the hallway.

"I can't leave," she protested even as her feet followed him through the twisting maze toward the exit. "The art show starts tomorrow. They can't know that I have a booth there."

"Would you risk your life to participate? They can track you now that we have connected." He scowled as though that thought displeased him, but which one? Their hook-up, or the fact that the bad guys could trace her?

"And how can they do that, exactly?"

He nodded at her wristwatch. "Through your vector device. Our priorities have changed. Escape is paramount." When she hesitated, he threw her a fierce glance. "They have worse things in mind for you than an accusation of theft and a stay in the local jail."

The guard's words from the museum drifted into her brain: *The Queen wants the female alive. There's a price on her head.*

Confusion warred with her sense of reason. Those drinks hadn't messed with her mind, had they? Maybe she was imagining all of this. How could it be real? A caped swordsman. An instant wedding ceremony. Breaking and entering an attraction and lifting one of its artifacts. Strange looking men with ugly features who'd attacked them.

Dazed and bewildered, she hurried after Magnor into the stairwell and up a set of concrete steps.

"Where are we going?" Her breath came short as they climbed from floor to floor.

"To the roof. Too many of the beasts patrol the lobby level."

"Are you crazy?" She dodged his sword, angled toward his rear. "We'll be trapped up there."

He stood aside to let her precede him. "These rooftops may be interconnected. Keep going. It isn't much farther."

They burst into the night onto a flat roof, where she huddled over to catch her breath. She wasn't used to climbing stairs. While her racing pulse slowed and her breathing eased, Magnor scouted the premises.

Neon lights from the Strip lit the sky so they had no need for added illumination. The front edge of the roof facing the street looked Viking in design, with a peaked surface and curved embellishments. Different levels attached to this one, but as they found shortly, the roof ended abruptly at an empty space.

The adjacent Mariner Resort, an aquatics themed complex, rose across a wide divide. Twenty-four floors below on street level, people scurried to their late-night shows, restaurants, and casinos. Traffic moved slowly, a ribbon of congestion, while in the distance, the lights ended and the desert began.

Magnor pulled out his portable scanner and reconfigured its settings. Peering at the screen, he cursed under his breath.

"We don't have much time. The beasts are headed this way."

Her eyes widened, and she made the mistake of glancing at

the empty space yawning before them. "We have nowhere to go except over the edge of this building."

"Correct." He eyed the roof hundreds of feet away. "That's our escape route."

"Are you crazy? We can't jump that far."

His eyes glowed momentarily, and he flashed her a grin. "Did I say we would jump?" He glanced at their surroundings, taking in the ventilation hoods, broadband satellite apparatus, and cables snaked along the rooftop surface. His gaze fixed on the latter. "I think that will do."

He grasped one of the cables and traced its connection while she crouched in place, wondering how she'd ended up in this situation. This had to be a nightmare. That explained it. She'd had one too many drinks and had fallen asleep in her room.

The desert wind whistled through the night, grit stinging her eyes and reinforcing reality. She wrapped her arms around herself, wishing she'd worn a more sensible outfit. Meanwhile, Magnor worked to make them some sort of tensile line.

She hoped he didn't expect them to bungee jump to the ground. Her heart would fail from fright.

Banging noises sounded on the other side of the door they'd come through, which he had latched shut.

"Magnor, we have company."

His brow folded. "I hear it. Look, this cable appears secure enough to hold our weight. Whether it will reach as far as the next roof is another matter."

She rose and advanced to his location. "Do you mean for us to leap off this building? What if the cable snaps?" She jerked her thumb at the great divide.

His eyes did that glowing thing again. "Consider it a leap of faith."

Hadn't she heard that phrase in an *Indiana Jones* movie?

She glanced at the exit door, where an orange outline was etching its way into an oval shape. The Trolleks must be burning a hole in it so they could storm the roof. She had a feeling being captured by them would be a worse fate than getting squashed on the ground if their makeshift rope failed.

"What are we waiting for?" She gestured impatiently.

I'm going to die, she thought after Magnor positioned himself at the edge of the roof, wound his legs around the cable, and instructed her to hold onto his back.

Standing behind him, she linked her arms around his chest, clasped her hands together, and sank her head onto his neck. His solid form felt reassuring as she pressed against him.

Her thoughts evaporated as they swung out into empty space. Her blood froze, and her breath stopped. She clutched Magnor as though her life depended on it, which it did. What if his wounded arm folded, and he lost his grip?

Wind whipped hair into her face and battered her skin. Magnor let go of the cable when they swung over the neighboring roof. As they tumbled, he rolled under her. She crashed atop him, her landing softened by his body.

They ended up face to face, sprawled on a rubbery surface. Her heart pounded as she got her bearings. Splashing sounds came from the near distance amid the glow of lamp light.

Magnor's arms wrapped around her. Startled, she realized her dress had hiked up, and her hips rode on a burgeoning part of his anatomy. He grinned up at her, clearly enjoying their compromising position.

Or was it the sense of danger that thrilled him more?

Nonetheless, their desperate escape and safe landing caused her to react without thinking. She lowered her head and pressed her mouth to his.

He stilled beneath her, as though surprised by her action, but then he responded by half lifting his head and deepening their kiss.

Angry shouts restored her sensibility. The man kissing her was a stranger, and a troop of security guards from next door was after them.

****

Magnor surfaced from a rising haze of passion. The woman had bewitched him with her skimpy attire and her tantalizing mouth. He pushed away, switching his focus to their escape.

His arm throbbed as he leapt to his feet. Erika stood and faced him with wide eyes, her curls rioting about her head. Observing how she trembled, he took off his cape and offered it to her as a wrap so she wouldn't get chilled.

"Wear this. We'll get new clothing later. We need to get out of here." He headed for the lighted area at a fast clip.

Assuming the Trolleks didn't follow them onto this roof, the beasts would be waiting downstairs at the resort's front entrance. He and his lovely wife needed to disguise themselves.

Even if some of the hotel shops were still open, they shouldn't linger in this place. Wishing to survey the entrance, he led Erika into an elevator. They emerged at a third-floor conference level with an outdoor balcony.

As he peered over the edge, he spotted a number of Trolleks patrolling the resort's exterior.

He returned to where he'd left Erika, who shivered in the night air even with his cloak around her slim shoulders. Resisting the urge to take her into his arms and provide comfort, he spoke in a gruff tone instead.

"This resort abuts a shopping center. We can escape through there. We'll emerge onto the street below where they won't be expecting us."

She followed him to the edge of the flat roof. "Don't tell me we're taking another leap of faith."

"Indeed. We can use that line strung between buildings." He pointed to a taut cable that stretched to the lower level next door. "It'll be easy."

He unwound his belt and looped it around the cable. After fastening the buckle with a knot, he then grabbed the part hanging down.

"Climb onto my back again and hold tight." As soon as her weight settled on him, he gripped his makeshift harness and stepped off the roof.

Chapter Five

Erika shut her eyes as they flew through empty space to the accompanying sound of a scraping noise, like chalk on pavement. At any moment, she expected the belt to snap and for them to tumble to the street below. But they made it safely to the other side, as the surface under her feet indicated.

While she stood regaining her composure, Magnor recovered his belt and looped it around his waist. She noted how he favored his injured arm. It must be hurting him, but the only indications were the fine lines around his mouth.

They entered the shopping mall through a rooftop door, descended three flights of stairs, and emerged through an emergency exit onto the crowded street.

Night was the same as daytime in Las Vegas—mobbed with people crowding the sidewalks, thronged with diners overflowing the outdoor cafés, and swarmed with folks seeking fun, food, and festivity. For some, it was a fantasy of lights, of dreams, and of hope. For others, it was a pit of despair and depravity.

Signage lit up the city like a neon forest against a pitch-black sky. Erika and Magnor melted into the crowd. She handed him back his cape, her black dress appropriate among the nightclub set.

Why didn't the thugs summon the police? She wouldn't think a resort's security force had any jurisdiction beyond the doors of their property. As long as she and Magnor kept out of sight of any uniformed cops, they might be okay.

Or not. The resort had her banking info, home address, and

other personal details of her life. She swallowed hard as they passed a jewelry store and an ice cream shop.

She couldn't retrieve the car she'd won and might lose the money she'd deposited into her bank account earlier. Although she had completed the transaction, the resort people could stop payment on the check. But she'd worry about that later, if she and Magnor didn't get arrested.

Then again, Magnor had returned the artifact he'd borrowed, so what crime had they committed? Unauthorized entry into an exhibit after hours? It didn't make sense that the goons would waste manpower on chasing them.

Another reason for their persistent interest must exist that had nothing to do with the display. She quivered at the notion, because it would confirm what she'd overheard in the museum. She and Magnor were specific targets for some other sinister purpose.

As soon as they reached safety, she'd ply him with questions. The man would answer them without any further evasion, or she'd—what? Strike out on her own?

At least she still had her purse strapped across her shoulder. Her credit cards would help her get home.

The tall towers of the next resort rose beyond a graceful entry of royal palms and a massive dancing fountain that spurted to music and colorful lighting. A tour bus roared past on the broad avenue, belching fumes. Outside a nightclub, a neon guitar flashed its invitation while cigarette smokers blew puffs at passersby. Erika wrinkled her nose at the smell of diesel exhaust mingled with beer.

Magnor had folded his cape and tucked it under his arm, but his sword still stuck out like a magnet for attention. People glanced their way but then hurried by, fixated on their goals.

A white stretch limo rumbled past with a group of young men hanging out of its open roof hatch and howling at the night. In the distance, a siren wailed. Real life existed beneath the city's surface, with urban problems like any other place. Only here, they were magnified by the thousands of visitors who mobbed the streets.

She tugged on Magnor's arm, bringing him to a halt. "Where are we going? We need a plan."

Adrenalin kept her moving, but soon it would dissipate, and then she'd collapse after the events of the day.

His formidable gaze snagged hers. "We need to disguise ourselves. Your hair stands out in a crowd."

"So does your sword, *my lord*."

He lifted his chin. "My blade is part of me. It stays. However, I will concede the need for some unobtrusive clothing."

She glanced down the Strip. They'd passed the MGM Grand and were nearly at the Parisian resort. Bellagio was across the street. They'd already walked a couple of blocks away from the Viking Vegas Resort.

"Let's go in here," she said, seeing shoppers coming out of Le Boulevard mall. "It's open until 1:00 am on Fridays."

"Perfect."

They ducked inside the impressive marble interior with its high ceilings, blue-tiled fountains, and maze of shops along a boulevard designed to look like a European street.

"Look for a clothing store that has menswear as well as women's outfits." She strode forward, past a newsstand selling magazines, snacks, and newspapers. Children's fashions, home accessories, perfumes and soaps, French wines and cheeses were useless to them. Finally spotting an apparel store, she led Magnor inside.

Thirty minutes later, they departed, pleased with their purchases. Magnor had surprised her by pulling a wad of bills from his pocket. Considering the designer labels on their clothing, she was glad he'd offered to pay.

He wore his same black pants, but an expensive blue French shirt graced his broad shoulders. It hid the ugly mark on his arm. From the way he'd winced when trying on clothes, she didn't think he would last much longer unless they got medical help.

Regarding the sword, they'd found a music store and he had bought a guitar case. The weapon fit inside. His cape and other gizmos went into a backpack from the boutique.

Erika had suppressed her natural tendencies to choose an attention-grabbing outfit. Instead, she'd selected dark brown pants, a bronze short-sleeved knit top, and ankle-high boots. With a scarf tied over her head and her handbag stuffed into a larger tote, she looked innocuous.

They emerged through Bally's next door since the malls interconnected. It appeared their new disguises were working as they crossed Flamingo and strolled up the street opposite Caesar's Palace. Erika's shoulders drooped and her eyelids sagged. As her adrenalin ebbed, fatigue set in. They'd been on the run for hours.

"We need a place to crash." She eyed a nearby bench under a shady tree.

"Not yet. The beasts can track you. We must keep moving."

The warm desert air dried her nostrils and brought the scent of cigarette smoke her way. Ugh. She padded on, feeling adrift in the city. Was this what homeless persons experienced? How awful to have nowhere safe to go.

Magnor poked her arm. "Don't look now, but people are staring at us. It started a moment ago, like a switch turned on in their brains. They must be confounded souls."

"What's that?" Alarm frissoned up her spine.

"They're spellbound by the Trolleks. We have to turn off that vector device in your watch. It doesn't matter what we wear. They can still find us."

Her skin crawled as she felt dozens of eyes aimed their way. "What can we do?"

He darted quick glances from side-to-side. People had started to congregate and move en masse toward them. The denizens had vacant looks on their faces. Soon she and Magnor would be surrounded, and they'd lose their chance to escape. Her heart rate accelerated.

"Quick, go down that alley." Magnor gave her a shove. "It may lead to a quieter side street."

Just before they turned to go, a charcoal Toyota Highlander skidded to a stop at the curb. The passenger window rolled down.

"Lord Magnor, get in! I'll take you to safety." The driver, an elderly woman with her gray hair in a bun, gestured urgently.

"And you are…?" He hunched his shoulders, a frown creasing his brow.

"I'm Edith, a Gatekeeper. Hurry!"

Strangers grabbed for Erika. Without waiting for Magnor's approval, she opened the rear car door and dove inside. The interior smelled like rich new leather. She sank back on the soft upholstery, creeped out by the encroaching crowd.

Magnor bumped her hip as he joined her. As soon as he'd slammed the door shut, Edith pressed on the accelerator. They zoomed forward down the main avenue.

The people seemed to snap out of their reverie and resumed their activities as though nothing extraordinary had happened. What could explain it? Erika sought a logical reason, but nothing came to mind.

She rubbed a hand over her face, too weary to think.

Magnor leaned forward and tapped on the older woman's shoulder. She'd left the main boulevard and drove with reckless haste through the city streets, charging through intersections.

"Edith, your name is familiar. Did you not aid my leader's mate, Nira Larsen?"

"Indeed, I did, milord. My kind has been aiding the Drift Lords for generations. I am honored you came in my time."

"And we are grateful for your interception just now, but how did you know we needed assistance?"

She glanced at him through the rear-view mirror. "We know many things. Like, I brought you a tissue regenerator. It should heal that nasty wound on your arm."

Magnor caught the instrument that she tossed to him, rolled up his sleeve, and panned it over his scorched flesh. As new, pink skin filled in, the taut lines around his mouth vanished.

Erika watched with narrowed eyes but didn't comment. Instead, she addressed Edith.

"Is this car yours? Because it looks very similar to the vehicle we won at the resort."

Edith gave an eerie chuckle. "You're very astute, missy. Yes, this is your car. I hope you don't mind that I signed the release form under your name."

"No, I'm grateful. They would never have let us take it from their garage."

The hackles on Erika's nape rose. Something struck her as odd about this woman. Had they made a mistake and gone from the frying pan into the fire?

****

Magnor observed his wife's anxious expression and knew that explanations were due. He'd rather wait until they were somewhere safe to reveal her role in the prophecy. More importantly, he had to contact Nira to see how to turn off Erika's vector device.

Each one of the prophesied Earth women had a wristwatch similar to the one Erika wore. It's what identified them, along with a birthmark between their right index and middle fingers. He'd already verified Erika's mark. That was more innocuous than the timepiece, which once activated, made her a target.

Hopefully, Edith would take them somewhere shielded from the Trolleks. He trusted her to an extent. Askr had claimed to be a Gatekeeper too, and yet the old man had turned out to be an agent of Loki. Magnor couldn't fully put his faith in these unnatural shapeshifters.

Although they drove away from the raucous city, he also knew he'd have to return to complete his mandate. Trollek recruitment centers were to be destroyed. He assumed the Viking Vegas Resort held one, although he had yet to find the portal there. Then he'd continue on his main mission after Nira translated the scroll.

Erika shifted beside him, and his attention skewed her way. A sigh escaped her lips. She must be confused and exhausted. A wave of guilt hit him in the gut. He'd dragged her into this quagmire. Now she was his responsibility.

He patted her hand. "We'll be all right, my *knesta*."

She moistened her lips. "Will we? I don't understand a thing. What happened tonight? Who are you?"

"I am your husband." Temporarily, at least. Regret rippled through him. He'd never be bored coupled to a lady like her, but neither did he have anything to offer her.

She cast him a suspicious glance. "It's possible you and Edith are in cahoots. Is this what you do, steal artifacts and sell them on the black market? How do I know you put back the real scroll? You might have done a switch and handed off the genuine article to your partner here. And now you're going to do me in so you can have the prize money, too."

She scrubbed her hands over her face. "Oh, God. Why did I let you talk me into entering that contest?"

"I told you, I don't want the money. My kewa stones—diamonds—bring me all the cash I need. As for your other allegations, they're absurd."

He sat rigid, insulted by her suggestions. How dare she believe him capable of such crimes?

And yet, hadn't he been accused of worse on his home world? Hadn't his lifelong friends believed his sister over him?

He stared out the side window, his jaw tight. Edith didn't say a word and concentrated on driving. She took them out of town on a highway heading for the hills.

Cactus and scrub brush dotted the dry land. Without the city lights, the night was black as pitch. Stars glowed overhead. Observing them, Magnor ached for the familiarities of home. Never again could he return to his mountainous haven on a distant planet. He'd been cast out, accused of a heinous crime. To go home meant death.

Eventually he became aware of Erika's steady breathing and risked a glance at her. She'd fallen asleep, her head bent at an uncomfortable angle. Against his better judgment, he put an arm around her and leaned her body toward his.

Her soft hair tickled his nose. He inhaled her scent, a tantalizing fragrance reminiscent of cinnamon. His loins stirred; he couldn't help it. Her warmth and closeness aroused him.

He stroked her arm. No matter what her opinion of him, he was duty-bound to protect her. She had no idea of the forces gathering to stop them.

****

Erika roused from her exhausted slumber to the sound of mumbled voices. She lay still, disoriented and uncertain of her surroundings. She'd been in a car, fleeing Las Vegas with the man she called husband.

Her eyelids fluttered open. She lay on a couch in a cozy living room. Magnor flopped in an armchair, his eyes half-closed, a police procedural playing on the TV.

"Where are we?" She forced herself upright.

He sprang to his feet, looking instantly alert. "What? Who comes near us?"

She ran her fingers through her tousled hair. "Calm down. There's no one else here." Her gaze narrowed. "Where's Edith?"

He waved a hand in dismissal. "She is gone."

Erika rose and stretched. Outside, the sky brightened as dawn broke in a tangerine sunrise.

Their car was parked in a dirt driveway. A quick surveillance told her they inhabited a small house at the end of an unpaved road and at the foot of a mountain. A few scraggly trees stood around but not much else. Her chest squeezed. She was alone with this madman, and nobody knew her location… except perhaps for those thugs who could track her.

She whirled to face Magnor, who'd turned off the TV. "Our car is still here. How did Edith leave? Did she fly away?" With all the weird stuff that had been happening lately, Erika wouldn't be surprised.

His mouth curved upward, and his eyes danced with mirth. "You might say that. Are you thirsty? Can I get you some water?"

"I could really use a cup of coffee." Her temples throbbed, and she rubbed her brow.

"Nira taught us how to brew the drink. I will make it."

Nira, again? She couldn't wait to meet this paragon. "Did you hear back from her about the translation of the scroll?"

"Not yet. You need not fear the Trolleks here. This place is shielded from their vector jumps." He turned about, presumably heading for the kitchen. "You'll find clothing in the bedroom if you want to change."

Their safe house was quaint, she noted upon inspection. It had a master bedroom suite in the rear, a modern kitchen, and an expansive living area. The latter's stone fireplace, rich wood trim, and Southwestern accents lent a cozy feel to the place.

While her warrior busied himself in the kitchen, Erika made use of the bathroom facilities. She took a shower, washed her hair, and then rummaged in a set of drawers where a variety of underwear rested in neat folds.

She selected a bra and panties that fit, rinsed out her own undergarments and hung them to dry, and chose a caramel cotton top and khaki pants from the closet. The air-conditioning unit strained in the background as she dressed, donning her newly purchased boots last. Her other new clothes she folded into the tote she'd bought.

Her hair took longer to comb out than usual. It was a mess of tangles and hurt as she yanked on the knots. Giving up in frustration, she found a clip and pinned the curls atop her head. Then she retrieved her purse, popped a cinnamon flavored mint into her mouth and applied her makeup. Thank goodness she carried the essentials along with her.

Magnor called that the coffee was ready. By the time she reached the kitchen, he'd heated some French toast from the freezer. Two plates, utensils, and syrup sat on the table.

A smile lit her lips, and she gave him an appreciative nod. He held out the chair for her and she took it graciously, as though this had been their morning routine for years.

His handsome good looks weren't lost on her, either. Her gaze feasted on his broad shoulders and muscular form as he seated himself in the opposite chair. He wore a clean shirt and his same trousers from the previous night. He'd trimmed his beard, and in the light of day, he had a rakish look about him that appealed to her.

"How long do we have to stay here?" she asked between bites. The French toast tasted a bit stale, but she could live with it. She gulped the coffee down after adding sweetener and a touch of cream from those little cups that don't need refrigeration. Someone had stocked this place well enough.

Magnor shrugged. He'd wolfed down half his food in the time it took her to cut her portion into pieces.

"We'll wait until I hear back from Nira."

She raised her eyebrows. "I'm due some explanations." *Including why you involved me in this mess.* "Start talking."

"Very well." He put his fork down, meeting her gaze squarely. "You've heard of the Bermuda Triangle? Just as the Earth has tectonic plates, dimensional plates exist on a cosmic energy level. These fuel an electromagnetic grid that intersects the planet at twelve geographic points named vile vortices. The Bermuda Triangle sits on one of these sites, known for their anomalous activity."

"Huh?" She'd heard stories of the Bermuda Triangle, wherein ships and planes vanished and compasses went awry. But the rest of his jargon didn't register.

He must have interpreted her blank look for curiosity because he continued. "When the plates grind against each other, the pressure forces open a door between dimensions."

She held up her hand in a stop sign. "Wait a minute. Between *dimensions*?" Was the man delusional, or did he watch too much science fiction on TV?

"Just listen." His voice edged with irritation. "Normally, the event horizon at this natural rift produces a substance called cors particles. When their mass reaches a critical level, the resultant pressure forces the rifts to close. But this time, the Trolleks have found a way to force the gateway open, and through it they have invaded Earth."

She pushed herself away from the table and stood. "All right, you're freaking me out. I know that things have been weird lately, but really? Tell me you're kidding."

"I do not jest." His eyes shone like two chunks of polished granite. "The Trolleks turn humans into mind slaves with a chemical transmitted through touch. They've confounded large numbers of individuals at all levels of society. Their plan was to activate these sleeper agents when their armies were ready to invade, but my team sealed the portals."

She shook her head. "This is too much, Magnor. I can't take it all in, never mind whether or not you're for real."

His brows folded together. "You have to understand. Your role is critical in defeating these beasts. The Trolleks who remain on this side of the gate may be stranded, but that won't stop them. And they're not the only threat. They serve a greater evil—the demon, Loki."

She rolled her eyes. "Yeah, right. I should have known the devil would enter into this equation somewhere."

"Loki is not a fallen angel like in your biblical fables. He was a companion of the gods until they banished him for his evil deeds. Nira can tell you more about him. She has studied the mythology."

"And who exactly is this wondrous woman? I can't wait to meet her."

"She is from Earth, like you. Note the inscription on your wristwatch if you doubt me. It identifies your place in the prophecy. The six daughters of Odin must unite with the six sons of Thor to prevent a coming disaster known as Ragnarok."

Erika sank into her chair, her head swirling with unfamiliar terms. None of this could be true, could it?

"So you're saying my job is to prevent this apocalypse?"

"Aye, that is so. Loki aims to cause the destruction of the multiverse so he can rule over the ensuing chaos. All six of you women have special powers, including the ability to resist the Trollek hypnotic spell."

"You said they take over people's minds through touch." She pointed at him, hoping to derail his fantasy. Either this guy was a sicko who needed to be committed, or else she'd fallen down the rabbit hole. "So how come you weren't affected?"

His face split into a wide grin. "I kissed you. Our mingling transfers your immunity to me."

"What? You kissed me to protect yourself against their magic spell?"

He waved a hand. "It isn't magic. As I mentioned, it's a chemical response—"

"I heard you. Can I not trust a single thing you say?"

Chapter Six

Erika couldn't believe he'd only kissed her for immunity against the Trollek mind spell. She didn't know how much credence she gave to his story, but still, hurt and betrayal wound a knot in her gut.

He rose quickly, nearly toppling his chair. His eyes sparked as he approached. "Do not mistake me, my *knesta*. I desire you more than what's prudent. You're brave, resourceful, and forthright. Under other circumstances, I might be proud to have you as my mate."

Her anger quelled under the longing in his gaze. She saw loneliness there, mixed with a heartache that spoke of some trauma in his past. Who was he really, and how did he come to be here? How much of his tale was true?

They'd been chased by ugly armed men, but those people could have been the security force at the resort. Maybe the hotel hired individuals with special needs to give them jobs.

But what about the women who worked there? They were all young, blond, and beautiful. Their free drinks were addictive and addled her brain.

Speaking of addling, Magnor's nearness made her body react in a disturbing way. Her heart raced, and her skin tingled. He stood gazing down at her, an uncertain expression on his face.

She wished he'd wrap her in his comforting embrace. Her glance roamed from his thick eyebrows to his straight nose to his dark, trim beard. The tiny braids on each side of his head swung with his movements.

A smile curved his sexy mouth. "If you doubt your effect on me, I can show you."

"Can you?" She rose to emphasize her challenge.

"We *are* married, you know."

"That's true." An irresistible urge to see him shirtless gripped her. Her fingers itched to trace the contours of his muscled arms and chest. Caution flew out the door. Either she was trapped here with a total nutcase, or else the world as she knew it was in terrible danger.

She didn't care about the horrors outside their door for the moment. After the harrowing evening they'd had, she sought succor in physical contact.

Lifting on her toes, she raised her face and brushed her mouth over his. He stood immobile, as though waiting to see what she would do next. She deepened the kiss, pulling his head down and increasing the pressure of her lips. Her body flared with sensitivity where they touched.

Satisfaction filled her as the bulge of his arousal met her belly. She rubbed herself against him, a spiral of need rising from her core.

She knew the moment his control broke. With a groan, he yanked her fully against him and plunged his tongue inside her mouth. He kissed her ruthlessly, while she wrapped her arms around him and savored his desire. They rocked together, hip to hip, until they parted to gain air.

He grinned at her, a predatory gleam in his eyes. Without saying a word, she reached up to unbutton his shirt. He remained still while she divested him of his upper clothing. Her top shortly joined his on the wooden floor.

"I'm sorry, I forgot about your wound." She glanced at his arm. The scorch mark had healed over. How was that possible?

His lips curved in amusement. "Edith supplied me with a tissue regenerator, remember? I'll mend quickly now."

Whatever. Her glance swung to his chest, and she sucked in a breath of admiration. He was all muscle, from his massive shoulders to his pecs to his taut abdomen. A tangle of dark hair descended in a line toward his belt.

While she splayed her hands on his powerful chest, he traced his fingers along the swell of her breasts. She still wore her bra, wishing to tantalize him with her cleavage and a bit shy about exposing herself to his hungry gaze.

He looked at her like a thirsty man might view an oasis with fresh, clear water. Where he stroked her skin, a fiery trail followed.

His fingers dipped into the valley between her breasts, rubbing up and down in an erotic motion that elicited a moan from her lips. He circled around her soft flesh, skimming her nipples and watching her reaction.

She resisted the impulse to rip her bra off and thrust herself at him. She wanted nothing more than to feel his hands all over her.

His gaze darkened, and he stepped back. "Are you sure about this?" he asked in a thick voice.

"Why not? We're here, alone. We are married. If we consummate the union, no one can challenge it."

"Why would you want that?"

"I want you, Magnor. God knows why, when we hardly know each other, but I do. I can't explain it."

"If you truly are the destined one, it is our fate. Say it now if you wish to retreat."

"Heck no. We're already talking too much."

"True." He undid his belt and tossed it to the ground. He'd just unfastened his pants when his wrist unit beeped. Cursing under his breath, he tapped a button to reply. "Magnor here."

"What is your status?"

So much for our moment of intimacy. Erika could hear the concerned male voice at the other end. Her companion needed to get a wireless earpiece.

Magnor redid his zipper as he spoke. "We're at a safe house in the desert, sire. Edith assisted us."

Sire? Was Magnor talking to his boss?

"Thank the stars. You're fortunate to have escaped that enemy camp."

"I may have to return there. Has Nira completed her translation?"

"Here, I'll put her on. She'll tell you the news herself."

Erika's head reeled. These people appeared to be buying into Magnor's fantasy. Could he actually be telling the truth?

A woman addressed Magnor, asking about his welfare. After he'd reassured her all was well, her tone lightened.

"Tell me about your companion, Lord Magnor. I'll bet she's as thunderstruck as I was when I met Zohar. Do you want me to talk to her?"

He glanced at Erika, who had retrieved her top and pulled it on while eavesdropping. "Maybe later. What have you learned?"

Nira's voice sobered. "The document contains a long verse about the ancient gods. It repeats the tales we already know but hidden among the words are a set of coordinates. I'm transmitting them now to your PIP."

"Have you identified the location?"

"It's in Copenhagen, at a place called Jolheim Gardens."

"A nature park? That's where I can find the sacred Book of Odin?"

"It's a popular tourist attraction."

His brow wrinkled. "Ah. Another Trollek recruitment center. That makes sense."

"Jolheim Gardens might only hold another clue, like the resort in Vegas. We have no time to waste. The Trolleks are preparing to launch an all-out offensive. We must obtain the weapon to stop them."

Magnor paced the room, while Erika rubbed her aching temples. Events were spiraling out of control, and she risked getting lost in the maelstrom.

"There's more." Nira's disembodied voice issued from Magnor's wrist unit. "A phrase puzzles me from the scroll's text. It says, *When the ground shakes, the dead shall walk the earth.*"

"What does that mean?" Magnor asked.

"I'm not sure. Here, Zohar wants to talk to you."

Their leader came online. "What is your plan?"

"I'll return to the casino. If it has a spatial portal, I can use it to vector to the coordinates Nira supplied, unless Paz can pick me up in the shuttle?"

Oh, Lord. Spatial portals? Shuttles? What's next? Erika shuddered. She sank into a chair as her knees wobbled.

"Paz is out of range for now but try to contact him later. Meanwhile, proceed with caution. We may have destroyed the dimensional gates, but we suspect the beasts are attempting to rebuild the rift generators from the other side."

"Our immediate concern is the Trolleks on this side of the barrier." Magnor paused. "Now that Algie has declared herself their queen, she is even more dangerous."

Erika latched onto the few familiar words. "May I interrupt? When I was alone in the museum and those guards came by, I heard them mention this person. She wants me alive."

Magnor relayed her words to his colleague. "With things under her control, Algie might accelerate her genetic program."

"Don't worry. Yaron's assignment is to track her movements and destroy her research. Be careful, Magnor. Guard your woman well. She's vital to our cause."

Great. He'd just confirmed what Magnor had told her. Either Erika had gone insane, or she had to credit Magnor's story.

Her stomach churned, making her wish she'd skipped breakfast earlier.

"Any luck finding the rune from the prophecy?" Magnor inquired, his tone softer.

"We've yet to find the verse that will dispel Loki back to his underground prison. He's been causing havoc with natural disasters. You worry about taking down the Trolleks. We'll worry about stopping Loki."

"And the others?"

Erika heard the strain in his tone. He must be missing his

friends. Were they his only companions? Or did he have a life back home? How little she knew about the man she called husband.

"Paz is reaching out to the Viden faction to see if they'll ally with us. Dal is targeting the recruitment centers we've identified, while Kaj is coordinating resources among global governments. He's made contact with Agent Monroe. Trollek sleeper cells have been activated in key governmental positions. The extent of their infiltration is widespread."

Magnor sighed, a weary expression on his face. He moved out of earshot, so she missed the rest of his conversation. When he returned, she attempted to make sense out of this madness.

"You're really considering going back to the casino?" she asked, voicing the first thought that popped into her head.

"I'll use the portal at the Viking Vegas Resort to reach the coordinates Nira supplied. That's the best alternative until I can raise Paz in the shuttle."

He set about packing supplies. She rose to follow him from room to room.

Finally, he halted to regard her with a tense expression. "I have to locate the Book of Odin if we are to defeat the invaders."

"Why is it your job? Who are your friends?"

"They are the Drift Lords, sent here to deal with the Trolleks. It is a calling they cannot deny."

"They? Aren't you one of them?"

"I'm a provisional member."

Were the Drift Lords a special ops team, then? Magnor must be a recent addition if he felt the need to prove his mettle. She scrubbed a hand over her face. It was all so bizarre. Afraid to ask the next question, she plunged on nonetheless.

"Who employs the Drift Lords? Are you, like, mercenaries?"

A mirthless smile curved his lips. "The League's role is to monitor Trollek incursions during natural rift events. They function independently of the Star Empire and other galactic alliances. It is their duty to protect mankind."

She gaped at him. "The Star Empire? Come on, you've given me enough material already for an entire TV season. You don't have to include extraterrestrials for my benefit."

"Indeed, our homes are light-years away."

Whump, whump, whump. A whirring noise from outside distracted her attention. What was that?

Magnor strode to a window and peered at the sky. Whatever he saw elicited a string of expletives from his mouth.

"We have to move, now!"

She snatched her purse and her tote along with Magnor's backpack, not wishing to leave behind their meager belongings. Magnor tossed his cape her way, and she stuffed it inside the larger sack.

An afterthought propelled her to the kitchen to add water bottles and nutrient bars to their stash. Magnor followed on her heels, buckling on his sword. He thrust open the rear door.

Before stepping outside, Erika propped a pair of sunglasses on her nose. Then she squashed her handbag and tote into the backpack and slung its straps across her shoulders.

The chopper opened fire as they left the house.

"Run!" Magnor charged for the hills, dust flying in his wake.

She sprinted forward as a huge explosion rent the air from behind. A blast of hot air impacted her spine and made her stagger to a halt. She glanced over her shoulder and winced. The house roared with flames along with her brand-new SUV.

Those bastards.

The copter circled as the pilot prepared to aim directly at them.

"Hurry!" Magnor signaled for her to move on.

The foothills were farther away than she'd thought. Her heart raced and her lungs burned as she strove to match his long-legged dash.

Gunfire pockmarked the earth around them. They weren't going to make it. They'd be cut down and left as fodder for the vultures.

Not if I can help it. The thought came unbidden to her mind.

As the aircraft neared, she turned to face her fate. Two figures rode inside the cockpit. They looked like normal men with blank expressions and headphones on their ears.

A dust storm would be handy right about now. Certainly, the ground was dry enough, the landscape sparse with an occasional scrawny shrub or a lone cactus. The greenery was less evident than at her Arizona home in the Sonoran Desert. A beetle scuttled by, unfazed by the heat.

The helicopter zoomed toward them. Before a hail of bullets issued forth, the dry dirt swept along in a gust of wind. Particles coalesced, spun, and boiled upward into a seething mass. Then, as if it had a mind of its own, the twisting cloud rolled toward the oncoming chopper.

She froze in place, watching in stunned disbelief.

Magnor stood beside her, his mouth gaping as the roiling cloud enveloped the helicopter and blinded its pilots.

The chopper exploded in a fiery display and a billowing tower of black smoke.

As suddenly as it had appeared, the sandstorm dissipated.

Erika's pulse pounded in her temples. Had she caused the phenomenon? Needing to test her theory, she stretched her hand out and visualized the dirt stirring.

Nothing happened.

Had it been her imagination that she'd brought the dust demon to life? Was this her unknown power? If so, how did it work? Willing it to happen didn't make it so.

One thing was certain—if she had a destiny to fulfill, those Trolleks and their minions were part of it.

Wind whistled through the hills, the only sound besides the crackling noises from the lingering fires. No one could have survived that crash, not from the looks of the charred remains.

"Now what?" She brushed her hair out of her face as she addressed Magnor with a calm she didn't feel.

He shaded his face with a hand. Sweat beaded his brow.

"Paz might be within range of our signal by now. I'll call for the shuttle. If he doesn't have time to take us all the way to Copenhagen, at least he can transport us back to Vegas." Magnor paused, his eyes narrowing. "But first, would you care to explain how that sudden cloud appeared?"

"What do you mean?" she asked with wide-eyed innocence.

He scowled at her. "It was convenient timing, don't you think?"

"I suppose so. How lucky for us." She cleared her throat, uncomfortable with the topic. "Go ahead and see if we can get picked up. I'd rather not linger."

Unless the two of them got out of there fast, they'd be stuck here at nightfall. The prospect didn't please her.

Thankfully, Magnor dropped the topic of their salvation and moved off to contact his colleague. Erika got out a water bottle and took a long draught. Droplets dribbled down her chin, and she absentmindedly swiped them away. Questions plagued her, but her brain was too weary to consider them. They were alive, and that was what mattered for now.

"So do we have a ride?" she asked Magnor upon his approach.

He stroked his beard, fatigue lines etching his face. "Paz will pick us up in the shuttle but not until later. He'll need a flat landing site, so we can't traverse the hills. We should head toward the city."

"Can't the bad guys track us wherever we go?" She tapped her wristwatch. "I thought you said this acts as some sort of beacon."

A sheepish expression washed over his face. "Oh, I forgot to mention it earlier. Nira said you can switch off the signal by turning the dials to noon and pressing the hour button twice."

"What? You knew this, and you didn't tell me?"

"It wouldn't have mattered. The Trolleks had already detected our location. Do it now, though." His face brightened. "Great Cosmos, if that's a vector device, you can transport us."

She tilted her head. "What do you mean?"

"The Trolleks have similar technology on their armbands. They use it to maneuver vectors within the space-time curve, parallel shifting themselves from one locale to another. Picture the place where you want to go."

"O-kay." Squeezing her eyes to slits, she imagined them back in Vegas. Zero response. "Well, forget that idea. How did I end up with a piece of their technology, anyway?"

"It's simple, my *knesta*. Your cells contain Trollek DNA."

Chapter Seven

"What do you mean, I have Trollek DNA?" Erika stared at Magnor, wondering if she'd heard correctly.

Magnor motioned for her to move along. She scrambled after him, resenting how he'd turned her life upside down. If he'd never turned up, she would be at the art show, exhibiting her wares and working toward her goals of opening a gift shop and getting an education degree. She didn't want to be here. Maybe she could ditch him somewhere and go home.

He squinted in the bright sunlight. "We have time now for more explanations." His steady pace was easy to follow. "Let me start at the beginning. Before recorded history, the Originals inhabited Earth. They predated your known ancestors."

"Where did they come from?" She watched her footing as they trekked along the dry ground, glad she'd worn closed-toe boots. A black insect scuttled under a nearby rock, making scorpions come to mind. The air, hot and dry, clogged her nostrils with dust.

"They came from out there." Magnor gestured to the heavens. "Their descendants took different paths on this planet. One group lived close to nature until mankind encroached on their territory. Those were the Trolleks."

She glanced at him. He wore a serious expression, like a schoolteacher aiming to ingrain a history lesson in his students.

"Wait a minute. What does *out there* mean?"

A muscle twitched in his jaw, but he didn't meet her gaze. "Do you truly believe life exists only on this planet? That your god created you for some divine purpose?"

She bristled at his derogatory tone. "I believe a creative intelligence designed the universe but then let evolution follow its natural course. So far, we've seen no evidence of sentient life elsewhere. Still, it might exist, despite the fact that we've gotten no response to our radio signals sent into space."

"Maybe the listeners chose not to respond."

Her mouth dropped open, and a gust of wind blew grit inside. She coughed and sputtered. "Where do you and your pals come from, Mister Magnor?"

He rounded on her, his sharp eyes flashing yellow. "We originate from a planet named Karrell, although some of my colleagues have homes on other worlds."

"Other worlds?" Dumbstruck, she could only stare at him. She stumbled over a rock and caught her balance.

His smoldering gaze captured hers. "You need to accept these truths, my lady, because soon the beasts will be upon us again. I have to know you will obey my commands without hesitation."

"Sure. Whatever." A breeze whistled through the forlorn terrain that stretched endlessly on all sides of them, the sun blazing overhead. She didn't have the energy to defy him.

He resumed his pace, sweat dribbling down his face. Maybe he should wrap his cape around his head for protection from sunburn and moisture loss. Erika wished she'd thought to bring a hat. It would have provided relief.

She shifted the straps of her bag, which weighed down her shoulders. There wasn't anything to do about it, so she trudged onward in silence.

If she complained, Magnor would take on the burden, and she didn't care to stress his arm that might still be healing. She swallowed, her throat parched. A drink would be welcome now, but it would be wise to conserve their water supply.

"Tell me more about the Drift Lords," she said as a distraction.

He shot her an approving glance. "The League formed eons ago when Trolleks first began invading Earth through the dimensional rifts. The warriors are called to arms only when an incursion happens. The rest of the time, they lead their own lives."

"What do you do when not deployed to dispel the enemy?"

"I have other duties."

"Such as?"

"That is not important now. You need to understand the danger in the present."

Clearly, she'd touched upon a painful subject. What life did he lead when not fighting with the Drift Lords? How did he come to be recruited into their team?

Hoping she would have time later to delve into his personal history, she sought explanations on a more familiar topic.

"How much do you know about the Trolleks?"

Magnor pursed his lips. "Humans persecuted them, and they were no longer welcome here. During a natural rift between dimensions, they passed through the gate to another world with pristine forests and fertile fields."

"So why do they want to invade us? Weren't they happy in that place? It sounds ideal."

He gave her a wry glance. "Were your Native Americans happy when they were forced from their land? The Trolleks felt this was their rightful place. In prior times, they made incursions during rifts, and the Drift Lords were able to force them back before the portals closed. This time, as I said earlier, the beasts devised a means to force the rifts open."

"But your team sealed them shut again?"

He nodded in acknowledgement, his braids swinging against his sober face.

"Stopping the invasion isn't our only imperative. With the rifts remaining open, the accumulation of cors particles would have breached the point of no return. The dimensional drift would have widened, causing a massive shock wave destroying everything in existence. That was Loki's original plan."

"He's the demon you mentioned?"

"Yes, and he manipulated the Trollek king into ordering the invasion." Lines crinkled around his eyes as though something else weighed on his mind.

"And now that you've sealed the rifts?" Could the Trolleks have another purpose besides taking back what was theirs?

"The main threat is from the beasts stranded here and from Loki, who grows more powerful. What he can't accomplish one way, he is now trying to bring about through natural disasters."

Erika wanted to ask him more, but her mouth was too dry and the heat had drained her energy.

The sun beat down upon them without mercy. Tying a scarf around her head provided relief, and her focus narrowed to their long and dusty trek.

"Let's rest now," Magnor said after another half hour or so. "It's best to conserve our strength during daylight."

He wouldn't get any arguments from her on that score. Erika sank onto a rock after eyeing the nearby soil for crawly things. She took a few gulps of water, craving more but rationing her portion.

Sitting next to her, Magnor covered them both with his cape to provide some shade. "I don't like how we're targets out here, but there's nothing we can do about it."

"Why not turn on your invisibility shield?"

"It would consume too much power to remain cloaked for so long."

"You should put on some sunglasses. You'll be blinded by the glare."

Her remark made him smile. She liked how it eased his worry lines and removed the tension from his posture.

"I have an inner eyelid. It's transparent so I can see through it, but it acts as a filter."

"You said you're from a planet called Karrell. What's it like there?"

"My home is in the mountainous region beyond the Hills of Agoora, where snow can be seen on the Great Crest peaks." His tone was so low, she could barely hear him. "At least, that's where I grew up. It is my home no longer."

"Why is that?"

He shifted his position, bumping her shoulder. "We'll use up too much moisture by conversing. Lean against me if you wish, wife." His arm went around her in a protective embrace.

Obviously, talking about his home upset him. Why was the man so reluctant to speak about his past?

****

Magnor folded the redhead against his hard length, every curve of her imprinted on his form. He fought the urge to covet her body and to bury himself inside her. She'd be repulsed if she knew the truth about him and would shun him the same way as his people. He could never reveal his shame and dishonor and wished she would cease her probing questions.

Why did she care, anyway? Their marriage was a farce that she'd nullify as soon as possible. Circumstances forced them together for now, but doubtless she'd want to continue with her life once the Trollek threat diminished.

The scent of her hair drifted his way on the wind, and he inhaled with longing. His dreams of a family had dissolved upon his banishment. Maybe it was for the best. Erika would never stay home and raise babes, like his tribeswomen. True, the females of the Tsuran battled alongside their men as warriors, but Erika had ambitions that went beyond home and hearth. She wouldn't be happy in a domestic role.

On the other hand, he admired her determination and her resilience in the face of adversity. She'd kept an open mind and had begun to accept her role in the prophecy.

The least he could do was to protect her from the personal threat posed by Dokter Algie Morar, the Trollek scientist who'd declared herself queen on this side of the rift. Algie had made it her mission to capture the women associated with the Drift Lords and use them as test subjects in her genetic experiments.

The only way to stop her was to find the secret weapon that would destroy the Trolleks.

He kept a wary stance as Erika dozed beside him.

Time passed until his ears picked up an engine noise from above. A spec appeared on the horizon and grew bigger. He nudged his companion.

"Erika, wake up. I believe our transport has arrived."

The shuttle descended in a cloud of dust as she roused. He helped her to rise, and then they headed across the dirt-packed surface to the boarding ramp.

****

"Erika, this is Paz Hadar," Magnor said to introduce them.

"A pleasure to greet you." The pilot gave her a broad grin after exchanging fist bumps with his comrade.

She murmured a polite response. Were all Drift Lords as good looking as these two? They could pass for reincarnations of the Norse gods. This one had engaging dimples and twinkling blue eyes beneath a thick head of caramel hair. The resolute tilt to his stubbled jaw suggested he viewed adversity as a challenge.

Hadn't Magnor mentioned the sons of Thor in that prophecy? Maybe they truly were descendants, and the ancient myths held more reality than people believed. That would make Odin one of her ancestors.

Shaking her head in confusion, she climbed the ramp.

Magnor's hand at the small of her back urged her past the hatchway. Paz plopped into the command chair at a console that reminded her of the space shuttle. She and Magnor had no sooner stepped across the threshold than the boarding ramp whined to a close behind them, and Paz initiated lift-off.

She grabbed at a metal bar on the bulkhead as her head spun, but it wasn't from the sharp angle of ascent. Amazingly, she felt hardly any motion at all. The flight deck held an array of gleaming instruments and dynamic displays labeled in foreign symbols. What kind of craft was this?

"Take a seat, Erika." Magnor indicated a row behind the two pilots' chairs. "If you don't mind, I'll sit by Paz so we can catch up." He rummaged through a cabinet onboard and tossed her a bottle of water and a bag of trail mix. Carting his own snack, he joined his companion up front.

Erika settled into a seat, the cap off the water before she'd even met the cushion. Water dribbled down her chin as she drank greedily before tearing into the nuts and dried fruit. Exhaustion claimed her, not only from the desert heat and the strain of their trek, but also from the shock of recent events.

Her appetite temporarily sated, she sagged back, yearning for some peaceful time alone.

"We'll touch down on the resort roof," Magnor was saying as she woke from a short nap.

With a jolt of alarm, she straightened to observe their approach to Las Vegas through a wide viewport in front. Why couldn't they just fly her home?

She voiced her request. Magnor twisted around to regard her, his lips pressed together.

"I'd like nothing more than to see you to safety, but you're coming with me. The threat isn't over. Even though you may have turned off your tracking device, the Trolleks know about you now. They will seek to capture you."

"Oh, that's great. I suppose those forms we filled out for our marriage certificate would tell them exactly where to find me."

His eyebrows raised, Paz glanced at Magnor. "What marriage? Did you leave something out in your report?"

Magnor cleared his throat. "Sorry, I haven't formally introduced you. Paz Hadar, meet Erika Sherwood—my wife."

"It's Erika Magnor now," she pointed out, "or don't the women where you come from change their names after they're married?"

Magnor glowered at her, as though the subject irritated him. "You haven't made the change legal yet. And why would you want to do so?"

She shrugged. "Good question, since you'll probably divorce me as soon as your mission is over."

"*I'll* divorce *you*? Excuse me, but you're the one who thought the wedding ceremony was a farce. You can seek an annulment."

Erika leaned forward and poked his arm. "Just because you tricked me, don't think I'm getting rid of you so fast." *You're mine for now, husband. Get used to it.*

Did she truly want him as a spouse, or was her statement due to the stipulations of her trust?

A flush of guilt washed over her. She hadn't mentioned the terms of her grandfather's estate to him, in particular the part where she had to stay married for a year to earn control of her funds. Magnor had been too busy telling her about the threat from the Trolleks who'd invaded her world.

She shifted her gaze to his broad shoulders, confident posture, and determined profile. Despite her efforts to learn more about him, she knew so little about the man. Yet he'd behaved honorably toward her, acted concerned for her comfort, and vowed to protect her.

His eyes narrowed, as though he sensed her mood and the secrets that silenced her. "Perhaps it wasn't I who tricked you, wife. Maybe I'm the one who was fooled."

Paz waved a hand in the air. "Can you lovebirds continue this later? We're approaching our vector."

Seething at Magnor's insinuation, Erika addressed the pilot. "Hey, here's another idea. Why don't you turn this thing around and fly us to Copenhagen? Wouldn't that be better than using a portal in that resort?"

Magnor faced forward again, his spine stiff. "Our orders are to destroy any recruitment centers we locate." He glanced at Paz. "Did you bring the supplies I requested?"

"Aye. It's too bad Dal is busy. He's our demolitions specialist," Paz explained for Erika's benefit. "I'll help you set the charges, but then I have to leave to continue my assignment."

"Where is your woman?"

"Jen is with Nira and Lianne. They're hunting the runic inscription that will banish Loki from this realm."

Erika swallowed as he banked their vessel. As they approached the Strip, she discerned the pyramid on the Luxor resort and the Parisian Eiffel Tower.

"We can go in cloaked, but I'll have to disable the inertial dampeners. Hold on." Paz punched in commands on his touch pad console. The craft jerked and then began a spiral of descent.

Erika gritted her teeth and clutched her armrests at the steep decline. She stared at the viewer in front as though in a dream. Surely this couldn't be happening to her. Maybe she'd still wake up and it would all be a nightmare.

If only!

Her life had become a kaleidoscope of events too bizarre to comprehend. *Better to go with the flow and worry about the consequences later.*

They made a clean landing onto a flat part of the roof at the Viking Vegas Resort. Had only one day passed since she'd met Magnor and they'd fled from this same site?

Wait, this was Saturday. She could still make the art show.

Or not. Her friends weren't planning to blow up the convention center too, were they?

The men stood and proceeded toward the exit.

"Here's the uniform you requested and a new case for your sword." Paz paused to hand Magnor a couple of items. "And this bag has the explosive charges. Be careful with it." He grabbed another sack for himself and hit the exit button.

Erika rose to join them. "Um, boys, aren't you forgetting about the innocent people inside this complex?"

"We'll make sure no humans are harmed," Magnor assured her. "You and I will locate the portal while Paz targets the casino."

"How can he lay charges with so many guards around?"

"Easy. He'll sit down at a blackjack table, for example, and slap a pack under the table. It'll stick on contact. No one will notice as he makes his way around the room."

"Let's hope the security cameras don't pick up on him." Her brow furrowed. So many things could go wrong.

Magnor tapped his friend's arm. "Signal me when you're ready. Erika and I will vector out from the transfer station right before you detonate by remote."

Paz gave him a grim look. "And the fire alarms?"

"We'll have to allow enough time for people to clear the place."

"What about the hotel and conference center?" Erika asked as they strode toward the rooftop door. Paz had cloaked the vessel behind them so it wouldn't be detected.

"Our goals are to disable the casino where the Trolleks select candidates and to blow the portal. Remember the man who broke into the Green Room during our competition? He screamed out a warning not to go downstairs. If this site is similar to others, the portal is located underground. That's where you and I are headed."

Magnor cracked open the door, his sword drawn and his face wary. He peered inside before giving the all-clear signal. Paz brushed past. The other Drift Lord gave them a mock salute and then disappeared down the stairwell.

"Would you like to make a brief visit to the art show to retrieve your wares?" Magnor asked.

She gawked at him. "You would do that for me?"

"I regret you will be missing the main event. We can at least make the effort to collect your items."

"But where would I put them? I don't have any luggage other than what I left in our hotel room. Wait, I have an idea. I could pay another vendor to ship the goods home."

Magnor sheathed his sword. "You can say your sister is ill, and you had to cancel your engagement at the show."

"My sisters are never sick."

Her cynical tone drew his curious glance, but he failed to

comment. "Nonetheless, this will be an appropriate story to gain cooperation."

"Yes, you're good at that, aren't you?" Why did this guy get under her skin so much? Everything he said, every action he committed, just made her itch to confront him. Or kiss him. "Let's get going, or Paz will be finished with his job way before us."

"I suspect he'll lift off before we're done at our end."

There goes our backup. Wondering what trouble they'd encounter this time, Erika followed him down a few floors and into a hotel corridor where they caught an elevator. Her ears entertained a low buzzing noise. What caused that? She'd forgotten to mention it to Magnor.

At the lobby level, he detoured into a men's room to change into the clothing Paz had provided. When he emerged, he wore a belted black tunic and tailored trousers to match. The sword was neatly hidden inside a long cylindrical container. He'd slung the strap over his shoulder. Nonetheless, wasn't he worried they'd be identified on sight?

"I like your team's outfit."

He grinned at her. "The fabric acts as protective armor against light projectile weapons."

As they entered the convention center and strode down the aisle where her booth was located, Erika spotted a pretty blonde chatting up her neighbor. Her neck prickled. The woman reminded Erika of the attendants in the casino. If her instincts were correct, that woman might be a Trollek.

It made sense the enemy would be interviewing people associated with her. She and Magnor might as well be wearing big red targets painted on their foreheads.

She grasped his arm. "They're watching my booth. We'll have to leave my things behind."

Those were some of her best sculptures, too. Swallowing her disappointment, she turned to go but Magnor stopped her.

"We can still employ someone to pack your things and mail them home." He found an amenable vendor a couple of aisles over, left the information, and paid the fellow an appropriate sum.

She'd meant to ask him about his source of cash, but not when he hastened her toward the casino.

"It's likely the Trolleks have concealed the entrance to their underground base somewhere nearby. That's their usual mode of operation."

Erika bowed her head, glad she still wore a scarf as they strolled between rows of slot machines. Patrons sat on benches, frowning in concentration at games that looked incomprehensible to her. She didn't spot Paz anywhere. Could he have finished laying his charges already? No, the Drift Lord would have signaled them. He must be keeping a low profile.

"How do the Trolleks get people to go below?" she asked Magnor in a hushed tone.

"They don't have to convince anyone. One touch, and humans respond to their commands."

"Then look for a bunch of people with vacant expressions."

They picked up the trail in the buffet restaurant, where Erika and Magnor had been invited to go for their wedding breakfast. Behind the lunchtime salad bar was an innocuous door labeled *Private*.

A regular stream of customers shuffled through this door. A costumed human employee stood by, nodding at each person who went past.

"Our turn," Magnor said, his eyes glittering. "Don't look so frightened. They'll know you're not confounded."

She washed her face of all emotion. "How's this?"

"Perfect." He clapped her shoulder. "Onward, my brave wife. Let us put an end to this enemy camp."

Chapter Eight

Magnor sweated as a beefy Trollek shook each person's hand at the bottom of a staircase. When had he kissed Erika last? Had it been less than twenty-four hours? His pulse accelerated. He'd hate to have come this far only to succumb to the Trollek touch.

When his mind remained clear and his will didn't subjugate to the beast, he breathed an inward sigh of relief. Her immunity still protected him, then. He hunched his shoulders and kept his face lowered, trudging along in line. The underground corridor led to more corridors, with closed doors on each side.

A sense of familiarity assailed him along with a musty smell. This underground complex was achingly similar to the one he'd first encountered at Drift World in Orlando.

They came to a fork in the tunnels. A Trollek sat at a desk, his fierce demeanor not cowering the spellbound humans who moved as though in a trance. He asked each person's name, age, and occupation, which he wrote down in a ledger. A disruptor rode at his hip and a shock stick on his belt.

"That way, *slogg*," the beast ordered a gray-haired man.

Another Trollek grasped the slave's elbow and shoved him along. Magnor's eyes narrowed. That particular line seemed composed of older humans, most of whom were likely over sixty. Why separate them out? This was something new.

Usually, the Trolleks only picked able-bodied humans for slave labor or their dastardly experiments. Same as at other sites, children were not among those enslaved. So why bother with elderly citizens?

His turn came, and he was relegated to the other side that held more fit subjects. Erika trailed after him, her red hair thankfully covered by a scarf. She gave a quick, indrawn breath as she approached the bureaucrat.

Upon questioning, Erika followed his cue and supplied a false name. Hopefully, the Trollek wouldn't notice the tremor in her voice. He exhaled with relief when the officer assigned her to Magnor's line.

Once they were sufficiently down the hallway and out of visual range of the Trolleks flanking their column, he bent as though to fix his boot. Without a word of warning, Magnor yanked Erika aside and into an alcove. The container holding his sword and strung across his back banged him from behind. The Trolleks hadn't searched anyone for weapons, presumably because they considered slaves to be harmless. His fingers itched to hold his blade, but he kept it sheathed.

He needed to find the portal, set charges, and vector to the coordinates Nira had supplied.

"Where are they taking these people? Why did you stop? And what are they doing with the old folks?" Erika's wide eyes and rapid respirations betrayed her nervousness.

"Sometimes they create villages which they screen from human view by means of a displacement field. They use the humans for slave labor and other things."

He mentioned the experiments conducted by Dokter Algie Morar's corps of scientists, the newly appointed queen's quest for humans whose genes were compatible with Trollek DNA, and her diabolical plan to reverse the sterility plaguing their males.

As he spoke, Erika's face paled.

"Is that why Algie wants to get hold of me? Because I have compatible genetics?"

He gave a curt nod, grinding his teeth at the thought of her being tortured in the name of science. Algie would be even more dangerous after seizing power.

A light blinked on his comm unit. "That's Paz's signal. He's ready to set off the fire alarm to clear the casino." He tapped a response before moving on.

"How do you know this so-called portal won't take us to a Trollek village instead of Copenhagen?" Erika hurried beside him, her slim body agile as she advanced.

"I'll enter the proper coordinates. We shouldn't have any trouble."

A coil of hair loosened from her scarf. She tucked it back inside the fabric, but not before an urge struck him to run his fingers through her mass of curls. They hadn't properly consummated their union, but at the rate they were going, they'd be lucky to live that long.

He took a reading on his PIP, confirming the presence of cors particles in the direction where the column of humans headed. Keeping close to the wall, he gestured for Erika to follow. They trailed the slaves toward a set of double doors guarded on both sides by armed Trolleks. The humans went in but didn't come out.

"We'll wait until the guards leave." He led Erika back down the hall in the opposite direction. "It's best to make our move when things have quieted down. I'm guessing the beasts process one group at a time. Likely, they give their victims a specific hour to report in upstairs. Otherwise, the portal's power would drain from constant use."

The sound of marching boots approached from around the corner. They'd be trapped between two contingents.

He twisted the nearest doorknob, grunting in relief as it opened into a storeroom. With a fluid movement, he hauled Erika inside and shut the door behind them.

Cleaning supplies, odd pieces of furniture, and various crates stood around along with a pungent chemical smell that made his nose wrinkle. A layer of dust told him no one came this way too often.

Erika split from him to explore. He lost her out of sight behind some piled-high containers when he heard her exclamation.

"Hey, there's a bathroom back here. Just what I need."

His ears picked up the muted sound of a door quietly closing. While Erika refreshed herself, he checked the nooks and crannies for surveillance cameras. Pleased to note the space was clean, he dumped his satchel from Paz and sword case on the gray concrete floor, then carefully lowered the pack with explosives.

He took a turn after she emerged, and then they sank together onto a worn sofa plopped among a jumble of discarded chairs, odd tables, and broken bookshelves. They ate nutrient bars and drank water. Not wanting to leave any trail behind, they packed their refuse in their bags.

Erika brushed a weary hand over her face. Her delicate features were pinched from fatigue. "How long until the coast is clear?"

He relaxed against the dusty cushion, appreciating the lumbar support at his spine. "The coast? We are far inland in the middle of a desert."

"It's a figure of speech."

"Oh, I see." He didn't understand the colloquialism but no matter. "I expect the guards in front to leave as soon as this group goes through. Then we'll see who remains inside the portal chamber."

"Won't Paz detonate his explosives in the meantime?"

"He'll wait until we're in place and the fire alarm has cleared the casino. We have a few minutes." His arm snaked around her. "Come, rest your head on my shoulder."

She settled against him. "How come you don't have a wife already, Magnor? I'd think plenty of women at home would show interest in a man as awesome as you."

She thought of him as awesome?

His loins stirred at her words and at the softness of her body nestled against his. He tickled her upper arm where her skin was bared.

"This world is my home now. I'm only concerned about one woman here, and that's you."

His line was as old as the hills of Agoora, but she must have liked it because she snuggled closer. Her face lifted, and her luminous green eyes regarded him with unabashed admiration.

Ignoring the warning bells that cautioned him against traitorous females, he lowered his head and brushed his lips over hers. Her succulent sweetness drew him back for another sweep. She sucked in a sharp breath and leaned closer.

Hunger consumed him. Aware of their precarious position and their time constraints, he still couldn't resist her allure. He deepened the kiss, pressing his mouth to hers in a silent demand. Erika parted her lips in response and wrapped her arms around him. His tongue plunged inside her welcoming warmth and danced a duet with hers while they clung together.

"Magnor," she murmured, her breaths coming faster.

Knowing he aroused her only ignited his flame. With a groan, he fully embraced her and crushed her body to his. His mouth plied her face with kisses and then settled again on her sweet lips.

Wanting to get closer, he nudged her onto his lap. When she faced him squarely, he grasped her nape and drew her head down for a long kiss.

Through his mental haze, he felt her body squirm atop his erection. Surely, she must feel it through their clothes. They didn't dare disrobe, but he yearned to feel her bare skin against his body.

His mouth melded to hers, while his hand roamed downward. She gasped when he touched her breast but didn't move away. Moreover, she seemed to want his touch by thrusting her bosom into his hands. He exerted all his resolve not to rip off her shirt right then. Instead, he slid his hand inside to trace her bra and the outline of her breasts. His heart thundered when he brushed her nipple, and it peaked under his strokes.

"I want you, my *knesta*," he whispered against her mouth. "You're mine to take."

"Don't stop what you're doing."

Her scent pervaded his senses, erasing his reason. Knowing he should halt before she made him witless, he obeyed her command.

****

Erika kissed her husband like tomorrow was doomsday and this would be their last chance to connect. She might be right. But oh, he made her feel so good. And this luscious man was *hers.*

When he touched her breast, need spiraled through her that wouldn't lessen until abated. She twisted her torso, centering the ache between her legs over the bulge in his pants. Her motion must have incited him, because his breathing became heavier. Her pulse raced through her veins, her heartbeat a staccato rhythm.

Empowered by how he reacted to her, she tangled with his tongue, savoring the taste of him. Her fingers traced the contours of his muscles, roaming from his powerful arms to his broad shoulders.

Oh, my. One of his thumbs circled her nipples, sending shocks of electricity along her internal wiring. His other hand crept downward, while her ache burgeoned into a raging fire.

He scraped her crotch, teasing her. She couldn't stand it any longer. She yanked his shirt loose and then unsnapped her khakis so he'd have better access.

She explored his bare chest after pushing his shirt out of the way. His hair-roughened skin was like a balm, offering nirvana and exciting her further at the same time. Splaying her hands across his broadness, she massaged his muscular outlines. Her fingers encountered his nipples, hard as tiny pebbles.

He shifted himself away slightly so he could reach inside her pants. Her palms stilled when his fingers dipped into her panties and met her sensitive folds.

"Ahhh, keep going." She exhaled the words on a long sigh.

"As you command, my lady." His hot breath fanned her cheek as his mouth left hers to nibble on her ear.

His practiced movements to the south narrowed her focus. Her desire intensified, shot toward the surface, and exploded in an eruption that had her jerking atop him. Her breaths came in short pants. Half-closing her eyes, she savored the sensation until it subsided.

Her limbs languid, she rested until her breathing returned to normal. Heat flooded her cheeks, reviving her energy. How could she have been so selfish as to accept her own satisfaction without returning the favor?

She rolled onto her side and grasped the tentpole over his groin. His head lolled back, and he groaned with pleasure. His hips moved as she stimulated him. Finally, he gave a muted cry as his release erupted.

Aware that time was slipping past, she rolled off the couch and straightened her clothes.

Magnor followed suit, towering over her and tenderly stroking her cheek. "I'll be right back, my *knesta*. Wait here."

She plumped the pillows on the sofa while he disappeared into the restroom. She'd just slung her backpack over her shoulders when voices sounded outside the door. Grabbing Magnor's sacks, she glanced around for telltale signs of their presence.

Her heart beating fast, she scurried toward the lavatory. Her knuckles rapped lightly on the door. "Someone's coming. Let me in."

"Where's my sword?" Magnor asked as she slipped inside.

"Omigosh, I forgot it."

Before he could make a move to retrieve his weapon case, the outer door burst open. Magnor shut the restroom door to a crack.

"Where do you suppose we're going to find a *maug* file box among all this junk?" a gruff male voice said.

"You got me, Warog, but the Leytnant said to bring him one. Stupid paperwork. I'd rather triage the humans."

"Me, too. When we're done here, *min drott* said to go upstairs. After the break-in last night, they want extra sentries by the secondary site."

"I don't see why. Humans aren't allowed near there."

"Visitors *are* right outside when the exhibit is open," Warog pointed out. "Those people aren't *sloggs* yet. It's a security risk, if you ask me."

Banging and thumping noises ensued as the soldiers sorted through the goods strewn about the room.

"I heard rumors a Drift Lord and his female were in the vicinity," Warog's companion said.

"I know. I'd like to catch them. The reward would buy me a nice plot of land back home."

His friend cursed. "We can't go home, remember? We're stuck here. But don't worry. This world is ours for the taking."

"It can't be soon enough. I don't know why the queen waits to give the activation order."

"She plans to finalize her experiments. It won't do us any good to conquer this world if our men can't populate it. We don't want our females to be the only ones to pass on our lineage, or our race will become tainted. Queen Algie's solution is our best hope."

"You sound like a Viden," Warog said, his tone accusatory. "Look how she usurped power from her husband, General Morar. I'm wondering if that wasn't her goal all along."

"You'd better watch your tongue. You're bordering on treason."

A loud crash sounded. "Here, I found the *maug* file box behind that chair. Someone should clean up this mess."

"A couple of *sloggs* would do. I'll suggest it to the Leytnant. We can beat the humans if they're too slow."

The pair guffawed on their way out.

Magnor signaled her. "Let's go. They'll be heading back toward the registration desk. This may be our only chance to reach the portal." He lifted his bags and retrieved his sword case, thankfully left untouched.

"What did he mean about Algie's experiments? How is that their best hope?" His earlier explanation hadn't answered all of her questions.

"Their males became sterile due to an impurity in the water on their world," he said after they'd slipped into the corridor. He spoke in a low tone so his voice wouldn't carry. "As chief scientist, Algie meant to find a compatible human genome to splice into theirs to solve the problem, but that didn't work. Her human test subjects kept dying when she injected them with Trollek DNA."

"Wait, I'm confused." She followed his lead and pressed her back against the wall as they crept along. "I thought Algie was their queen."

"She is now." His expression hardened. "Normally, females don't hold positions of power on Jak'tar, the Trollek home world, but Algie is a clan chieftain's daughter. Her father sits on the Council of Elders and has the king's ear. She received favorable treatment in being appointed chief scientist."

"Didn't I hear she was married to a Trollek general?"

"True. She helped Paz kill him so she could seize power. Now that we've sealed the rifts, no one opposes her."

Magnor peered around the corner and indicated it was clear to proceed. They padded silently toward the double doors at the far end and flattened themselves on either side while Magnor used his PIP to check the interior.

"It's safe. No one is inside. Come on."

Once in the room, Erika stared at the huge white arch from which wires and cables snaked everywhere. Four columns supported this structure, raised on a platform. Was that the portal?

She moistened her lips. How did it work? Would it scramble her molecules like the transporters on *Star Trek*?

Magnor strode directly to one of the columns and examined its control panel. Wearing a thoughtful frown, he entered a code onto the touchpads.

"So, Algie is going for conquest over science now?" Erika said to clear the muddle in her head.

"Not exactly. Her latest initiative is a dual-pronged effort, but never mind that for now. Get onto the platform."

He removed the charges from the sack Paz had provided and

stuffed the empty bag into his satchel. Then he set about clamping explosives to the columns. Once done, he sent a message ostensibly to Paz on his wrist comm.

"Let's go. We only have a few seconds."

Erika stood beside him on the dais, grateful when he grasped her hand in his. The buzzing in her head increased to a throbbing intensity.

The room shimmered, and her vision blurred. Everything in sight spun and vanished into a vortex that sucked her in.

Panic gripped her as she lost her sense of balance and felt herself falling. Magnor's strong grasp tied her to reality.

An instant later, images coalesced, and her feet landed on a solid surface. They stood in a room under another arched canopy next to a wall.

They'd been transported, but to where?

Chapter Nine

The room where Magnor and Erika arrived was similar to the one they'd left, except for the position of the portal. They were lucky no Trollek guards or human *sloggs* were present.

Eager to proceed, Magnor dropped Erika's hand and stepped off the dais. Had they reached the proper location?

He took out his PIP and did a quick calculation. His brow wrinkled into a frown. These numbers didn't match the coordinates he'd entered on the control panel.

"Give me your backpack," he told Erika in a terse tone.

"I don't mind carrying it. Your arm—"

"Is fully healed. Please do as I say."

"Fine, it's all yours." She withdrew her purse before handing him the sack.

He pocketed his PIP, removed his folded cape from the backpack, and then transferred over his supplies from the satchel. After slipping the sack's straps over his shoulders, he fastened on his cape and sword. His final order of business was to use his phase weapon to vaporize the satchel and empty cylindrical container.

"What are you doing?" Pausing halfway to the exit, Erika gaped at him.

"We're not in Copenhagen. I don't want to leave any evidence of our arrival."

"Then where are we? Could this be one of those Trollek villages you'd mentioned?"

"We appear to be in California." He strode to the door and

cracked it open. "It's clear. Let's see why fate has brought us here. If we meet anyone, pretend you're confounded."

They proceeded along a corridor and up a flight of steps to a closed door. Boisterous voices sounded from the other side.

Gritting his teeth, he twisted the knob and pushed the door open. They emerged into a lively gift shop crowded with people.

A pretty blond woman gestured to him from behind a sales counter. "Hello, I didn't expect any others to come through. Are you the last?"

"Yes, mistress." He bowed his head in obeisance.

She pulled out a ledger. Around them, customers chatted and browsed the souvenirs. Why were they so animated? Were they free from mind control, or had they been instructed to act that way?

His glance rose to a placard above the counter. It gave ticket prices for standard, deluxe, and VIP tours of Kevlin Meyers Studios.

Erika poked him. "Omigosh, we're in Los Angeles. This is KM Studios."

"Ah, it's another theme park." Enlightenment dawned. The controls back at the portal must have been fixed to these coordinates. But why send people here?

"Please put your index finger into this scanner, and then I'll issue your tickets," the attendant said in a flat tone.

When Magnor complied, something scraped his skin. The clerk examined her monitor with narrowed eyes. He hoped the analysis didn't expose his identity.

"You qualify for the VIP tour. So do you, Miss," she added after Erika had done the same. "Take these tickets, go outside and find your tram."

Could selected individuals from the casino be relegated here for further testing? What did it mean to be assigned to the VIP group?

There was only one way to find out.

They jostled their way past racks of logo tee shirts, baseball caps, framed photos of film stars, and other merchandise. Magnor sniffed the aroma of brewed coffee from an adjacent café.

Outside, boarding areas for the different types of tours were identified by signs on posts. He showed their tickets to a man in uniform who swept them onto the rear of a tram. All the other seats were already filled.

"Welcome to the VIP Studio Tour," their thin-faced male guide said into a microphone as the driver took his seat. "We'll be going on a two-hour journey into the imagination where you'll see backlot streets, soundstages, crafts shops, and more. If you look sharp, you might even spot a celebrity."

Magnor adjusted his sword on the narrow seat of the open-air motorized cart that held twelve people. An overhead canopy shaded them from the California sun. No one paid attention to them or noticed his strange garb. The other tourists stared straight ahead with vacant eyes.

Meanwhile, other guests boarded the standard tour tram to their left. This group spoke in loud voices with excited expressions. The men pointed cameras while the women studied guide maps. They appeared to be a normal bunch of tourists.

He squinted at the farthest queue, where there didn't appear to be a single person under sixty among them. Like the others in his tram, they didn't react to the bustle around them.

Glancing back, he saw the building they'd come from had been the Tour Center. If he needed to reach the portal again, this would be the place. Curious to see why they'd ended up at this particular locale, he decided to explore before moving on to Copenhagen. Besides, their directive was to destroy any recruitment centers, and that might apply here.

Erika leaned toward him. "Our group looks like they've been spellbound. Have you noticed?"

"Yes, and I'm wondering what the purpose of this place might be besides serving as a possible recruitment camp. Let's see where this tour goes."

"Our first stop will be Orientation for a brief film on the history of KM Studios," their guide said before taking a seat.

Their tram zoomed ahead through the main gate leading into the studios. Multi-story brick buildings lined the broad avenue beyond. According to their host, this section served as an inner-city street exterior. Magnor marveled at how real it looked with chained trash cans, graffiti-stricken walls and scraggly trees surrounded by wire fencing.

After rounding a corner, they pulled up in front of an old-style cinema. Other trams had stopped here too, ones that must have emptied earlier.

As directed, their group lined up to enter single-file. Inside the double doors, a uniformed attendant shook each person's hand and gave them a set of plastic framed eyeglasses.

"That woman touches everyone who passes through here," Erika whispered close to his ear. "Are you okay?"

"I believe so."

They took seats in the darkened theater, whereupon he stole a quick kiss as insurance against the Trollek mind spell.

"Stop it. You're not supposed to behave that way."

"You're right." He glanced around but the humans on either side of them stared straight ahead. "I don't see any of the older people here, do you? I wonder where they went."

A female voice over the loudspeaker system distracted him. "Welcome to KM Studios. Please put on your 3-D glasses and the adventure will begin. This innovative technique brings cutting-edge virtual reality to your studio experience. When you are done, you'll be ready for the next stop on your tour."

What? This was some sort of indoctrination? He steeled himself against the possibility that he'd be affected.

"At the conclusion, follow the instructions of the guide on your tram. This person will be your kabak, and you'll obey his commands. When you leave the studio and return home, resume your normal activities and wait for further orders. In the meantime, tell your friends how much you enjoyed touring KM Studios and encourage them to visit. Now sit back, relax, and enjoy learning about movie-making magic."

The 3-D film started with a montage of hit movies filmed at the studios then segued into a documentary-style description of the production facilities.

"This historic ninety-acre lot contains twenty-five soundstages, including one with an in-ground water tank that holds up to two million gallons." Images accompanied the male narrator's voice. "Our eighteen-acre backlot can double for a scene set anywhere, from a tropical rainforest to a bustling urban center.

"KM Studios is a global leader in the creation, production, distribution, licensing, and marketing of creative content and its related businesses, across all media and platforms. Every aspect of the industry is included, from feature films, TV, and home entertainment, to DVDs, animation, comic books, and more. Now let's talk about how it all started."

Despite his resolve to remain alert, Magnor got drawn into the video. When the film finished, he couldn't wait to see the production facilities in person. He blinked as the lights went up and the interior brightened.

Outside, his group boarded the tram for the next segment of their tour. They wound through various street sets—a Midwestern town with a white church, a broad New York avenue, an inner-city precinct, and a picturesque New England village.

As they trundled down a suburban street that looked so real, he could have sworn someone would emerge to cut the grass, he noticed the rear of the structures consisted merely of scaffolding. That's not the only illusion in this place, he thought with a twisted smile.

Magnor didn't believe in coincidences. He meant to discover what had brought him and Erika there.

At intersections, they spotted other trams snaking along. Those seemed to hold normal tourists judging from their dynamic expressions and lively voices.

Again, he wondered where the gray-haired group had gone. They weren't in sight anywhere. Nor did he spot them as their tram stopped at intervals and they got off to walk through cavernous warehouses holding props and costumes or various craft studios.

Their next stop took them onto sets for shows under production. Inside one of the buildings, Erika pointed to a boisterous crowd rounding the corner ahead.

"Look, those folks are on the standard tour. Why haven't they been confounded?"

"The Trolleks can't turn everyone who walks through the doors here into mind slaves. This place has to appear legitimate to outsiders. They're dividing people into three groups. VIP people like us have already been confounded and came through the portal. I'm assuming a preliminary scan at the Viking Vegas Resort shows these people to be candidates for further genetic testing. Hence the finger scrape at the ticket booth."

"And the others?"

"A certain portion of park visitors is left untouched. Some are probably assigned to a VIP tour to be newly confounded. And older humans are being segregated for unknown reasons."

He caught a snatch of dialogue from the regular group's escort, a lean young man in a logo blue polo shirt and navy trousers. His uniform colors matched the trams with their cobalt exteriors.

"Next we'll view the set for *Forensic Times*," the fellow said with a broad gesture. "This show is my personal favorite, and you'll be the only group to see where they film."

Magnor's eyebrows shot up. "*Forensic Times*! We have to join them. That's my favorite crime drama." His mission temporarily forgotten, he grabbed Erika's hand and tugged her their way.

"What are you doing? The guide will notice our absence."

"We'll say we got lost if he catches us. I don't want to miss this opportunity."

Erika hurried beside him along a corridor strewn with props. "Are you crazy? This isn't on our agenda."

He gave her a chagrined glance. "I have to see this set. It

won't take much of our time. We'll catch up to our group afterward."

"You must be an avid fan." She couldn't have sounded more astonished if he'd transported her to his planet.

"Why is that so unusual? Isn't watching television what males do on your world? We should fit right in."

****

Would wonders ever cease? Erika kept pace next to him, astounded by his behavior. Her great and mighty warrior liked crime shows on television?

"Why detective stories?" She spied the group ahead just as they disappeared behind a wall that didn't reach the ceiling. It must be the back end of a set.

Magnor glanced at her with a wry expression. "My people aren't familiar with a scientific approach to crime. They've never heard of trace evidence, fingerprints, or blood spatter. A hearing before the tribal council based on witness reports is considered justice. Many rulings might have gone differently if we'd practiced these techniques."

"O-kay." His bitter tone hinted at a personal interest in the subject. So did the hard glint in his eyes, but she'd pursue the topic later.

Meanwhile, she should remind him of their mission. What was it, again? To go to Copenhagen and find some ancient book that would tell him how to destroy the Trolleks? They'd ended up here instead. What other purpose did this movie studio serve besides another place to recruit human mind slaves?

A thrill of excitement shot through her. She'd settled into a reasonable routine in life, hoping to live up to her family's expectations. But she'd had to suppress her curiosity, the part of her that wanted to discover adventure around the next corner.

Now she had an opportunity to save the world. Had chance brought her to this juncture, or had the quest for more always been in her blood?

They caught up to the tail end of the other tour.

"We've lost our group," Magnor explained to the last man in line.

The guy eyed him up and down. "You're in luck. We have a couple of empty seats on our tram. But don't you belong on one of the sets here? That's a great costume."

Magnor gave a mirthless chuckle. "It's from my Halloween collection. I thought I'd dress up for the occasion."

"Sure, buddy." The fellow nodded as though humoring him. "Quiet, now. I don't want to miss what the guide is saying."

"Stage Nine holds the headquarters set for *Forensic Times*. The interrogation room, offices, and morgue are all there." The guide led them through a corridor with pipes overhead and unused furniture pieces leaning against the wall.

A faint banging sounded in the distance. Erika's nostrils clogged with dust. She supposed things were always being built or dismantled here. The soundstage was a warren of structures representing scenes from various shows, with fake walls, staircases going nowhere, elevated platforms, and spotlights aimed from overhead. Piping lined the perimeter of stark concrete walls.

"The characters' apartment complexes and the labs are also on Stage Nine," the guide explained, leading them forward.

"Where do they film *Ambulance Chase*?" a young woman with Asian features asked. She wore a backpack, as did the other young adults accompanying her.

"Stages One, Two, and Three. Watch your footing, please."

They stepped over wires taped to the floor before passing through an arch into another area. The young man stopped at a set featuring brick apartment building facades bordering a central courtyard. Trees, green plants and a working water fountain gave the impression they were outdoors.

"Here's where the characters live on the show. Let's go inside this house. You'll see how the interiors are interconnected."

Erika glanced around the first furnished home. A cozy living room held a couch, a cocktail table, a couple of armchairs, an area rug, and a fireplace. Magazines and coffee mugs lent an authentic touch to the scene.

The kitchen looked like she could cook a meal there, with its gleaming appliances and full array of cookware. She could have sworn that sink must work.

The attention to detail amazed her. Even the hairbrush on the dresser in the bedroom made the room come alive.

"Great Cosmos, I didn't realize how much labor goes into your entertainment vids. An army of people must work here."

Her lip curled in amusement at the look of awe on Magnor's face. "A movie studio needs actors and crews for each show, plus the administrative staff, writers, producers, and directors. I assume they can't all be confounded."

He gaped at her in horror. "What if they *are* all spellbound but have orders to go about their business and behave normally? These shows have enormous influence. Could the Trolleks have found another way besides direct contact to manipulate people?"

Fingers of dread iced her blood. Was the threat from these invaders even more insidious than they suspected?

"When they shot the pilot," the guide continued, "they went on location to an actual apartment complex that looks like this one. It was cheaper to film that way in case the show didn't get picked up. Later, they built these sets." He led them back to the courtyard. "A lot of this foliage is real, but some of it is fake."

Erika had to admit her to own fascination with the process. But they weren't here to sightsee. Did she have to remind Magnor of their purpose?

Before she could nudge him, their group headed en masse out an exit. In an asphalt lot, the guide pointed out parking places of stars. "And that's our Dumpster, labeled *Forensic Times*." His mouth broadened into a grin. "You know your show has arrived when you get your own garbage bin."

"Now what?" Erika regarded Magnor, who looked every inch a warrior with his stern bearded profile, his hand on his sword hilt, and his cape flowing behind him in the mild breeze. "If you're looking for proof that this is another recruitment center, I'd say it was that orientation film."

"Is that so?"

"The blond woman at the door shook everyone's hand as we walked in, and then the briefing instructed people to wait for further orders. What more do you need?"

Magnor spied a tram rumbling by and pointed at it. "Look, that vehicle is filled with older people. I want to see where they go. They've been singled out for some reason." Gripping Erika's elbow, he steered her in that direction.

"Why don't you tell your team to follow up on this place? I thought your mission was to find the Book of Odin."

"It is, but we landed here for a purpose. I'd like to determine what's going on besides the usual Trollek recruitment activity. Then I may let Dal deal with the demolition aspect." His gaze zoomed in on a golf cart parked in front of another soundstage door.

"Oh, no. You're not going to steal that vehicle."

"Indeed, I am. Come on, get in. We can catch up to the tram faster this way."

She hopped into the passenger seat while he retrieved his mobile unit, fiddled with the settings, and aimed it at the ignition. The engine sputtered and started.

"When can I get one of those PIP thingies?" she asked in a sugary tone.

He shifted gears and backed out of the parking space. "Sorry, they're special ops issue only. Hold on."

The sharp turn made her grasp her seat for support. Then they whisked forward down the street. She could just make out the tail of the tram ahead before it sped around a curve.

Chapter Ten

Magnor brought the golf cart to a halt as they rounded the corner and spied the tram parked dead ahead. Its occupants had already disappeared inside the building labeled Warehouse Number Ten.

Was that anything like the Tent Ten at Trollek camps where Nira and Jen had undergone interrogation?

Using his PIP, he shut off the ignition. He and Erika exited the vehicle and entered the building through an unlocked door. His quick scan didn't detect any surveillance.

"They must be pretty sure of their victims' compliance," he told Erika, keeping his voice low.

"We don't know yet if they are victims." Stray coils of red hair flitted against her face in the air-conditioning.

He hated risking her in this venture but admitted he liked having her company. A swell of affection made him long to plunder her mouth and sweep her into his arms, but they'd have to save that for later. Her gaze lowered as though the same thought had entered her mind, and a becoming blush heated her cheeks.

"You should wait here," he said, already knowing her response. An adamant shake of her head followed.

"No way. Listen, do you hear voices?"

Muted chatter mingled with clanging noises in the distance. They edged forward until meeting a fork in their path. Magnor hesitated. Which way should they go?

He chose to follow the sounds. The path led them down a series of twisting corridors. His boots echoed on the concrete floor as they covered ground. They finally emerged through another door into a cafeteria filled with patrons dining at long tables.

Where had the gray-haired individuals gone? These must be guests from the standard tour, judging from their younger ages and animated expressions. The smell of bacon made his mouth water.

Erika put a hand on her stomach. "I'm hungry. We should eat while we have the chance. And I need to use the ladies' room."

He frowned. "Make it quick. I have a bad feeling about this place. The people we were following are nowhere in sight."

They must have taken that other route back at the fork. From the plate glass windows fronting the street, Magnor assumed he and Erika had entered this establishment through a rear door.

He used the men's facilities, ignoring the looks of curiosity shot his way. People probably thought he was a cast member but didn't want to risk embarrassment by asking questions.

Erika waited for him at the head of the food line. He selected chicken parmesan and she got a large salad. How could she sustain herself on a stack of greenery?

"You should eat something more substantial," he said as they searched for seats. "We don't know when we'll have another meal."

"This has goat cheese and walnuts. That provides enough protein."

For you, maybe. It wouldn't fill my stomach.

They found a couple of vacant seats and claimed them. Magnor cut into his poultry and chewed a morsel, savoring the juicy flavor. The chicken on this world reminded him of pamadore back home. His tribesmen had made a sport of hunting the fowl in the wild.

Now he was hunting information instead.

"How do you like the tour so far?" he asked the pudgy fellow sitting next to him. He kept his tone light and conversational.

"It's fantastic, man. We got to talk to Ellen. Did you see her?" The guy's gaze lit with excitement.

"Uh, no." Magnor swallowed to cover his ignorance. She must be someone famous if everyone knew her name. "Have you noticed anything unusual during your rounds?"

"Like, what isn't?" The man pointed to him with a grin. "Look at you, dude. Are you on one of those, like, medieval shows? Sorry if I don't watch them."

Magnor chuckled. "I'm partial to crime shows myself. We got to see the set for *Forensic Times.*"

"Awesome. Are you a visitor then?"

"Yes, I thought I'd dress up for the occasion. Maybe I'll get discovered by one of the casting agents."

"Good luck with that." The man turned back to his companion, busy stuffing a burger into his mouth.

Erika coughed as though to alert Magnor that he didn't exactly blend in with the locals. His lips compressed with irritation. He wouldn't hide his sword. It was his trademark weapon and as much a part of him as his right arm. Besides, in this place, costumed characters were part of the scene.

He glanced at her prim expression, reminded again of her differences from his tribeswomen. They fought alongside their men in battle, showing prowess in combat and courage against stronger odds. Erika might not have the same fighting skills, but she exhibited bravery and resilience in the face of adversity.

However, the women of his tribe wouldn't dare challenge a man's decisions.

Maybe not, but the females of the Tsuran used more subtle methods to get what they wanted.

His fingers gripped his water glass. He'd never forget his sister's betrayal. And if he let down his guard again, he'd be subject to similar treachery.

Already Erika's charms tempted him away from his mission. He chewed vigorously while she scooped salad greens into her delectable mouth, which even now urged him to kiss her.

He tamped down his desire, forcing up a mental wall to guard him against his baser needs. He needed her to make the prophecy come true, and then he'd leave once his work was done.

But where would he go? Despair swept him. He couldn't go home. He'd been banished from all that he held dear.

He hung his head, not wanting her to see his shame. Even if he could truly trust her, he wouldn't have anything to offer. He'd lost his title and with it, his future. There wasn't any point to getting involved when their relationship had to end.

****

Erika sensed his withdrawal from the way his shoulders tensed and his jaw tightened. Had she said something to offend him? Perhaps he'd detected her negative opinion of his costume. It may look great on him, but he stood out like gold among clay. If he was hoping to avoid attention from their enemy, he'd gone about it the wrong way.

Too weary to argue her case, she rose and tossed her trash into the bin. They'd wasted valuable time but had to maintain their strength.

"Now what?" she asked Magnor.

Her stoic companion finished clearing his space. "Now we find out where that other group has gone."

His cape billowing behind him, he stomped off toward the rear entrance to the cafeteria. The noise from the commissary became muted the farther they went into the structure. At the same fork in the path, they took the alternate route.

Erika jumped when booted footsteps resounded from behind.

"Move along," a gruff Trollek voice commanded. "*Maug* humans. No wonder we're getting rid of you. You're too slow."

Magnor hauled her toward a shadowed recess. "It must be another Deluxe tour group coming through. We need to stay out of sight."

"They'll see us here. Try that door ahead."

He twisted the knob, and it opened readily. Inside the narrow space were cleaning supplies. They'd barely squeezed in among the mops and brooms when the group shuffled past.

Erika peeked out through the crack they'd left open and saw the older crowd being herded along like sheep, a Trollek bringing up the rear. She ducked back, nearly kicking a bucket over. Magnor righted it with his foot before it rattled.

Sucking in a breath, she stood rigidly beside him, neither one touching the other. Her nerves were acutely aware of every movement he made. She tried to ignore her thumping heart and racing pulse. Being near him did that to her, while she wondered what she'd done to displease him. So what if she thought he should dress more conservatively? It made sense, when they wanted to blend in.

Maybe wearing that outfit was his version of making a statement. Or maybe he equated it with his sense of identity. No problem, if they were on his home world. But here, he should make more of an effort to adapt.

She folded her arms across her chest, reprimanding herself for even thinking they could remain married for a year. Who was she kidding? He'd want to lose her as soon as his team defeated their enemy. It was obvious he couldn't stand being leashed in any way. And she didn't want a guy who wouldn't compromise.

After the group passed and they'd waited a safe interval, she eased open the door. At Magnor's nod of consent, she slipped into the corridor. He followed, moving with the stealth of a ninja.

His nostrils flared when the overhead lights dimmed and then reset. She put a hand to her forehead. That incessant buzzing had started up again.

"I hear that damn noise in my head. Why do I get it whenever I'm around these thugs?"

His brows drew together. "It means cors particles are nearby."

"Aren't cors particles produced at a rift?"

"Yes, but they also occur during vector shifts. If you hear a buzzing sound in your head, it means either Trolleks are vectoring into this site, or there's a portal in the vicinity. Or maybe you're allergic to the beasts." His teeth gleamed white in the harshly lit interior.

She slowed as they approached an open doorway ahead. "Isn't the portal back at the tour center where we first arrived?"

"Maybe there's another one here. Let's find out."

Or not. The sound of booted footfalls had them scrambling for a hiding place again. Magnor yanked her around a corner just before the group's escort headed back down the corridor toward the warehouse's side entrance.

Finally, they could proceed. Magnor had grabbed her hand, and he let go as though she'd given him a firebrick from her kiln. A wave of despondence hit her like a punch to the gut.

"What's wrong, Magnor? Have I said something to anger you?"

He threw her an impatient glance. "What do you mean?"

"You've shut yourself off from me. I'm not going anywhere until you explain."

His gaze hardened. "We don't have time for this now." He plunged down the hallway.

She scuttled in his wake. "Typical male," she muttered. "We're married, Magnor. It's important for us to communicate our needs to each other."

He stopped and glowered at her. "Our marriage may be necessary for now, but it's only temporary."

"Of course, you'd have no reason to stay with me once your mission is done." Was she so undesirable? Was that it? Or had he decided she wouldn't fit the bill for a suitable wife? Too bad their wedding ceremony hadn't truly been a sham.

Without another word, she moved forward. Hereafter, she'd treat their relationship like a business arrangement. But she couldn't help the pall of depression that settled over her.

Inside the room ahead, an arched canopy covered a dais

much like the portals they'd seen before. Four columns supported this arch, too, with cables snaking everywhere.

Magnor strode directly to the control panel and tapped the keypad. Then he withdrew his PIP and entered some calculations. As he read the display, stunned shock crossed his face.

"These people are being selectively eliminated," he said, his voice hoarse. Staring at her, he pocketed his mobile device.

"What?" She couldn't have heard him correctly.

"The last coordinates would put them in deep space."

"I don't understand."

He hopped off the platform, took her elbow, and steered her to the door. "This portal is fixed to certain coordinates like the one at the Viking Vegas Resort that brought us here. Let's go before we're discovered."

"But what do you mean?" she asked as they scurried back down the hallway toward the warehouse exit.

"They're sending those people to their doom."

"Deep space?" She finally grasped the concept. "Oh, God. You mean they're taking old folks and getting rid of them?"

The notion was so horrific, she couldn't speak. Her throat constricted. The Trolleks were even more monstrous than she'd thought.

Magnor's braids swung as they rounded a corner. "The beasts haven't deployed this pattern before. I'll have to contact my team."

He made a ferocious figure, his cape flowing behind him, his shoulders wide. A scowl creased his face. She kept on the opposite side of his sword, not wishing to get poked.

"Is this a new strategy on their part?" Fear put wings on her as she flew ahead.

The corridor walls seemed to narrow, enclosing them inside a death trap. At least the people in that particular tour group had been confounded. They wouldn't be aware of their fate.

"Algie must have decided the elderly population didn't suit her needs. Who's next, Earth's children? We *have* to find the Book of Odin to stop her."

"You'd think someone would notice people have gone missing." How far ahead was the exit? They veered around another corner. Had they come this way before?

"Someone has noticed. The federal government assigned a task force to investigate. Paz encountered Agent Monroe in Hong Kong. His people believe humans are being kidnapped by aliens."

"Huh, they're not so far off the mark."

Magnor's gaze chilled. "The dangers go beyond missing persons. Diplomats in high positions have been compromised. The invasion is more insidious than we'd realized."

He stopped as they reached the exit. Contrition washed over his face as he placed a hand on her arm. "Listen, I want you to know that I appreciate your company. You've been amazing ever since we met."

"Gee, thanks." His regard sent a warm glow through her. He glanced at her mouth, and she wondered if he meant to kiss her.

Wait a minute. Did he hope to soften her for a smooch, so he could protect himself from the Trollek mind spell? She couldn't remember if he'd told her how long the effect lasted.

"We should keep moving." She pushed beyond him to crack open the door. Humidity from the outside air hit her full blast. "Uh-oh."

"What?"

"A couple of those brutes are examining our golf cart."

"Shut the door. We'll have to use the front entrance by the cafeteria."

They whipped around and hastened down the corridor.

"You still haven't told me why you're acting so distant," Erika reminded him.

"I've no idea what you mean." Magnor cast her a sideways glance.

"One minute you can be passionate, and the next you're shutting me out. Are you afraid of what will happen if you let anyone in?"

"This discussion is irrelevant. I suggest we focus on an escape route."

"All right, be that way. But I'll dig deep until I learn more about you, *husband*. Don't think I will give up so easily."

Like it or not, they were wed until either one annulled the marriage or filed for divorce. She wouldn't be the person to do it, at least not for a year until she'd earned control of her trust fund. That is, if Magnor didn't get rid of her first.

In the meantime, she intended to probe until she learned his secrets. A reason must exist to explain why his moods shifted so abruptly. She sensed he craved love and acceptance but didn't feel he deserved them. What had happened in his past to cause these doubts?

And why did she care enough to want to know?

****

Magnor gritted his teeth, annoyed with Erika's probing questions and determined manner. At the same time, he admired her persistence. She could accomplish much when she set her mind to it. He didn't care to be the target of her inquiries, though. They made him too uncomfortable.

After his sister's betrayal, he'd not allowed another female to get close. His amorous relationships had been brief and casual. Yet here they were, married not even a week and arguing like a seasoned couple.

It irked him how they needed each other for protection. He required her immunity from the Trollek touch, and she needed his sword arm and fighting skills.

Could have been worse.

He might have met a woman wearing a wristwatch like hers who dissolved into tears at the slightest adversity or who harangued him endlessly. Instead, he'd encumbered himself with a worthy mate who should have wed a more reliable man. Not one like him, who'd lost his family name and led a nomadic lifestyle.

At the first opportunity, he should give her a divorce so she could find someone more appropriate.

Was that why he kept withdrawing emotionally like she said? Because he didn't want to get involved, only to have to leave her at the end?

Chances were that she'd leave him once she learned he'd been convicted of murder.

Torn between wanting her and reaching for a goal he could never attain, he didn't at first notice the shaking beneath his feet. The sound of glass shattering and people screaming sharpened his wits.

"Omigosh, it's an earthquake." Erika dove for the door leading into the cafeteria, shoved it open, and plunged through.

Inside, pandemonium reigned as the tremors increased. Glassware crashed to the floor and metal utensils rattled. Trays fell off their tables, landing with a clang on the floor.

Everyone crowded the double doors, pushing and shoving to get outside. As they joined the melee, he heard frightened talk.

"This isn't the first one," a fellow said to his friend. "These quakes have been getting stronger."

"Yeah, and I heard Mount Saint Helens is giving off warning signs again. That's not good."

"Did you hear about the tsunami that hit Indonesia? Natural disasters are causing damage everywhere these days."

This was Loki's work. The demon's original plan for conquest through the Trollek invasion had failed, so now he was bringing about disaster via natural catastrophes. Magnor had forgotten California sat on a fault line.

His gaze swung to Erika. Her power couldn't have caused this tremor, could it?

Unlikely. She hadn't been personally threatened, a factor needed to trigger her ability. He remembered very well the dust storm in the desert that had downed the helicopter.

They made it outside, where a crevice divided the road, its cracks spreading like ripples in a pond. Buildings swayed as he stood frozen. People scattered, running in panic to avoid falling debris.

"Magnor." Erika jabbed his arm. "We're in trouble."

"I can see that. How long does a tremor last?"

"That's not what I meant. Look over there. They're heading right toward us."

His heart leapt into his throat as he spied the troop of armed Trolleks bearing down on them.

Shoving his cape out of the way, he drew his sword.

Chapter Eleven

Erika grabbed him and kissed him. "For good luck," she said. And for protection against the Trollek mind touch.

Stepping away, she dodged behind him to allow his sword arm free play.

These Trolleks didn't disguise their evil intent. The six brutes wore military uniforms and bristled with armaments.

Erika's heart thumped and her pulse raced. Had her wristwatch given them away? She'd thought she had turned off the tracking beacon.

"Do not struggle. Fighting us is useless," said the Trollek with the most decorations on his uniform. He reminded her of a dog with his pudgy nose and hanging jowls.

"Come any closer, and I will slay you." Magnor stood firm, his legs apart, his sword lifted.

"Make a move and these unfortunate humans will suffer."

At his nod, the five others each grabbed an innocent bystander and pointed a knife at their throats.

"Look," a passing tourist said, nudging his companion. "They're staging a fight scene for our benefit. That guy wearing a cape and sword must be part of their act. Let's watch."

"It's not safe." His friend glanced around nervously. "Aftershocks might occur. We should go to the bus."

"I suppose you're right. Come on."

Avoiding broken awnings and shattered glass that littered the pavement, they hastened off down the street. In the wake of the tremor, most visitors remained unaware of the real drama unfolding in their midst.

None of the humans grabbed by the Trolleks looked frightened. Erika assumed they'd been confounded as soon as the nearest Trollek touched their skin.

"Throw down your weapon and be sensible," the enemy commander ordered.

When Magnor refused to budge, the leader gestured to one of his soldiers. The trooper drew his blade across a captive's throat. As the man toppled over, none of the others reacted.

Erika clapped a hand over her mouth. Oh, God. They'd killed an innocent.

"Sersjant Krok, do you wish me to get rid of this puny female?" another soldier asked with an eager grin. He held a young woman who looked to be in her early twenties.

"You want to see another die, Drift Lord?" Krok's lips curled in a snarl. "Surrender yourself, now."

Magnor threw his sword to the ground with a curse. The officer grunted with satisfaction and pointed a futuristic gun at him. Erika wished she knew how to operate the vector device on her wrist. Then she could whisk them away.

"Do not fear." Magnor glanced her way as the thugs closed in. "I'll find a way to save us."

Let's hope so. "We'll both figure out an escape plan," she said with a bravado she didn't feel.

Sersjant Krok sauntered closer and scanned her from head to toe. "Be glad I have orders to bring you in unharmed. In the meantime, you'd be wise to obey me." He took one of those sticks she'd seen other Trolleks carry, flicked a switch on it, and jabbed her in the side.

White-hot pain shot through her. She doubled over, her nerves seizing in agony. The effect lasted moments but left her breathless. At her side, Magnor growled and tensed.

"No," she rasped. "Don't do anything foolish."

"I suggest you heed the female," Krok said. He turned to her. "You will follow my commands. Understand?"

"Yes," she replied through gritted teeth.

"It's yes, my *kabak*. You may not be confounded, but you're still my catch. The queen awaits your presence in Tent Ten, but maybe she'll let me have you when she's done—if there's anything left." He gave a low chuckle.

She'd noticed Magnor's shoulders jerk at the alien's words. Was he alarmed that Algie, the Trollek scientist and self-proclaimed queen, would finally have her? What did that mean, *Tent Ten?*

The ranking officer confronted Magnor with a sneer. "As for you, Drift Lord, the Brigader has some questions for you." He stooped to retrieve the fallen sword.

"You have a military brigade here?" Magnor asked with a hint of surprise.

"What, this is news to you? Your team may have destroyed our dimensional gates, but we'd already brought in enough troops to conquer this world. We're only waiting for the queen's order to launch our offensive."

Sersjant Krok gave orders to the spellbound hostages on where to report and then signaled his troops to move out. They took positions flanking her and Magnor.

Erika swallowed past a lump in her throat. Now what? She didn't dare speak and draw the leader's attention. He might stick that rod in her side again. The pain had lessened but the buzzing in her ears was an omnipresent annoyance.

That was minor compared to what might be in store for them. Magnor faced torture to tell what he knew. And she… what would the Trollek scientist do to her?

Her stomach churned and her breath came short. If only she'd had a chance to talk to Nira Larsen in person, she might have learned more about her power. Then again, she couldn't reveal what she didn't know.

She marched beside Magnor, taking comfort from his resolute presence. He'd taken her hand, whether consciously or not, and she cherished his warmth and strength. Very likely, they'd be separated. It would be up to her to manage her own escape.

Good Lord, she wished she'd paid more attention to learning useful skills instead of filling her house with pottery and plants.

As they wound through the studio streets, avoiding rubble from the tremor, she hatched a plan. Well, sort of. She had a budding ability about which she knew little, but it had served her in a tight corner before. She only needed time to practice it.

Unfortunately, time was the one commodity in short supply.

A horrifying thought struck her. What if *she'd* caused the earthquake? Perhaps the event had been the result of her subconscious. Did that mean she could lose control at any time and wreak havoc?

Probably not. According to recent newscasts, natural disasters were occurring with alarming frequency all over the world. She may have had nothing to do with this one.

Speaking of the shakes, her body was trembling so hard she had to clench her teeth to keep them from chattering. Her fingertips felt icy and her heart pounded so hard she feared it would burst from her chest. Where were these soldiers taking them?

She glanced at Magnor, his body rigid, his face grim. Her gut wrenched at the thought of him suffering pain at the hands of their captors. How could she help him?

They'd entered one of the backlots, a suburban street that held houses in a colonial New England style. The two-story buildings looked peacefully sublime, like the setting for a sit com. Manicured lawns, white picket fences, and painted mailboxes gave the scene a serene ambiance. Even the afternoon air, warm and mildly spiced, added to the atmosphere.

On a far hill sat a pristine white church that looked to be real, unlike the fake fronts on the dwellings. Oh, no. They were aiming for that hilltop. Surely the Trolleks weren't operating an interrogation center out of a church, albeit a set piece?

She whooshed a sigh of relief when they went past. A tram rattled by behind them. Were those riders normal tourists? Could she call for aid?

She wouldn't endanger them even if she could. Erika and Magnor had already caused the death of one man and the enslavement of others.

Bowing her head, she shuffled along while feeling the weight of responsibility on her shoulders. Whatever she did from now on would have ramifications. Why, oh why, did this have to happen to her?

Be careful what you wish for, a voice in her head admonished. She'd wanted to be special. She'd wanted to be noticed. She'd wanted adventure. And oh my, had all three come true, albeit in a bad way.

Magnor squeezed her hand. She shot him a glance from the corner of her eye. He twisted his lips in what he must have meant as an encouraging smile, but it came out as a grimace. She squeezed back, giving him a nod. It was important he didn't worry about her. Then he could think of a way out of this fix.

He focused his gaze ahead, and his jaw tightened. Glancing in that direction, she gulped in dismay.

They'd passed a New York City street and headed toward a fake cemetery. Beyond it on a rise was a creepy mansion. Like the church, this structure didn't have scaffolding behind it.

Her steps faltered. She knew beyond a doubt that was where they were headed, because if screams emitted from that place, no one would think twice about it. They'd believe it to be part of the tour.

The Trollek nearest her growled and swung his stick around. She hastened her pace, sweat beading her brow. Either the humidity had thickened, or her shortened breaths came from fear.

Be brave. Face your fate like a daughter of Odin. Wasn't he a Norse god? Was she truly descended from one, if such a being actually existed? How else could she explain her ability?

As they neared the spooky three-story house, she noted peeling paint, missing roof tiles, dented gutters, and other signs of neglect. Her headache intensified. She could barely drag her feet up the steps onto the front porch.

The Trollek officer rapped his thick knuckles on the wood surface of the door. It swung open. The troops divided, allowing her and Magnor a direct path ahead.

Her stomach somersaulted. What horrors awaited them inside?

"I'll take it from here," said the uniformed officer facing them from the front stoop. He had a humped nose, oversized ears, and whiskers jutting from his chin.

"Kaptein Parug, may I present you with the Drift Lord's sword?" said their escort's leader.

Parug accepted the tribute before surveying his prisoners. "Did you search him for other weapons? Never mind," he added at his subordinate's chagrined expression. "He won't have the opportunity to resist. Step inside, humans."

Copying Magnor's example, Erika strode forward, her chin held high. He'd let go of her hand as soon as they reached the steps. She missed the contact, feeling forlorn without his comforting touch.

How would she manage to keep her cool without him?

His stern profile only made her more afraid for his well-being. He'd be courageous until the end, she thought, her throat clogging. She shouldn't have challenged the man and put roadblocks in his way. Her stubbornness could prove a fatal distraction to him. When he'd urged her to remain someplace safe, she should have listened.

It was too late to change things now. Better to make the Trolleks believe they cared little for each other and only worked together as temporary partners. Then they couldn't barter her life to him in exchange for information.

"What do you want with us?" she asked the captain, hoping he couldn't detect the tremor in her voice.

"We have important guests who are looking forward to meeting you." His sinister tone raised her anxiety level.

Another Trollek closed the door behind them, the thud bringing home their predicament. Her heart racing, she squared her shoulders and put on a brave mien.

To their left rose a staircase while off to the right was a living room. Discarded drink cans and food wrappers showed it to be in use. Did this house serve as military headquarters for their recruitment center, or for the entire region?

A pair of Trolleks formed on each side of her and Magnor. So they were to be separated.

"Don't worry about me," she told him. "I'll be fine."

"I've no doubt. You're resourceful and will survive." His mouth lifted in a wry grin, and then the troops led him away.

The Kaptein faced her. "We're using the basement as Tent Ten. You're to go there. I probably won't see you again. No one lasts long under Dokter Algie Morar's ministrations. Er, I mean our queen. We are unaccustomed to her new title."

His nostrils expanded, and he snorted with clear displeasure. Erika averted her gaze while wondering if she could use their personnel conflicts to her advantage.

They proceeded down the hallway and into the kitchen. Dirty pots and pans, soiled platters, and empty ale bottles littered the counters. The goons must not have any workers assigned to cleanup duty. Her gaze zoomed in on a rear exit that was bolted shut. Not so the cellar door that stood wide open. As they approached, she swallowed the rising bile in her throat.

Beyond the door was a flight of steps, barely lit by a single overhead bulb. The stairs led downward into the gloom.

She hesitated, balking at being trapped below. Once there, she might never surface again.

The sting of the shock stick prodded her from behind. She staggered forward, her heart galloping. A fall down those concrete steps might be fatal. She grabbed the handrail, tears pricking her eyes.

Her spine burning where she'd been jabbed, she began her descent.

****

Magnor, having been disarmed by his escort, climbed the staircase toward the third floor. At least they'd let him keep his boots, after confiscating his phase pistol and dagger.

His mind wandered to Erika, wondering what would become of her. He'd heard the other Drift Lords describe the trials their mates had overcome at Algie's hands, and his fists curled in helpless rage. He couldn't bear for Erika to be subjected to the same torment.

Unfortunately, there wasn't much he could do for her at the moment.

The troops prodded him up yet another staircase to the attic. As he emerged at the top, he glanced around. The space had been completely rebuilt into a loft, cooled by a noisy air-conditioning unit. A musty odor prevailed along with a coppery smell.

His senses heightened. *Blood.*

The man seated behind a wide mahogany desk rose with a smile and gestured for him to come closer. A single armchair faced the desk, and as he neared, he noticed the shackles and the stain on the wood planked floor.

His jaw clenched while remorse swept him. He should never have let Erika accompany him. He should have insisted she remain behind in safety while he completed his mission. Now he'd not only failed her, but his teammates also. Without the Book of Odin, they had no hope of quelling the Trollek invasion unless Prince Zohar assigned another to his task. But each of their assignments was invaluable and none could be spared.

Wait a minute. Wasn't Yaron, their medic, supposed to be sabotaging Algie's experiments and destroying her research? Maybe his colleague was in the vicinity if he'd been tracking the scientist, who now called herself queen.

Or not. Yaron's other assignment was to develop an antidote to the confounding spell by analyzing the components of Nira's blood. He might be back in the lab.

Nor could Magnor count on the others. Paz was busy coordinating resistance efforts among their allies. Zohar was helping Nira search for the ancient rune that would bring the prophecy to fruition. Kaj was working with Agent Monroe to identify compromised individuals within the global governments. And Dal, their demolitions expert, would be occupied targeting enemy recruitment centers.

"Why are you standing there, Drift Lord? Be seated."

The Trollek behind the desk spoke in a commanding tone. At his signal, the troops came forward, grabbed Magnor by the arms, and hauled him to the chair. They fastened him down with leather straps around his wrists. He faced his interrogator, washing any emotion from his expression.

"I am Brigader Omeron." The Trollek puffed out his chest, various medals flashing on his belted uniform tunic.

The officer wore a disruptor at his side along with a curved knife and the usual shock stick. A tall male, he had husky shoulders, a thick neck, and a peppery beard. Bushy eyebrows partially obscured his sunken dark eyes, while a mole dotted his elongated nose.

"A brigader usually commands a brigade. Are there many troops stationed here?" Magnor asked in a mild tone while doing a quick mental calculation. If so, several thousand soldiers might occupy the studio premises. Where could they be billeted?

Omeron rose from his chair. "I will ask the questions, Drift Lord. From your manner of dress, I assume you are the one they call Lord Magnor? You weren't on our original roster for the team. When did you graduate the Academy?"

"I never went through League training. I'm only an apprentice."

Omeron raced forward in a blur of speed and swatted him on the head. "Come now, do you think I'm a fool? You fight like a skilled warrior."

Magnor strained against his bonds. "I am a tribesman of the Tsuran."

"What is that? Some new branch our enemy has established?"

"No, we are natives of Karrell. We live in the mountainous

regions and rarely show ourselves to outsiders. I, uh, left my home to seek adventure elsewhere."

"So how did you join the Drift Lords? You don't possess their special trait?"

"That is correct." He saw no harm in telling the truth. "I do not share their ability to detect cors particles. I was hired to protect Prince Zohar from his political enemies."

"You lie. The Drift Lords allow no one else into their ranks, and yet you work in concert with them. Do not tell me you're a mere bodyguard."

"At first, that was my assignment. If you don't believe me, ask Algie Morar. She'll confirm my story. Is she in charge here? Also ask her what happened to her husband and how she seized power right after his death."

"You are not to speak against our queen." The brigader's fist connected with Magnor's jaw, snapping his head back.

He bore the blow stoically. Maybe he could plant seeds of distrust among the enemy.

A swishing noise came from a darkened corner. Magnor caught the frightened glances of his escort. What was back there, a leashed animal?

"My colleague, Paz Hadar, fought a battle against General Morar while the other Drift Lords destroyed the spearhead gateway your people were building. Algie helped him win so she could take command. She's looking out for herself, Brigader. You'd better watch your back."

"Insolent fool!" With a growl of rage, he pummeled Magnor about the head and face, with a final punch to the gut for emphasis. "Now tell me your mission and how close your team is to fulfilling the prophecy."

"My mission is to defeat your entire race, you son of a liver-bellied *wagmire*." His face bruised and his gut throbbing, Magnor spat a wad of blood from his mouth. "You want to know my role with the Drift Lords? Very well, I'll tell you. They seek to grow their ranks. Being able to detect cors particles will no longer be the sole criteria for acceptance into the Academy. I'm their test subject. If I succeed in my mission, I'll achieve full status as a Drift Lord. And then many more will follow."

The brigader guffawed, jiggling his thick lips. "So far, you are failing admirably. We need not worry on that score. Now answer my question. The prophecy says that the six daughters of Odin must unite with the six sons of Thor to utter the ancient words and prevent the coming apocalypse. Have you found the relevant rune? Have the six sisters come together?"

Magnor shook his head, his jaw throbbing. "I won't tell you anything further. Do your worst or kill me now. I'll die before I talk."

"Oh, you'll wish you could die, Drift Lord. You may claim you're an apprentice, but you're a capable warrior in your own right. We have methods for men of your ilk."

"You won't break me, even if you use your infamous boratus worms."

Paz had described this interrogation technique from his sojourn as a guest of General Morar. Magnor shuddered at the thought of the wriggly creatures boring their way into his nerve ganglia, but he'd bear the pain if necessary.

The officer smirked. "Ah, but it isn't I who will continue your inquisition. *He* awaits the glorious opportunity."

Brigader Omeron pointed to the corner, where an ominous shuffling sounded. "Leave us," he said to his troops, "or risk your lives. Not many can withstand the Prince of Darkness."

The armed Trollek soldiers scuttled from the room as if a fireball had erupted. Magnor wondered what manner of monster approached him.

He squared his shoulders, prepared to face his doom.

Chapter Twelve

"I'm Algie Morar, Chief Scientist and Queen of the Trolleks. I've been eager to meet you." The blond-haired woman at the bottom of the basement steps greeted Erika with a grin.

She didn't look like a mad scientist in her clingy black dress and low-slung heels. Stunningly beautiful, Algie had clear blue eyes that shone with determination. She grasped Erika's hand in a firm shake. Golden hair cascaded to her shoulders in soft, layered waves.

"You will lie on that table and follow my orders," Algie said, observing her with a sly expression.

A sweet scent drifted into Erika's nostrils, weakening her resolve. Alarm bells rang in her mind.

She jerked her hand away. "I don't think so."

Algie nodded. "I had to make sure you could resist my confounding. You *are* one of the prophesied six." She walked over to a wall, took a tan lab coat off a hook and donned it.

Erika's heart thudded as she surveyed the laboratory with its single treatment table covered by a ragged sheet, counters strewn with metal instruments, and other pieces of equipment.

"Come inside," Algie said with an ingratiating smile.

"No." Erika dug in her heels.

"Please don't make this difficult." Algie held up a hand as the officer behind Erika raised his arm, meaning to strike her again with that pain-inducing rod. "That won't be necessary, Kaptein. You and your men are dismissed."

The Trollek pounded his fist against his chest. "As you wish, my queen." Turning on his heels, he stepped onto the lower rung of the stairs.

Her voice called out more softly. "Good work, Parug. This pair has eluded us before. I feared they might slip from our grasp again."

The kaptein hesitated. "Our surveillance caught them when they entered the studio grounds. How they got here or learned about this compound are yet to be determined."

"Indeed, the Brigader will be asking the Drift Lord those questions. I need the woman for more important matters."

Kaptein Parug inclined his head in acknowledgment then retreated up the steps along with the rest of Erika's escort. The door to the kitchen slammed shut after him.

Algie's lab assistant lumbered forward when summoned. He was a huge male with an ugly pockmarked face and a smell like a dead animal. Or maybe that odor didn't emanate from him. Erika sniffed, her nose wrinkling. Traces of bleach rent the air.

"Lie down, and we'll get started." Algie gestured toward the table.

Erika sought to delay the inevitable. "Why do these soldiers obey you? I understand you're the first female of your race to wear the crown. Have you had an official coronation?"

A flicker registered in the assistant's gaze then extinguished as Algie shot him a glance.

"We're not on Jak'Tar here. In this realm, we recognize the worth of our females. Don't we, Croft?"

"Aye, my queen." Her assistant gave a slight bow.

"Unlike that fool, King Jorg, I openly acknowledge our alliance with the Dark Lord. At first, I didn't agree with his methods, but I've come to see its advantages."

"Who do you mean? What methods?"

"Sit down, and we'll talk. If you act reasonably, force won't be necessary. I promise you won't be restrained." Algie patted the table's surface.

Erika walked over and sat on the edge. Her knees were

wobbly and her body trembled. Nonetheless, she maintained a confident air.

"I don't know if your companion explained the rationale behind our incursion into your world." Algie clasped her hands behind her back and paced the room.

Erika remained silent, wanting to hear what the self-appointed queen had to say. Besides, she didn't want to inadvertently give away information Magnor's team might deem sensitive. Wishing she'd met the other Drift Lords, she pressed her lips together and waited.

"Over time, we noticed our reproductive rate had been declining." Algie's brow wrinkled in concentration. "An analysis showed the water on our world contained an element that reduced male virility. This led to two choices: we could raise the incidence rate of childbirth by having our females mate with human *sloggs*. Or we could correct the problem."

"Wasn't there some way to remove the contaminant from the water reservoirs?" She sympathized with their plight but not with their solution.

"No, we tried every means, and the results were the same. We could identify the specific element causing the problem, but we couldn't locate its source to shut it off."

"What about a countermeasure?"

"We tested every possible angle, from filtration to binding agents. Nothing reversed the effects."

"So you gave up?"

Algie nodded. "King Jorg urged the Council of Elders to claim what was rightfully ours—the clean waters on Earth. We devised a means to force open the rifts. Our scouts came through to set up centers of operation."

Erika scrunched her forehead. "I don't understand. Did you want our resources, or our men to mate with your females?"

"Intermating would dilute our bloodline. That wasn't the ideal solution. I had a better idea. Once upon a time, we all descended from the Originals who inhabited this planet. Some humans might still possess remnants of these traits. If I could find a compatible strand of DNA, perhaps I could splice it into our males to restore their virility."

"Hence your experiments, which mostly failed from what I gathered." Was it wise of her to say so?

"Until recently." Algie's eyes fired with enthusiasm. "I realized we could approach the problem differently. Why try to fix the males of our species? Instead, we should test humans and mark the ones with related genes. Then we could suppress their human DNA and turn them into Trolleks like us. That would sufficiently increase our genetic pool."

Erika's blood chilled at her casual tone. It sounded like something out of a horror movie.

"If you have a solution to your problem, why do you need me?" She hunched forward, her back aching.

Algie wagged her finger. "Because you, my dear, along with your five sisters in the prophecy, share certain strands of our DNA. You're the best test subjects we could have."

"Rumor says we're descendants of Odin. Did the gods really exist?"

Algie chortled. "The Originals may have seemed godlike to their future generations. Some of them did have unusual traits. You inherited their abilities."

"And this dark lord whom you follow? Have you considered the possibility that he may be using you for his own purposes?" She rested her hands on the treatment table for support.

"I'll ask the questions here, Erika. I'm hoping to gain your understanding. Your cooperation will help my race to survive and our people to thrive. You wouldn't want to be responsible for our extinction, would you?"

Heck, yes, if it meant ridding the world of your kind.

Erika darted a glance at the attendant, who stood by with his arms folded across his chest and a scowl on his face. "If you're so intent on saving your species, why did you seize power and declare yourself queen? Is it true you helped a Drift Lord kill your husband?"

Algie stalked over and slapped her with a stinging blow to her cheek. "Do not challenge my authority. Action needed to be taken. The Jorgonauts, followers of King Jorg, would merely have us conquer each world and enslave its populace.

"I, on the other hand, will swell our numbers with new blood. Rather than make *sloggs* out of the humans, I will turn them into Trolleks. Once I've perfected my techniques, we can apply them to your entire species."

"Yes, but at what cost? Won't any offspring still contain human DNA, even if it's been suppressed? Who knows when down the road those traits will resurface? You risk the very survival of the race you're trying to save. Are you sure you're serving science now, or your own aims?"

"Science still offers our best solution. We won't have to confound your people when we can subjugate them by other means."

Erika glanced at the guard, noting his interested mien and hoping he was a Viden, one of the Trollek factions who'd supported Algie and her scientific solution. If they thought their queen had taken power for her own ends, they might oppose her cause.

"What about your alliance with the power behind the throne? What are his goals? Does he even care about your people? Isn't he aiming to destroy the universe, including all of its inhabitants?"

Algie moistened her lips, shooting an anxious glance around the room as though a hidden force might be listening. "The Dark Lord has sworn to protect us in exchange for doing his bidding. Already one of his promises has come true. He said we could rule this world, and it's nearly ours."

"Yes, about that." She shifted her position. Her hands had started to go numb from too much pressure. "When will you be activating the government officials under your control?"

"What do you know of our subversive efforts?" Algie's eyes gleamed with malice as she stood in front of Erika.

Erika realized she'd revealed too much. "Not a lot," she lied. "I've only caught snatches here and there. The Drift Lords know you're after world domination." Who knew a villain that wasn't?

"Not world domination, Erika. We're going to take the universe. This planet is only the beginning."

"I gather your plan is to either confound people or turn them into Trolleks like you. What about the elderly? Why are you sending them into deep space?" She caught Algie's startled glance. "Oh, yes, we found the portal. Have you no use for the aged population?"

Algie's gaze hardened. "The elderly, the infirm—we might as well get rid of the contamination from the start. We will purify our line and thrive in a new world order."

Led by you, of course. This same refrain of racial cleansing had been repeated throughout history.

Erika pushed herself off the table and stood. She couldn't keep sitting there with her legs dangling. Her feet tingled from lack of circulation.

Algie pursed her lips. "We need to get started on your tests." She moved to a counter and lifted a syringe. "Menig Croft, put her on the table."

"Aye, my queen." His jaw clenched, the soldier advanced.

Erika slipped sideways. "Let's be sensible about this. Our scientists could help you develop a cure for your people's problem. Why don't you ask for help?"

"It's not our way." Algie gripped the syringe in one hand and wheeled over a metal pole with the other. An IV bag hung from a hook, its tubing twisted and secured.

"No!" She wouldn't allow the Trollek scientist to experiment on her.

As Croft grasped her arm, Erika remembered the dust dervish in the desert and how she might have been responsible. Using visual imagery, she delved through the ground's surface to its virtual layers beneath, to the substrata, to the tectonic plates. If only she'd studied geology, but earth sciences had never held her interest.

Ignoring Croft's fingers that dug into her flesh, she pictured herself grabbing hold of the mantle underlying the earth's crust. She yanked on it in her imagination, but nothing comparable happened in reality.

Her concentration broke when the brute lifted her and flipped her onto the table. Spine down, she stared at the ceiling and gritted her teeth.

This time she gave a more violent mental shake. Ripples extended upward through layers of substrata until reaching the surface.

Again, no corresponding response in real time. Was she wrong about her power possibly being related to the earth?

Croft's shadow fell over her as he lifted one of the leather restraints prior to clamping it onto her wrist.

Desperation clawing at her, she imagined herself grasping fragments of clay deep underground and kneading them together. They coalesced into larger clumps and melted in the heat coming from the magma below. Molten material surged upward through the cracks she'd created in her mind.

A low rumble sounded in the cellar, and the ground jerked.

"It's another earthquake," Erika said, jubilant that her theory had worked. "Quick, we have to get outside."

A crevice split the concrete floor, racing toward Algie and Croft. Sounds of glass shattering and objects thudding from above reached them. Instruments fell off the metal tray, crashing to the floor with a loud clang.

Gathering her wits, Erika yanked her arm free from Croft's grip, rolled off the table on the side away from him, and dashed for the stairs.

A blur of motion followed her.

"Not so fast," Algie said from behind.

Damn, hadn't Magnor mentioned they moved with super speed? The door was just ahead, up a flight of steps. A few more feet, and she could make it.

She turned and kicked at Algie to keep her away. Croft, a

snarl baring his teeth, thrust his queen aside and jabbed his shock stick at Erika.

Erika dodged the blow while wondering if offense might be a better defense. As she whirled to spring up the steps, she brought forth her mental imagery and gave the underlying layers a sharp yank. The ground shook side-to-side, making Croft stumble.

She still faced a closed door at the top of the landing. Would it be locked?

She'd taken her first steps upward when the door burst open. A large figure ranged in the doorway, blocking her access.

****

A hairy gray beast lumbered into Magnor's view, its eyes glowing and its fangs exposed. His heart pounded as he imagined those teeth ripping out his throat. The beast's size was larger than any canine he'd encountered. It prowled closer, sniffing his legs while Magnor's blood curdled.

"Meet Fenrir, the mighty wolf who slayed Odin at the battle of Ragnarok," Brigader Omeron said. "He's a shifter like his sire, whom he serves now. As do we all."

The animal opened its mouth and spoke in a gruff voice. "Until our lord regains his true form, I speak on his behalf. Behold the magnificence of Loki, companion to the gods."

An inky cloud separated from the shadows and approached from the opposite side of the room. The dank smell of rot accompanied it.

Magnor searched his memory for the myths Nira had taught him. Loki, if he recalled properly, was a frost giant's son fostered by Odin. He'd caused endless trouble for the residents of Asgard, home of the Norse gods.

Loki had three children, Fenrir being one of them. The sea monster, who lived in the waters surrounding Midgard where humans dwelled, was another. And so was Hel, ruler of the dead.

After Loki caused the death of Balder, one of Odin's sons, he was banished to a cave and chained to a rock beneath a serpent who dripped poison onto his face. He'd remained in this prison until Ragnarok.

Magnor had to make sure history didn't repeat itself.

"Loki, I thought you were stuck in an underground cave. Is this really you or an embodiment of your evil?"

The thunderous cloud roiled and twisted like a wraith from hell. When the wolf responded, its voice echoed throughout the attic.

"Until I am free, my visits to this realm are limited to this shadowy mist. The walls of my cavern crack and widen even as we speak. Soon I will regain my strength, and then I will unleash a catastrophe the likes of which you cannot imagine."

Magnor tried unsuccessfully to wrench his hands loose. "We've sealed the gates. There will be no further accumulation of cors particles at the rift horizons. Without the widening dimensional drift and the resultant blowout, how do you plan to free yourself from your prison?"

Fenrir cackled, an eerie sound coming from a wolf. Drool slobbered from his mouth as he ranged back and forth in front of Magnor. "The dimensional plates underlie the tectonic plates of this world. Disrupt one, and I disrupt the other."

Magnor's heart raced as he gleaned Loki's purpose. "We will stop you. So the prophecy states. So shall it be."

"The prophecy calls for the six sons of Thor to unite with the six daughters of Odin to recite the ancient rune. I have you and your lady. That leaves only five of each. The prophecy will not apply."

"Untrue. I wasn't born with the genetic trait inherent to the Drift Lords. Nor have I been accepted officially into their League. Who's to know if they'll find another warrior to join them, one whose latent power becomes evident?"

"We have the woman."

"Yes, but is she the rightful one?"

"Have you found the prophesied rune yet?"

"Maybe." A cramp in his lower back made him shift his weight. *Maug* hard chair.

Fenrir approached, salivating next to Magnor's ankle. One chomp from that beast, and he'd limp for the rest of his life.

Never mind what else they'd do to him. He'd been trained from childhood to resist torture. His people might be farmers, but they'd fought neighboring tribes in an ages-long struggle. He had learned to wield a knife in battle before using one as cutlery.

His gut clenched at the thought of Erika somewhere below, a captive of Algie. The Trollek scientist might believe she was in the right to save her people with her genetic programs, but that was an excuse to maim and kill thousands of humans. Even now, she might be infusing Erika with her latest compound, causing the twisting, excruciating pain that often resulted.

If only he could get to her. What he faced might be no less, but he'd die with honor. Erika might die in screaming agony, and he couldn't prevent it.

Her defiant green eyes and plush lips floated into his mind. His nostrils flared at the remembered scent of her. He'd kill these *doniks* if they hurt his woman.

His woman. Aye, he couldn't deny it. Destiny meant for them to be together. He'd suspected as much from the moment he had walked into that casino and spotted her. It seemed an improbable outcome, considering his origins and her personal goals. And now they'd never get the chance to explore their future.

Cold dread tore the veil of his thoughts. The black vapor had seeped across the floor and oozed up his leg toward his chest.

Shadowy fingers extended from its midst and dove into his flesh. The entity squeezed his heart until suffocating pressure stole his breath. Blood suffused his face. He bent forward as far as his bound wrists would allow but it didn't ease his breathing.

A voice entered his head. "Tell me, Drift Lord, what know you of the rune? Where does your team plan to assemble with Nira Larsen's sisters to recite the words?"

"You'll never find out." He spit the words from his dry lips. "We'll say the verse and you'll be gone forever."

The illusory fist tightened, and his vision tunneled into a red haze of pain. He sucked in just enough air to avoid passing out.

"Tell me where to find the rest of your team."

"Go. To. Hell."

"I will gladly send you to my daughter, Hel, after you talk," the insidious voice rasped in his head.

Vaporous arrows lanced his kidneys, eliciting a moan from his throat. Loki's incorporeal fingers twisted and probed, intensifying his agony.

He clenched his teeth so hard that his jaw throbbed. While he awaited the next torment, his heart raced like an out-of-control train.

Then to his surprise, the assault lessened.

"I am not at my full strength yet. Perhaps the wolf will have better success in convincing you to cooperate."

Fenrir bit down on his ankle, and his vision went black.

Chapter Thirteen

Awareness filtered into Magnor's consciousness. He remained in the chair, where his head had fallen forward. He didn't move, concentrating on breathing slow and deep. The awful pressure was gone from his chest. But what of his leg?

"Your eminence, we have a report from Togura Island," said a man in a voice he didn't recognize.

"What is it?" Loki demanded.

So, the demon is still here. What about the wolf?

"A shuttle from the *Protector* is flying reconnaissance over the volcano, my lord."

"I thought our allies had destroyed Prince Zohar's ship."

"They must have launched their spacecraft before then."

Loki cursed in a foreign tongue. "I'll see to it. Come, Fenrir. Let us determine what brings the Drift Lords to our island. Omeron, you may continue the interrogation."

Magnor must have drifted off again because a painful prod to his side roused him.

"What portal led you to this place?" Brigader Omeron's words penetrated the fog in his brain.

Magnor blinked his eyes open. He was still bound to his chair. Dust motes floated in the air as the late afternoon sun penetrated the attic from a far window. A glance downward showed his leg to be intact. Had he imagined the wolf biting his ankle?

Loki must have been playing mind tricks on him. He winced at the remembered torment. What was it he'd just heard? Oh, yes, the messenger had mentioned Togura Island, the Pacific isle where Paz and Jen had crash-landed after leaving Tokyo. It housed a volcano in imminent danger of eruption.

"How did you get to Los Angeles?" Brigader Omeron repeated, jabbing him in the ribs with a shock stick.

Magnor gritted his teeth against the flare of pain. "We went through the portal."

"Which one? You were last seen in the Nevada desert."

"We used the transfer platform at the Viking Vegas Resort. We'd returned to the city." *And somehow, we ended up here instead of Copenhagen.*

Omeron snapped his fingers. "Send for Kaptein Parug. I have an order to transmit."

Magnor sagged in his chair, pretending to be weakened. He'd make a move when the opportunity presented itself, but first he had to be alone with the brigader.

"*Min drott,*" Parug said after offering his salute, "I have cleaned the Drift Lord's sword, if you wish to keep the trophy."

Omeron snatched the blade from Parug's outstretched hand. Avarice in his gaze, he examined the steel blade and its sturdy hilt. Done with his inspection, he placed the prize on his desk.

"A gross negligence has occurred," the brigader said to his subordinate. "This warrior came through the portal from our Vegas command post. I've had reports of explosions there. The destruction will set back our operations for weeks until we can rebuild. Does their commanding officer still live?"

The kaptein bowed his head. "Aye, min drott."

"His failure must be punished. Take the major into the desert at dawn and stake him out. Pin his eyelids open. Either the sun will burn him blind, or the carrion birds will pluck out his eyeballs. Then leave him and return here."

"As you command." The kaptein clapped a fist to his chest before turning toward the exit.

Brigader Omeron's nostrils flared as he regarded Magnor. "Why did you come here, to this particular site? What is your mission?"

"Reconnaissance."

"Liar. We know your team is targeting our recruitment centers. Have you planted charges yet?"

"Do you think I'd tell you if I did?" His muscles bulged as he attempted to break free. The restraints were too secure. But wait, one of the chair arms had creaked. Could it have a loosened bolt?

Omeron sneered at him. "Tell me before the Dark Lord returns, and it'll go easier on you."

"Forget it. I'll never talk."

Omeron's face purpled. "You have no idea what he is capable of doing to you. You've only had a sample. But if you wish for me to force the answers from you, I'll be happy to do so." He glanced at the soldier on the staircase landing. "Menig, go fetch the worms."

Not those! He'd better make his move now, while he had the chance. They wouldn't be alone again. Loki or his monster son might return at any time.

"You're right," he said after the trooper had left. "I have set charges. The remote is in my bag." His backpack lay on the floor where his captors had tossed it earlier.

As the brigader brushed past, Magnor rocked his chair sideways and crashed into him. Both tumbled to the ground in a tangled heap.

Before the officer could scramble to his feet, Magnor broke off the chair's arm that had cracked on impact. His wrist still secured to a piece of wood, he grabbed the knife from the officer's belt and plunged it into the brigader's gut.

Without a word, Omeron slumped over.

Magnor used the blade to slash through his bindings. As soon as he was free, he leapt to his feet. He retrieved his belongings before moving out. Unfortunately, his phase pistol and dagger were nowhere in sight.

Fear for Erika's safety propelled him downstairs. Where might they be holding her? Presumably, she'd been taken to Tent

Ten, like Nira and Jen under captivity before her. But would the lab be inside this building?

If it were elsewhere, Erika would have been taken there by now. Hoping he was wrong, he did a quick survey of the upper level to make certain she wasn't held in any of the bedrooms or converted offices. It was less likely she'd be on the first floor, where lower rank soldiers roamed.

Maybe there was a basement. After all, the Trolleks favored their subterranean habitats. A cellar would be the perfect place to set up a discreet laboratory.

He crept down the stairs toward the ground floor. Loud guffaws of laughter reached him from below. Before hitting bottom, he flicked on his invisibility shield. This allowed him to do a quick search of the ground level without being detected. He hoped that wolf didn't return. The beast might be able to sniff his scent and reveal his presence.

Trolleks lounged in the various public rooms, off-duty soldiers enjoying a moment of respite. He wondered where they bunked. For such a large contingent, they'd require facilities like any other military base.

It's not your mission to investigate. While it was his duty to destroy any recruitment centers he happened upon, this time he'd not let it interfere with his prime directive to locate the Book of Odin. He'd pass on these coordinates to Dal and let him follow through.

The Book of Odin. Did it really exist? Supposedly it was a companion to the *Codex Regius*, a thirteenth century manuscript preserving the *Elder Edda*, an older body of verse. One of the poems was the "Völuspá" that warned Odin of a great war before Earth's rebirth.

The newer volume he sought contained a verse saying history would repeat itself and offered a means of dispelling the invaders. Would it lead them to a super weapon? Or was the verse itself a spell to defeat the Trolleks? If so, why hadn't it been used during their earlier incursions?

Was this book where the legend had arisen, stating the six sons of Thor had to unite with the six daughters of Odin? Nira searched for the rune believed to hold the key to banishing Loki. What if they both reached for illusory goals?

But no, Nira had said the museum scroll he'd found in Vegas directed them to Copenhagen. Why else would that location have been written in the ancient text if not to provide a clue?

Blind faith wasn't something he had in abundance, and faith was what this mission required. He preferred fighting Trolleks like the ones snoring on that couch, he thought as he slipped past the living room.

Heading toward the kitchen, he dodged a cluster of troops milling about in the foyer.

A couple of human slaves had begun preparing the evening meal. Busy chopping vegetables by the sink, they didn't look up when the ground shook. He clutched the wall.

Another quake?

Dishes rattled, and a porcelain mug crashed to the floor as the tremors increased. He braced himself as the ground jerked violently. Something fell with a huge thud outside. Soldiers cursed in the distance, while he hoped his escape wouldn't be noticed in the confusion.

Meanwhile, the cooks continued unfazed, blank expressions on their faces.

Spotting the basement door, he dove in that direction, hoping it would be unlocked. The knob twisted easily. Dim lighting illuminated a staircase leading below. He stopped a moment to listen, his heart pounding in his chest.

He didn't hear Erika's voice. Had Algie already extracted what data she needed and killed his bride before he'd even had the chance to tell her he cared?

It didn't matter that his destiny rode in the stars. If she survived, they'd find a way to be together.

His fingers twisted the dial on his belt, and his shield dissipated. If she was there, he wanted her to see him.

Another tremor shook the earth as he clutched the handrail. A figure sprinted into his line of vision. Erika stood at the base of the stairs, staring at him with wide, frightened eyes.

"Magnor! Oh, thank God it's you. For a moment, I thought you were one of them blocking the way."

"My *knesta*, are you alright? How did you…?"

She rushed up the steps. "Never mind that now. Let's get out of here."

He grabbed her hand. "The earthquake has caused chaos. We can take advantage of the commotion to slip outside."

Troops congregated on the front lawn where they'd gathered after the tremors. A wide crack split the hillside, and a fallen tree blocked the road. He and Erika ducked around a corner and fled.

As soon as they had put enough distance between themselves and the soldiers, he let go of her hand and gave her a quick scan. She looked disheveled, her hair askew and her clothes rumpled, but she seemed intact otherwise.

"Did they hurt you?" he asked, relieved when she gave a negative response.

"You?" She pointed to his chafed wrists and the bruise on his jaw.

He lifted his chin. "I am trained to resist interrogation. However, the session with Loki was unpleasant."

"Loki was there? In person?"

"He was more like an evil presence, but he could affect events all the same. Fenrir the wolf showed up, too." He related what had happened to him, including his encounter with Omeron. "We need to leave the premises before the body is discovered."

A squad of troops marched by at an intersection, and they hid in a recess between buildings on one of the backlot streets.

"Can you use your belt to make us invisible?" she asked, her back pressed against a brick wall.

"It won't work if Fenrir is in the vicinity. He'll detect my scent. At any rate, Algie will still be after you. She's probably set a cordon near the portal."

"She won't be too pleased to learn you killed her commanding officer."

"I wish I could have taken out more of the beasts."

She placed a hand on his arm. "Look, in case we don't make it, I want you to know I'm glad we shared this adventure."

"Me, too. But don't give up yet. I've faced worse battles."

"I'm sure you have, but I fear we are severely outnumbered."

"They underestimate us." Unable to resist, he swept her into his arms for a passionate kiss. "I should check with Zohar to make sure he still wants us to go to Copenhagen," he said, breaking away. "He might want us to deal with Algie instead."

Stepping back, Erika met his gaze with a somber expression. "She's even more dangerous than we thought. Her latest plan is to exterminate the old and the sick, and to either confound humanity or turn people into Trolleks. I suspect this is what you meant when you said her latest initiative is a dual-pronged effort?"

"It's mass genocide, any way you look at it. The human race as we know it would disappear."

And a worse threat remained. If Loki succeeded in achieving his power, he would annihilate all life in the multiverse, including Algie and her minions.

When he reported in via his wrist comm, Zohar confirmed his original orders.

"The location of the weapon is paramount," said the Drift Lord captain. "Yaron will pick up Algie's trail from there. You go on ahead to Copenhagen and find the book."

"Brigader Omeron was in charge of this operation. You might want to send Dal to investigate the extent of their troops. Plus, he'll need to take out their orientation station as well as the portals." He told his leader what they'd learned.

"Stick to your mission," Zohar reiterated. "It'll be easier to defeat the demon once we remove his allies."

After Magnor signed off, they headed down the backlot street.

"When am I going to meet the rest of your team?" Erika said with a sideways glance in his direction.

"I hope to have you safely home before that is necessary."

"You're not eager to introduce me as your wife?"

The thought hadn't occurred to him. "Since we won't stay wed, there's no point in getting you further involved in our troubles."

"Oh, like I'm not involved enough already? I should have figured you'd dump me as soon as possible."

"That's not what I meant." What did he mean? He'd like to see her safe and reunited with her family. Wasn't that what she wanted, too? "You are important to me, but we have other concerns right now."

Her eyes narrowed. "And to think I feared for your well-being in that house! I knew you always had it in your mind to get rid of me."

He snatched for her hand, but she jerked it away. "You've got it all wrong. I do care. That's the problem."

She stopped at a crossroad, glancing from left to right. "Oh, so now I'm a problem? Maybe you shouldn't take me to Copenhagen. I'd only be a burden."

"Don't be absurd. We have to stick together."

"Yes, because of the prophecy, not because you want to be with me."

Great Cosmos, he was terrible at understanding women. He hadn't meant to make her feel unappreciated. Perhaps it was just as well. When she learned about his disreputable past, she would want nothing more to do with him anyway.

It occurred to him that he was the one betraying her trust, and not the other way around.

"I do want you, my *knesta*. Very much. And from the way you kissed me back a moment ago, I believe you desire me as well. But we have to put aside our personal needs until we complete our mission."

"Don't try to smooth talk me, husband. You only want me

in your bed. I won't deny I'm attracted to you in that way. But I'd hoped… well, never mind."

The sound of approaching footsteps reached them. "We need to move on. They'll be spreading out to find us." He pointed in the opposite direction of the soldiers and took off.

Erika matched his pace. Wisps of reddish hair floated about her face which held a pinched expression. His heart squeezed. He'd alienated her without meaning to do so, but they'd have to resolve things later.

They wound their way through the fake city streets, down another section that looked like a warehouse district, and past the massive soundstages. But as they approached the main gate into the Studios, Magnor halted.

Erika had seen them too, a contingent of guards in front of the gate, now shut tight. On the other side was the tour center. Fenrir patrolled the parking lot where people boarded the trams, now emptied of passengers. It was late, and the park must have closed for the day. Hopefully, the wolf wouldn't pick up their scent from this far away.

"Can we use your invisibility shield to get past them?" Erika said in a low tone.

"Fenrir will sense us. We dare not take the chance."

"He's a monster. You didn't tell me he was so big. That's no ordinary wolf."

"Believe me, I know." He tugged on her sleeve, and they hustled into the shadow of a building.

"Now what?" She sagged against the wall, her face weary.

"We'll have to find another way out of this complex." He surveyed the grounds, weighing different possibilities. All of them came with risks.

"If we can make it beyond the gate, we could circle around to the tour center's rear door and from there reach the portal," Erika suggested. "They won't be expecting us to get that far."

"That's true. The quake might have loosened a section of fencing. Let's see if we can find a break." A troubling thought entered his head. "How did you get away from Algie, anyway? A tremor hit right before I met up with you."

"Later." She strode along the perimeter. "Look, there's an opening. It looks big enough for us to squeeze through."

She twisted past the ragged edges, and he followed. They steered a wide swathe around the tour center to avoid detection. Where had Fenrir gone? The wolf was nowhere in sight.

"Fenrir must have been summoned away," he said. "That's a relief." Or else the shapeshifting beast was lying in wait for them. He didn't mention this possibility to Erika.

They made it to the side of the building without being spotted. He led the way forward when the air suddenly wavered in front of them. He halted abruptly, hand on his hilt.

A dozen or so people shimmied from the ground, clods of dirt still clinging to them.

The emaciated men wore ragged clothing that hung off their bony bodies. Instead of eyes, they had empty orbs. They walked with jerky motions, as though controlled by a puppeteer. In their skeletal hands, they held farming tools like pitchforks and shovels.

Magnor's muscles tensed as he prepared for battle.

Chapter Fourteen

Erika's heart pounded as she surveyed the armed mob facing them. Those men had seemed to spring from the ground, if her eyes hadn't deceived her.

Or could they be using a similar technology to Magnor's invisibility shield? Perhaps they'd been here all along, and when their prey appeared, they'd shown themselves.

Magnor thrust her aside and drew his sword.

She clucked her tongue. "And here I thought our escape had been too easy."

"What do you mean?

"Algie may have let me go so as to discover our mission."

"I doubt it. Her experiments are her prime concern. But just to be sure, I'll scan you after we're away from here to make certain she hasn't planted a tracking device."

Erika nodded at the mob encroaching on them. "Why don't you make us vanish again?"

"Good idea. It's best if we save this battle for later."

He sheathed his sword, twisted toward her, and grasped her hand. Then he turned the dial on his belt.

The beings with vacant eyes halted in unison. They seemed stymied by their quarry's vanishing act.

Magnor urged her toward the tour center's rear. She hurried along beside him. Any minute, she expected to see the monster wolf reappear.

Her heart pounded as Magnor passed the back end of the structure and kept going. At the opposite side of the building, he stopped and pointed to a nearby tree.

"We'll go in from the roof. They won't be expecting us that way. How are you at climbing?" He let go of her hand and switched off his shield.

Discerning his intent, she swallowed her doubt. "The only thing I've ever climbed is stairs."

"Those branches look sturdy. You go first."

They made it with only a few scrapes and scratches. At the rooftop, Magnor found an unlatched door. Soon they found themselves on the ground floor inside the building. Erika gave a whoosh of relief that no troops waited to ambush them. Magnor led her along a corridor and downstairs to the lower level.

"Assuming I can reset the portal's coordinates, we can transport from here to Copenhagen." He moved forward with the grace and agility of a trained hunter, even though they were the hunted in this case.

Wondering how her life had fallen into such disorder, she stood by while Magnor fiddled with the control panel on the column supporting the portal's arch. When he signaled to her to step onto the dais, she complied without hesitation. Did she really trust him so completely?

She trusted the man to look after her safety. No matter what he planned to do once they defeated the invading beasts, he cared about her well-being.

On the dais, she steeled herself as the disorienting sensation of a vector transfer encased her. Time and space swirled around her as she tumbled into a void. Her heart fluttered as a momentary panic seized her.

Then objects clarified and they were in a similar room but different. Instead of a single overhead light, this place had recessed lighting. A desk sat in one corner with a computer and a blanked-out monitor.

Her ears buzzed, and her equilibrium wavered. She drew in a long breath. Feeling steadier, she glanced at her companion. Magnor had stepped off the dais and taken out his PIP to confirm their location. She admired the impressive figure he made with his somber bearded face and his powerful physique.

Whether he liked it or not, they were wed. And one of these days, she really wanted to see what that meant in the classic sense.

"Why do you dawdle? Let's go." He gestured for her to follow him toward the door.

"Where are we? Did we make it to Copenhagen?"

"Yes, this time we landed in the right place."

"Hallelujah!" Her voice burst out like air from a balloon. What an awesome way to travel—no hassle with the airlines or ticket prices. Despite the uncomfortable falling sensation, she could get used to this means of transit.

He paused to smile at her, and the transformation to his face took her breath away. "You haven't traveled much, have you?"

A purse strap slid off her shoulder, and she slung it back on. "My pottery studio has kept me busy, plus I haven't had the time or money to travel. At least, I didn't have the funds until we won the contest back in Vegas. I hope the money is still in my account. I need it to earn my education degree."

"Have you no thoughts of a family?" His gaze deepened and slid to her mouth.

Heat rose in her cheeks. "Marriage means someone else criticizing me like my parents and older sisters. I hadn't considered it until I met you."

Oh God, had she really said that aloud? Yet when he looked at her like that, her bones melted and her resistance faded.

Regret etched his features. "As much as I'd like to continue this discussion, we must move on. If this place runs true to the other portals, it's located in a tourist attraction that serves as a recruitment center."

"If I recall, your friend Nira mentioned Jolheim Gardens. That would suit the purpose."

He twisted a dial on his PIP. "Before we go any further, let me scan you for surveillance devices. I doubt Algie planted anything on you, but we should be certain." A pause. "Good, you're clean. I didn't think she'd have let you go so easily." His eyes narrowed as he regarded her, and she knew he waited for an explanation of how she'd gotten away.

Leaning past him, she opened the door. "It's quiet for now. Come on, we have a mission to accomplish." Aware he'd pursue the topic later, she stepped into a windowless, winding corridor that branched in several directions.

"If this is like other Trollek recruitment centers, we're underground." Magnor's cape flapped behind him as he quickened his pace. "I doubt the clue I need is down here."

She scurried to keep up. "You're looking for a clue and not the actual book?"

"I'm not sure. We need to see where we are once we surface and take it from there."

The complex appeared deserted, making her wonder what time of day it was in their current locale. They found a flight of steps, pushed open the door at the top, and exited into a vacant gift shop. She heaved a sigh of relief that it wouldn't be a repeat of their experience at the film studio.

Shortly thereafter, they emerged outside in the temperate night air. She gaped at the sight before them.

Thousands of tiny white light bulbs decorated the leafy trees overhead, casting sparkles of light over colorful flower beds and fairytale-like buildings. Beyond a central lake rose the curves of an enormous rollercoaster.

"This has to be the amusement park," she said.

Magnor peered around with a frown. "We could search the premises now, but daylight would be better." His gaze zeroed in on her. "Besides, you look exhausted. It's been a trying day. Let's get lodgings and return in the morning."

He calls being chased and captured by the enemy a trying day? Her shoulders sagged as fatigue set in. Now that they'd reached their destination and weren't under imminent attack, she experienced an overwhelming need to rest.

"I'm with you, husband." She accompanied him past a carousel with miniature Viking ships instead of horses and an Arabian-style palace housing a restaurant. Suppressing a yawn, she proceeded toward the main exit.

Considering the confusing layout of the place, it might be helpful to get a map before they returned. She should see about picking one up at the ticket booth.

Suddenly Magnor stopped and cursed.

"What's wrong?" Alarm jerked her to full wakefulness.

"I forgot to see which building we left, the one with the portal."

"Oh." A puff of air escaped her lungs. She'd thought those zombies might have popped up from the ground again. Jumpier than she'd thought, Erika resumed walking. "This place might have multiple entrances to the complex below. I wouldn't worry about it."

"You're right."

Once at the main entrance, they climbed over a barrier. She spied a price list at a ticket window and gulped.

"Ah, Magnor, how are we doing for cash? We're going to need to buy tickets during peak hours. I can use my credit cards but then our location could be pinpointed."

He reached into his pants pocket. "I still have a supply of kewa stones. Will that suffice?"

"We should get some local currency." She stared at an urban vista of tall buildings and broad avenues in front of them. "It must be the middle of the night," she guessed from the paucity of traffic.

Magnor made an adjustment to his wrist unit. "Local time is three o'clock in the morning."

"No wonder I feel so zonked." She scanned the ticketing counter, but no maps were available. Maybe their hotel would have a business center where she could look up the information.

Now they only had to find a place with a vacancy.

They crossed the street and strode along an empty sidewalk. Streetlamps lit the night as Erika shivered. She didn't care to be out and about on a lonely street. No telling who, or what, might emerge from the dark to accost them.

Magnor pointed. "There's a hostelry we can try."

She noted the fancy hotel sign up ahead. The brick building looked to house a bastion of European formality. Aware that every moment they lingered outside was one in which they could be attacked, she hurried in that direction.

The painted gray hotel with white trim had five stories and resided on a corner of the wide boulevard. A cornerstone gave 1890 as the year of construction. To their left was outdoor seating for an adjacent restaurant. Its red awnings provided shade, and a row of planters offered a semblance of privacy.

Since the front door was locked, they rang a bell. A sullen staff member appeared to allow them entrance.

Inside, a brightly lit lobby faced them. They padded across the patterned green carpet to the elegant reception desk, manned by a single gentleman at this late hour. Various armchairs with tangerine upholstery sat about the expanse while tables held colorful bouquets of fresh flowers that scented the air. Crystal chandeliers provided lighting for the modernized interior.

"Hi, do you speak English?" Erika asked the sleepy-eyed clerk. "We need a room for the night. Our, uh, train had an unexpected delay and we got in late. Our luggage, unfortunately, got left behind, but we'll sort it out in the daytime."

The young man tugged on his rumpled suit jacket. "We have one room available, Madame. All of the rest are sold out. However, we offer free wireless Internet and cable television." He mentioned a high price.

Erika turned to Magnor. "We'll have to use my credit card until we can find a bank in the morning."

"All we need is a jeweler," he reminded her. "We'll take it," he told the clerk.

The man gave him a strange look. But then, who wouldn't think it odd when a fellow wearing a cape and sword walked into their hotel?

Erika filled out the registration form and offered payment. She'd feel safer once they were upstairs and Magnor put up his perimeter defense, if he'd kept the rods in his backpack.

The room was tastefully decorated, with a king-sized bed, a desk and chair, a TV console, and two nightstands.

Heavy drapes covered a wide window. The same color scheme as the lobby prevailed, with a green carpet and orange accents. Lamps provided subdued but adequate illumination.

Radiators stood by the windows but she didn't see a thermostat. Great, they had heat but no central a/c. Luckily, the temperature was comfortable, and they'd only have to tolerate the lack of circulated air for one night.

She flopped her bag on the desk and then sank down wearily on the bed, kicking off her shoes.

"I'm ready to collapse. If you don't mind, while you set up the defense network, I'll use the bathroom."

"Go ahead." Rummaging in his backpack, he grimaced. "We both need a good night's rest."

And so they got one. Erika fell asleep before Magnor even joined her on the bed. By the time she awoke, sunlight streamed through the curtains.

Lying on her side, she blinked her eyes open. Magnor faced her, his beard scruffy and his gaze observant as he leaned on one elbow.

"Are you watching me?"

"Indeed, I am, wife." His lips curved upward. "You look delightfully cozy in your nightshirt."

She stretched and groaned. Without having any sleepwear, she'd gone to bed leaving her shirt over her underwear.

"Does this place have a coffeemaker? My head feels heavy, and my nose is stuffed." Although the air felt comfortable, she bemoaned the lack of ventilation.

"We have water bottles on the desk, compliments of the hotel. Shall I get you one?"

"I'd rather have a jolt of caffeine."

"What is that?"

"It's the substance in coffee that wakes you up." Noticing his blatant stare, she drew the sheet all the way to her neck.

"Come now, don't be modest. We are married. Look, I'm not shy." He sat, letting the coverlet fall away.

His bare chest, ridged with musculature, reminded Erika of her wish to consummate their vows. Her body responded with instant heat.

"Wait there. I'll be right back."

She lunged from the bed and hastened to the bathroom to freshen up. When she returned, she noticed he'd folded the top bed covers down. He lay in a tantalizing position on the sheet clad only in his briefs. Her gaze zoomed to the bulge at his groin, and her pulse accelerated.

"Come closer, I won't bite… unless you want me to." His light, teasing tone both surprised and pleased her.

A coil of answering warmth rose within her. "Shouldn't we prepare for our excursion today?" she asked, while her body prepared for something else entirely.

"By all means. However, we should discuss our plans first."

His slow perusal made clear what plans he had in mind.

"So we should. What do you think we might do first?" Several naughty ideas popped into her head.

"You'll understand better if I show you."

He slid from the bed and strode toward her. His broad shoulders and sculpted arms produced a responsive need to be held in his embrace. Heavens, he was handsome in a wild warrior sort of way.

You need to be wed to him for a year, an inner voice reminded her. *Best satisfy him so he'll want to stay.*

Most women would be glad to bed a hunk like him, and the man was hers for the taking. Did it matter that he'd leave her in the end? Never mind how long they might have together, at least she'd experience what it meant to be a wife. And it wasn't as though inexperience held her back. Why not share one morning of bliss with him before chaos erupted again?

"I'll bet you're tense after last night," he said, moving to her rear. His hands lit upon her shoulders. "Allow me to ease your discomfort." Kneading motions followed, making her sigh with pleasure.

He'd found her one weakness. She leaned against him, closing her eyes as he dug into her knots and eased her muscles. Ah, it felt so good. The outer world fell away from her consciousness as his hands worked their magic.

Lower, she wanted to say but kept silent. Her breasts ached from wanting his touch. When he sniffed her hair and blew gently into her ear, a shiver of delight coursed through her.

She curled her fingers, resisting the urge to touch him in return. He was nearly naked, his chest brushing her back. If she reached behind, she could grip his… oh, my.

Too many barriers remained between them. In one swift action, she divested herself of her shirt.

"Oh, heck, why not?" Giving up all pretense of modesty, she stripped off the rest of her clothing and turned toward him.

Chapter Fifteen

Magnor sucked in a breath as Erika tossed her clothing onto the carpet. He hadn't expected her to be so responsive. Lying in bed watching her sleep, observing her wakefulness, and then seeing her sensual awareness blossom, made him frenzied with lust. And now she stood before him totally naked.

He didn't understand why she was giving him this gift, but he wouldn't stand around arguing. An instant later, he'd removed his briefs and stood perusing her. She looked lovely with her enticing eyes, plump lips, and curly red hair, like a pixie from the Fae world come to tempt him. He'd read about those Earth legends in his cultural studies.

But she was flesh and blood, and from the way her nipples peaked, he'd say she was as aroused as he. He stepped forward, smiling at the expectation in her eyes. She appeared both eager and somewhat hesitant at the same time, a charming combination. His wife exhibited none of the sultry airs that the women of his tribe had put on to attract his attention.

Thankfully, she didn't know what they knew about him. He had a chance with her, or at least an opportunity to make their marriage a real one in the biblical sense of her people.

He lifted her chin and lowered his head, brushing his lips across hers in a teasing touch. He made another foray, flicking his tongue out, pleased to hear her responsive gasp. Her breasts were inches from his chest, but he resisted the urge to fondle them, instead wanting to build her passion first.

On the next round, he lingered longer on her mouth,

supporting her nape with his other hand. Their bodies barely touched, but his skin burned and his veins filled with fire. From the corner of his eye, he saw the bed, its sheets rumbled from their restless sleep.

Envisioning what they'd be doing there next hardened his already stiff shaft. Erika swayed her hips against him, sending bursts of pleasure along his nerves at each point of contact. He deepened the kiss, reining in his raging need, savoring the taste of her.

She parted her lips and allowed his tongue to plunge inside. Her sweetness elicited a moan from his throat. He crushed his mouth to hers, drawing her closer, pressing his body against her softness. His hands roamed the slender planes of her back while she clutched at him as if her life depended on it.

He couldn't wait much longer. Nudging her toward the bed, he kept his mouth clamped to hers. She's mine, he exulted inwardly. Who would have known a fountain of passion lay beneath her saucy exterior?

A moment of doubt assailed him. How many lovers had she known? Her movements were bold and confident, lacking a virgin's fumbling responses. Does it matter? another voice answered in his head. You're wed to her now. Whatever her background, she could be yours forever. Or at least until she divorced him.

No, he thought, tumbling onto the bed and pulling her after him. He'd make her want him. He'd make her want to keep him by her side.

Desperate to prove himself, he ranged his kisses across her face, down her neck, and to the crevice between her breasts.

"You're beautiful, my wife," he murmured, burying his face there. Ah, she gave him a glimpse into heaven.

She squirmed and thrust her bosom forward. Sensing her need, he brushed his lips across her soft flesh and took a nipple into his mouth. Her back arched, and she cried out as he suckled her and circled the peak with his tongue. He ministered to the other one next, pleased to hear her murmurs of pleasure.

Then he withdrew and rolled her supine under him. He

raised himself above her and stared at her loveliness. Her cheeks flushed under his scrutiny while her flame-colored hair spread out on the pillow. With a low growl, he claimed her mouth again, kissing her with wild abandon while he lowered his body. Pressed against her, it took an effort of will not to push her legs apart and enter her right then and there.

He curbed his impatience and instead let his hand roam south toward her belly. His target drew near, and when he flicked his fingers across the apex of her thighs, she jerked under him. He cupped her fully, proud to claim her as his, knowing this pleasure they shared for one morning wouldn't be enough. But it was all they had for now, and he'd make it memorable.

He tickled her inner thighs, every now and then brushing his fingers across her feminine folds. She heaved toward him, murmuring his name. But he wasn't about to give her satisfaction yet. Her slickness called to him, and he left her mouth to leverage himself downward. Pushing her legs apart, he dove toward the core of her sweetness.

"Please," she gasped when he flicked his tongue across her swollen nub. "I can't take any more."

"Yes, you can, my *knesta*."

She writhed as his mouth worked on her. Aware he was bringing her to the brink, he withdrew and slid a finger inside her moist tunnel, rejoicing in her readiness for him.

His finger slid inside and out while his thumb continued to stroke the sensitive spot above it.

A spasm gripped her followed by a cavalcade of waves. Her head thrust back, and her eyes closed as pleasure flooded her.

His lust surged. Unable to wait any longer, he shifted his position and entered her.

****

Erika was still in the throes of her release when he thrust inside her. She opened for him, spreading her thighs and letting him fill her completely. Then she wrapped her legs around his torso and matched his movements, giving him the gift he'd given her. She rocked under him, wanting him to know how much he fired her inner kiln.

She'd never known such bliss. None of her previous lovers had excited her to this degree or had treated her like a cherished treasure. She had merely been their means to satisfaction. Magnor, on the other hand, focused entirely on her, as though she were the center of his universe.

Her body, slick with sweat, writhed under him. His rhythmic motions increased in intensity and initiated another coil of pleasure from her core. She reached up and pulled his head down to kiss him, rubbing her breasts intentionally against his chest. His last thrust dove deeply, and he jerked atop her, his mouth stilling as his seed spurted forth with his climax.

Erika spasmed again, her need so great that her body's heightened responses drove her over the brink. Then they both sagged until finally, he rolled off her and onto his side.

The stickiness between her legs recalled her to reality. They'd forgotten all about protection. Or maybe the men of his tribe didn't subscribe to birth control. She really needed to learn more about his customs.

His serious eyes regarded her as he leaned on one elbow and stroked her arm.

"Now we are truly wed, my bride."

"So we are. What does that mean on your world?"

Her face heated as he surveyed her nude body. She traced swirls on his broad chest while waiting for his answer.

"When a man and woman join in the coupling ceremony, their bond lasts forever. Our marriage was an act to win the casino contest. It doesn't bind me according to the laws of my people. However, as long as I remain on Earth, I'll abide by your rules. But be aware the ultimate decision is yours."

Decision about what? Did he want to stay or not? After all they'd experienced together, she had felt a connection between them. Was it folly to believe he shared the feeling?

"What do we have to do to make our marriage real under your laws?" she asked, eager to ensure his commitment. "We've just had unprotected sex. I'd like to know we are legally married in the eyes of your people as well as mine. You know, in case the unexpected happens." *And I'd better buy some supplies next time we go shopping.*

"I will show you what we do." Grasping her palm, he muttered some words in a foreign tongue. "You are my beloved, now and for eternity. Do you accept me as I am?"

"Yes, but what about you?" she said, shifting the responsibility to his shoulders. "Do you mean to stick around after we fulfill the prophecy? You could go home once your obligations here are done."

He dropped her hand and averted his gaze. "I have nowhere to go, my *knesta*. I cannot return to my tribe."

"Why not?" She smoothed her fingers along his arm, hoping to coax him to talk. "Tell me about your homeland."

"Very well. You should know the man you've wed." He gave her a hooded glance before looking away. "I had a peaceful life on Karrell, if you call fighting the neighboring tribes on a regular basis to be peaceful. We farmed the land, a deep valley nestled between tall mountain ranges that few outsiders could access."

"Karrell is your planet?"

"Aye. My people remained relatively isolated, stuck in our ways but happy. Territorial disputes had the various tribes in constant warfare. Attempts to unify the disparate groups always failed, so our warrior skills were instilled at a very young age. We trained in combat before we learned to work the soil."

"That doesn't sound so idyllic to me."

"We were a close-knit community, looking out for our brothers, solid in our beliefs and values. Our materialistic needs were simple. Give us a roof over our heads, a good crop, and a day without battle, and we were content."

"Then why did you leave?"

"I was shunned and driven out as a criminal." He spoke in a challenging tone, as though she'd be chased away by his words.

Her fingers stilled. "How so?"

She couldn't imagine him doing a vile deed. To a man like Magnor, honor would be paramount. Maybe what passed for a crime on his world wouldn't be considered one here.

He settled onto his back, put his hands under his head, and stared at the ceiling. "The Council of Elders convicted me of murder. Evidence pointed my way in my brother-in-law's death. I was imprisoned, judged, and sentenced. If I return home, I'll be killed. They sent me through the mountain pass with nothing except the clothes I wore and my sword for self-defense."

"B-but did you kill the man? What happened?"

An extended silence followed.

"Please, Magnor. You can tell me anything. I'm not going to leave you."

"There's no reason for you to be encumbered with me once our mission is done."

"Is it so hard for you to believe someone might care for you? Do you think so little of yourself? If so, that sentence had the designated effect. It stripped you of your life and any hope for a future."

His frosty glance met her compassionate gaze. "And so it has, except for the Drift Lords. If Primer Pedar hadn't hired me to protect Prince Zohar, I'd be adrift. His royal highness has given my life meaning again. I must not fail in my mission."

"You won't, Magnor, but you don't have to work alone anymore. You have your friends, and you have me."

Clearly, by his troubled expression, she could tell he wasn't used to relying on others. Well, tough for him. If he wanted to be accepted by the Drift Lords, he'd have to become a team player. A thought struck her.

"Speaking of your team, have you checked in lately? Shouldn't you report that we've arrived here safely?"

"I will do so shortly."

His curt response made her realize she was losing him. "So how did your brother-in-law die?" she said in an encouraging tone. Rolling to her side, she trailed a finger up his inner thigh. A smile curved her mouth at his body's response.

"Stop that." He gave her a menacing scowl that she ignored.

"Why should I? According to my laws, I'm your wife. Like it or not, you belong to me. This is mine." She closed her fingers on his shaft.

"You're a witch." His voice thickened along with his body part.

"I'll ask you once more. How was your brother-in-law killed? Tell me, and I'll relieve your tension." She stroked him lightly, brushing her hand over the tip where a bead of moisture hovered. She took it and danced her fingers up and down his engorged flesh.

"My sister stabbed him." He bit the words out, his breaths growing heavier with her actions.

Her jaw dropped. "Say again?"

"Nalyse called me over one day." He brushed her hand away and sat upright. "You want to know the sordid details? Very well. When I walked into her kitchen, I saw blood everywhere. Nalyse crouched over her husband. He was dead on the floor, a knife in his chest."

"Omigosh. What happened?"

"Nalyse claimed her mate had abused her, and she'd killed him in self-defense. Their marriage had seemed so perfect that I'd no idea anything was amiss. As her older brother, I should have detected her unhappiness earlier."

"How would you have known? Did she ever show up with unexplained bruises or suffer so-called accidents with injuries? Those are signs of spousal abuse."

His brow wrinkled. "Not that I recall, but her clothing may have covered up such evidence."

"Even so, it wasn't your fault if she didn't let on."

He leapt off the bed and pulled on his briefs. Pacing the

room, he clasped his hands behind his back. "Yes, it was. My duty as head of our household was to protect my sister, even after she'd wed. I failed miserably. While wondering what to do about the body, I noticed the weapon looked like one of my hunting knives. I took it out to verify the blade was mine. Before I could determine what that might mean, the authorities arrived and took me into custody."

"You?" Her eyes widened. "Why not your sister?"

"They assumed I'd killed my brother-in-law, and she didn't correct them. I accepted the blame to protect her. The Council decided I'd wanted their land that abutted mine. As my sister's only remaining relative, I'd take charge of her husband's property. But even if I had wanted to prove my innocence, no way existed except for Nalyse's word."

"She allowed you to be accused of murder in her place?" Erika had trouble wrapping her mind around the concept.

Halting in place, he glared at her. "This had been her plan all along."

"Huh? I'm not following you."

"She lied to me. While I languished in prison awaiting my sentence, she visited one day. There she confessed she'd wanted her husband out of the way so she could be a wealthy widow. When I was banished, she'd gain my lands as well as her own. Her husband had never abused her. She had only said that to gain my sympathy."

"I'm so sorry." Erika slid out of bed and stood, covering herself with the sheet.

"Don't be. Nalyse played me for a fool, knowing how honor would compel me to protect her. No one believed me when I tried to tell them the truth thereafter." His jaw muscle twitched, while the sharp glint in his eyes could have cut glass.

"Was there a trial? What kind of justice system do you have on your world?"

He shook his head. "Remember, my mountain tribe is isolated from the rest of civilization. We are not so advanced. The scene of a crime along with any witnesses are all that matter."

"Didn't you have any friends to vouch for your character? Or other relatives to come forward and testify on your behalf?"

His grim silence gave her the answer. A surge of sympathy made a slight cry escape her lips, and her heart went out to him. No wonder he was so reluctant to trust others. He'd learned the hard way to rely only on himself.

"I was fortunate Primer Pedar offered me a job," he said at last, plowing his fingers through his hair. "It's rare for our tribesmen to pass beyond the boundaries, but our legendary skills are known far and wide. Now I stand with my brothers against a new and yet old enemy."

She pounced on his words, her eyes misting with emotion. "Exactly, Magnor. The Drift Lords are your family now, plus you have me. You're not alone."

"We'll see." He grabbed his bundle of clothes and strode into the bathroom, his movements tense.

Dear Lord, how could she convince him that she meant to remain by his side? First, she had to convince herself. Did she really want to stay wed to him, once they'd saved the world? What if she didn't have that condition set on her trust fund?

After a brief interval, he emerged from the bathroom fully dressed and looking every inch the dangerous warrior. Erika, still clutching the sheet to her body, cleared her throat.

"Uh, Magnor, as long as we are in confession mode, there's something I have to tell you."

He waved a hand. "Enough chatter. We should dine to maintain our strength."

"I agree, but—"

"Well, don't just stand there. Get dressed, woman."

She bristled. "You can't order me around. And we need to talk. You see, I—"

"I'm removing the perimeter rods. You don't want to be caught unawares if the Trolleks vector in here. Get yourself clothed." He snatched his sack from the closet.

Annoyed by his hard-nosed attitude, she retrieved her

clothing and marched into the bathroom. Why was he being so obstinate?

She pondered the reasons while she showered and applied her makeup. He'd been betrayed by his sister and shunned by his people. The fact that he'd confided in her meant they'd achieved a step forward in their relationship, but then he'd shut her out again.

Was he afraid to get too close, because he might be disappointed again? If so, learning she'd used him to gain control of her trust fund money would be comparable to his sister's deceit. He'd despise her without listening to her rationale. And did she have one? Why else would she stay married to a stranger from the stars?

Then again, he'd used her as well. He had tricked her into marriage, and why? To protect her as he claimed, or to acquire her immunity from the Trollek mind touch?

Her feelings jumbled when she thought about what he meant to her. His protectiveness, his courage, and his sense of honor had earned her respect and admiration. But that wasn't what made her breath come short and her skin tingle in his presence. He aroused her like no other man. She yearned to ease his longings and to fill the emptiness in his soul.

Yet once this mission was over, he had little to keep him here. He'd go where his duty took him. The Drift Lords were his family now. She meant nothing to him except a warm body in his bed and an inconvenient bride.

Chapter Sixteen

Magnor folded his perimeter rods, packed them away, and then strapped on his sword. Although he avoided looking at his wife, he'd already seen her baffled expression. She wouldn't understand why he had turned from her, but curse it, if he gave in to his desires, he'd never complete his mission. She seduced away his reason and stole his purpose.

His only hope was to focus solely on his intent and forge ahead. If he allowed himself one iota of feeling, he'd admit how much he yearned to lie with her again, to feel her smooth skin beneath his fingers, and to hear her soft moans as he stroked her.

Great Cosmos, even those few thoughts had made him hard. He tightened his jaw, firming his resolve. Their mission came first. So what if they had explored each other's bodies? Marriage was based on more than sex. And Erika hadn't given him any indication she wanted him to stay for other reasons.

He gritted his teeth as he inspected the room for any remnants of his gear he might have forgotten. She deserved better than him anyway. He was a man without an honorable name, a man cast out from his own kind. Forced to roam the stars, he had nowhere to call home.

Yet she'd overturned his expectations in one aspect. Magnor thought she might regard him with revulsion after hearing he'd been accused of murder. Instead, she'd been sympathetic. Her lustrous eyes had grown dewy and soft as he related his sister's betrayal. But then, criminals in her culture were innocent until proven guilty.

Their scientific approach to crime solving fascinated him. If his people had these investigative techniques when he'd been apprehended, perhaps the Council's ruling would have been different.

No use arguing over tilled soil. What's done is done.

"Are you ready?" He glanced at Erika, finger-combing her layered hair at the dresser mirror.

She'd done her best with their meager belongings. He'd expect no less from his tribeswomen who trained as warriors alongside their men. Pride swelled his chest. His wife could hold her own among them. She may not possess combat skills, but she had other talents.

His eyes narrowed as he remembered one topic they hadn't discussed. What exactly was her power? Had she used it to escape from Algie?

When they met up with his team, they could review those issues. Nira Larsen, Zohar's mate, would be able to advise them. For now, he had a job to do.

Following Erika's suggestion, he printed out a copy of the Jolheim Gardens map at the hotel's computer center. Then he reported in to his team leader.

"The situation is bad." Zohar's voice issued from Magnor's wrist unit. "Seismic quakes are damaging city infrastructures and causing worldwide tsunamis. Volcanic activity has increased. Government officials have responded to these disasters by declaring emergency status and taking control."

"The Trolleks must have activated their sleeper agents." He glanced at Erika, checking her email at another computer. From the way her head tilted, he could tell she was listening. Magnor really should request one of the team's earpieces. It would allow for more private conversations.

"In some areas, the Trolleks are even making an overt appearance and assuming command."

"That's not good. How are the others progressing?"

"Yaron is getting closer to refining an antidote to the

confounding spell. Don't ask me to explain the science. And he's been keeping track of Algie's movements since your last update."

"Sabotaging her research should be a priority."

"Agreed. Dal continues to destroy their recruitment centers, while Kaj is working with Agent Monroe to expose the compromised individuals within the government. As for Paz, he's contacted the dwarfs and wrestled an alliance from them."

"That'll be helpful."

"He'd hoped to gain the Videns' support among the Trolleks, but they're backing Algie. They still think her scientific approach is better than all-out warfare."

"Don't they realize she's seized power for herself?"

"Some of them do. Paz is working on it." A pause. "Is anything else going on that I should know about?"

"What do you mean?"

"Yaron seems distracted, and he has consulted Dal and Kaj on more than one occasion. When I've come upon them, they fall silent. I get the impression they're keeping something from me."

Magnor rolled his shoulder, a bit stiff this morning. "If true, I am not privy to it. How are you and Nira doing with your tasks?" he said to distract his commander. If Yaron had secrets, it must be for a good cause. Perhaps their medic didn't care to add to Zohar's burdens.

"We've been back to the island where Nira and I first saw the temple ruins. She was able to copy the runic inscription on the pillar this time and is studying it."

"Good luck to you both, sire. Have you any further orders for me?"

His superior's voice grew grim. "Just find that *maug* weapon to destroy the Trolleks."

"I'll do my best. Peace be with you."

Magnor rang off and suggested to Erika they take the time for a proper meal.

Once they'd placed their orders at the adjacent café, he filled her in on each team member's role. She kept silent during his explanation. What was there to say? Their success depended upon each person's contribution.

After a filling repast, he unfolded his Jolheim Gardens map at the table. They sat outside where birds chirped, traffic droned, and patrons chatted in a pleasant semblance of normalcy. Aware that could change in an instant, Magnor focused on the task ahead.

He squinted at the layout of attractions filling the twenty-acre expanse. Pedestrian walkways led between open-air theaters, amusement rides, and restaurants. To the left of the main entrance was a lake with boats for rent.

Erika, who'd been perusing a tourist brochure from the lobby, set down her pamphlet on the table.

"I have a suggestion." Her tone indicated she felt strongly about her opinion.

"What is it?" he said, keeping his expression bland.

"We should go to the park when it's crowded, later on in the day. In the meantime, we can go shopping. It would be wise to disguise our appearances in case Algie has put out a bulletin for us." She scanned his uniform, cape and sword. "We're not exactly unobtrusive, unless you plan to scout the place using your invisibility shield."

Observing the wisps of flame-colored hair feathering her face, he could think of a more pleasurable way to pass the time.

"My device would use too much energy. Your idea has merit." He pointed to the broad avenue where cars whizzed past. "Let's explore while we determine our strategy."

Deciding Erika was right about their need to blend in, he removed his cape and folded it into a neat bundle. While she charged the bill to a credit card, he slipped the cape inside his backpack before slinging the straps over his shoulders.

Although they'd paid for additional nights at the hotel in case they had to return, he'd insisted on keeping his belongings close at hand. There wasn't much he could do about the sword at his hip, unless he bought a container to hide it.

Traffic hurtled around a busy town square, where they browsed window displays. Erika's eyes brightened as they strode past shops selling wool sweaters, pewter items, and teakwood tableware. Lunch hour had brought out the tourists, and the streets were getting crowded.

"Man, I wish I could afford some of this stuff." She gazed longingly at a Royal Copenhagen porcelain figurine.

"You can if you still have our prize money in your account."

"Those funds are meant for more important things. Besides, we're not here to shop for souvenirs. Let's look for a clothing store."

****

Too bad they didn't have time to tour the city, Erika thought as they moved on. If they survived the upcoming apocalypse, she'd insist Magnor bring her back here to see Christianborg Palace, the Danish Resistance Museum, and Rosenborg Castle.

Then again, he might be long gone by then. She'd resume her lonely life, although new goals would keep her going. A sigh escaped her lips. What would it be like to have a husband who supported her dreams?

But what was she thinking? By his own words, Magnor had confessed to being a convicted murderer. If he was as innocent as he'd claimed, that meant his sister had betrayed him. How would he feel when he learned she had reasons of her own for wanting them to stay wed?

"Listen, Magnor, we have to talk. I need to tell you—"

"About your power and how you got away from Algie?" His narrowed gaze scoured her. "I was wondering when you'd bring that up. Save it for later, when we can consult with Nira."

Erika pressed her lips together. Why wouldn't the man let her speak? Fine, if he was going to be that way and interrupt each time, she'd save it for later all right. And it was getting annoying how often he mentioned Nira Larsen's name.

Then again, none of this would matter if they didn't succeed in their purpose.

Erika took out the brochure she'd acquired at the hotel. "This says Jolheim was created in 1863, so it's been around a while. Do you want to get tickets only for the restaurants, grounds, and entertainment, or for the rides also?"

"Everything. Here's a jewelry store. We can trade a kewa stone for local currency."

She went inside with him, browsing the showcases while he spoke to the proprietor. The gleaming gold pieces drew her attention. She'd never coveted fine jewelry, preferring chunky necklaces and semi-precious stones. But something drew her to the wedding rings and diamond solitaires as she twirled the fake gold band on her ring finger.

"Which set do you like?"

Magnor's low, sensual tone flared along her nerve endings. She hadn't realized he had come up behind her.

Erika pointed to a band with a brushed gold design. "That one is nice."

"Too plain." He moved toward the next case with glittering anniversary rings. "I understand women on your world value kewa stones as adornments. Sir!" he called to the owner, who bustled over. "Can you show us some of these, please?"

"Magnor, we don't have time."

He waved a hand dismissively. "This won't take long. It's the least I can do."

"But these are costly, and it's unnecessary, especially when..." She couldn't finish aloud. *When you're going to leave me,* she meant to say.

"Nonsense. I have more than enough currency now to cover our expenses. Since your culture values these rocks as symbols of unity, allow me the pleasure to purchase you a proper ring."

Unity, he'd said. *Not love.*

She bit her lower lip as the store owner reverently withdrew a velvet case holding a variety of diamond rings and proceeded to measure her finger.

How did Magnor's people symbolize the union between man and woman? She'd ask him but didn't want the shopkeeper to overhear.

For all she knew, his tribesmen might gift their women with necklaces made from an enemy's teeth. She understood so little about her husband's background. They were worlds apart in so many ways, and she didn't see how they could reconcile their differences.

Yet he'd been banished from home. Where else would he go after he'd completed his mission? Maybe she could discover a way to keep her warrior, but first Erika needed to do some hard soul searching of her own. Did she truly want him to stay? Was the trust fund merely an excuse to hang onto the man?

She shrugged aside her musings. Now wasn't the time to ponder their problems. They had an artifact to locate.

"How about you?" she asked, pointing to the band on his finger. "Do you want a new ring?"

Hadn't she been cautioned to make him wear that one at all times? The memory jiggled in her mind. Sylvia, the teen with a blond braid who'd helped her prepare for the televised ceremony, had advised her thus. *Tell him this will protect him against the coming darkness.* A shiver racked her. It sounded ominously like a prophecy.

"This looks real enough." Magnor had the jeweler examine the ring. The fellow verified it was fourteen carat gold. Her husband slipped the band back on his finger. "I'll keep this one. It reminds me of Vegas, where we first met."

Fifteen minutes later, Erika walked out of the shop wearing a two-carat diamond anniversary band. She couldn't stop looking at it. Pride swelled her bosom. This handsome hunk was hers, and by God, she wanted the world to know.

She hooked her arm through his, smiling at his startled glance, while they headed down another street bordering the river. Spying a drugstore, she hastened over.

Inside the shop, she grabbed necessities off the shelves like a child in a candy store.

Several doors down, they entered a boutique to buy some new clothes. Erika couldn't convince Magnor to hide his sword, but at least he traded his military cut uniform for a sport shirt and jeans. She got herself a practical pants set in brown tones while twisting her hair under a scarf.

Outdoors, a boat plowed the river parallel to their street while the afternoon sun blazed overhead. Workers jostled past them on the sidewalk. Looks could be deceptive, she reminded herself as they headed toward Jolheim Gardens.

Hidden behind the peaceful facade were evil beings bent on conquering Earth and turning everyone into slaves.

Erika gripped her purse as they approached the ticket window. Leaves floated to the ground from an oak tree as they stood in line.

After they'd passed through the turnstile, she opened the guide map given to her along with their tickets. "Where should we start?"

Magnor scratched his jaw as he studied the printout he'd brought from the hotel. "We should look for anything related to Norse mythology or the Viking era."

"That makes sense. But then what? Are we searching for the book itself or a clue to its whereabouts?"

"It could be either."

"I'd place my bet on any kind of item with runic lettering. It'll be hard to find if planted in plain sight among other details." She squinted at the map. "There's a train ride called the Odin Express. Or how about the Grote Mine? The Grotes are little people like dwarfs. Or here's a Journey to Hel ride."

Magnor took her elbow and moved her along. "I'd also like to find out which attraction they use to confound humans, so I can pass the information along to Dal."

They strolled by a restaurant with diners eating outside at clothed tables. Planters with greenery and large red flowers dotted the perimeter. Colorful blossoms sprouted everywhere throughout the park, delighting Erika with their brilliance.

"Look, that sign says Jolheim Jackpot. Do you suppose they have gambling here?"

Magnor released her arm. "Perhaps, but I'd prefer to avoid visiting another casino."

She caught his wry tone. "The one in Vegas is fresh in my mind, too." They passed an open-air amphitheater for pantomime acts. "Ugh, I've never been a fan of mimes or clowns."

Her words got drowned out as a marching band came into view. Costumed figures paraded past to a blasting rhythm.

"Which way should we go?" Magnor spoke loudly to be heard over the booming noise.

"Let's keep to the left. The other side borders the park and holds mostly restaurants. I have a hunch our goal may be found on one of the rides."

Erika dodged a couple of mothers pushing strollers.

"There are certainly enough places to eat," she said, indicating a gaudily decorated Chinese restaurant, a regal palace offering Danish cuisine, and a European café. Biergartens appeared at regular intervals along with stands selling fast food. None of them related specifically to ancient Norse history, so she passed them by as possibilities for clues.

"Where are the rides?" Magnor asked, a disgruntled look on his face as they encountered more eateries, a concert hall, and an ornate outdoor stage designed in an Asian motif.

"Toward the back. Come this way."

She steered him from the glistening lake where people could rent swan boats. The first attraction they encountered was a walk-through haunted house with moving stairs, hanging bridges, and switchbacks. It sounded like a Danish version of Hogwarts.

Magnor wanted to go inside to see if this was the place where Trolleks confounded people. They showed their tickets at the door and entered. The dark interior made her clutch his arm. Scary music set her nerves on edge.

"The attendant at the entrance didn't touch us, so this can't be where they confound people." She watched her footing, wary of hidden trapdoors.

Magnor tensed at her side. "Nonetheless, we must be vigilant. Trolleks could be anywhere."

She shivered, thinking of the zombie-like figures at the movie studio. They'd fit right in at this place.

The corridor dead-ended and they faced a blank wall. Suddenly, the floor tilted and a panel opened in front of them. They stumbled into the next room, where a winged creature with fangs flew at them. Erika spied an opening at the opposite end.

"Over there!" She ducked as the thing dived at them, its wing brushing her shoulder.

Magnor grabbed her hand and hauled her across the room before the creature swooped down again. Its glowing eyes glared at them as they leapt across the threshold. A pitiful cry came from its mouth as a panel shut behind them.

"That thing looked real." Magnor glowered at her in the dim lighting. "Prince Zohar spoke of creatures called pfrells that are much like this one. They inhabit the Trollek home world."

"Maybe these are modeled after them. Come on, let's get through this place. Keep your eyes open for anything that might relate to the Book of Odin."

Although they encountered more monsters, spooks, and illusory effects, nothing hinted at the sacred tome.

They emerged into a gift shop and then out the exit into the bright sunshine. Magnor squared his shoulders as though invigorated by the experience, while Erika breathed a sigh of relief. Her heart gradually calmed from its rapid, thudding beat. She didn't like dark, enclosed places. And just because they hadn't met any threats so far didn't mean the Trolleks weren't biding their time, waiting to pounce.

"What's next?" Magnor glanced around them, his hand on his sword hilt as if he, too, expected the enemy to pop out of nowhere.

She studied her map. "We could probably skip the Ferris wheel and the kiddie rides. You can go on this rollercoaster called Demon's Revenge if you want."

He shook his head. "It would be difficult to spot clues when going so fast. You'd mentioned something about a mine?"

"The Grote ride might be worth a visit."

This attraction was popular judging from the line snaking around a corner. The sun beat down on Erika's neck as they edged forward. Once inside the cave-like setting, they boarded a tram. As before, the attendant didn't touch anyone at entry.

She settled into her seat. Hopefully, this ride would be slow-moving, giving them plenty of time to examine the details.

"We should go on the Odin Express next," she suggested. "It's a train ride, and we might see something relevant along the way."

"You're right. Pay attention for now. We're moving."

Short fellows with big eyes and funnel-like ears waved at them on their journey along the track. The small folk, busy digging for glowing rocks, wore friendly smiles under their miner's helmets.

They got so close to one that she could see its eyelashes. Admiring the detail, she noted the sad look in his eyes, the smile that appeared more like a grimace, and the tear that streamed down one cheek. A tear? Water must be leaking from somewhere above.

Lively music with an Irish lilt made her think of Leprechauns. As they appeared to descend deeper underground, a fiery glow ahead grew brighter. Their tram car whipped around a curve and a treasure room filled with gold rocks came into view.

Steam blew out of the dragon's nostrils who guarded this chamber. A chain wrapped around its neck. It roared at the intruders, blasting fire at them but the flame blew short, missing their tram. Frustrated, the dragon stomped its feet.

The rail shook and their tram tilted, but they made it around the next bend. The Grotes waved at them as they zoomed toward the exit.

"I didn't see anything noteworthy." Erika dismounted the ride, wondering how they'd ever find the fabled Book of Odin. It was akin to looking for the proverbial needle in a haystack.

The hairs on her nape prickled as people strolled past them outside. Anyone of these folks might be under Trollek mind control and could turn on them in an instant. Feeling exposed, she grabbed Magnor's hand and tugged him forward.

Chapter Seventeen

After passing a pirate boat ride for children, Erika and Magnor stopped at a tall tower where tiny overhead cars on cables whipped around at high speed.

Magnor nudged her with a grin. "We'd have a good vantage point over the whole park on that ride."

"That's not for me, but it's a good idea. You go. I'll wait here."

"No, we stick together."

She pointed forward. "Look, the Odin Express is up ahead."

The train ride didn't produce any useful clues. As they disembarked, she rubbed a hand over her face. Maybe this park represented a wild goose chase. At this rate, they'd never find anything. It might be wise to expand their reach and not exclude other types of attractions.

An operetta at a concert hall and a variety show with jugglers did not hold the key to their target.

"Most of the other rides are on the far side of that food palace," she said, her tone weary.

"Let's eat. I'm hungry."

Erika got an open sandwich with smoked salmon while Magnor ate a schnitzel dish. Afterward, they strode past several thrill rides including one where people sat in harnessed seats while hoisted upward and then plunged upside down. Erika hurried past so Magnor wouldn't get the notion to try it.

"Here, this has to be the place." Magnor halted beside a popular ride. "Loki's Lair is an appropriate title for our quest."

"Yes, it is." A smidgen of unease clawed at her.

The guidebook didn't say too much except the attraction was an adventure into the mythological past. Children couldn't go as there was a height requirement. Nonetheless, a line snaked toward an entrance designed to look like the mouth of hell.

Fake stalactites hung down at the entry. Red glitter reflected the sunlight, casting images like flames on the surrounding rock walls.

The sounds from the park muted as they entered the dark interior. Here guests were forced into narrow aisles until they shuffled along single-file. Careful not to bump into the people ahead of her, Erika grimaced as she passed dimly lit dioramas of torture and suffering. Wails reverberated from somewhere ahead like ghostly residents howling a protest at the intrusion.

"Delightful place," Magnor murmured in her ear.

She'd taken the lead, peering around each curve in their path, wary of what might be around the next corner. Then the route widened, and they emerged onto a landing where people boarded boats presumably on tracks. Shadows played against the stony walls while torches flickered on sconces. Smelling smoke, she marveled at the authenticity of the setting.

A figure dressed like the Grim Reaper and holding a scythe shook each person's hand before issuing directions for which row to take prior to boarding. Next to him stood a lovely assistant, a blonde wearing dominatrix black leather that drew men's glances. She was meant to be a distraction, Erika realized.

This was it. They must be Trolleks.

Erika whirled around and lifted on her toes to kiss Magnor smack on the lips.

Before she could explain her action, their turn came.

The blond woman grasped her arm and said something to her. When Erika shook her head in confusion, the attendant spoke in English. "How many are in your group?"

The Trollek female's tantalizingly sweet scent made Erika want to lean closer. With her sexy outfit, she'd easily snare any red-blooded human male in the vicinity.

"Um, there are two of us." Erika's voice came out a squeak.

Meanwhile, the hunched figure in the robe reached for Magnor, who had been watching Erika with a perplexed frown. The hooded host snagged his hand for a firm shake.

Magnor shot her a panicked glance. She gave him a reassuring smile in return. He should be all right if her immunity had transferred to him, but they should play along.

"Row number four," the husky Trollek ordered.

Magnor cast his gaze downward in mute obedience and proceeded to the labeled spot.

Erika followed while surreptitiously glancing at others standing in queue. Besides assigning rows according to the number of people in a party, it didn't appear as though any different selection process was at hand. Perhaps it happened at the end of the ride, or in the inevitable gift shop.

Would old folks be parted from their loved ones and sent to their doom? Would strong, healthy adults be selected for slave labor? Or would a covert scan provide new subjects for Trollek experiments? With luck, they'd all be sent home with orders to wait for activation in Algie's army.

An empty boat appeared from around a curve to their left. It must have disgorged its occupants at another station and then rode the track to collect its new load.

Erika stepped into the vessel, a narrow design with pointed tips at either end, reminding her of Viking ships she'd seen in history books. They sat in rows of two and donned harnesses. Thankfully, she and Magnor were in the last seats. She wouldn't want to be in front, in case there were dips ahead.

She stashed her purse in a net under her feet, wishing they'd learned more about this attraction before entering. Her spine tingled in dread of what might come.

Their boat jerked into motion and glided along, picking up speed toward a dark maw that loomed ahead. She clutched the rail in front of them, gritting her teeth as they ascended a steep incline into darkness. A cool breeze blew tufts of hair into her face while a voice spoke in a foreign tongue.

"What's he saying?" she asked Magnor. He'd told her about his implanted universal translator. Could he understand Danish?

"It's a story about the early Danes and how they settled disputes, and how crime and punishment have evolved over time. We're going to get a glimpse of what happens to the souls of dead criminals."

"Oh, great. Like, this is supposed to be hell?" Those earlier dioramas of torture came to mind.

"This attraction is called Loki's Lair. The evil spirit wants to bring hell on earth to everyone who lives there."

"How appropriate."

At the top, a three-headed creature glared at them and spat angry words.

"What's that? It looks like something out of mythology." She didn't recall such a monster from Norse myths, but her knowledge wasn't that extensive.

"It's saying we have sinned and we'll be punished like all who have transgressed. Our humanity alone has earned us an eternity of suffering."

At those words, their boat whizzed around a curve and plunged downward into total darkness. Erika's breath whooshed from her lungs in a shriek.

She closed her eyes as their vehicle looped and dipped through an endless, twisting speed ride. Her head reeled and she lost her sense of orientation. The brochure had said nothing about this! Then again, they were supposed to be spellbound. She held her breath, her grip on the rail so tight that it dug into her skin. Her heart pounded like a racehorse on the turf.

They zoomed down another steep slope then climbed up again and careened around a curve. She gasped in a breath, praying this nightmarish ride would soon be over. Her neck stayed locked in the harness while her mouth opened in a silent scream. They plummeted downward, her stomach knotting with each motion.

Her body sagged against the seat, flung this way and that but held tight by the restraint. She didn't care what happened at the end, only that she reached it intact.

Just keep breathing, and you'll survive.

Her pulse thundered in her ears. No wonder people died of fright.

"Are you alright?" Magnor nudged her with his elbow at the same time she realized they'd slowed.

Her eyes blinked open. Their vehicle glided toward a landing. Shaking, she could only nod in response.

A voice emitted from a speaker near their ears, rattling off a series of words in a foreign language and then repeating them in English.

"Please proceed to your right where you'll be given a souvenir key ring. Go home and tell your friends what a wonderful time you had and urge them to visit Jolheim Gardens."

Erika could barely lift herself from the seat let alone place her foot on the platform when it came time to disembark. Magnor took her arm and hauled her up.

"You're trembling like a glitter bug. Can you manage?"

"Yes, I'm fine. That wasn't my kind of ride."

Inside the inevitable gift shop, they headed with the others in their group to obtain their free souvenir. Directed to reach into a dispenser, Erika exclaimed aloud when her finger encountered something sharp.

"Ow, what was that?" She snatched her hand away, the key ring somehow ending up in her palm.

Magnor, who hovered behind, nudged her. "Ssh, you're supposed to be confounded, remember? This must be where they take DNA samples."

The staff wouldn't let them exit immediately, regaling the group with a sales pitch. When Erika noticed a uniformed man heading their way, she dodged past the speaker toward the door with Magnor following at her cue.

Outside, she held her stomach and sucked in a shaky breath. The warm air, flowered scent, and bright sunshine helped to dispel her anxiety. Hopefully, the attendants wouldn't come after them out here.

Spotting a trash can, she tossed the key ring inside, not wanting to take any chances it might be more than it seemed.

"What now? You didn't see any clue to the book in there, did you?" she asked Magnor, her gaze alighting on a colorful bed of purple and white pansies.

"No, but it must be here somewhere." He cast a narrowed glance around them. "At least we have confirmation this theme park acts as a recruitment center. I'll notify Dal so he can neutralize the underground complex once we're finished here."

"Will we have to use the portal again?" She'd rather not transport to their next destination that way and risk encountering a troop of armed Trolleks down below.

"It depends on where we have to go from here."

Erika glanced at her watch, surprised to see it was four o'clock local time. Man, she could use a drink.

"Let's take a break. I need one after that last ride."

They chose a bar overlooking the lake. She got a glass of chardonnay, while Magnor ordered a beer. They strolled along the pavement while sipping their beverages. Music blared from a nearby concert stage.

Magnor's face scrunched in thought. "Perhaps we've been thinking about this the wrong way. How could anyone have hidden the Book of Odin at the theme park? This land would have been forested in early times."

"That's true." She considered the possibilities. "Maybe we should look for it at the base of a tree or under a rock. Too bad we're not more familiar with the geology of this area."

His pace slowed. "What if the Trolleks utilized a system of natural caves to build their underground tunnels? We shouldn't exclude the possibility of looking there."

"Speaking of caves, I got a weird feeling inside the mine attraction. Those little men seemed awfully real."

Her glance rose to an overhead ride where baby dragons on

cables flew passengers around a central tower. A much larger dragon had been chained inside that fake mine shaft.

"So? What's your point?" Magnor finished his ale and discarded the bottle in a trash bin.

Erika sidestepped a gaggle of teens munching on popcorn and cinnamon-scented almonds. "We should go back and take a closer look. What if the Grotes are not audio-animatronic figures? They could be actual people enslaved by the Trolleks and controlled to please the crowds."

He squinted at her. "We have a mission to accomplish, and it doesn't include freeing Trollek slaves."

"I know, but they might be able to tell us where to search for the book. At least, let's go see if I'm right. And if not, then we'll examine the park's natural surroundings."

His mouth compressed. "Very well, but afterward, I intend to inspect every tree and bush, every stone upon the ground. There's a reason why we were directed here."

A swell of excitement surged through her. "I agree. We'd better hurry. I have a feeling our time is running out."

She drained her plastic wine cup and dumped it in a receptacle. A hunch told her they were doing the right thing.

****

Magnor resettled his backpack on his shoulders as he strode beside her toward the mine attraction. He ignored the curious glances sent his way. Although this site didn't have costumed characters roaming in public like at other theme parks, a sword wasn't totally out of place. For all anyone knew, he could be a ride attendant taking a break.

Surely the Trolleks had noticed him by now. They must be waiting to discern his purpose. Algie would want to get her hands on the book once she understood his mission. Or had she already learned why he was there? Maybe Loki had figured it out and told her. In that case, they'd want him to find the legendary Book of Odin before attacking.

He didn't conceive how those short little fellows on the mine ride could be real, but if true, they might be just the thing he needed to create a diversion.

They entered the attraction and boarded the mine car without mishap. With a lurch, it zigzagged off on its route through darkened tunnels and past scenes of miners hacking at rocks for gold. He waited until they'd entered the chamber with the dragon and then he poked Erika who sat by his side. Her tense posture and worried look betrayed her anxiety.

"Look, there's a path that parallels the track for emergency evacuation. We need to leave the ride."

Their tram would pick up speed once it left this room and entered another so-called shaft. This was their best chance. They'd asked for the last row on the tram so no one would notice their departure.

She clutched her purse in her lap. "It's dark up ahead. The other people won't see us if we hop off there."

He leapt after her, landing on the obscured path and ducking down until the tram passed out of sight. Another one would soon follow.

Signaling for her to join him, he hastened to a faux calcite column and huddled behind it. The sound of hammering came from where the miners labored. As another tram rattled past, the dragon spewed flames in its direction. Magnor felt the blast of heat on his skin.

As soon as the tourists were gone, Erika lunged toward the scene. "Yo, boys! Over here."

Heads turned their way. The dragon swung its neck, its nostrils flaring. Scales glistened on its huge body. The chain restraining it pulled taut. Magnor gazed in astonishment at their response. Erika must be right about them.

"Who are you?" the nearest Grote said. He had big round eyes, a knobby forehead, and funnel-shaped ears. They all wore work clothes, plaid shirts and dirty trousers.

Magnor stood proudly. "I am a Drift Lord, come from the stars to save humanity from the scourge known as the Trolleks."

The little guy looked around fearfully. "Shush, you moron. You'll bring the beasts down upon us. We don't want to be punished. We've felt their shock sticks enough times."

"We want to help you." Erika advanced stealthily, her hair askew. She'd lost her scarf in their hasty leap from the tram.

The dragon growled. "I haven't eaten, humans. Talk fast or become my meal."

Erika and Magnor exchanged startled glances. The dragon could speak?

"Why would you want to assist us?" the Grote spokesman said with genuine curiosity. "People stare at us and laugh."

"They think you're here to entertain them," Magnor replied. "Guests don't know you're prisoners and that your kind exists."

"So how are you different from them?"

"We're part of the prophecy concerning the ancient legends." He did a quick introduction. "You've heard of Ragnarok and the Norse gods? We seek the Book of Odin."

"Listen," Erika added, "perhaps you can help us in return for your freedom."

"You see?" The dragon snorted fire. "They will use us, like the others."

Magnor elbowed her and spoke in a low tone. "If you release them, they'll run away and we'll have gained nothing. We need their cooperation."

"We're not going to get it without haggling. Let me do this my way."

A rumbling vibration heralded the arrival of another tram car. They ducked out of sight until it passed, then Erika moved within range of the dragon's fiery breath.

Maug stubborn woman. Would he be stuck continually doing damage control in her wake instead of carrying out his duty?

He had to admit sweet-talking as a tactic could be useful, especially when that fire-breathing beast tilted its head and sniffed her. If they'd forged ahead as he had wished, they might be toast by now.

"What's your name?" Erika halted beside the dragon.

"I am called Shayna," the creature replied in a reluctant tone. Its tail swished, making a wide swathe on the packed dirt ground.

"Tell me, how did you end up here?" Erika petted its thick hide with a trembling hand. "I mean, you're such a big, beautiful thing. You're meant to soar high in the skies. How did you and your friends get captured?"

Shayna issued a pained howl. "The Trolleks attacked my nest one day when I was out foraging. They took my babes. Upon my return, they threatened to kill my children if I didn't go with them."

That ride with the flying dragons—those creatures must be Shayna's offspring, Magnor realized.

"What purpose do you serve?" Erika asked, stepping away. "The Trolleks could have faked this attraction same as the other rides."

Shayna lowered her head. "I turn the water wheel at night when the park is closed. It provides power."

"For what?" Magnor moved closer, keeping his sword arm free in case the dragon took a dislike to him.

"For machinery. I don't know its purpose, but it takes up an entire hall."

That amount of energy could fuel an inter-dimensional rift generator. If he could see it for himself, it would confirm Zohar's theory that the Trolleks were rebuilding the portals his team had sealed. If reopened, they'd allow for a massive invasion of Trolleks from Jak'Tar, their home world.

But would Algie approve? She'd taken advantage of the vacuum in power to declare herself queen. Was a faction of Jorgonauts—followers of King Jorg—defying her?

"You claim you're a Drift Lord?" The spokesperson approached, his beady eyes studying Magnor. "What are you doing in this place?"

"As I said earlier, we're here to recover the legendary Book of Odin. Either the book itself or a clue to its whereabouts is hidden on these grounds. It holds the key to destroying the Trolleks."

The fellow stretched to his full height, a good foot shorter than Erika. "If you free our friend there, you free us. She'll fly us out of here."

"And why were you captured, mister…?"

"Ribald. We're relatives of the dwarfs. Everyone has heard about how one of the Drift Lords rescued our chief courier and second cousin to the king."

"That would be Paz. He escaped from the dungeon at Shirajo Manor with a dwarf named Smitty. Do you have the same abilities as your relations?"

Ribald shook his head. "We do not possess the magic to turn inanimate objects into gold. Our job is to guard such treasures."

Magnor leaned forward. "Is that why you're here then, to watch over something important?"

"We've always been here to guard the treasure, but it's not this pile of fake rocks. When the Trolleks discovered our presence, they tried to confound us. Their attempt failed as we are immune to their spell. But they knew our weakness." He pointed to his shorn hair.

Magnor remembered Paz saying something about the dwarf's vulnerability. "The Trolleks cut your hair, the source of your strength?"

"They did the deed while we slept. When we woke up, we were chained and unable to break the links."

"And what treasure is it that you are guarding? Did the Trolleks know your reason for being here?"

"Despite their attempts to make us talk, we've kept silent. They are not the ones meant to find it."

"What is it?" Impatience edged his tone.

"We guard what you seek, Drift Lord. The legends are true. Our kind has been waiting for generations to meet you."

A vibration underfoot indicated a tram about to approach. Magnor glanced around the cavern. "Take cover," he said to Erika, grabbing her hand.

They ran behind a plaster stalagmite until the cars passed.

Erika's eyes shone with zeal as she regarded him. "We have to free these people, Magnor. How can we break those chains?"

"Our chisels won't work," Ribald said, overhearing her. "These chains were forged in Jak'Tar. Nothing will break them."

"What about dissolving the metal?" Magnor asked.

"You see?" Ribald addressed his brothers, who'd halted their labors to watch them. "He has the ingenuity, the inquisitiveness and the courage. If he passes the test, he is the one we've been expecting."

Magnor pointed to the dragon. "How about your saliva? Does it have acidic properties?"

Shayna snorted a cloud of steam. "We've already tried. It didn't work."

"There's only one place where you can get the acid that will dissolve these chains," Ribald said with a grimace. "If you succeed, we'll give you the information you need. You will have proven yourself as our destined savior."

Erika kicked at a pebble on the ground. "With all these delays, we'll never find that stupid book."

Another tremor shook the cavern, and Magnor gripped a rocky outcropping as the ground shifted under him. "That's no train coming this time."

"These quakes have been happening more often lately," Ribald said after the motion abated. "Loki is growing stronger. You must hurry and free us. My kind can help you in the final battle, but only if we get word to them."

Magnor gave him a wry glance. "Where do we find the required acid to dissolve your chains, then?"

The dragon snickered as though doubting his ability to accomplish the task.

"It won't be easy." Ribald stroked his stubbled chin. "You have to collect the sweat of Balhogg the Ogre."

Chapter Eighteen

Erika felt of a mind to let Magnor chase after the ogre by himself but stuck by her wifely duty to accompany him. So it was they left the theme park to wait for nightfall in the safety of their hotel room.

Magnor nixed her idea to explore further, concerned the Trolleks might try to grab them. He believed they were being left alone so as to reveal their mission. But if Algie had already gotten wind of their target, she might become impatient. He didn't care to risk exposure until it became necessary.

They spent the rest of the afternoon enjoying each other's company and ordered room service for dinner. By nightfall, Magnor was ready for action, dressed once more in his uniform.

Public transportation brought them to the outskirts of the forbidden woods known as Giant's Glen. For ages, the forest was said to be inhabited by a monster. People who ventured inside the dense thickets were never seen again.

"What exactly is an ogre?" She admired the handsome figure Magnor made in the moonlight, his cape billowing behind him and his hand on his sword hilt. He looked every inch the warrior with the proud tilt of his head and his erect posture.

A warm tingle spread through her as she remembered the tender gleam in his eyes back at their hotel room, the soft words he'd murmured in her ear, and the passion he'd stirred in her heart. If she weren't careful, she'd grow dependent on his presence, and then it would hurt all the more when he left.

His eyes flashed with that otherworldly glow. "From what

I've heard, an ogre is a mean and hideous monster, larger than a man but not as big as their cousins, the giants."

"Giants?" She raised an eyebrow. "You speak as though they're real."

"Ask Nira Larsen to tell you the Norse creation myth when you meet her. She will explain how two races evolved from the void, the giants and the gods, and how they always battled."

"O-kay. It's likely there's something menacing in these woods, but that could mean any type of animal. Don't you think I should have a weapon, too?"

She'd been amazed he hadn't insisted on going alone and leaving her behind for safety. Instead, he had seemed to welcome her company. This was a surprising change for the man. Perhaps he was coming to accept her in his life.

"You're right. Tuck this knife into your belt but be aware its use requires close combat. Hold the blade this way when you make a thrust." He showed her what he meant and then gave her the knife while describing the best places to jab someone.

"Can't we sneak through the forest using your invisibility shield? We can find the monster that way."

He located the head of a path leading into the interior. "It will smell us. I'd rather not waste the energy." His eyes took on a faint luminosity as though he could see in the dark.

They started on the path, the cooler air making her grateful she'd changed clothes earlier. She wore a pair of black jeans, a long-sleeved top, and a pullover sweater. Magnor had donned his uniform that must have insulating properties as well as deflective armor against light projectile weapons.

The forest seemed to breathe on its own as she listened to the crunch of their footsteps on dead leaves, to the crickets singing their nightly chorus, and to the occasional howl of a wild beast.

Never mind ogres and giants. She was afraid enough of normal predators. Her hand gripped the flashlight she'd brought, which she panned back and forth across the trail.

An earthy aroma brought home the smells of fresh clay and fire-kilned pottery from her studio. A sense of calm descended over her as though she'd entered her natural habitat. And perhaps she had. Whatever special power she possessed seemed related to the earth.

"Careful," Magnor said as he dodged a large root ahead.

Fallen tree stumps, rocks, and dead branches obstructed their progress as they edged deeper into the preserve. Leaves rustled off to their right, and the hairs on her nape elevated. Could Loki, that shapeshifting evil spirit, be following them even now?

He wasn't really a spirit, she reminded herself. Not quite a god and yet living in their realm, he'd been banished to an underground prison. Like Lord Voldemort of Harry Potter fame, he attempted to recover his full form. In the process, he intended to destroy the multiverse.

But he wouldn't have the Trolleks as allies if she and Magnor had any say in the matter. As soon as they found and deployed whatever weapon was mentioned in the fabled Book of Odin, the sooner she could go home.

Maybe she could use this quiet interlude to tell Magnor about her need to stay married for a year.

"Uh, husband, there's something we need to discuss."

He halted abruptly and raised his hand. "Do you hear that?"

"What?"

"The sound of branches snapping."

Damn, every time she went to tell him, they got interrupted.

"Magnor, you need to teach me how to defend myself," she found herself saying instead of what she'd meant to confess. Erika didn't want to destroy his budding feelings for her, emotions he wouldn't admit to having but that she saw in his eyes and in the way he no longer tried to avoid her company.

He gave her a surprised glance. "You wish to learn the ways of a warrior?"

"I wouldn't go that far, but I could benefit from some self-defense training."

"I will be happy to oblige." The cracking noise grew louder. He unsheathed his sword, creeping forward at a steady pace.

She shut off her flashlight as a precaution. Peering into the gloom, she couldn't discern any threats but still her nerves prickled with unease.

At first the shadowy form blocked a clump of trees from view. But as the creature lumbered into a shaft of moonlight, she gasped at its size. Its big head, mane of unkempt black hair, and distorted features told her this must be the ogre. He wore animal furs around his muscled torso and carried a log club. Fangs gleamed when he opened his mouth to emit a howl.

Erika's throat went dry. Any hope of reasoning with this being fled when he raised his arm and swung the club at them.

Magnor shoved her aside. As she fumbled to recover her balance, he leapt out of the ogre's path barely in time to avoid the blow. He whirled around, his dark green cape flapping behind him, and thrust upward with his blade. The steel gleamed in the moonlight filtering through the trees.

The ogre swatted Magnor away as though he were a fly. He crashed into a cluster of bushes but quickly regained his feet. Sword in hand, he approached the beast, his wary glance gauging its abilities.

How could they fight this thing?

We don't need to defeat it, she reminded herself. *We only need to collect a vial of its sweat*. She'd brought a small jar along for that purpose.

Her lapse in attentiveness cost a price when the beast's large fingers flicked her into a tree trunk. The impact knocked the breath from her lungs. Stunned, she slid to the ground.

"Come here, you liver-bellied son of a *snipeling*." Magnor waved his arms and danced in front of the creature. "Leave her alone."

Erika sucked air into her chest and scrambled around to the other side of the thick trunk. Her boot dug into a pile of dead leaves, exposing something white in the moon's gleam. Glancing down, she squinted at the strange object. Was that a bone sticking out?

She kicked the debris away and shivered with revulsion. One of the ogre's conquests, perhaps? The bone looked human but could have belonged to some unfortunate animal.

The beast snarled at Magnor, who dodged another swing of its club and thrust his sword into the monster's side. Roaring with rage, the ogre lifted him in the air. Magnor wriggled but was trapped in the beast's grip.

"No!" Erika flung herself forward, yanking the dagger from her belt.

She rushed across the expanse, heedless of the danger. Her only intent was to distract the ogre from hurting her husband.

Her knife pierced its tough skin at the Achilles tendon. The beast threw its head back and roared, the sound reverberating throughout the woods and dropping leaves from trees. The ogre's grasp must have loosened, because Magnor writhed free and tumbled to the ground. He rolled sideways, yanked his sword from the beast's flesh, and sprang to his feet.

Erika backed away as the creature swung toward her.

"Balhogg is your name, isn't it?" she remembered suddenly. "I'll bet it gets lonely in these woods."

The beast paused, tilting its head to regard her, its eyes puzzled. Could it possibly understand her words?

"Look, we didn't come here to harm you. We need your help."

"Erika, are you insane?" Magnor gestured to her. "Get out of the way and let me do my job."

"Please," she told the creature, while ignoring Magnor's command, "listen to me. A big war is coming that will involve everyone, even you. Put down your club and let's talk about it."

"Arrrrrgh." It thwacked her on the shoulder.

Flung backwards, she landed on a bed of leaves. The soft ground cushioned her fall, but the force of it knocked the wind from her. She curled on her side and gasped for air.

Issuing a battle cry, Magnor charged the beast before it could approach her again.

His sword plunged into the ogre's spine.

The beast stopped, his eyes widening, and then he whirled.

"Magnor, watch out!" Erika, having regained her breath, dragged to her feet.

With the sword stuck in his back, the ogre stomped toward Magnor. Unfortunately, it didn't appear as though the wound had damaged anything vital. The beast's innards must be as tough as his hide.

A ray of moonlight gleamed off a gold medallion Balhogg wore that Erika hadn't noticed before. The beast swiped at Magnor, who dived across the ground and bounced up again.

Her heart galloped as the beast sped forward and forced Magnor against a tree. With no weapon handy, he assumed a fighting stance.

Balhogg reached down with both hands and grabbed Magnor by the shoulders. Magnor punched him, but his blow had no effect. The ogre bonked him against the nearest tree, repeating the action until Magnor's head lolled and blood rolled down his face.

Erika's heart slammed against her ribs. Dread coursed through her veins, especially when the beast tossed Magnor aside like a piece of laundry. He fell to the ground, motionless.

Balhogg roared his triumph. He clomped over, licking his lips at the prospect of a tasty meal.

How could she distract him?

Her gaze fell upon a nearby rock. Remembering David and Goliath, she picked it up. If only she had a slingshot of some sort, but her aim would have to do.

"Hey, Balhogg, over here." She pranced into view, keeping her hand hidden.

The beast stiffened, spun around, and flashed angry eyes at her. Its snarl revealed fangs dripping with drool.

Then Balhogg stormed in her direction, his heavy footsteps shaking the ground.

Erika tensed her muscles, drew back her arm, and threw the rock with all the force she could muster.

Her makeshift weapon smashed into the beast's nose. He stopped, holding a hand up to the injury. His fingers came away bloody. For a moment, he peered at the blood as though wondering at its source. Then his lips curled back as he refocused his attention on Erika.

Damn, she'd missed her target between his eyes. All that move had done was to enrage the ogre. His tall form blocking the trees, Balhogg beat his fists against his chest and roared. Leaves cascaded to the ground.

The dirt under her boots shifted and moved. Was it another quake? No region of earth was immune from the disturbances.

She backed against a tree, glancing at its low branch. Could she scamper up there in time to avoid the ogre's wrath? Probably not, and anyway, he could knock her out of the tree with brute force.

Her pulse pounded in her ears as Balhogg advanced toward her.

This was it. They were to be slain by a beast in the middle of the woods of a foreign land. And without the weapon to defeat the Trolleks, the Drift Lords would fail to save Earth.

There had to be something she could do.

A gust of wind swept by, stirring the soil and lifting debris from the ground.

Wait a minute. She *could* affect the outcome.

In her mind's eye, she envisioned that swirl of soil growing larger. It writhed and twisted, picking up more dirt and zigzagging across the turf in real time. Twigs and other debris swirled into a growing cloud.

Balhogg hadn't noticed. He stopped in front of her and raised his arm holding the club.

Erika cringed, covering her face with her hands.

For a few moments, all she heard was heavy breathing and angry, choked grunts.

Peeking past her fingers, she noticed particles of soil flying around the beast's head, obscuring his vision. With a growl of frustration, he flailed his arms attempting to clear the air, but grit bombarded his eyes and thick skin.

A series of thumps followed, then a crash and a ground tremor. Something hit her foot. She jerked her leg away even as the cloud of dirt dissipated.

The ogre lay dead on the ground, Magnor's sword buried in the top of its head.

Magnor, atop the beast, withdrew his weapon and wiped it clean on the ogre's furs. Then he jumped to the ground and sheathed his sword.

"Magnor, I thought you were a goner." She rushed forward to embrace him.

"Gone where?" Comprehension dawned. "Oh, I was faking it." His arms opened to welcome her, and she buried her face in his broad chest. "I was merely stunned. You distracted the beast long enough for me to gain the advantage."

Setting her aside, he gave her a speculative glance. "Interesting how the wind picked up and caused that flurry of debris. It made the ogre pause at just the right time."

Her cheeks heated. "Yes, I noticed. Strange, wasn't it?" She pointed to the body. "Are you sure it's dead?"

"I'd better make certain." His eyes narrowed, as though he knew she'd distracted him on purpose. Nonetheless, he strode over and felt for a pulse. "He'll threaten no more wanderers in these woods. Hand me that jar you brought. We'll collect our specimen and leave this cursed place."

He unwound the medallion from the ogre's neck, looped it around his own as a prize of war, and then stripped away the monster's coverings to gather the precious drops they needed.

"Let me see your injury," she said after he'd collected the sample. Trails of dried blood and grime soiled his face.

He brushed away her fingers when she probed a sensitive area under his hair. "We can assess the damage later." Gesturing for her to follow, he headed for the forest's edge.

"Are we going directly back to the theme park?" She pushed a hanging vine from her path as she kept pace.

"Not yet. The dragon will be working the water wheel. We'll have to wait until morning. We should rest in the meantime." He gave her a weary but fond smile that made her heart somersault.

Inside their hotel room, Magnor erected his perimeter defense while she dove into the shower. The hot water streamed down her slick skin. Her body ached in places she hadn't known could hurt. Bruises would soon become apparent, but they would heal. Magnor was the one who concerned her.

She wrapped herself in a towel and then padded into the bedroom. Magnor sat at the desk, his eyes half-closed.

"Are you alright?" She tapped his shoulder, relieved when he lifted his gaze in response.

"My head hurts, but I've had worse. You?"

"These scratches will disappear in a few days. Let me see your wound. The ogre smashed you pretty hard against that tree."

He waved his hand in dismissal and stood. "It's nothing. I'll get cleaned up. You should sleep."

"Don't be stubborn. You were very heroic today, but heroes need to learn when to accept help." She didn't wait for a reply and began lifting his shirt over his head.

Her breath stole from her upon the sight of his bare chest. She couldn't keep herself from splaying her fingers across his skin. Warmth spread up her arm and into her body.

"Great Cosmos, wife, you tempt me beyond reason." He stepped back. "At least let me get washed first."

"In a minute." She caressed his shoulders, admiring their breadth and enjoying the sensation. Her hands roamed to his upper arms where she explored the contours of his muscles.

Standing on her toes, she pressed her mouth to his in a hungry kiss. "Go take your shower, but be careful of your head wound, or it'll bleed again."

By the time he rejoined her, she'd donned a nightshirt and had rummaged through her purchases for first aid supplies.

"I have a nasty gash," he admitted, sitting on the edge of the bed where she'd directed him. "Too bad we don't have a tissue regenerator. I lost the one Edith gave me."

He'd done a decent job of washing his hair and cleaning away the excess blood, but the wound remained exposed. After fastening a nude-colored bandage over it, she stood back to survey her handiwork.

"Your hair covers most of it. I hope that's the extent of your injury."

"You worry too much. And while your concern is appreciated, I'll be fine." Magnor grasped her by the waist and pulled her close. "In fact, I can show you how fit I am if you wish."

She raised her face toward him. "Oh yes, husband. Please do."

Chapter Nineteen

A ringing noise jarred Magnor from deep slumber. With a groan, he tapped his wrist. No answering voice emitted from his comm unit. Cracking his eyes open, he rolled over and fumbled for the receiver on the nightstand. He'd been dreaming of home and felt momentarily disoriented. What was the proper cultural greeting on this planet?

"Hello?" he said into the unwieldy mechanism.

"Mr. Magnor? You have a visitor downstairs in the lobby."

His cobwebs of sleep evaporated at the news. "A visitor? Who is it?"

"The lady wouldn't give her name, sir. She insists you come down right away."

Magnor glanced at Erika asleep beside him. She looked so vulnerable, her coils of hair spread out on the pillow, her face peaceful in repose. The rods would protect her if he left for a few minutes.

"Very well, I'll be down shortly." Maybe Edith, the Gatekeeper, had come by for some reason. That was the only female he could think of who might come to see him.

But when he arrived at the lobby, nobody stood by whom he might have recognized. A few businessmen sat about, reading newspapers or consulting their tablet devices. He glanced at a wall clock. It was nine o'clock on a typical weekday.

He approached the desk clerk. "I received a call that a woman was here to see me?"

The young man gave him a stony glare. "You're Mr. Magnor?"

"Yes, that's correct." His gaze darted about, seeking exits and evaluating the occupants as he went into defense mode.

"Your visitor went to the restroom. She said for you to wait here."

"Very well, thank you." His inner alarm jingled. Something wasn't right.

He paced the lobby, his nose sniffing coffee and toast from the adjacent café. His hackles rose when he walked behind one of the men sitting in an armchair. The fellow's newspaper was upside down.

Then he noticed the blank stares of the other occupants.

Great Cosmos, these people were confounded!

His hand went to his side but came up empty. He'd left his sword upstairs along with his other equipment.

Erika. His heart slammed into his throat. They hadn't come for him. They wanted her.

She'd be safe as long as she stayed in the room and didn't open the door. But if she woke alone and heard a knock from outside, she might think it was him.

He sped toward the lift and pushed the button with frantic fingers. What was the room number? He should call in the meantime and warn her.

But when he punched the code into his comm unit, no one answered.

Desperation drove him to rock on his feet until the elevator reached the lobby and opened. He dashed into the lift and jabbed his floor number on the control panel. Up and up, the elevator creaked while his nerves strung taut and his fists curled with impatience.

As soon as the door opened, he sprinted down the hallway. He'd gotten out his key card when he rounded the corner and stopped abruptly. Outside their door stood two Trolleks, swiping the lock which kept reading red.

Relief washed through him. Thank the stars he had arrived before these two beasts forced open the door.

His flying kick hit the first one in the kidney and doubled him over.

The other fellow turned toward him with a snarl. Magnor's uppercut punch caught the guy on the jaw. The impact hardly affected him. The Trollek bared his teeth in a sneer of contempt. His blow knocked Magnor into the opposite wall.

He rebounded quickly. Ducking to the side, he dodged the Trollek's meaty fist and aimed a kick at the fellow's thigh in a crucial spot where a hit would disable him. In a blur of speed, the Trollek lunged past, avoiding his blow but striking Magnor on the elbow along the way.

Pins and needles wove down his arm, useless until his nerves recovered. Resisting the urge to cradle his limb, Magnor feinted to one side and then came back with a fist to the beast's gut. The Trollek grunted, but it felt like hitting a board. His eyes gleaming, the tall lout reached for him.

Meanwhile, the other fellow lurched to his feet. Soon the two would fight him in unison. His head throbbed where his wound might have reopened. He'd better end this fast.

He backed down the hall, preparing for a tactic he'd learned as a youngster. Hopefully, he could still pull it off.

As the two of them started after him, he squared his shoulders and took a couple of deep breaths.

With a screaming battle cry, he flipped onto his hands, righted himself, repeated the move, and ended up with a flying kick, both legs stretched out. His two feet landed on his opponents' chests at the same time. The move shoved them against the wall and winded them.

Recovering swiftly, he jabbed the heel of his right hand under one fellow's nose. Hearing a satisfactory crack, he whirled to the other guy and snapped his neck in a single move. They both went down.

Breathing heavily, he shook out his arm that was still tingling from the nerve pinch.

He stepped past their bodies, swiped his key card, and let

himself into the room. The television was blaring and the bathroom door was closed. A rush of water sounded from within. Erika must be washing. She wouldn't have heard a thing.

With her safety secured, he turned his attention to removing the evidence of a fight. If only he'd recovered his phase pistol from the movie studio, he could have vaporized the *riffs*. Instead, he dragged them to a utility closet down the hall and stuffed them inside. Hopefully, he and Erika would be long gone before the housekeeping staff discovered them.

He was buckling on his sword when Erika emerged from the lavatory. Clad in her underwear, she looked delectable. Too bad they couldn't afford to linger.

"Why did I hear that buzzing sound in my head, Magnor? It lasted a few moments and disappeared."

Not wishing to alarm her, he decided to keep the Trollek incident to himself. Instead, he gave a casual shrug.

"I wouldn't worry about it. Let's check out of this place and move on. I'd rather not stick around."

She peered at him. "Are you bleeding again? I should change the bandage."

He switched on the TV while she put on a smaller adhesive. Increased seismic activity around the globe concerned the newscasters.

"Hurry and get dressed," he advised when she had finished. "It's getting late." He couldn't help his curt tone. Natural disasters were rising in frequency, and he still hadn't found the weapon to disable Loki's allies.

Hopefully, he and Erika wouldn't be accosted on their way to Jolheim Gardens, but this morning's incident had proven the enemy was everywhere, waiting and watching.

****

Erika wondered what was wrong as they bought snacks in the gift shop for a makeshift breakfast and set off for Jolheim Gardens.

200

Magnor wore his backpack, his cape folded inside. The sword bounced at his hip. He strode forward with his bearded chin lifted and a determined gleam in his eyes while ignoring the curious glances directed his way.

He'd added one new addition to his outfit, the gold medallion previously worn by the ogre, Balhogg. On its surface were angular markings similar to the ones on her watch. She wanted to ask him what it meant but not when he was such in a tense mood. Did it have to do with his stepping out earlier?

When she'd awakened to an empty space beside her, alarm had flared inside her chest. Spying his gear nearby, she realized he must have left the room to make a call without disturbing her. If he'd reported in to his team and received unpleasant news, it would account for his terse manner.

She bit her lower lip and scurried along the sidewalk toward the river and the theme park beyond. Business people hurried to their destinations, while joggers dodged past mothers pushing baby strollers. The morning sky appeared overcast, cloudy with a peculiar yellowish tint.

Having put on a clean shirt under her sweater, Erika shivered in the fifty-some degree temperature. Tiny white particles fluttered in the air like a swarm of insects.

She gestured upward. "Look at the sky. Wildfires back home often produce a haze like this, but I don't smell smoke."

Magnor glanced at her from beneath his thick brows. "Iceland had another volcanic eruption. The ash fallout has closed airports throughout Europe."

"Oh, my. That's what these things are floating in the air. We shouldn't be outdoors."

"Don't worry. We won't be sticking around here much longer."

She let him pay for their park admission tickets in cash. Once through the turnstile, they veered around a marching band parading down the main street. The odd weather hadn't diminished the crowds. Young couples sauntered along holding hands. A foursome of friends laughed and jostled each other. A group of tourists strolled by behind their leader, who held up a flag.

She and Magnor rushed toward the mine attraction. There wasn't any line yet so they boarded easily. At the scene with the dragon, they slipped away same as before. Magnor gave a wary glance around, his hand on his hilt, once the tram had departed.

"What's the matter?" She could tell something bothered him from his cautious expression. A twinge of anxiety struck her. Maybe he feared betrayal by the Grotes.

Shayna the dragon roared fire when she saw them. "You came back! I didn't believe you would keep your word, humans." She lowered her head and peered at Magnor with large, slitted eyes.

"I told you he'd return. He's a Drift Lord," Ribald said.

Chained to his post, the stout Grote had been chiseling away at the rock, sweat streaming down his face. His labor was real even though his job didn't involve actual prospecting.

Magnor's posture relaxed. "Look, we only have a few minutes before the next tram arrives." He withdrew the jar from his pocket. "Here's the sweat from Balhogg the Ogre. Now fulfill your part of the bargain and tell us where to find the Book of Odin."

Shayna lashed her tail against a wall, sending rocks cascading to the ground. They bounced as though made from rubber. "Not yet, Drift Lord. We must prove its effectiveness."

Ribald stretched out his hand. "She's right. Give it here."

"I don't think so. Our deal was for you to provide the information in exchange for this sample."

"For heaven's sake, Magnor, we can wait a few more minutes," Erika chided him. "How can we leave without seeing if the acid works?"

A vibration heralded the arrival of another tram. She and Magnor ducked behind a faux calcite column until it passed. The place looked so real that she had to keep reminding herself the scenes were fake.

"For all we know, you filled that vial with water." Ribald glared at them after they showed themselves again. "Once we test the liquid, we'll know for sure if you are the prophesied one for whom we've been waiting."

Erika's heart went out to the captives. They'd been here for years, with no way to break free until now. She and Magnor were their only hope.

She grabbed the jar from Magnor's palm and dashed forward. "Here, take it."

"Erika, stop! They could be tricking us," Magnor called.

"No, I believe Ribald. Let me do this my way." Didn't the man possess an ounce of tact? Barging in here and making demands wouldn't get them anywhere.

She handed the container to the Grote who flashed her a grateful grin. Grasping the prize in one hand, he twisted the cap open with pudgy fingers. His eyes scrunched in concentration as he gingerly dripped a single drop onto a critical juncture of his restraint. For a moment, nothing happened. Erika peered close to watch as the liquid sizzled through the metal links. The chain broke away with a clatter to the floor.

Ribald pumped his fist in the air with glee. "It works. I am free!"

A rumbling noise indicated the imminent arrival of another tram. "You'd better pretend otherwise," Erika said before ducking for cover.

After the last car rounded a curve, the dragon thumped her tail, causing the ground to shake. "Use it on me. I must release my children from their bondage."

"There are people on that ride. At least wait until they disembark," Erika pleaded, not wanting any innocents to get hurt.

"Hold on." Magnor drew his sword and strode forward, a stern look on his face. "Keep your end of the bargain, Ribald, or I'll smash that jar into pieces."

Damn the man. Subtlety wasn't in his nature.

Ribald glanced at his companions who nodded to him in

return. "Very well. You have acted with honor, Drift Lord. This test confirms you are our destined savior. Listen carefully, for we have been guarding these words for eons. What you seek is hidden in the splinters of time."

"What? That's it?" Magnor sheathed his sword, a puzzled frown on his face.

"Can you be more explicit?" Erika swiped her forehead. The steamy temperature made it hard to breathe. Firelight from sconces flickered against the stone walls.

"I have told you what you came to learn." Ribald applied the acidic solution to his brothers, who rubbed their chafed skin after their chains fell away.

"You'd better use that stuff on Shayna," Erika told him. "It's getting hotter in here."

The dragon curled her head down to Erika's level, allowing Erika to note the details of her tawny irises and the fine scales around her mouth.

"You make a worthy mate for the Drift Lord, lady. Go now, while you can." Shayna snorted, steam issuing from her nostrils. "Come, Ribald, it is my turn."

Ribald waddled around to the dragon's side. Her heavy chain strung taut to a pole disguised as a stalagmite. It took a few drops of the precious liquid to eat through the thicker metal.

Freed at last, Shayna stretched her neck to its full height and roared. The chamber shook from the reverberation.

Erika's gaze zeroed in on a fissure off to their left. Had that been there before?

"Be careful, or you'll bring the roof down upon us. How do you plan to get out of here? For that matter, how are we going to slip past the ride attendants?" she asked her husband, not having considered this aspect.

"I have an idea." Ribald, his eyes gleaming, pointed to where the mine car ride curved around a bend and vanished from sight. "We'll put a clog on the tracks so the tram will malfunction. The distraction will give us all time to escape."

"But Shayna is so big," Erika protested. "People will notice her, especially if she takes flight."

"Leave it to me," the Grote insisted. "You can use the emergency exit."

The ground jerked sideways, and the crack in the floor widened. Erika gulped. She hadn't caused that movement, had she?

"I think we're about to get the diversion we need." She grabbed Magnor's arm. "Let's not linger."

They fled to the street. Outside, pandemonium ruled when a genuine quake shook the park. People screamed as buildings swayed.

After the tremor stopped, guides warned everyone that rides would have to be tested before anyone was allowed back on. Erika and Magnor lost themselves in the milling crowd. Many people streamed toward the main exit but others stood around, waiting to resume their activities as though earthquakes happened every day.

"Where do we look for your clue?" Erika stopped by the lakeside. She wasn't convinced the quake hadn't been her fault. Her power was still a mystery, and despite her theories, she had no idea how to control it.

Magnor gazed into the distance, his jaw resolute. He looked every inch the stoic warrior. "What we want is hidden in the splinters of time. What does that mean?"

Erika's brow wrinkled. She felt exposed out in the open. At any moment, guests could turn against them. This place that had appeared so pleasant at their first arrival now creeped her out. And they hadn't even investigated the tunnels beneath the complex where the Trolleks kept their portal, or that machinery Shayna had mentioned. Hopefully, Magnor's team could follow up in that regard.

What had Ribald meant? The fragrant aroma of pastries wafted in the air from a nearby vendor as she considered his words.

Over by a rotunda where concerts were held, a heavy tree branch had fallen. As she watched staff members work to remove it, an idea formed.

She turned to Magnor, enthusiasm in her tone. "Listen, splinters of time could refer to wood. Look at all the trees around here. See their thick trunks? I'll bet they've been here for years."

"What's your point?"

"The clue may be hidden among the trees. We might be able to spot it from an overview."

He caught on and indicated a ride by the rear boundary. "That tower is the highest location in the park. It's operational again. Let's go."

Erika balked when she saw it was a bungee-jumping attraction. Riders rode an elevator to the top where they were strapped into harnesses. Then they free-fell toward the ground, stopping short right before a safety net.

"Oh, no. I am not riding on that thing."

"It won't be necessary." He urged her to join the line of people waiting their turn. "All we need to do is access the top to gain a view."

"Fine, you go. I'll wait here."

"It is not safe for you to be alone." He hesitated as though meaning to tell her something else, but then he pressed his lips together. "You'll come with me." His tight grip on her elbow steered her along.

Her heart thumped as they rode the lift and emerged onto an elevated landing. The height made bile rise from her gut, until she recalled how they'd survived a leap off the roof in Vegas.

Magnor, his feet on the solid platform, rested his hands on the guard rail. "All I see is greenery everywhere. It's nothing unusual."

She joined him and studied the park's perimeter, the city beyond, and the winding river. Then her gaze returned to the gardens and the pattern of trees.

"Look, the trees are laid out in a certain way." She

rummaged in her purse for a notebook and pen and then drew a diagram.

If she hadn't lost her cell phone, she could have snapped a photo. She'd forgotten all about replacing the device. She ought to get one and notify her family she was okay, although they probably assumed she was still on vacation.

Magnor snatched the notebook from her hands. "Great Cosmos, you've drawn a map. I recognize these geographical features. We need to go north. I'll summon the shuttle so we don't have to use the portal again."

"Good idea. I have no desire to encounter Trollek soldiers, and they'll have patrols down below."

He glanced at her, his expression chagrined. "I didn't want to mention this before, but they made an attempt at the hotel to grab you. Since Algie didn't launch an attack at Jolheim Gardens during our last visit, I assumed she wanted to wait and see what we found. She must have gotten impatient."

Erika's heart accelerated at his mention of the Trollek scientist. "Don't keep secrets from me, Magnor. I'd rather be warned than taken by surprise."

"I didn't want to worry you. I'll feel better when we're gone from here."

"Me, too. Go ahead and call for transport."

Before Magnor could tap his comm unit, a flap of wings stirred the air. Shayna banked into view, her children following in her wake. The dragons, flying free, made a beautiful sight.

"Hop on my back, humans. I'll take you where you want to go."

Chapter Twenty

Shayna related how she'd escaped the park. She had crashed through the roof of the mine attraction and zoomed to the ride where her babies were enslaved. With a single swipe of her long tail, she had knocked the central post to the ground and freed her children. She'd timed her arrival after a group of riders had disembarked, so no one got hurt.

The people below had pointed and cheered. They thought her exploits were part of the show. Even now, guests stared upward as Magnor and Erika climbed onto the scaly humps along Shayna's spine. Maybe they thought she was some sort of hot air balloon. The creature soared into the sky, her young following.

They aimed north to colder weather. Shayna rode the air currents while Magnor and Erika clung to her back. His insulated uniform protected him from the drop in temperature, but Erika's shivering concerned him. She sat behind him and had a death grip around his waist.

Shayna spiraled through dizzying heights. Grayish flecks flew into Magnor's eyes as their visibility became increasingly obscured. He risked a glance backward. Shayna's children struggled to keep up in the wind.

"Where will you go after you drop us off?" Magnor hollered to Shayna.

"We are the last of our kind. I will find a place for us far from human eyes and away from the Trolleks. Know that this fulfills my obligation to you, Drift Lord."

Her words made his chest swell with pride at having saved

her, but soon the glow dissipated. He'd only be truly worthy of his title if he completed his mission.

"You're not alone, Shayna. We know of one other." He told the beast about Paz's encounter in Hong Kong with a descendant of the legendary dragon, Fafnir.

"Thank you, human. I will seek him after we make a home for ourselves."

The sharp wind stung his eyes and bit into his flesh, reminding him of the ordeals yet ahead.

"We might freeze to death before we get anywhere," Erika shouted into his ear.

He gazed at the stark landscape below. "It's hard to see landmarks with all this snow."

Ducking his head, he squeezed his eyes shut, his inner ear telling him when Shayna began a spiraling descent. Wind battered his face, fine particles stinging his skin.

Finally, Shayna touched ground with a dull thump. "I dare not risk going farther, humans. I must see my babes to safety. Good luck to you and thank you again for gaining our freedom."

Wrapping one arm around Erika, he waved as Shayna careened into the sky and vanished from view.

Erika's teeth chattered. Her lips had turned blue and her face was as pale as the ash that obscured the sun. He had to do something to warm her, or she wouldn't survive.

He retrieved his cape from the backpack and unfurled it around her. "This will shield you from the cold. Watch your footing and stay close to me." The snow-covered ground could mask crevices and other hidden dangers.

Glad they'd both worn leather boots, he inched forward. Through the haze, he discerned lumpy shapes in the distance. Mountains? He advanced cautiously. Rocky outcroppings, snow mounds, and icy patches slowed their progress.

"How do you know where to go?" Erika asked in a tremulous tone.

"The pattern of trees at Jolheim Gardens told me." He

paused to scan their location with his PIP. "Do you see anything recognizable?"

He spoke loudly to be heard over the force of the chill wind that bombarded his face. His nose felt cold, the air icy. He spared a glance at Erika, whose pallor concerned him. They needed to find shelter.

She pointed to a pile of jagged boulders. "Over there."

He stowed his PIP and led the way across the frozen turf. Up ahead, he barely discerned a dark shape outlined against the rocky rise.

"Come on, move faster. My fingers are numb." Erika nudged him with her elbow.

As they approached, a crevice became distinguishable. The dark maw grew wider the closer they came. Icicles dangled from an overhang at its entrance.

He wanted to smile at the sight, because it represented his goal. They must be meant to go inside. However, his frozen flesh wouldn't cooperate.

"It's more than a cave. Be careful." Erika put a hand on his arm, her face tilted toward him. Her eyes looked large in her ashen complexion. "You'll need your sword."

He drew his weapon in a fluid movement. "Why? What is it?"

Maybe Algie had anticipated their destination and sent troops who hid in ambush. But that was impossible. Even if she or Loki had determined his mission, how would they have learned of this location?

"Maybe there's a bear or another wild animal inside," Erika said, although her tone suggested she believed otherwise.

"I don't see any tracks on the ground, unless a beast hibernates in there. We'll soon find out. Let's get away from this *maug* wind."

As he eyed the icicles over the entrance, his scalp prickled. It might be wise to cut them down before proceeding. Those things were weighty enough to kill someone.

He signaled for Erika to wait and swung his blade. The metal clanged against the ice without making a single dent. Strange. He tried again, and his sword bounced off the impermeable ice.

It made no sense. He stamped his feet to ward off the cold then lunged upward from a different angle.

"It's no use, Magnor. For whatever reason, the ice won't break." Her voice dripped with weary resignation, and her shoulders slumped. "Let's go inside. I can't stand this wind another minute."

Alarmed for her health, he sheathed his sword, prepared to duck under the entry first to test its safety.

Erika grabbed his arm. "Wait, I'm thinking about what Ribald told us. *What we seek is hidden in the splinters of time.* That might have more than one meaning."

"How so?" His foot met the threshold.

Without warning, Erika shoved him from behind and leapt after him as the icicles descended en masse. He covered his head with his hands as icy needles and slush from the impact flew in every direction.

"Have you heard of ice splinters?" Erika gasped from the soft ground where they'd landed. "This must be the right place if that opening was booby trapped."

He scrambled to his knees to examine her. She'd been directly behind him. Had she been hit by one of those falling missiles?

She sat upright, brushing off her clothes, but she appeared unharmed. He picked up his cape from where it had fallen, shook it out, and fastened it over his shoulders. She wouldn't need it in here. Already the air felt warmer.

He peered into the gloom, his eyes adapting. His natural vision would compensate for the dim lighting. The walls of the cave glowed with luminescent crystals, providing enough illumination so Erika could see their path.

"The Book of Odin has to be here. It makes sense that the Originals would establish precautions against intruders. We might encounter more obstacles."

"I agree." She edged up beside him. "Thank goodness we're out of the wind. I'm beginning to thaw out."

"Come here, let's share our body heat for a moment." Magnor drew her into his embrace, where they stood until her shivering stopped. He parted from her with reluctance. Color flooded her face again, and she appeared more at ease.

They ate energy bars and drank their fill of water from the supplies they'd brought.

He couldn't keep the eagerness from his voice when he spoke. "We're finally closing in on the legendary book. Perhaps the weapon itself is hidden here, where the Originals might have walked."

"We'll see." Her eyes sparkled in the iridescent glow. "Watch out for any other kind of splinters."

"You know I wouldn't have gotten this far without you." He didn't bother to disguise the admiration in his tone.

"That's for sure." She grinned at him, her ripe lips tempting him to kiss her.

Ignoring her allure, he reaffirmed his resolve to complete their mission. He would consider Erika's role in his life later, once they'd defeated the enemy.

He adjusted his sword. "We should move on."

"I hope we haven't been followed. If Algie had her minions observing us, they might be waiting until we obtain the artifact for them."

Magnor nodded at her wristwatch. "I doubt that's an issue. You've turned off your tracking beacon. Too bad you can't operate the vector component. We'll need a lift out of here when we're done."

He gestured for Erika to be silent as they headed farther into the cave, lit with tiny crystals embedded in the rock. The air had a fresh ozone smell but at least it wasn't freezing cold. His breath didn't elicit a cloud of steam.

The trail led them on a steady decline. At times, they had to squeeze between narrowed rock walls or crawl beneath a low ceiling. In that case, his sword clanged on the ground as he dragged himself forward. As they went deeper into the mountain, a faint grating noise made his breath quicken.

"What's that?" Erika said from behind him. They crouched single-file in a tight corridor surrounded by rock walls. The surface was slick with moisture as water trickled from above.

"Let's hope it's not a pending earthquake. Keep moving."

A gap presented itself directly ahead, beyond which the path widened. He rose and stretched in the broad space.

Suddenly Erika shoved him sideways. "Get down!"

He flung himself to the ground as a wave of spears flew at them from up ahead. The deadly weapons struck the surrounding rocks and clattered downward without hitting their target.

Letting out a whoosh of relief, Magnor stood. "Look at those bones. I didn't notice them earlier." He indicated a pile of white remnants by the opening. "We're not the first visitors."

"Perhaps your predecessors were here?"

"You mean previous Drift Lords? If so, their knowledge was buried here alongside them. Be wary. Those spears were made of wood."

Her eyes widened as she caught his meaning. "Oh. More splinters of time. What's next, arrows?"

Further ahead, they came to a narrow bridge over an endless chasm. The bridge consisted of stepping stones, five wide and two deep then a short hop to the next set.

"Hold it, Magnor." Erika held up a hand. "I've seen enough *Indiana Jones* movies to know there's a pattern here."

"I agree." He picked up a hefty rock and tossed it forward onto a random stone. A blast of fire shot downward from the ceiling with a roar and a crackle of heat. It would have incinerated anyone standing there.

Erika tucked a strand of hair behind her ear. "This book is meant for a Drift Lord to find, right? If there is a proper sequence, it must be one only you can determine."

"Hmm." He racked his brain. "The League's training ground is on Karrell, the sixth planet from the sun."

"That's only one number. How many light years is it from Earth?"

He told her. "That combination might work, assuming this stone on the left is the first. But what if it's the other way around? Not every culture reads from left to right."

"What about runes?"

"They can go either way." His lips compressed. "I'll test it. You stay here."

He placed the weight of one foot onto the first rock. Nothing unusual happened. Still wary, he stepped onto the next stone. So far, so good. Feeling more confident, he tiptoed across the rest of the appropriate stones, finally coming to a halt at a small ledge between sets.

"Follow that exact combination," he said, fearful for her safety. What if only the Drift Lords were meant to proceed?

She gingerly moved forward. Her progress unimpeded, she made it the rest of the way. With caution, they repeated the process until they faced a blank wall at the opposite end.

"Now where do we go?" Erika said in dismay.

"Look at these etchings." His fingers traced the angular marks drawn on the rock. "They're similar in design to the inscription on your watch. It must be runic writing."

"Which neither of us can interpret." She shifted her purse, fatigue clearly wearing her down by the taut lines around her mouth.

They had to keep going. Reaching their goal was the only way they'd achieve a normal life again.

Was that what he wanted, to live a domesticated lifestyle with this woman on Earth? He had vowed never to trust another female after his sister's betrayal. Splaying his fingers on the wall, he pretended to examine the markings while he explored his future.

When they were together, he felt as though he'd come home. Erika erased the emptiness plaguing him since his expulsion from the tribe. Although this world was foreign to him, certain similarities existed. Family units and loyalty among friends grounded her culture. They shared the same value system in that regard. But could he settle here and be happy?

Pursing his lips, he focused on the task at hand. Again, thoughts of Erika had distracted him. *Maug* woman. He couldn't think straight with her so near.

Emotions have no place on a mission. They make you soft and leave a man vulnerable.

He straightened his spine. Despite his banishment, he'd always be a warrior of the Tsuran. He must remember his creed.

"I think I've found something!" She poked him. "See this set? This part matches the figures on my watch."

Squinting at the rock face, he examined the markings. "You're right, and that one looks like the lettering on Nira's timepiece. What if this entire line represents the six daughters of Odin? Over here are six other sets that could stand for the sons of Thor in the prophecy."

"And they're the Drift Lords?"

He nodded and pressed on the second set. Nothing happened.

"Try pushing on your symbol alone."

"Mine?" He gazed at her questioningly.

"You're a Drift Lord now. What number are you?"

"I'm the last to join the team, so that would make me number six. They had two other members upon their arrival on Earth. Rayne was murdered and another was killed in battle."

"Is that all of you?"

"Normally, the Drift Lords work in teams of seven." He recited what he'd studied when he had accepted the job as bodyguard to Prince Zohar. "The Sacred Seven represents earth, fire, water, air, time, space, and the Wise One, creator of all."

"Your team is lacking its seventh member?"

"For now. And we're all that's left. During the seventeen years of the Great Purge, the Drift Lords were persecuted and outlawed. They trained in secret on various non-aligned worlds, but their numbers still diminished. The inherent trait that makes a Drift Lord has become increasingly rare."

She leaned forward. "Wait a minute. The Great Purge?"

"A dark time in the Star Empire's history. Zohar's widowed father, the king, was seduced by a Trollek female. His new queen initiated a terrible age of tyranny. Prince Zohar—heir to the throne and a Drift Lord due to his ability—fled the palace with a price on his head. Once the queen died and his father passed, Zohar appointed a regent in his place instead of taking the crown."

"Why didn't he ascend the throne?"

Magnor swiped a hand over his face. "Our prince was afraid of falling prey to a Trollek female in the same manner as his father. Nira helped him see that he is stronger than the old king. He's decided to accept his destiny after we conclude our mission."

His sense of loyalty swelled. Zohar had accepted him and offered him back his honorable name. He wouldn't disappoint his leader.

He pressed on the wall, targeting the sixth mark in the second set. His pulse accelerated when the granite moved inward an inch or two with a scraping noise. Encouraged, he pushed harder with the heel of his hand.

"Uh, Magnor…?" Erika's voice sounded strained. She must have felt the same vibration underfoot.

Then the ground beneath them opened and they fell into empty space.

****

Erika screamed as she tumbled into a void. This was it. They'd triggered a booby trap and were about to die.

But in the next instant, her body landed on something soft. She lay spread-eagle on the spongy surface, gazing up at the round gap in the ceiling through which they'd fallen. Her breath came in pants, while her heart thundered in her chest.

"Are you hurt?" Magnor scrambled to his knees and peered into her face, alarm in his eyes.

"No, I'm fine, just stunned." With a groan, she rolled to her side and pushed herself upright. Her bruises must have multiplied, judging from the various places she ached. A week of rest would be welcome, but they didn't have that luxury.

They'd ended up in a vast cavern dotted with boulders and piles of breakdown—fallen rocks that had cracked on impact. Soft dirt had cushioned their fall. The sound of water sloshed in the distance, and a rusty smell permeated the air. Crystal flowers decorated a section of wall.

"Approach, humans."

"Holy shit." She jumped at the disembodied voice.

"Who goes there?" Magnor demanded, hand on his hilt. He glanced around, his eyes showing that unearthly glow.

"It is I, the Sentinel. I have been waiting for you, Drift Lord. Come closer."

Magnor relaxed, moving his hand away from his weapon. They advanced toward the voice at the opposite end of the expanse. Knobby rock formations and mounds of rubble inhibited their progress. Erika hoped there weren't any more bones scattered around. She'd had enough unpleasant surprises for one day.

Life had certainly gotten more exciting since she'd met Magnor. No longer was she stuck in a small Arizona town, eking out a living from her pottery classes. If only her older sisters could see her now.

They won't see you again unless you pay attention. Who knew what this sentinel intended?

"Move forward, my children."

An old man emerged from the shadows, his white beard matching his hair. His hawk-like eyes watched them approach.

"We've come for the Book of Odin," Magnor stated. He looked every inch the warrior with his flowing cape, solemn face, and wary stance.

"I know. You have passed the tests to get here, but I have bad news. Long have I waited to tell you."

"What news? Where is the sacred book?"

"I regret to inform you that it has been stolen."

Chapter Twenty-One

"Hel has stolen the Book of Odin." The sentinel shook his head, sadness in his eyes. "I could not prevent her. She used the powers of darkness to circumvent my traps and overwhelm me."

"Hel? Who is that?" Erika asked, aware the name sounded familiar.

"She is goddess of the underworld and daughter of Loki," Magnor reminded her.

The sentinel pointed a bony finger at him. "If you intend to retrieve the sacred Book of Odin, you must travel to the land of the dead."

"To the underworld? Are you daft?"

"You must go alone, Drift Lord. The queen of death will yield this treasure to no one else. But she won't give it up easily. You'll need a bargaining chip."

"Great Cosmos, what would that be?"

Erika gazed at him in dismay. This just got worse and worse. How would he even get to the underworld? Didn't you have to be dead to go there, if it really existed?

"She would value a flask of mead from the dwarfs. Made of blood mixed with honey and imbued with magic, the elixir instills wisdom upon all who drink it."

Magnor glanced at Erika in consternation. *Oh, no, not another quest,* she could almost hear him saying in her head.

His mouth thinned. "Paz has a contact among the dwarfs. We'll return to Florida. I need to catch up with my team's progress anyway."

He spoke in a melancholy tone, as though he blamed himself for this setback. It wasn't his fault. He should be proud that they'd made it this far.

"My time is at an end. I have done my duty. Safe journey, my children." The sentinel's legs folded, and he collapsed.

"Wait!" Magnor rushed forward and knelt by the old man's side, but the fellow didn't stir. Magnor felt for a pulse. "He's dead." His voice held incredulity.

Erika signaled. "Let's leave this place. We're done here."

Magnor rose and swept his cape behind him. His hand found the hilt of his sword as habit. "The sentinel neglected to tell us the way out."

Erika strode to the wall of solid rock and walked the perimeter. She didn't see anything that might be construed as an exit. No outlines in the granite, no knobby protrusions, no etchings in the stone.

Magnor caught up and placed his hand on her shoulder. His intense dark eyes captured hers. "I have an idea. The old man said, *safe journey, my children*. He addressed both of us."

"So, what does that mean? I'm supposed to go to Hel with you?" Considering what had happened lately, she wouldn't be surprised.

"That is my task. But the sentinel knew we have to work together. I assume he also knew of your powers. You hold the key to our escape." He glanced pointedly at her wristwatch.

"You're forgetting one thing. I don't know how to use it."

"Concentrate. Take us to Orlando, Florida."

"Yeah, right." Her feet picked up a low vibration, and she stiffened. "What's that?"

The ground jerked. Then the entire cavern shook with a violent tremor. A jagged stalactite broke away and crashed onto the dirt. Boulders wavered, threatening to topple across their path. Debris rained down upon them.

"Cover your head!" Magnor swept his cape over them both as they crouched against a wall.

Erika peered out as dust clogged her nostrils. A huge pillar cracked. She felt the blood drain from her face. If those support columns failed, the entire mountain might crash down upon them.

"Do something," Magnor urged, his face grim.

"I-I'll try."

She squeezed her eyes shut as the tremors continued. Bits of soil and stones flew through the air. A loud thud indicated a heavy rock being unseated. Soon more would follow. Something thwacked her on the arm.

There had to be another way out. They couldn't have come all this way only to be trapped here. More rocks tumbled down, piling up around them, entombing them.

A loud cracking sounded overhead followed by a series of thuds. Magnor cried out with an exclamation of pain.

His arms, which had been wrapped protectively around her, went slack. Her heart racing, Erika thrust the cape aside to see the damage. Blood seeped down her husband's pale face. A gnarled stalactite lay nearby.

"No-o-o," she howled, cradling him in her arms. If only she could transport them to safety. If only—

Something smashed her on the head, and all went dark.

****

"Magnor, wake up!" A woman's familiar voice roused him. "Come on, open your eyes." She prodded his arm.

With a groan, he stretched and obeyed. Erika stared down at him, her flame-colored hair feathering her anxious face. She looked pale and drawn, a mat of dried blood on her temple.

"What happened?" He pushed himself upright, pausing as his head whirled dizzily.

"We were in the cave, remember? The tremors loosened rocks all around us. We both got conked out. When I came to, we were here. I-I think we're back in the States."

Bright sunlight hurt his eyes, which he shaded with a hand.

One glimpse of the palm trees, the lush greenery, and the traffic, and he had an idea of their location. His PIP confirmed it. With a grimace of pain, he pocketed the device and dragged himself to his feet.

"Here, let me help you." He hauled Erika to her full height, examining her with a critical eye.

Aside from that fresh bruise on her head, she appeared all right. Her clothing, ripped and dirty, was another matter. His lips curved upward. Despite everything they'd been through, she still held onto her purse strapped tightly on one shoulder.

"We made it to Florida. Good work, wife."

Erika gazed at him askance. "Florida? How is that possible?"

"You must have activated your vector device. And good targeting, too." He pointed down the residential street of attractive one-story homes and manicured lawns. "Our safe house isn't far."

Her eyes scrunched. "How would I even know that?"

"You must have gotten the information from me."

"Like, we have some sort of mental connection? That would explain how I knew those answers in the casino contest. I'd wondered how the correct responses popped into my brain."

"It's my Tsuran blood. We forge a strong bond to our mate."

They stared at each other, weighing what that meant.

Magnor readjusted his backpack. "Come, I must report in to my team. If Nira is here, you can meet her at last and exchange news."

But as they started down the street, doors opened and residents emerged. Their blank expressions raised his hackles.

Tires screeched to a halt beside them, and the passenger window rolled down on a black sedan.

"Get in," Paz hollered from the driver's seat. "We've changed the safe house. This one has been compromised."

They tumbled into the rear seat and then Paz took off in a cloud of dust. Magnor let his muscles relax. He took Erika's hand, drawing circles on her palm while she sagged against him. At least now he'd be able to take better care of her. She'd been a true warrior, and he would be proud to introduce her to the Drift Lords.

"We picked up your wrist comm locator a short while ago," the communications officer said to Magnor. "You've been off the radar for quite some time."

"I have a lot to tell you."

"How are you holding up, Erika?" Paz asked, glancing into the rear-view mirror.

"I'm managing, thanks. It's been an adventure."

"I can imagine. Prince Zohar has called a strategy meeting since we're all present."

Magnor gave a terse nod. "Good, because we have dire news. I've hit a roadblock in my mission."

Zohar greeted him with relief upon his arrival at their new headquarters, a nondescript house on another homogenous street. His dark brown hair brushed back from his forehead in his usual authoritative style, Zohar regarded him with somber eyes after giving him a brotherly slug on the shoulder.

"It is good to see you safely among us again, Lord Magnor. So, this is your lady?" His eyes crinkled in warmth as he turned to Erika and held out his hand.

She took it with a smile and offered a firm handshake. "I'm Erika Sherwood." Although married, she hadn't had time to change her legal name. But why bother if she meant to get a divorce? She had no obligation to Magnor beyond their mission.

"Erika, this is Zohar Thorald, Captain of the Drift Lords and Crown Prince of the Star Empire," Magnor said.

She bowed her head. "I am honored, your highness, sir."

Zohar chuckled. "No formalities, please. Come inside, you both look like you could use some attention from our medic."

Erika strode through the front door, her chin lifted. Magnor had no doubt she could hold her own in this crowd.

He spotted a familiar face and rushed forward. "Kaj, it's good to see you! You are well, I hope?"

The young man offered him a rare smile. "Yes, I am fine, thanks. May I introduce you to Maggie Holten?" He signaled to a stunning brunette who joined them.

"I see you've been busy in my absence. You'll have to tell me your story." Magnor yearned to hear how Kaj had escaped captivity and paired with Maggie.

"Later. Zohar wants to hold a briefing."

Magnor drew Erika forward and introduced her.

"Looks like you need some healing," said Yaron, the team medic, as he strode over. A shy young woman accompanied him.

It appeared Kaj's tale wasn't the only one he'd missed, but his friends would have to fill him in later.

Yaron attended to their wounds and pronounced them fit for duty. He and Erika were allowed to wash up, change into clean clothes, and get a snack.

The team gathered in the family room with its entertainment center. Zohar took command, pacing back and forth. He scraped a hand through his hair as he began the session.

"Lord Magnor, you're the last one here, so your news is the freshest. You can start."

Magnor came forward, unencumbered by his cape or sword that he'd left in the bedroom. His jaw taut, he faced his commanding officer.

"Sire, I regret to inform you that I have failed in my task to find the fabled weapon that will destroy the Trolleks."

"What? I thought you'd discovered the hiding place for the Book of Odin."

"Indeed, we did. A sentinel stood guard over the relic for many eons, waiting for a chosen one to appear. We passed the trials to enter the cavern where the book was kept. But when we met him, the old man gave us the bad news that Hel had stolen the artifact."

"Oh, no." Nira, who'd been seated on the couch, sprang to her feet. A redhead like Erika, her hair had a lighter tint and was much shorter.

"This is bad." Zohar held his gaze. "How long ago did this theft take place?"

"The sentinel didn't say. He collapsed soon after imparting his message. With his death, a quake commenced. We escaped the cave and headed back here."

"We need that weapon now more than ever." Zohar's eyes narrowed. "How did you obtain transport to Florida?"

"Erika used her vector device. It was a subconscious effort on her part. She needs some lessons in that regard."

"I'll be happy to oblige." Nira smiled approvingly at Erika.

Zohar held up a hand. "Let's backtrack a bit. Tell us what happened from the first time you and Erika met each other."

Magnor paced the room while recanting the start of their adventure. Snickers sounded when he mentioned the contest and how they'd gotten married on live television.

"I'd noticed her wristwatch and recognized the markings as similar to the ones on Nira's timepiece. It seemed the best way to keep Erika close and protect her. From then on, things happened fast."

"You sent me a copy of the scroll from the museum exhibit," Nira reminded him with a thoughtful pout. "While I deciphered the writing at this end, where were you?"

"We were under pursuit. The Trolleks chased us into the streets. Then a strange thing happened. Ordinary people turned on us like robots."

Kaj jumped to his feet, his gray eyes blazing. "That's because the enemy is activating their army of mind slaves. Confounded people everywhere are being called to duty. The scope of infiltration into world governments is beyond anything we've imagined."

"How did you get away?" Zohar prompted Magnor.

"Edith came by and gave us a ride."

Nira's eyebrows arched. "Edith Marsh? A gray-haired lady?"

"Yes, the Gatekeeper aided us." They exchanged a significant glance. Magnor remembered Nira's story about meeting the shotgun-wielding rune caster who lived in an isolated cabin outside Cassadaga.

"Edith is the person who first related the prophecy to me," Nira explained to Erika. "The six daughters of Odin must unite with the six sons of Thor to chant the ancient words and prevent the coming darkness."

"Will that get rid of the Trolleks and stop their invasion?" Erika asked.

"No, we were hoping Lord Magnor would take care of that problem for us. The verse we're after will dispel Loki back to his underground prison. The inscriptions on our wristwatches hold the key to the rune."

Magnor tilted his head, grateful Yaron had healed his lacerations with a tissue regenerator. "How are you ladies progressing in your research?" he said to Nira.

"We're trying to make sense of the markings we've put together. Erika's piece may complete the puzzle."

"We'll discuss this aspect later." Zohar gestured to him. "Magnor, continue with your report. Where did Edith take you?"

Magnor clasped his hands behind his back. "She drove us to a safe house in the desert. Shortly thereafter, I spoke to Nira. She'd interpreted the scroll and gave us the coordinates for Copenhagen."

"Right, and I picked you up in the shuttle and took you back to the resort," Paz said. Beside him sat a lovely woman who wore her raven hair in a twist. Jennifer Dyhr, a fashion designer, had a figure like one of her models.

Magnor focused on his story. "We accessed the portal there and ended up in Los Angeles. This locale turned out to have another Trollek recruitment center inside a popular movie studio, but we also discovered a military command post."

"You wasted time by taking a detour," Zohar chided him. "If you'd gone directly to Copenhagen, you might have beat Hel to the Book of Odin."

Erika, who'd been looking increasingly distressed by their

discussion, leapt up from her perch. "Don't blame him. He's been wonderful. You won't believe the things we've had to do to reach the sentinel."

Zohar gave her an imperious glance. "Why don't you fill us in then, Miss Sherwood?"

"Actually, I suppose it's Mrs. Magnor now, although I haven't officially changed my name."

Magnor's gaze swung toward her. Did she truly intend to stay wed to him? Why would she want to remain his wife?

Regardless of her motives, he doubted she had considered the consequences. He could be called to duty at any time if another threat emerged. And in the intervals when his Drift Lord duties didn't occupy him, he had no place to call home.

She must have spoken in haste. Surely, she wouldn't care to tie herself to a man condemned by his failures.

Nonetheless, he tuned in to what she had to say with bated breath.

Chapter Twenty-Two

Aware of the rapt faces watching her, Erika related the entire story of her adventure with Lord Magnor. The expressions of his companions ranged from disbelief to astonishment to horror. Even the women gasped when she explained Algie's master plan to space old people and turn the rest of humanity into Trolleks.

The man who'd treated their injuries sat forward. Yaron had soulful eyes and a dark beard. "I can confirm this observation. Algie is very close to achieving the means to accomplish her objectives."

Zohar grimaced. "Supposing Algie succeeds in her experiments to suppress human genetic material, how will she distribute this biological weapon to the population at large?"

Paz answered. "My informants among the Viden faction have suggested atmospheric dispersal of some sort."

"With all that volcanic ash in the air? Impossible. Besides, Algie's plan will be pointless if Loki succeeds in causing a cataclysmic event. It'll wipe out everyone, including his allies. Togura Island is the epicenter of his activity. Once Nira interprets the runic verse, we'll assemble there."

"We've encountered another complication." Magnor told them about the zombie-like beings who had popped into existence at the movie studio.

Erika surveyed the other men while he spoke. Her husband looked a formidable figure with his wide shoulders and agile form, but then so did his friends. They could sell a lot of calendars with all the beefy muscle between them.

Nira turned a bleak face to Magnor. "It sounds as though Hel has unleashed her dead walkers. It's another sign that Loki grows more powerful. They're spirits of the underworld who have received the gift of reanimation."

"How can we stop them if they're already dead?" Erika asked. Those creatures could have come from a bad horror movie.

"Once they disable you, they suck the iron from your blood. It strengthens their powers, but it also makes them vulnerable to anti-magnetic fields."

Kaj, the engineer, piped up. "If that's true, I could rig a defensive shield using the anti-mag generator from our shuttle."

"Make it so," Zohar agreed, his brows drawn together. "We'll need every weapon at our disposal in the coming battle."

"Speaking of weapons," Magnor said, stroking his beard, "Hel has the Book of Odin. I can still go after it. The sentinel suggested I offer an item in trade, such as a flagon of mead from the dwarfs."

Nira shook her head. "Hel isn't likely to give up the Book of Odin if it leads to her father's banishment. She and the wraiths in her dominion wait for Loki's summons to battle. She'll prevent you from taking the book."

"Nonetheless, I will complete my mission if you grant me leave to do so, sire."

Zohar gave him a curt nod. "Take a day or two to gather whatever equipment you'll require."

Magnor turned to Paz, who sat fiddling with his PIP. "Can you contact Smitty and ask how I can acquire the mead?"

"Sure, I'll get on it."

Nira strode over to Erika's side and examined her wristwatch. "Your inscription says you are Six of six. Now that we have your final letters, we should be able to interpret the symbols. It isn't easy. Runic lettering can be read from left to right or vice versa, plus letters can be jammed together. To complicate the issue, runemasters often wrote in secret codes."

"We need a cryptologist on the team," murmured their

demolitions expert. Dal was a wiry fellow with a gaunt face and a bodybuilder form. He sat next to Lianne, a brunette with long, wavy hair who wore a maxi dress and sandals.

"Paz has a gift for languages. He's our linguistics expert," Zohar reminded Nira. "If you need an extra set of eyes, ask him to help. Meanwhile, Paz, bring me the emblem, please."

Paz put away his PIP, stood and stretched, then sauntered from the room. He did everything at his own pace, Erika noticed. A few moments later, he returned holding a wrapped package that he gave to Zohar.

"Lord Magnor, it is my pleasure to bestow this honor upon you." Zohar motioned for the others to rise. "Wear this patch proudly upon your uniform sleeve. You've achieved full status as a Drift Lord. Congratulations!"

Magnor's eyes widened as applause sounded around the room. "But why now? I have yet to succeed in my mission."

"You have already proven yourself, brother. Success comes in degrees, and we recognize your valor. Accept this offering and join our League, but know the obligations that come with it."

Erika inwardly urged him to pluck the embroidered badge from Zohar's outstretched fingers. Why was he hesitating?

Magnor accepted the token with a slight frown. "What will happen to the Drift Lords once we strip Loki of his power?"

Zohar gave him a puzzled glance. "We resume our former lives until summoned again. When we finish here, I shall assume my place as emperor of the Star Empire. I am likely to need help beyond the boundaries of Imperial Space Command. The League would come in handy performing such a function, but that would mean expanding our duties beyond battling Trollek incursions."

"Like a special forces team," Nira clarified. "I can think of dozens of ways we could be useful in that regard."

Zohar wagged a finger at her. "We? Your days of adventure will be limited to ruling by my side as queen."

"That doesn't mean we won't be together again as a team. You're still the group's captain."

"That may change when I ascend the throne. I mean to open membership to new recruits. It is imperative to swell our ranks, and removing exclusivity is the best way to do so. The prior requirement to possess our special trait will no longer apply. But first, we must avert the threat of Ragnarok. Then we can discuss our plans."

Erika wandered toward a corner, where the team's medic had roamed to study a bookshelf. Kaj sidled up to him.

"What about the other prophecy?" Kaj said quietly to Yaron. The engineer looked like a fitness model with his muscled physique. "The future won't exist if that one comes true."

"I'm working on it." Yaron cast a guilty glance at their commander. "There's no need to worry the others."

"We might be cutting off the snake's head by getting rid of Loki, but that won't stop the body of evil he's spawned."

"I know, but it's better for us to deal with this alone."

Kaj put a hand on his shoulder. "Dal and I will be there when the time comes."

Yaron's face softened. "Thank you, brother. The curse must be lifted before we can make our next move." He nodded at his lady who'd moved off to stare out the window. She had alabaster skin, golden hair, and wistful blue eyes.

After Yaron returned to the woman's side, Erika considered their words. What did Kaj mean by another prophecy? Were they hiding something from Zohar and the rest of the guys?

Zohar requested a few moments alone with his team to discuss strategy. Nira led the women into the dining room where they sat around a rectangular wood table.

"What will you do after the show is over?" Erika asked her newfound friends, curious as to how they would fare without a worldwide threat to distract them.

"Zohar and I will get married once things are resolved," Nira said quietly in response. "Then after I finish my doctoral studies in mythology, I'll join him on Karrell. The man will need his empress, and I'll keep busy helping him establish reforms. I'm looking forward to my new role, although it'll be challenging."

"Paz is going to move into my place in Manhattan." Jennifer Dyhr fingered the chunky turquoise necklace around her neck. "He plans to quit his job in telecom and work on his private research project."

"What about you?" Nira addressed Erika.

Erika's cheeks flooded with heat. "Magnor and I haven't discussed our future together. I don't know if he'll want to stay married to me."

"Believe me, if destiny has brought you this far, you'll be inseparable. I've seen the way you look at him, and vice versa. I am glad for him. He was so stern when we first met, and sadness haunted him. You've brightened his life."

"Well, let's see if any of us have a future first. Tell me about Ragnarok," Erika said to divert their focus.

Nira clasped her hands on the table and leaned forward. "In the legends, the Norse gods battled monsters and giants at this great battle. The wolf, Fenrir, defeated Odin. Thor fought the sea serpent who resided in the waters surrounding Midgard, where humans dwelled. He killed the serpent with his hammer, but not before the monster fatally slashed him with poison."

"That beast is still alive," Jen said. "Paz and I encountered it after we escaped from Togura Island in a Chinese junk."

"That's a whale of a tale for later," Nira told Erika with a broad grin. "At Ragnarok, Loki battled his nemesis, Heimdall, guardian of the Bifrost Rainbow Bridge that connected the realms. The two of them killed each other and Bifrost collapsed. Each of the nine realms fell into the abyss. Fires, earthquakes, and tidal waves swept across the Earth and wiped away the human race. Consumed by fire, Midgard sank into the sea."

"If everyone died," Erika said, "how can we be Odin's descendants?"

"The Earth reemerged from the oceans, and members of the Aesir gods who'd had no part in the battle ruled again at Asgard. Balder, a son of Odin who'd been killed through Loki's trickery, came back to life and took his seat on the divine council along with his brother, Hoder. Two of Odin's other sons and a pair of siblings also survived."

"And humanity?"

"A man and a woman lived and founded a new human race."

"Like Adam and Eve?"

"You could say so. The 'Völuspá' is a poem that holds the words of a prophetess who spoke to Odin. She predicted that decadence would be followed by a new generation of gods. The world would rise anew, and peace would prevail. This poem is in the *Elder Edda*, a body of verse in a manuscript called the *Codex Regius*. It's kept at an academic institute in Iceland."

"What else did this prophetess say?"

"The twilight of the gods is nothing more than an episode, and the end of the world is succeeded by another."

"So history repeats itself."

"Yes, that is the implication."

"Then what is the Book of Odin?"

"It's a continuation of the prophecy from after the Great Peace, but this volume holds the means of breaking the cycles."

"I thought it mentions a weapon to defeat the Trolleks?" Restless, Erika shifted in her seat. Were they doomed by destiny to fail? Or could they break the chains of fate?

Nira swept her hand in a broad gesture. "Loki's minions pose a major threat to our efforts. They're like gnats that must be swatted away so we can concentrate on the bigger insect."

"How is Magnor supposed to obtain the sacred book?"

"We'll figure it out."

"Tell me about the vector device on my watch. How do I control it?" While she had Nira's attention, dozens of questions came to mind.

"You concentrate on where you want to go." Lianne, seated across the table, regarded her with dewy eyes.

Erika examined each woman in turn. They seemed so different. How could they possess any shared traits?

Lianne looked like an earth goddess with her long dress and

soft, wavy hair. Maggie, a Southerner from her telltale drawl, was Kaj's girlfriend. The brunette had a sweet, wholesome look about her and a winsome smile. Jen was ultra-sophisticated, like the models who wore her fashions. Nira came across as a practical downhome type of girl, while Yaron's woman exuded an air of mystery.

"It helps to direct the vector device if you shut your other thoughts behind a mental door," Nira suggested. "The only open passageway leads to your destination. Picture yourself walking across the threshold."

"I'll try that next time." Clearing her throat, Erika addressed another topic. "Um, do any of you understand the powers we have been gifted?"

The mythologist nodded. "I believe our talents relate to Odin's shapeshifter ability. Maggie is a jewelry designer who manipulates metal. Jen works with fabric. Lianne can influence water. And so on. We each have a specialty related to the basic elements. Mine is air, or more precisely, oxygen molecules."

"Like the Drift Lords? Magnor told me they normally operate in teams of seven. Members represent earth, fire, water, air, time, space, and the Creator."

"That's right. For example, Maggie's ability to stir metal relates to the space element. If you think about our planet, at its core is molten iron."

"I get it. Jen's power corresponds to the fabric of time?"

"Uh, huh. And she can start fires," Nira said, pointing to Yaron's girlfriend.

"I made a dust storm appear in the desert when we were being threatened. Is that what you mean?"

"Your power must be related to the earth."

"Who correlates to the Creator?"

Nira quirked her eyebrows. "That remains to be seen. Maybe she'll make an appearance when Zohar adds a seventh Drift Lord to the team. Presumably, the prophetess recorded our births in the Book of Odin and predicted that each one of us would wield a special power. We're identified by a birthmark between our right index and middle fingers."

"Hey, ladies, come here," Paz called from the family room.

Hearing the urgency in his tone, they scurried over. The men sat staring with furrowed brows at a big orange blob on the TV set. A weatherman reported on the news.

"It's not even official hurricane season yet, but this storm has sprung up in the Atlantic and is heading northwest toward Florida. Hurricane hunter aircraft will be assessing the winds soon. Geologists say it's the increased thermal activity of undersea vents that have raised ocean temperatures."

He went on to quote statistics and to advise residents in the storm's potential path to stock up early on supplies.

"The weather is screwed up everywhere." Jen's eyes reflected her worry. "My parents live in Palm Beach. I'd better call them."

Zohar's mouth tightened. "This is Loki's doing. Before long, he'll be unstoppable. We have to be one hop ahead of him."

"You mean, one step ahead of him, big guy." Nira tapped him affectionately on the chin.

They parted ways to carry out their assignments. Erika hoped she'd have a chance to join the five women again when things calmed down. They had a lot to learn from each other.

Magnor caught up to her in the hallway. "Here you are. I hope you had a chance to ask Nira all your questions."

"Some of them, but not all. I wish we had more time to get to know each other."

"There's never enough time." His hooded gaze raked her over, making Erika wonder if he referred to their relationship.

"I still need to hear how Kaj freed himself from imprisonment by the Trolleks. Zohar said our engineer had already fled by the time he and Dal arrived. How Kaj met Maggie or where Yaron found his lady are tales for another afternoon. Zohar's orders are to focus on current tasks."

"Congratulations on being made a full-fledged Drift Lord."

He lifted one shoulder in a half-shrug. "I have yet to earn the honor by completing my mission. We journey to the dwarf kingdom. Paz has contacted his friend, Smitty, to provide transport. Gather what you need and meet me in the foyer."

"Do you believe the dwarfs will simply hand over a flask of mead without asking for anything in return?" She plucked at a piece of lint on her pants, pleased Magnor wanted her along.

"They hate the Trolleks as much as we do. Paz considers them our allies." His mien, all business, gave nothing away of his personal opinion.

"I hope he's right."

"If not, we'll still get what we need." He patted his sword, strapped onto his hip once again. His cape flowed behind him. He wore a fresh black uniform that gave him an air of authority. She noticed he'd fixed the emblem on his sleeve.

"I'll get my purse." Heaven forbid a woman should leave the house without her handbag.

Minutes later, they stood outside by the curb while Erika glanced anxiously up and down the residential street. She felt exposed out here, where any one of their neighbors might turn into a puppet under Trollek command.

Magnor's hand snaked into hers. "I'm glad you had the chance to meet my friends."

"They're a great gang." She smiled at him.

"This could end badly. Maybe you should stay here. I'm being selfish in wanting your company."

His voice held such a note of longing that she lifted on her toes and kissed him. "You can't get rid of me that easily. I'm your wife, remember? We belong together. Besides, this is the most excitement I've ever had."

But as the ground vibrated and a sudden screeching sounded, she wondered if her foolhardy sense of adventure had displaced her common sense. A dust dervish arose mere feet from where they stood, obscuring the cause of the commotion.

From the settling cloud emerged a short, bearded fellow

wearing a plaid shirt, loose trousers, and pointy boots. Beyond him sat an open tram, bits of dirt and pebbles streaming onto the ground from its surface. Where had that conveyance come from? Or him, for that matter?

"Well, don't just stand there. Get in," the dwarf ordered in a gruff tone.

Paz banged open the front door of their safe house and rushed down the sidewalk.

"Smitty, you old devil! Thanks for coming. These are my friends, Lord Magnor and his wife, Erika."

A thrill twirled through her at the introduction. Being married still seemed unreal. Maybe when she returned to Arizona and found the marriage certificate in her mailbox, it would bring home the reality of their hasty wedding.

She threaded her arm through Magnor's, reassured by his presence. At least he appreciated her value. His warmth seeped through her. How could she ever part from him when he completed a segment of her she hadn't known existed?

The dwarf scowled at Paz. "Where's the reward you promised me?"

"Your hair has grown longer," Paz pointed to the dwarf's scraggly dark hair that reached his shoulders.

"Aye, and I've got my powers back, so don't make me angry."

Paz offered him a kewa stone, while Erika gawked. Did every Drift Lord have a supply of these uncut diamonds?

Smitty gazed at it with a grimace. "Why would I want this worthless rock?" He scanned Erika and Magnor from top to bottom then pointed to the gold medallion around Magnor's neck. "I'll take that necklace as my price. Give it to me!"

Magnor's hand flew to the trophy he'd won from the ogre. "Will this ensure we get the flask of mead?"

"It'll ensure I take you to my king, human."

"Very well." Magnor lifted the gold chain over his head and handed it to the dwarf. "But you'd better not betray us, little man, or you'll feel the wrath of my sword."

Smitty grabbed the item of jewelry and hung it around his neck. "Don't argue with me, or I'll take your weapon, too. Climb into the transport. I don't have all day."

Magnor assisted Erika to enter the ore car before he squeezed in beside her. They sat on a bench seat behind Smitty who rode in front. The driver flipped a switch, and their vehicle rose vertically into the air.

Smitty spared them a glance over his shoulder. He grinned, showing a row of tiny, pointed teeth. "You'd better hold on. The ride can be rough." And he thrust a lever forward.

Erika barely had time to grip a hand bar before they dove straight down toward the ground.

Chapter Twenty-Three

Erika screamed as a crevice opened in the earth and swallowed their tram. Like a crazy ride at a theme park, they careened through a series of underground tunnels seemingly designed for their means of transport.

Cool air blasted her face as they sped along so fast that everything became a blur. After a grinding, twisting, and frenzied ride deep beneath the earth's surface, their vehicle skidded to a halt. Trembling violently, Erika had trouble loosening her white-knuckled grip on the hand bar.

She sneaked a glance around. They'd arrived at a deserted landing inside a small cavern. Fires burned in braziers set into wall sconces. Wasn't that dangerous? Couldn't the flames ignite flammable gases trapped underground?

As she stepped onto a packed dirt surface, she sniffed a rusty odor. That didn't tell her much. Carbon monoxide and other substances had no detectable smell.

"Uh, excuse me. Smitty?"

"Yes?" Their guide, busy tethering their tram to a tall post, glanced at her. His dark eyes gleamed in the flickering light. Shadows danced upon the walls around them.

"Couldn't there be, like, methane gas or something down here? How can you burn fires with potentially explosive compounds in the air?"

A grin split his mouth. "Don't worry. We have a system of vents. The air is clean."

"Oh. Well, that's a relief."

The dwarf raised his eyebrows as though she heralded from an inferior race that would never understand his people's ways.

While she and Magnor trundled along in his wake over a wooden boardwalk, she wondered at the evident signs of civilization. This wasn't a mine shaft like any she'd seen in movies, nor did it resemble the Grote attraction at Jolheim Gardens.

Plants bordered the walkway, while decorative fountains sprouted streams of clear water like on a garden path. Tiny yellow wildflowers poked their heads above the greenery. The walls sparkled from crystalline formations in the rocks while a pleasant tinkling sound brought to mind delicate wind chimes.

The temperature was comfortable, and a light breeze caressed her arms. This far underground, she might have expected it to be colder. However, geology wasn't her forte. Maybe if you were nearer a source of magma, it got hotter. Surely, they hadn't gone that many miles, but she'd lost all sense of direction.

They crossed caverns with mineral formations that glittered like a fairyland. The beauty of it stole her breath as did the raw gemstones exposed openly as in a natural history display.

When they stopped at a ledge, she gasped at a different sight. Far below spread an entire city constructed of white stone. At the opposite end of a hill stood a magnificent golden palace.

"Great Cosmos, what is this place?" Astonishment claimed her husband's features.

"It's our capitol city, where King Tiberius resides." Smitty gave him a supercilious glance. "You'll make your appeal directly to him. I must warn you to behave. Our liege doesn't take kindly to interlopers."

"Did you tell him we were coming?"

"Of course. Watch your step, now."

Smitty led them down a rocky trail toward the settlement below. Along the way, they passed a contingent of dwarfs wearing leather aprons and carrying sledgehammers. Like Smitty, they sported long beards and pale, lined faces. From their lack of surprise at seeing humans in their domain, Erika guessed that must not be so unusual.

As they reached ground level and proceeded toward the city, she gazed with awe at a bustling marketplace. Short, hunched females haggled over prices while vendors hawked their wares. Where did they get those fresh vegetables? The aroma of vine-ripened tomatoes and green peppers made her mouth water.

Narrow streets merged, defining residential lanes where stone block dwellings dominated the landscape. Flowers grew in planters along the road, their bright colors contrasting to the stark white of the buildings. Mica must have been embedded in the stone, because the exteriors glittered.

A wooden chest with a flat top stood by the curbside at each house.

"What's that for?" Erika asked, pointing.

"Valet trash service." Smitty cast a bemused glance her way. "We like our amenities. In case you're wondering, we have running water, sewers that lie below the city, an air filtration system, and a recycling center. Our power comes from a hydroelectric generator."

Closer toward the palace, a commercial district was lined with shops, clothing emporiums, and more. Nearly everyone wore colorful loose-fitting tunics over baggy pants while going about their daily routine. Down here, how did anybody know day from night? Erika couldn't conceive of an entire population living under the earth.

Overhead, wires strung with electric lights supplemented lanterns on posts that provided illumination. A low vibration hummed in the background, likely from the generator. Erika peered into a couple of shop windows, admiring the tablecloths embroidered with gold and silver thread, the gleaming copper pots and pans, and the gardening implements.

"Oh, my, look at those sculptures." Her mouth dropped open at a display of porcelain designs.

Magnor hustled her along. "We're on a mission, remember?"

They crossed an arched bridge over a rushing stream and trekked up an incline toward the palace at the opposite end of the city. The palace's gold surface was so bright that it made her squint. Her heart thudded in her chest and her palms grew sweaty as they neared their destination. How would the king receive them?

They rounded a corner and came upon a chain of humans shoveling sludge from a roadside ditch. The gang was a bedraggled bunch, their clothes ragged and their faces smeared with dirt. On closer examination, Erika noticed shackles around their ankles.

She poked Magnor. "Who are those poor souls?"

"Slaves," he murmured from the corner of his mouth. He took her elbow and propelled her forward. "Keep moving."

"Slaves?" Her breath hitched. "How did they get here? Don't tell me the old fairy tales are true about dwarfs stealing children in the night?"

"Those refer to trolls, and they are true, at least for the Trolleks during their incursions into our dimension. Dwarfs don't normally keep people captive unless they've earned the king's displeasure."

"Good to know." Her wry tone hid her attack of nerves. "What if his majesty denies our request?"

"That's unacceptable. Just follow my lead."

She was more than happy to comply as a set of double doors swung wide to receive them. Attendants wearing fancy court dress escorted them forward. At least the dwarfs in the inner guard didn't bear arms, Erika thought, entwining her hand in Magnor's.

The likelihood of this being a trap frightened her. What if they'd been sold out? What if Loki had gotten to King Tiberius first? After all, the demon had persuaded King Jorg, the Trollek leader, to believe his lies. Jorg assumed he was acting in his people's best interests while Loki pulled his strings. The same thing could have happened here.

If Loki had turned the dwarf king against them, would she

and Magnor be enslaved like those humans outside or killed outright as spies?

Magnor moved closer as though sensing her doubts. His natural mantle of authority reassured her. How horrible it must have been for him to be dragged before his tribal council as a criminal. The dishonor and shame must have wounded him more than his sister's treacherous actions. He wouldn't take well to imprisonment again.

Her knees wobbled but she kept her chin high as they strode through chambers decorated with gold. Silk covered the walls while woven tapestries and painted portraits adorned the rooms. Electric lamps provided subdued lighting in the air-freshened environment. A slight citrus scent pleased her. Clearly the king didn't lack for luxuries.

A treasury of gold surrounded them, not only in the gilt work but also in the ornamental vases and bowls and statues scattered throughout the place. She wondered if any of those slaves outside had been thieves who'd heard about the treasure below and sought to raid their stores.

Smitty strutted ahead, his chest puffed with pride. Erika tapped him on the shoulder.

"Where did all this gold come from? Do your people mine the ore and process it?"

Smitty laughed. "We have no need to hunt gold in the rock when we can transform metals ourselves."

"So tales of alchemy are true?"

"To some extent." He strode onward without elaborating.

Magnor nudged her. "His people are goldsmiths and metal workers. They weave magic into their creations."

"I see." She didn't really, but what did it matter? Still, she wondered what the dwarfs mined if not gold or diamonds.

"What of this elixir we're supposed to obtain?" Magnor asked, his voice low. "Did Nira say anything more about it?"

Erika nodded. "It's called the mead of inspiration. The dwarfs made it after a war between the gods."

"That would be the two factions, the Aesir and the Vanir."

"Whatever." She shrugged, not as well versed on mythology as Nira but remembering the story she'd been told. "The gods spat into a cauldron to seal their peace, and out of the pot rose a giant. He was a wise poet who hoped to teach with his gift. Instead, the dwarfs killed him and distilled his blood with magic and honey to produce the mead. This elixir provides wisdom and poetic inspiration to anyone who drinks it."

Smitty rounded on them, his eyes furious. "Odin wanted it for the gods, and he stole it from us."

"Yes, after your people murdered the giant. So how did you get the mead back from Odin?"

"We didn't. That giant wasn't the only wise creature who existed, so we simply made more."

Erika fell silent, not wishing to incite him further. Odin couldn't have pleased the dwarfs by his actions, and supposedly her lineage was derived from him.

Their escort halted just before the throne room. A collection of armaments lined the walls of this antechamber. Swords, axes and shields, wheels made of pistols and cutlasses, maces and other lethal weapons made up the display. Erika supposed they were meant to intimidate visitors.

At a signal from a page, they proceeded forward. Enormous crystal chandeliers lit the great hall, bordered by a series of velvet-upholstered chairs. The courtiers who'd assembled there wore jewels that glittered more brightly than the light fixtures. Accent tables held sparkling silver pieces, while marble busts on pedestals dotted the expanse. Gold gleamed from the lowest baseboards to the highest moldings.

A moss green carpet led to a dais ahead on which sat an ornate throne. The pudgy dwarf who occupied it wore a crown set with faceted gemstones. He addressed a young woman who stood before him with her head bowed and with shackles binding her wrists. Blond hair streamed down her back.

Smitty held out a hand to halt their approach. "Wait here until the king summons us forward."

Erika cringed at the stares directed at them. Or more precisely, at her. Maybe the dwarfs didn't get redheaded visitors that often. The villagers had been more polite, averting their gazes after a quick glance. But these nobles had no such manners, or else their sense of superiority entitled them to indulge their curiosity.

The king glowered at his prisoner. "For your serious crime against us, you are sentenced to labor in the coal mines until the breath in your lungs clogs with dust and the blood in your veins turns to sludge. You will learn what it means to take what is ours without asking."

"I didn't do it," the young woman squeaked. "My friend tricked me. Track him on the surface, and you'll see. He left me to take the fall."

"You're a liar as well as a thief. You had the goods when we found you. Consider it fortunate that we don't chop off your thieving hand. Guards, take her away to the dungeon until the next transport arrives."

Erika sidled closer to Smitty. "Coal mines? I thought you said a hydroelectric plant provides your power?"

"Not everywhere, lady. Some of our outer settlements use more primitive sources of fuel."

Feeling compassion toward her fellow human, she couldn't help her next question. "Doesn't that girl get a trial? Does the king serve as both jury and judge in your realm?"

"Silence in the court!" the king thundered. His beady eyes inspected them. "Or perhaps you'd like to join this one in the mines?"

Smitty fell to his knees and gestured for her and Magnor to do the same. "No, my liege. Begging your pardon, but my friends are merely curious about our customs."

The ruler's mouth turned down. "You may approach."

They scrambled to their feet and obeyed.

"So, humans, my Chief Courier there claims you need a favor from us? Tell me, why should we give you a single drop of our precious mead?"

Beside her, Magnor squared his shoulders. "Great king, we desperately require your assistance. As you may be aware by the recent seismic disturbances, our world is endangered. Not only the world above, but the entire universe."

"The demon, Loki, threatens us all," Erika inserted. She clasped her hands while facing the stern monarch. Her knees quaked and her stomach fluttered. If this went south, they might not see the sky again.

"Your help in this struggle will make a great difference," Magnor added. "I understand you've agreed to be our allies."

"We will join you in the final battle, but that has nothing to do with your request."

"Yes, it does." Magnor's eyes scrunched as though he could convince the king by sheer willpower alone.

Maybe he could, Erika thought, wondering at the extent of his mental abilities. What if she demonstrated her own?

Bad idea. If she so much as stirred a speck of dust, they'd probably clamp her in irons like that poor girl.

"Hel is daughter to Loki." Magnor held himself erect, his palms outward. She wondered if he'd faced his tribal elders in a similar non-threatening manner. "She holds the key to eradicating the Trolleks. In an ancient text lies a clue to defeating them. She's stolen this book, and I need an item of value to trade for it. I'm told she would appreciate a flask of your mead."

The king signaled to an attendant who brought him a bowl of grapes. He popped them one at a time into his mouth as he spoke.

"The Trolleks are being led by Loki, are they not?" King Tiberius said, munching. "Why would Hel go against her father? She has no love for the gods, who forced her to dwell in the underworld."

Magnor leaned forward. "The Trolleks are trapped on this side of the dimensional gate since we sealed the rifts. Their chief scientist has declared herself Queen. Her research has given her the means to subjugate the human race and turn everyone into Trolleks. Do you truly want those beasts to rule the Earth? You know they won't stop there."

The king's face reddened. "I've heard nothing of this preposterous claim."

"Hel has the only means for us to stop them. Yes, we'll need your assistance in the battle against Loki, but first help us destroy his minions. Otherwise, we're all doomed. Loki wants nothing less than the destruction of the multiverse."

"Hmm." King Tiberius appeared to mull over his words. "It goes against my grain, but I fear you may be right. It will not be easy to wrestle this book from Hel's grasp. And then what?"

Magnor's posture eased. "It depends on what we find in the text. Supposedly, it mentions a hidden weapon."

A sly look came over the king's face. "Is that so? Very well, we will assist you in this cause. But what will you give us in return?"

"Excuse me?"

Erika's spirits fell. The dwarf king wasn't about to let them go without bartering. She elbowed Magnor.

"Give him a gift," she suggested in a low tone.

"Oh. I'd be happy to offer you this technological wonder in appreciation of your gracious assistance." He withdrew the PIP from his pocket, did a few quick calculations, and held it up for inspection.

The king made a dismissive gesture. "Bah, we have no need of such gadgetry. However, your sword will make a fine addition to our collection."

Magnor jerked upright. "What? No!"

The ruler's eyes narrowed and his mouth thinned. He stood, his expression menacing. "You would deny us?"

Erika stepped forward, wishing she had something of value to offer. They wouldn't want her wedding ring, so what else might entice them?

"Perhaps you would like my husband's cape instead?" she said with a sweeping gesture. "It's made of a fine fabric that would look magnificent on your shoulders, great leader."

"That would merely get in my way. His belt buckle shines

nicely though. I'll take that, too. Give it to me." He pointed to Magnor's waistline.

Magnor backed away, his hand on his hilt. The guards around the room stiffened. They held no weapons, but somehow Erika knew they could defend their king if necessary.

"An offer is already on the table," Magnor stated in a firm tone. "I'll give you my sword."

Carefully, he pulled the weapon from its sheath. He turned it around and handed it by the grip to the nearest attendant.

The king settled onto his throne with a satisfied smirk. "Bring the mead," he commanded one of his subjects.

Once Magnor held the sealed vial containing a golden liquid, the ruler dismissed them. "Escort them to the boundary and see that they leave the premises. Do not trouble me again, humans."

Magnor gave a deep bow after stowing the precious vial in an inner pocket. "If I may, your majesty? Might we have a tour of the palace before we leave, so I may extol its magnificence to my brethren? Truly they should know what a great contribution your eminence will be making to our cause."

One of the king's men whispered in his liege's ear.

"Very well," King Tiberius said. "Rok'by, you take them. Make sure you show the Drift Lord and his lady every corner of our home."

Erika didn't like the way he emphasized that one word. What did it mean? What had that other fellow said to him?

Suspecting treachery was afoot, she swallowed gamely and followed their designated guide from the chamber.

Magnor strode alongside her, his empty scabbard banging against his hip. A feeling of foreboding crept up her spine at the conniving look on his face.

Chapter Twenty-Four

Magnor held his tongue, other than uttering appropriate words of admiration, during their tour of the dwarf king's palace. When Rok'by, their guide, led them to the dungeon, he bit back his surprise. Hopefully, this segment wouldn't lead to a permanent visit.

But why would King Tiberius trick them? He'd want to show magnanimity, so the Drift Lords would value his worth. Then again, for all Magnor knew, inside the stoppered vial could be apple juice rather than ambrosia. He'd had to give up his sword to obtain the prize, and he wouldn't leave without it.

A plan had hatched in his mind earlier, but this detour hadn't been part of it. They'd entered a lower region carved out of rock and gloomy with sparse lighting. Two guards let them through a heavy iron door into the detention area beyond, where a single light bulb glared overhead in the central lane.

Barred cells lined either side of the corridor. Bedraggled occupants, mostly other dwarfs, stared at them with despair as they passed. Erika held a hand to her nose. It stank down here, from mildew and urine.

"What crimes have these people committed?" Magnor asked Rok'by, whose scowl indicated he was none too pleased about this visit, either.

"They're thieves, mostly, who've grown too greedy for their own good. They get a flogging commensurate with the value of the goods stolen and then are locked down here until space is available in one of the forced labor camps. More serious crimes are punishable by death."

"I didn't steal nuthin'," one of them shouted. "He's lying. I spoke against the king's taxes, and this is where it got me."

"Is that true?" Erika asked in a tremulous tone.

Rok'by shrugged, while Magnor wished Smitty had been allowed to accompany them. Probably the king feared his chief courier might become tainted by too much exposure to humans.

A clanging noise distracted him, and he twisted toward the sound. The blond woman who'd faced the king's sentence rapped a tin cup against her bars. "Help me! I'm innocently accused."

"According to the evidence, lady, you're a thief," Rok'by sneered. "You'll get your lashes on the morrow. That'll teach you to steal from the dwarfs. Come on, humans, we've seen enough. Let this serve as a warning not to cross us."

"Wait." Unable to stop himself, Magnor approached the girl, who looked to be in her twenties. "What are you accused of taking?"

The prisoner gazed at him with frantic brown eyes. Her wrists no longer bound, she clutched at the bars, her pale face upturned toward him.

"Please! I'd come exploring with my partner. We're archeologists, and he'd found references to a place that might have been the lost city of Atlantis. But it was a trick. He'd learned of the great treasure here and meant to raid it. He left me behind when we were discovered so I'd get the blame."

Magnor's brows drew together. Was there any truth in her words? He scoured her dirt-smudged face but could find no trace of guile. With the foul odor in this place, it was impossible to detect Trollek pheromones. Wouldn't the dwarfs have tested her at first confinement?

"What was this evidence you found against her?" he asked their reluctant guide.

"She was caught red-handed in the treasure room. It appeared as though she'd tripped on a step and hit her head when she fell, while her partner got away without knowing she wasn't directly behind. A patrol found her lying there with jewels in her hand."

"That's it? Didn't your fellows think maybe she'd been telling the truth? A real partner would have come back for her."

Rok'by glowered at him. "Be wary, human, or her beauty will confound you. Oh, she's not a Trollek," he said upon Magnor's inadvertent step backward. "We checked to be sure. But she may be an agent of the demon himself, sent here to spy on us."

Could she be confounded and acting on Loki's behalf? If so, why? To determine where the dwarf king's loyalties lie?

"Perhaps the whipping will kill her," Rok'by added in a nonchalant tone. "Then she won't have to slave in the coal mines. She's a frail thing. It would be a blessing."

The woman choked on a sob, while Magnor's fingers curled. He clamped his lips tight to avoid betraying his emotion.

"May I have a moment to pray with her?" he asked, forcing his face into a mask of compassion.

Rok'by gave him a startled glance, while Erika's eyes narrowed. She knew him well enough by now to tell he was up to something.

"I suppose it wouldn't do any harm but keep your hands where I can see them." The dwarf stepped back, gesturing for Erika to do the same.

Magnor waited until they were out of earshot before leaning inward. "How do I know you're being truthful and are not simply trying to gain my sympathy?"

"Oh, sir, why would I lie?" The woman's voice held a pleading note. "These creatures won't listen to reason. How could John do this to me?" Her eyes filled with tears.

"Was he your lover?"

"John is my brother. He's always had a penchant for trouble. I should have learned my lesson when he took those Canopic jars from the tomb outside Cairo. Why did I trust him this time?"

Magnor was no stranger to betrayal. He'd have to take the chance that she wasn't already a mind slave to the Trolleks. "I'll get you out. Pretend you're distressed by your fate."

"It's no pretense." She grasped for him but met empty air. "Thank you, sir," she said in a loud voice, "for bringing me comfort. At least I'll go to my doom knowing my soul is at peace."

"May the gods forgive you." Magnor backed away, his head bowed while he altered his earlier plan for this new ripple.

He didn't want Erika anywhere nearby in case he failed. In that event, it would be her job to deliver the mead to Hel and retrieve the Book of Odin.

Was this detour worth his mission? Was he being foolish in hoping to recover his sword and rescue this woman? Should he turn his back on them both and proceed?

He gnawed on his lower lip as Rok'by led them out of the dungeon, back into the palace with its brightly lit chambers filled with gold and works of art, and out toward the city gates.

He could no more turn his back on the imprisoned female than he could detach himself from his blade. This choice wasn't one he consciously had to make. It was done for him by his past experience. Hopefully, the outcome wouldn't make the Drift Lords sorry they'd accepted him into their fold.

Smitty arrived to see them off with a grumpy farewell. As soon as he and Erika were out of sight of the two dwarfs, Magnor increased their pace. He had the route to the surface on his PIP now. A towering cliff of sheer rock bordered one side of the narrow path leading upward, while a precipice dropped away on the other.

"What's wrong?" Erika said after they reached the ledge where they'd first viewed signs of civilization below. She halted to regard him. Water dribbled down the wall behind her, glistening on the rock face.

"I'm going back." He took the prized vial from his pocket and handed it to her. "Take this and keep it safe. Go on a little farther until you find a comfortable spot to wait." He checked the time. Had so many hours passed already? "If I'm not back by midnight, get to the surface and use your vector device to return to my team."

Her mouth gaped. "Are you crazy? What are you planning?"

"I want my sword. And there's that woman."

"What, the prisoner?" She raised her hands to heaven. "Now I know you've gone bonkers. Why, Magnor?"

His lips thinned. "She stands accused of a crime she didn't commit."

"Ah." Comprehension lit her features. "But you don't know that for a fact. She could very well be guilty. And why risk your mission for a stranger? Doesn't the good of the many outweigh the good of the few, or the one?"

"Huh?"

Her shoulder lifted and fell. "It's a quote from a movie. But seriously, you need to stick to your mission and use this vial to obtain the Book of Odin. Rescuing a prisoner from the dwarfs and retrieving your sword isn't in the game plan. You'll risk alienating the dwarfs, and they're allies."

"Then they should have given me the elixir freely without imposing conditions."

"It's not their way." She brushed a strand of hair from her face. "Think clearly, Magnor, with your brain and not with your emotions. You're blinded by your past in the case of that girl. Let it go."

"I cannot. She is to be whipped tomorrow and might not survive the flogging. If there is any chance she is innocent, I must act to save her."

"Then I'm coming with you."

"No, you are not. You will obey me, wife."

They faced off, staring at each other. As he gazed into her lustrous green eyes, he imagined sending her a mental message of how much he cared and wanted her to be safe. She'd be a distraction if she accompanied him. The words wouldn't come to his lips so he transmitted them that way. His eyes took on a glow. He saw them reflected in her own.

Some believed his tribe had telepathic powers, from the way wild animals left them alone and from how they coordinated attacks on their enemy. Part of it was due to their ability to see well in the dark, but he'd had experiences that could almost verify this ability.

Erika dropped her gaze. "All right, but you'd better stay safe. I don't want anything to happen to you."

No one else had ever said those words to him. Unable to resist, he swept her into his arms. He planted a kiss on her forehead when what he really wanted to do was ravage her mouth.

"Do not worry, I have a plan. The city has a sewer system, remember? That's my way inside."

He left her his cape for warmth and to unburden himself in case he had to crawl through small spaces. He'd noticed a treatment plant in the distance and would head there to find a point of entry.

****

Erika dozed off as she waited, huddling on the cold ground of a distant cavern. She'd followed the path until it had widened into this chamber. When she awoke, hours had passed. She stretched and yawned, then shook out Magnor's cape which she'd used as a mat. It smelled of him, woodsy and masculine.

Her throat was parched, so she took a drink from the water bottle Smitty had supplied before they left. A nutrient bar gave her energy. Aware of a gnawing sense of disquiet, she stuffed the empty wrapper into her handbag.

Magnor was late. She'd overslept his deadline by two hours.

Standing, she raked her fingers through her tangled hair. Could Magnor trust the captive woman not to betray him, assuming he had sprung her from prison? Maybe she'd been a plant by the dwarfs, a test to see if he was trustworthy. If so, then by now he would have taken her place in the dungeon.

Erika understood his motives. He'd been wrongly accused and couldn't stand to see others face the same injustice. But this was the wrong time to let his personal hang-ups get in the way of their mission. Too much was at stake.

Should she continue to wait for him despite his orders?

She reminded herself of what was at risk if she delayed her departure. Without the Book of Odin and its fabled weapon, the dark wave of invasion would spread across the globe.

All the while, Loki stirred, fueling the embers of distrust on the surface while feeding a writhing monster below that would burst free in a violent cataclysm. This would set off a chain reaction to shatter the dimensional barriers, widening the drift as Loki had intended from the start. The multiverse would be consumed in a great cosmic blast, and all because she and Magnor had been too selfish to focus on their goal.

Her shoulders slumped, and despondency seeped into her bones. Maybe Magnor would have been resistant to the plight of the female prisoner if she hadn't come along. Her influence softened him and could lead to his undoing. She should have stayed behind.

She bent her head and took a few faltering steps toward the opposite end of the chamber.

Give yourself some credit, girl. He's a full-fledged Drift Lord now, thanks to you. He wouldn't have gotten this far without your input and encouragement. You strengthen him.

Her chin lifted, and her resolve firmed. By God, she was letting her old doubts take hold of her again. She thought she'd learned to ignore her sisters' disparaging remarks and live life in her own manner. Evidently, old grievances were hard to let go. She could say the same for Magnor.

The two of them were more alike than they knew.

Determined not to leave without him, she paced back and forth, worry eating her innards and churning her stomach. Where was he?

She'd just decided to head back toward the city to gain intelligence when footfalls approached.

Hastening behind a column, she held her breath.

"I think she's gone," Magnor's voice rasped. "It's beyond our rendezvous time. We'll meet up with her on the surface."

"No, Magnor, I waited for you." With a whoosh of relief, Erika rushed forward from her hiding place.

He looked magnificent, standing in the archway leading into the chamber. The bedraggled prisoner stood beside him.

Erika stopped short of embracing him. "I was almost ready to go on. I'm so glad you're here."

"Erika, this is Imogene. We must make haste. The dwarfs are not too happy with me at the moment."

She pointed to the sword strapped onto his hip. "I see you retrieved your weapon."

"Yes, Grimshaw is mine again."

"What? You have a name for your blade? Why didn't you mention it before?"

He gave her a sheepish grin. "There was no need. And then there's our tribal belief that sharing a name weakens a man."

Imogene snorted. "Ha, that's true for the dwarfs, too. But cutting their hair is what makes them vulnerable. They lose their power of invisibility along with their strength. If I'd had a pair of shears, I would have made my escape sooner. As it is, I have your warrior to thank for rescuing me."

"That won't last long if we don't hurry." Magnor gestured for them to move along.

"The dwarfs can become invisible?" Erika swallowed nervously as she glanced over her shoulder.

"Yes, so let's go. We set off an alarm, and they aren't far behind. I suspect they won't follow us into the daylight. It'll be dawn by the time we surface."

They accessed the tunnels, climbed across ridges, and squeezed between boulders. Careful not to trip over the many protrusions in her path, Erika kept silent. She didn't want to discuss sensitive information in the stranger's presence.

Voices echoed from the path behind them for a while but then trailed off. Their pursuers must have given up, glad to be rid of the interlopers. She hoped the king wouldn't hold Magnor's actions against his team as a whole. They needed the liege's aid in the coming battle.

Another hour passed while they maneuvered their way past various obstacles. Finally, a dim light gleamed up ahead. It grew as they neared, and Erika cried out in relief when she saw the trees outlining the cave's entrance.

The cool morning air chilled her skin, but she'd given the cape back to Magnor. She folded her arms across her chest while they paused to take stock of their surroundings. Ahead rose an evergreen forest in hilly terrain. Wind whistled through the pines, rustling branches and blowing hair into her face.

"I'll find my own way now," Imogene said with a grateful smile. The chilly temperature didn't seem to bother her despite her ragged clothing and slight figure. "But first, I have a gift for you." She lifted her skirt and removed an item strapped to her leg.

Erika peered at her with suspicion. "Didn't the dwarfs search you when they took you captive?"

"They gave me a brief inspection, that's all. Here, this horn will assist you in your quest." She offered a shiny gold instrument in her open palm. "It blows a warning when your true enemy is near. Bring it with you to Hel's realm, Lord Magnor. You will have use of it there."

Magnor grasped Imogene's arm. "This item possesses magic properties? Did you steal it from the dwarfs? And how do you know my mission?"

"I overheard your plea for assistance to King Tiberius. My only intent is to return the favor you've done me," Imogene said in a sweet voice.

Magnor dropped her arm as though the contact burnt him. "That may be so, but it doesn't explain your possession of this golden horn."

"Milord, what is that American expression? Don't look a gift hog in the mouth."

Erika's lips curved. Despite her doubts, she was beginning

to like the woman. "It's horse, Imogene. Don't look a gift horse in the mouth."

Imogene glanced over Magnor's shoulder. "We don't have much time. A friend is picking me up, and he'll be here soon."

Had Imogene known Magnor would arrive to rescue her? That indicated it might have been her plan all along to get captured.

Worried about her trustworthiness, Erika almost missed the woman's next question.

"Tell me, Drift Lord, how do you plan to breach the gates to the underworld?"

He pointed to Erika's wristwatch, while she wondered how Imogene had gotten word to someone to meet her there. "I was hoping my wife could take me."

Imogene shook her head, loose waves of hair framing her face. "Only one way exists to enter Hel's domain, and you must go alone."

"What's that?"

"I'd think you would have guessed. Very simply, you have to die."

Chapter Twenty-Five

"I have to die?" Magnor grabbed Imogene by the shoulders and shook her. "Are you crazy?"

She gave him a level gaze. "How else do you think you can reach the realm of the dead?"

Erika snagged his arm. "Don't listen to her. She's trying to trick us."

His mate could be right. He considered the possibility that he'd had made a gross mistake in rescuing this woman from the dwarf's dungeon. Perhaps she was a thief like they said or even an instrument of Loki, trying to eliminate another Drift Lord to obstruct the prophecy.

Imogene twisted free from his grip. "Here, use this." She withdrew a small container from a pocket. Flipping it open, she showed him the white tablet inside. "It'll be quick. You won't suffer." She noticed their looks of incredulity. "Is it so strange I carry poison in case my torment became too much to bear? I had no idea when you would arrive."

"So you *did* know we were coming," Erika stated. "What are you, one of those Gatekeepers who pop up now and then to help the Drift Lords?"

Imogene gave her an enigmatic smile. "You must be prepared to revive him. You'll discover the means among the Fae."

"Who?"

"You know them in your culture as fairies."

"Oh, sure. Why not?"

"It's important that you believe me." Imogene spoke in an earnest tone. "Think about it. You've known about them much of your life. You depict them in your porcelain figurines."

"My designs come from my imagination."

"Do they? You must act without delay once he takes the pill. Time passes differently between the realms. What seems like seconds to you will be hours to him when he is gone."

A cloud of dust arose down the street. Magnor's hand clamped on his hilt. "Someone is coming. We have to go."

"Oh, don't worry, luv. It's only my ride."

As Imogene spoke, a vehicle clattered toward them. It looked like an automated rickshaw. The driver, an elderly fellow with a beard, hooked his finger at Imogene.

"Come now, Imogene. You mustn't linger."

"But, Dikibie, I still have so much to tell them."

"They must discover these things for themselves. Foreknowledge is dangerous in the face of prophecy. You've said your piece. I hope it didn't go too badly with the dwarfs?"

"No, he arrived right when I was giving up hope. Now the clock is ticking again."

"Dikibie, aren't you the shapeshifter whom Jen and Paz encountered in Hong Kong?" Magnor said, recalling their story.

The fellow gave him a dismissive wave. "That's me. Look, we've angered Loki." Lightning flashed in the sky, the rising sun obscured by swollen clouds. "We'd best be gone from here. Do not tarry, Drift Lord. Your destiny waits."

Imogene climbed into the passenger seat. Then Dikibie turned the vehicle around and careened down the street. The pair vanished into a gray mist, leaving Magnor and Erika alone.

Magnor stood in stunned silence for several minutes until he realized he held the golden horn in one hand and the pill box in another. He pocketed them both before addressing Erika.

"We have to return to Florida so I can consult Nira and Zohar. I'd rather fight my battles while still alive."

"Wait, I may be able to help." Her anxious gaze pinned him.

"At home, I work with different types of clay, and one of the things I design is figures of fairies. I've always had a compulsion for them. Maybe they'll show us the way to the Fae."

"You're as insane as Imogene."

"I'm just saying, let's go home to my place in Arizona."

She might have a point, much as he hated to concede it. And he couldn't keep running back to Zohar. He had an assignment and should be able to complete it on his own.

Had he really come to rely on his team that much? From an early age, he'd been taught to stand alone. Nothing brought that home as much as when he'd stood accused before the council. No one had spoken in his defense. They didn't have lawyers in his tribe or methodology based on science. Their justice system needed modernization along with most of the archaic institutions on Karrell. That day wouldn't come if the Drift Lords failed to complete their goals.

At first, his task had been to protect the crown prince of the Star Empire. His skills suited the job of bodyguard. But Zohar had gradually integrated him into the team. He appreciated how each team member treated him as an equal, not as a pariah who'd deserved banishment. Their respect meant a lot to him.

No, it meant everything to him. It had restored his sense of self-worth. And so did Erika's affection. Her steadfast devotion made him whole again and showed him that his sister's betrayal was uncommon. Thanks to his wife, he'd gained stature as a Drift Lord. He should value her opinions in return.

"Very well, let's go." His warm smile of admiration brought a flattering blush to her cheeks.

"How? We're stuck here." She swept her hand in a broad gesture. "Where are we, anyway? Can your PIP tell us?"

After a few calculations on his handheld device, he showed Erika a map. "We appear to be in Northern Ireland."

"Interesting. The Irish believe in leprechauns. Maybe they've seen dwarfs from time to time and that's how their legends arose."

"It's possible. Here, you're shivering." Wrapping his cape around them both, he drew her close and nuzzled her hair. "Use your vector transport to take us to your home."

"I'm not sure I can summon the energy when I'm so cold."

"Then let me see if I can address both those issues." He tilted her chin up and lowered his head.

His lips sought hers, and she met him eagerly. Their surroundings melted into a blur as he kissed her with all his pent-up passion. His tongue darted out in an exploratory effort. When she parted her lips, he dove inside, wanting to meld with her, to be closer.

He shut his eyes, relishing the taste of this woman who had bewitched him. Lost in the haze of passion, he exalted at the wondrous sensation of transport, as though the two of them were alone on another plane. The hunger he felt for his wife was so strong that it displaced his reason.

An inner warning bell recalled him to duty just as an odd sensation impinged his mind. It weighed him down and instilled in him a sense of dread.

He broke the embrace. "Did you feel that?"

She gazed at him with concern. "What?"

His hands smoothed her arms. "A heaviness, like something was tugging at me." He glanced around at the unfamiliar landscape. "Do you recognize this place?"

They stood on the corner of a residential street, where mixed adobe-style and Mediterranean homes stood back from the road on wide swathes of property. Varieties of cacti and shrubbery graced the landscaping along with palo verde and mesquite trees and yellow-blossomed snakeweed.

In the far distance, mountains rose as a bluish shadow on the horizon. The warm, dry air brought the smell of dust to his nostrils. From the position of the blazing sun in a cloudless sky, it appeared to be late afternoon.

"Omigosh." Erika bounced on her feet. "I can't believe it. We made it home!"

"I am not surprised, my *knesta*. You have many talents."

His words seemed to please her as a smile curved her mouth, a mouth reddened by his kisses. Masculine pride swelled his chest, and he wanted nothing more than to sweep her into his arms again, but sensibility prevailed. They had a job to do.

"Come on, I'll show you my place." Erika gestured for him to follow. "I can't wait to take a shower and get into some clean clothes."

She rushed along the sidewalk while he marveled at the way flowers bloomed in the heat. The terrain brought home to him their different backgrounds. A pang of yearning struck him for the shady forests, green hillsides, and cool breezes of his mountainous origins.

To his surprise, she didn't head for any of the homes on this street. They turned the corner at the next intersection, and she aimed for a plot of land standing on a rise by itself. Further along, he observed a fuel station and a shopping strip.

Erika turned up a walkway toward a modest house with a red barrel tile roof. Lantana shrubs and bougainvillea plants provided bright splashes of color against the beige structure. His discerning gaze noted the painted wooden bench, metal donkey, and other eclectic art works that decorated a patch of gravel between the garage and the front door.

"My sisters say the place looks cluttered," Erika said, while retrieving a set of keys from her handbag. "They don't appreciate the artistic touch, but then again, they've never accepted my lifestyle."

He absorbed her words while indicating a separate building with the lettering, *Erika's Emporium.*

"Is that your pottery studio?"

"Yes, I converted my casita. What I like about this piece of property is its mixed zoning. I have enough land to add a gift shop. Visitors to the area like cozy little boutiques."

Her gaze grew wistful, and she hesitated before inserting the key in the lock.

"What is it?" he asked, hoping this detour wouldn't be a time waster.

"Before I met you, I was thinking my life was dull and I'd be stuck here forever. But after our adventures, you know what? I agree with Dorothy in the *Wizard of Oz*. There's no place like home."

He tightened his mouth, not wishing to remind her that they had no safe haven until they'd ended the threat from the Trolleks. But he didn't want to spoil her homecoming.

She unlocked the front door and preceded him inside. A foul odor struck his nose as he entered after her.

"Oh, no. Things must have spoiled in the refrigerator." She strode into the kitchen and glanced at the blinking light on a phone set. "I'll bet I have a ton of messages. As long as we're here, I should go through my mail, call my parents, and—"

"Erika, we don't have time." He faced her with a stern expression, sorry he had to alter her plans. "Every minute that we delay increases our danger. You'll have to perform these mundane tasks another day."

Her shoulders sagged. "You're right. Besides, I'm exhausted. That brief nap in the cave has only made me more tired. I need to take a shower and lie down." She wrinkled her nose. "It feels as though I've been wearing these clothes for a week. You don't smell so good, either."

He gestured to his uniform. "I've been through the sewer with these, literally. I should probably get some rest myself and wash up. Do you have any men's clothing I can borrow?"

"I think my dad left a few items here. I'll go get them. They might be loose on you, but you can tighten your belt."

After a quick shower in the guest lavatory, he donned the black jeans and dark gray polo shirt she'd provided. He folded his dirty uniform and cape into the canvas backpack she'd supplied until he could clean them later. Forget about polishing his boots, but at least he'd scraped off the worst of the grime.

Scowling with impatience, he wandered into the living

room. He scanned the tasteful furniture, his gaze lingering on a set of bar stools with colorful bird carvings. The chairs matched her coffee table and a framed mirror on the wall.

He sank onto the couch while waiting for Erika and dozed off before even realizing he was sleepy. He awoke with a jerk, conscious of every lost moment.

Rising, he moved to study the knickknacks on her shelves until she entered. He was glad to see she looked refreshed in a teal top, cocoa pants, and sensible sandals. She'd washed her hair, her springy curls still damp with moisture.

"Do you like my kachina dolls?" she asked.

He gave a noncommittal grunt then pointed to an item on a pedestal. "I prefer that bird with its outstretched wings sitting on a rock. It reminds me of the *hagrets* back home."

"The eagle is one of my horsehair sculptures. Can I get you a drink or something to eat?"

"No, we need to decide how to proceed. You'd said you might find a way to the Fae among your figurines?"

"Yes, let's go to my studio. I can't wait to show it to you anyway." The phone rang. "Drat, let me get that. I've been gone so long people must think I'm dead."

She lifted the receiver. "Hello?" Her mouth turned down. "Oh, hi, mom. Yes, I'm home."

A voice screeched on the other end. Magnor turned away, not wishing to intrude.

"I'm sorry, but I couldn't contact you. I'll explain later." A pause. "What, you filed a missing persons report? Why did you do that?"

While listening, she glanced at Magnor, who studiously avoided her gaze. "Sure, we can come over." She checked her watch. "Yes, we'll stay for dinner."

He waggled his eyebrows, attempting to signal her that they couldn't spare the time. She didn't pay attention.

"Yes, mom, I said *we*. Um, I'm with a guy." She winced at the response. "Listen, you'll understand after I tell you everything, but we can't stay long. See you soon." She slammed down the receiver. "Sorry about that."

A few steps brought him to her, and he placed his hands on her shoulders. "Your parents must be worried about you. I can understand their concern. You went to Vegas and disappeared without contacting them."

"Huh, when has my family been concerned before? Usually, they don't even notice my absence. This would be a first."

He planted a kiss on her luscious lips, pleased by how she seemed reluctant to part. "Do not worry. I'll be with you. Together, we can face anything."

She lowered her head. "You know, I've been thinking. When this is over, what do you plan to do? I mean, you can't go home, right? And we are married. I've kind of gotten used to having you around."

He tilted her chin upward, while hope blossomed in his chest. "Are you asking me to stay?"

"We could try to make it work, Magnor. We're good together. I-I might not be what you were expecting in a wife, but it's a place to settle in between your special ops jobs."

"Let's discuss this later." He spoke in a gentle tone, hoping to delay a decision. "We have many battles yet to fight. Let's be sure the outcome is a positive one before we commit to anything."

She broke away. "But assuming we survive, there's something I have to tell you. My grandfather—"

Magnor's comm unit beeped. "Hold that thought." He tapped the respond button. "Magnor here."

"We lost your tracking beacon for a while." Prince Zohar's solemn voice came through loud and clear.

Magnor went outside for privacy. "We had an audience with King Tiberius of the dwarf realm."

"Did you accomplish your task?"

"Aye, we got the mead."

"Good. So why are you in Arizona and not pursuing the Book?"

"There's been a slight complication." He told his leader about the advice he'd been given.

"That woman named Imogene told you that you have to die? That's absurd. Come back to Florida. We'll figure out another way for you to approach Hel. In the meantime, I have news. Nira has put together the inscriptions from the women's watches. She finally deciphered the rune they make when combined."

"And?"

"It's a sentence with six words. The rune says, *Silence is a treasure beyond words*."

"What does that mean?"

Zohar snorted. "We have no idea. The ladies are working on it. What about your, er, wife?"

"She sculpts mythical figures. We were hoping to find a clue to the Fae among her figurines."

"Fairies are not part of our universe, to my knowledge."

"They could come from another dimension," Magnor suggested.

"True, we'd thought the spontaneous tears in the space-time continuum would close once we sealed the rifts, but perhaps not. In that case, things are worse than we thought. Creatures could still slip through from other streams into our reality."

"That's assuming Imogene wasn't lying." Magnor's eyes narrowed as the air by the street shimmered. Was it the heat causing that image, or something else?

"Her plan is too risky," Zohar said. "I don't want you to—"

"Sire, we've been made. I'm signing off."

He loped inside the house and rushed through each room until he discovered Erika watering some wilted plants in her kitchen.

"Trolleks. We have to go."

"What? Where?" She put down the sprayer in her hand.

"Outside. They're vectoring in."

"Now that you mention it, I hear that annoying buzzing sound in my head again."

"They must have had someone watching your house. Probably Algie planted her agents here to wait for you."

Erika grabbed her purse lying on a counter and slung the strap diagonally across her shoulder. "I understand how this watch operates now. We'll go to my parents' place. They're expecting us, and I don't want to disappoint them."

"The Trolleks might have them under surveillance as well, so we'd better not linger. You wouldn't want to put your family in danger."

Her face paled. "Oh God, what if the Trolleks have already gotten to them? They might be confounded."

He grasped her hand. "We'll find out soon enough. Take us there."

Chapter Twenty-Six

They whisked through the void toward their prescribed destination. Erika would never get used to the sensation of imbalance that vector shifting caused. She focused on Magnor's presence, grateful for his reassuring solidity as her vision spun dizzily.

Before nausea had the chance to grip her, she met the ground with a resounding thud. It took a few seconds for her senses to reorient.

They stood atop a hill before a familiar split-level house. A fantastic view of the mountains spread before them. Erika swallowed a lump in her throat. She'd never tire of the fabulous desert scenery, painted with a palette of colors like the ones she used in her studio.

"It's beautiful," Magnor said, letting go of her. "The house, the view, even the desert vegetation. I can see why you like living here."

"Mom and Dad custom built this place. We moved in when I was eight." She pointed to a separate building. "They use their casita as a guest cottage."

The polished wood front doors opened at their approach, and her mother rushed out to embrace Erika in a tight hug.

"Erika, we were so worried about you. I can't believe you're home safe." Brooke stepped back, brushing a strand of strawberry-blond hair off her face. She wore a simple sheath dress and pearls.

A pang of guilt tore through Erika. She hadn't thought anyone would notice her absence, and she'd been wrong.

"Magnor, meet my mother, Brooke Sherwood. Mom, this is, uh, Magnor." It sounded strange without his first name. How had he signed the marriage certificate? She should have opened her mail at home. The document must have arrived by now.

Aware of her mother's scrutinizing glance, she surreptitiously covered her ring finger. Erika needn't have worried. Brooke's gaze fixed on the sword at Magnor's side.

"How do you do?" Brooke politely offered her hand as years of society etiquette prevailed.

Magnor took her hand and bowed. "It is an honor, madam. Your daughter and I—"

"Shall we go inside?" Erika knocked her mother's hand away and tugged him forward.

If her parents didn't know about her nuptials yet, she'd rather enlighten them after dinner. Truth be told, it was Magnor's ire she feared in that regard. Their lawyer would have to be notified that she was fulfilling the terms of her grandfather's trust. What would her husband think of her then?

She stepped inside the house, her knees quaking. She should have thought of this before accepting Mom's invitation.

Massive dark wood furniture greeted them inside the great room, a combined living and dining area. She'd never liked the heavy style, preferring lighter woods and southwestern accents instead. Paintings adorned the walls, but they weren't what drew her attention. When had her mother put Erika's sculptures out for display?

She hadn't observed them around the house before. In fact, she'd stopped giving her family any of her work because they didn't seem to appreciate her talent. But instead of donating the items to charity as she'd suspected her mother had done, Brooke must have stored them somewhere. Did she bring them out after Erika had gone missing?

Erika trailed behind her mother as a realization blossomed in her chest and threatened to choke her. Could Mom care more than she'd ever let on?

"Your dad and sisters are on the patio." Brooke headed toward a set of French doors leading outside. "We're all eager to hear where you've been and why you didn't call."

They stepped onto the tiled terrace with its barbecue grill and chimney built into a stucco fire pit. A fond memory surfaced of how they'd sat around the fire and roasted marshmallows when she was young. Her mouth watered at the fragrant aroma of grilled chicken and vegetables.

She swallowed as her sisters rushed to greet her. After they finished with the obligatory hugs, she turned to her father. Even dressed in casual clothing, he wore a mantle of authority on his broad shoulders. Dad regarded her with both affection and reproach. His dark hair had turned grayer since she'd seen him last.

"So, the prodigal daughter returns."

She quelled a bubble of nervous laughter. "Dad, I'd like you to meet my, uh…" Her voice trailed off but then she rallied. "Magnor, this is my father, Alan Sherwood."

They shook hands. Then Alan pointed to Magnor's sword. "Are you trying out for a role in the Renaissance Festival?"

Magnor chuckled as though sharing a joke but said nothing in return. This couldn't be easy for him, Erika thought. He was an alien who'd married their daughter. How could he explain his origins?

Thank heavens her family acted normal and not under Trollek mind control, although that wasn't a guarantee they'd been untouched. Still, it would be nice for a change if she and Magnor could relax through the meal. Her rumbling stomach agreed.

"The food's almost done. Go take a seat." Her father grabbed a spatula and attended the grill.

Magnor gazed at her questioningly as she led him to the table. "Let's eat, and then we can leave," she said in an undertone.

He pressed his lips together in mute acquiescence for which she was grateful. They sat around a circular table set for six with cutlery and paper napkins. A candle flickered in a glass jar in the center.

Erika introduced Magnor to her sisters, who gave him curious glances but made polite conversation until the meal was served. Brooke placed a dish of steamy rosemary potatoes on the table, while Alan brought over platters of grilled chicken and roasted red peppers, zucchini, mushrooms, and onions.

Once they were all seated, Erika passed a pitcher of iced tea to Traci on her left.

Thirty-four years old with short blond hair and sharp blue eyes, Traci was a prosecuting attorney and still single. From her trim form and sculpted arms, Erika surmised she kept up with her workouts. Or maybe Traci had simply been playing more tennis with that boring corporate lawyer she dated.

"What do you do, Magnor?" Traci asked, breaking the ice as they ate.

Magnor answered with equanimity. "I'm a Drift Lord and former warrior of the Tsuran."

"Oh, my. What a wicked sense of humor." Erika's eldest sister, Crystal, tittered with laughter. Tall and willowy, she was an events planner for a five-star resort. Erika wondered where her husband and their two sons were this evening.

"I do not jest," Magnor retorted.

"Of course, you don't." Brooke exchanged warning glances with the others.

Their conversation turned light until dessert was served. By then, the sun was setting, emblazoning the sky with a burst of tangerine and crimson.

Crystal set down her water glass. "So, Erika, why didn't you notify anyone where you'd gone? Mom called the hotel. They said you had changed rooms and then left abruptly."

Erika twisted her ring under the table. She'd been careful to keep it hidden, hoping Magnor would catch on and do the same.

"I know, and I'm sorry." She glanced around the table. Curiosity mixed with concern in her family's expressions. "I met Magnor, and I got caught up in—" Her voice faltered.

"My investigation," Magnor inserted, leaning back in a casual posture.

"Oh? Are you in law enforcement?" Traci's eyes sparked.

"You could say that. We're on the trail of a terrorist organization. You can blame me for Erika's involvement and lack of communication. Secrecy is essential to my mission."

"Yes," Erika caught the thread of his story. "And we may be putting you in danger by coming here. That's why we can't stay."

"I wish you'd sent us a message," Brooke said. "I thought the worst had happened when you disappeared. Vegas can be a pit of sin."

"Honestly, I didn't even think you'd notice." Erika hadn't had this frank of a conversation with her family in a long time. Maybe that's why Crystal had come alone. Her mother had wanted to sort things out between them.

"You always act so flippant about life, but you're the one who doesn't notice things." Brooke's accusatory finger pointed at her. "You don't respect our values. It's almost as though you've meant to draw attention to yourself by acting rebellious. Is this why you live such an unorthodox lifestyle? You want to be noticed?"

Old childhood hurts resurfaced. "If so, it's because no one ever listens to me."

"Come on," Traci said, "you blazed your own trail without any regard for our feelings or how it would affect us."

She half-rose from her seat. "Your feelings? How about all the times you've put me down? Nothing I do is good enough or compares to your brilliance. I'll only succeed in life if I get a nine to five office job. Well, that's not who I am."

Magnor cleared his throat. "May I interrupt? Mrs. Sherwood, your daughter is an amazingly resourceful and brave woman. Perhaps she doesn't fit into your family mold, but she's an incredibly talented and caring individual. I would not have survived the trials of my mission without her."

No one responded, because their gazes swung from the

sun's gleam reflecting off his gold wedding band to the diamond anniversary ring on Erika's hand, exposed in her distress.

Uh-oh. Here it comes.

"What do those rings signify?" her father demanded.

She steeled herself. "It means we got married in Vegas."

Alan's face registered disbelief followed by anger, while Erika felt like sinking into the floor.

Brooke clapped a hand over her mouth. "Oh Lord, did you get drunk and end up in bed together? Or did the hasty wedding come first? What puzzles me is why you didn't seek an annulment right away. You're not pregnant, are you?"

"No, mom, I'm not pregnant." *At least, I hope not.* "Listen, everyone, this isn't what it seems."

"Oh, I get it." Brooke's eyes narrowed. "You married the poor sap so you can satisfy your grandfather's will. Did you even tell him about the clause in the trust? Or is he ignorant about the real reason why you hooked him?"

Magnor peered at her. "What clause?"

Erika felt the color drain from her face. "Um, this is what I've been trying to tell you. My grandfather left me a trust fund, but I have to be married for a year to gain control of it." She cast a disgruntled glance at her family for outing her.

Magnor's eyebrows drew together like laden thunderclouds. "You married me for money and neglected to tell me about this critical factor?"

"I tried to explain, but we kept getting interrupted. Besides, you knew I wanted the cash reward from the casino. What's so different about this?" She told her family about the contest they'd won. "It was your idea," she reminded him.

"Yes, but that was because I needed to keep you close."

"Oh, right. You felt it was your duty to keep me safe, while you really needed me to protect you from the Trollek mind touch." She shot him a scornful glance. "We both had our own reasons for getting hitched."

His icy expression made a shiver run down her back. Where had the man gone who'd made such tender love to her?

"You said nothing about being married for a year."

"What, that's too long for you?" She threw her napkin on the table while her family watched the drama unfolding with horror. Tears of humiliation pricked her eyes.

"Great Cosmos, I figured to offer you freedom once our mission was complete, but you never intended to let me go. No wonder you suggested I stay."

She winced at the look of hurt in his eyes. "The trust fund may have been my motive at first, but not now. We have something between us—"

"We have nothing between us except lies." He scraped his chair back and stood. "I see your scheme now. Well, consider our union dissolved. You can keep the cash from the contest. Maybe that will satisfy your greed."

Without another word, he pivoted and stalked away.

"Come back here," she shouted, torn between explaining to her parents and running after him. "We have to file for divorce in this country. You can't cast me off in so many words. Stop, Magnor."

But he'd already left and didn't hear her desperate plea.

****

Magnor fumed as he strode away. If he were an engine, steam would be issuing from his ears. A grievous sense of betrayal gnawed at his gut as he descended the hillside.

She'd used him. Here he had believed Erika cared for him, and it had all been a show. Memories of that initial day in Vegas came to mind with her smiling face and tipsy manner. Had she been playing him for a fool ever since then? Had she truly consumed all those drugged drinks, or had she been putting on an act for his benefit?

She must have zeroed in on his outfit and correctly surmised him to be a newcomer to town, someone gullible whom she could target. What an easy mark he'd made. Why else would she have consented to entering the contest and then moving into the honeymoon suite with him, a perfect stranger?

He pounded the pavement, his sword bouncing against his hip as he walked blindly on. Reason argued with him, saying she did wear the wristwatch and carry the power of the Six. Even Algie had taken aim at her. But while Erika's role in the prophecy might be real, they weren't destined to be together as soulmates. She'd taken advantage of him for her own ends.

Memories of his sister's betrayal clogged his throat. He'd resolved to guard himself against a woman's wiles. How could he forget the pain that had forged his decision? For a brief interlude, he'd thought the illusive dream of having a loving family might be his to claim.

He should have known better.

Magnor whipped around a corner, ignoring the houses on either side of the dusty street, hating the desert. It was as dry as his heart.

The Drift Lords wouldn't understand this split between him and Erika. They'd all joined happily with their destined mates, but their women weren't vipers like her.

An image of a poisonous snake floated into his mind, and he knew what he must do. He patted his pockets, realizing with a sense of dismay that he'd left the poison pellet from Imogene in his uniform pocket. He'd have to return to Erika's house to retrieve the backpack he'd left there.

Death would come as a sweet escape from the despair gripping his soul. Assuming he awoke in Hel's lair, he'd follow through on his mission.

The only problem would occur if he obtained the Book of Odin and Erika didn't revive him. What would happen in regard to her inheritance if she became a widow? Would that nullify the clause requiring her to be wed for a year? If so, it would be to her advantage to let him stay dead. And then all their efforts would have been for naught.

Loki would win. The world would end. And he'd no longer have to worry about a future without love.

****

"I have to go after him." Erika rose from the table and grabbed her purse.

"Hold on." Alan gave her the glare that, as a child, had made her quake. "You owe us some explanations."

"I can't stay. He needs me."

"He's angry. Leave him be for a few hours. If he's been hurt, he'll come around when he thinks things through."

"You don't understand. None of you do. I care for him. At first it was only about the money, but not now." Even as she said it, she knew those words were untrue. Something had connected between them from the start.

Her gaze lifted to the horizon, which had grown hazy in the twilight. A breeze whistled through the shrubs hugging the hillside. Barbecue aroma inhabited the warm night air, but now it mixed with the scent of dust like before a storm.

"Sit down," her mother commanded. "Tell us everything."

The resistance melted out of her. She sank into her seat, unsure how to convince Magnor of her sincerity when she'd kept the truth from him. Considering how his sister had betrayed him, it was likely he'd turn a deaf ear to her. She wouldn't blame the man. Maybe her family *could* offer some advice.

For the first time in her life, she found herself sharing her innermost feelings and thoughts with those people closest to her. But what astounded her more was their willingness to listen and not condemn. They'd been quick to react before, but that had been her fault. She'd acted exactly as they had expected.

Now she told her story in a rational, calm manner, answering their questions along the way. But when she got to the part about Magnor being a warrior from space who'd come to Earth to fight an invasion, they stared at her as though she'd sprouted wings.

Erika raised her hand. "Don't talk, just listen. I said earlier that you might be in danger because of your association with me, and that's true. Now I need some answers. Where did this watch come from? Let's start there, because it marks me as one of the women in the prophecy. So does this birthmark between my fingers." She spread her palm for them to see.

"The six daughters of Odin?" her eldest sister sneered. "You truly expect us to believe this fairy tale?"

"The wristwatch came through the mail." Brooke squinted as the breeze blew ashes from the fire around. The tiny gray flakes rode the air currents like snow. "An anonymous note said for you to have it on your sixteenth birthday. I thought it might be a gift from my brother, who didn't like to acknowledge his family ties but every now and then sent birthday presents for you girls."

"I'll bet Uncle Bob didn't send it."

"That may be true, but you can't expect us to believe your story about dimensional rifts and life on other planets? And here I'd thought you had finally come to your senses."

Alan shook his head. "Erika, you always did have an active imagination, but this time you've gone too far." He thrust his thumb toward the exit. "And it looks like you sucked that poor fellow down the rabbit hole with you."

Traci examined her fingernail. "I don't think so, Dad, he seemed as nuts as her. Didn't you see his sword?"

"We may have other problems." Alan stood and flicked on the flat-screen TV mounted on a brick wall under the covered portion of the patio. A buzzer sounded with a weather warning flashing across the screen.

Erika blinked as the wind blew grit into her eyes. The breeze had become stronger and more uncomfortable.

"Maybe we should go inside," she suggested. A paper cup tilted over and rolled off the table, followed by an unanchored napkin.

"Omigod." Brooke jumped to her feet, pointing at the TV screen where a roiling, thick cloud from the distant hills headed for the city. "It's a haboob."

"Sandstorm. Get indoors." Erika leapt up as her sisters did the same.

They stared at the horizon, obliterated by a rapidly advancing mass that charged forward like an angry bull. This wasn't an anomaly she'd caused. She felt it in her bones. Loki was flexing his power.

Her father directed the others to push the furniture back and grab the cushions before they rushed inside the house. He hovered by the door. "Erika, why are you just standing there?"

"Don't worry, I'll be okay. Shut the doors and move away from the glass."

"You're crazy. You'll be injured. Come inside."

"This is my chance to prove I'm telling the truth."

Alan stepped out and shut the French doors behind him. The women's faces pressed up against the insulated window panes as he returned and yanked on Erika's arm.

"Stop this insanity. You don't have to prove anything to us."

The TV screen went blank as the raging cloud neared. The wind picked up, whipping her hair into her face and lifting her shirt. A utensil rolled off the table and crashed to the tile.

"Stand aside." Erika shoved her father behind her and faced the massive brown wall headed their way.

Lifting her arms, she summoned her power. A tingling sensation began at her toes and rose to her fingertips. Blood surged through her veins along with a sizzling energy that enervated her. A chant began somewhere in her head.

"Silence is a treasure beyond words. Silence is a treasure beyond words." Magnor had told her about the runic phrase Nira translated from the markings on the six women's watches.

Her arms trembled as the high wind hit, particles pelting her skin. But then the churning mass separated. It blew past on either side of her and bypassed the house.

One minute the dust storm surrounded them, and in the next instant, the air cleared. The last vestiges of a crimson sunset showed over the distant mountains.

Erika's limbs sagged. Her father caught her and eased her into a chair, while her sisters and mother burst outside.

"You did that?" Brooke gazed at her with awe.

"It's related to the power I inherited from Odin. This is the first time I could actually control it."

"It's all true." Traci gaped at her, while their older sibling seemed at a loss for words.

"Yes." She studied her sisters. "Now you see why I have to go after Magnor. He needs me. We're meant to be together."

"You like him, don't you?" her mother said, compassion in her eyes. "I've never seen you this devoted to a man before."

"He's wonderful, Mom. He treats me with such gentleness, appreciates my value, and tolerates my quirks. And the poor man is so lonely. He deserves happiness."

She hated herself for causing him more pain. If only she'd told him the truth from the beginning, they wouldn't have come to this morass.

Brooke tipped her face upward. "Do you love him? Is that why you want to hang onto him?"

Tears filled her eyes. "I don't want to lose him. I was so afraid he'd choose to leave me after his mission was done, but you heard him. He meant to offer me freedom, thinking I'd want a divorce. We were so wrong about each other."

"So go tell him."

A weepy smile lit her face. "Really?"

"What are you waiting for?" Alan said, gesturing. "If he's the one for you, go hook him and reel him in, and your grandfather's clause be damned. Getting your husband back for the right reasons is more important. We're behind you one hundred percent."

Her throat constricted. She'd never been more grateful to have her family's support. They crowded around her, making her feel loved and accepted for the first time in her life.

No, not the first time. Magnor had made her feel that way.

It was time to let him know how she felt about him.

Chapter Twenty-Seven

Magnor felt no pain as his body slid into permanent sleep and his soul separated. His essence hovered above his form lying on the floor in Erika's studio where he'd taken the poison pill.

He'd had no choice. There was nothing left for him now other than failure if he didn't finish his mission. He pushed aside the unhappy thought that his plan depended upon Erika to revive him. He'd survived so far. Maybe he could find a way out of Hel's domain on his own.

A pinpoint of light showed in the periphery of his awareness. It brightened into a flare that sucked him in.

His essence flew into a tunnel with walls of swirling colors. He spun and twisted through the wormhole-like corridor until his mind reeled.

The journey ended when he landed with a whump on a hard surface. His hip took the brunt of the impact.

Wait, only a corporeal body could feel the cold ground beneath him. In the dim light, he lifted a hand and poked at it with his other. He felt that. What did it mean? Breath rose in and out of his chest as though he still had lungs. All right, he didn't understand how that was possible, unless it was an illusion born from his brain. But hadn't those cells expired with his demise? Perhaps this represented another level of consciousness.

Did it matter? What counted were the heavy iron gates that rose in front of him. Beyond the gate was an arched bridge paved with gold. It crossed a raging river. The sound of rushing water echoed loudly in the darkness, barely illuminated by torchlight.

Was that the River Styx he'd read about in his cultural studies of Earth? Or did he have his mythologies confused? Perhaps the afterlife appeared to a soul in accordance with his beliefs. If so, that would be the river Gjoll. Beyond was Helheim, where Hel resided in a palace and ruled over her subjects.

His nape prickled at the uneasy feeling of being watched. He focused his night vision, and soon he could discern humanoid shapes hovering nearby. He wasn't alone, then. Were these people other souls like him, waiting to move on?

He shoved to his feet, surprised to find his sword still strapped to his hip. More important was the vial of mead inside his pants pocket. He'd left the backpack behind, certain he couldn't take earthly belongings along. Perhaps his garments were another illusory effect.

As he brushed off his clothes, a bell tolled from somewhere beyond the opposite riverbank. It must have been a signal of sorts, because the forms around him inched forward, revealing themselves. They looked like normal humans except for the bewildered looks on their faces. They formed a line facing the iron gate.

With a shrug, he joined them. Turning to the fellow behind him, he asked, "Hello, why are you here?"

The bald man's gaze lifted to meet his own. "I was on my motorcycle and got hit by a truck. What is this place? Am I dead?"

Magnor grimaced. "I believe so, yes." Not wishing to hear more, he faced forward. A heavy vibration shook the earth.

Across the bridge, an immensely tall woman approached them from the blackness beyond. The giantess had skin the color of ash and glacial blue eyes.

"Welcome to Helheim. I am Modgud, guardian of the Gjoll." She towered over them all, an intimidating figure to those who might resist her authority. "You may cross if you properly state your name and business."

Her voice boomed across the expanse to her mesmerized

audience. "Be unafraid. Helheim is not a place of punishment. Those who've done bad deeds go to Niflhel, a lower level where the evil dead suffer endless torment. You are more fortunate. Here you will reside until Hel summons you to battle on her behalf."

Not too reassured by these remarks, Magnor watched the giantess insert a key into a lock at the gate and twist it. She shoved the massive gates wide open, her large body quivering from the effort. Then she lumbered through to their side.

"A word of warning. You'll get three chances to state your correct information. If you fail, you'll be condemned to linger in this never-world forever. Now let us begin." She snapped her fingers, and two hunched figures appeared out of the gloom to set a desk and chair on the supplicant's side of the gate.

Modgud crooked her finger at the man leading the queue.

The thin fellow stumbled forward. Facing the desk, he leaned over and muttered his response to the giantess while she picked up a quill pen and dipped it in a bottle of ink. She gave him a nod, wrote his information on a piece of parchment, and then waved him through.

Her minions stood on either side of the opening to make sure unauthorized souls didn't charge past the gates. The line progressed slowly, while Magnor seethed with impatience. Every minute that he lay dead in the real world lessened his chances of revival. But even if Erika meant to do her part, how would she know he was ready to return? If she brought him back to life too soon, he wouldn't have had time to accomplish his goal.

If they'd have been able to discuss strategy, he might have devised some sort of signal. Now he would just have to take his chances. That is, assuming he got past this first barrier.

"State your name and business," Modgud said when his turn came.

He lifted his head proudly. "I am Lord Magnor of the Tsuran. I wish to see Hel."

Modgud's flat eyes stared at him, and her lips thinned. "Wrong answer. Try again."

Magnor's brow folded. Ah, he should have remembered he'd lost his title after being disgraced at home.

"I am Magnor," he stated simply. "I'm here on a mission for the Drift Lords."

"Hmm. You're still not getting the point."

"Well, what is it then?"

"Your full name is required, and the true reason why you are here. Look beyond the mundane."

"The true reason? I gave it to you."

"One more try is all you get."

He glared at the misshapen female. Was he to reveal his mission, or confess what he was trying to prove by joining the Drift Lords? And what was that, exactly?

He supposed he had wanted to lessen the humiliation he'd felt in front of the council, his hurt that no one believed him, and his betrayal by a loved one. They'd done more than take away his honorary title. His name would no longer be spoken or acknowledged among their people. He would be like a shade that passed unnoticed in the night, forgotten in the light of day.

Primer Pedar had given him the chance to recover his self-respect when he'd hired Magnor as Prince Zohar's bodyguard. Magnor had redeemed himself in that capacity, but had it been enough?

He swatted himself on the forehead. He hadn't believed Erika when she said he mattered to her. Instead, he'd assumed she meant him ill and never gave her the chance to explain about the trust fund or to admit her true feelings for him. He'd been guilty of the same injustice of which he'd stood accused.

He lowered his gaze to the ground. Truly, he was still unworthy.

"I have no name," he mumbled. "And I am here to regain my honor."

Modgud's mouth curved into a slight smile. "You're on the right track, but unfortunately, that was your third try. Remove yourself from the line. Next!"

"What? Which part of that was right? Tell me! And why don't I get another chance?"

The two heavyweights stepped forward, grabbed his arms, and hauled him aside. A trembling woman took his place before the giantess.

Magnor, stuck on the sidelines, considered his response. Should he have spoken his full name? Would that have worked? He'd only experienced shame at its mention because the council had made it so. No one else should be able to dictate what resided inside a man.

He staggered back as the truth hit him with the force of a meteor. Great Cosmos. The worth of his name hadn't been taken from him. He'd done that to himself. He'd allowed the council to strip away his pride. Who were they to tell him whether he was honorable or not? The truth showed in his actions. The elders had reduced his self-worth to shreds, and he'd believed them.

His true purpose became clear. It was to seek justice against people who'd been falsely accused.

Now he knew what to do once he completed his mission for the Drift Lords.

A curtain lifted from his mind. He didn't have to hide his name in shame. He had the right to shout it to the stars.

"I know the answers!" He raced forward, but the two guards blocked his path. They looked as though they'd like nothing better than to toss him into the seething river.

The giantess pointed to him. "You've lost your chance. Accept your fate."

He hung his head as the reality of her words sank in. He'd lost more than his chance to gain access to the bridge. He had lost Erika's regard by hurtling accusations at her. Yes, she'd not told him the truth about why she had married him. It was a sin of omission, not a lie. And she had tried to tell him several times, but he'd ignored her.

Maybe she had started out having an ulterior motive like him, but then she had begun to care for him.

And now he'd lost his one chance to have the family he'd always wanted. Coming to Earth had given him more than a job. It had given him the opportunity to reclaim his life.

He swallowed past a painful lump in his throat. As Erika would say, he blew it.

Or not.

He could still make amends, if he ever got out of here. Was there such a thing as cheating death?

He'd never find out by standing there. He receded into the shadows, away from the line of lost souls and their pitying glances in his direction. He'd been the recipient of those looks before. This time, he wouldn't accept them as his lot.

His night vision discerned the rough walls of the enclosed chamber. Water trickled down in little streams, nothing compared to the tumbling flow of the river. He'd already eliminated climbing the gate, jumping into the river from above, and attempting to swim across. That would be folly. He would be swept along in its current, ending up who knew where.

No, he had another plan. He smoothed his palm along the rock, feeling the indentations and ridges. It might work.

When he was far enough away from probing eyes and newly arrived souls who wandered about, he hoisted himself upward. Using the rocky outcroppings and dents, he slowly made his way to a height with a good overview. Down below, the line snaked toward Modgud at her desk and the gleaming gold bridge beyond, lit by torches for the crossing.

Magnor would be crossing by other means.

Feeling like a fly on a wall, he slowly inched at a diagonal. He didn't want to go too much farther in an upward direction or he'd be hanging upside down from the ceiling. Unlike insects, he didn't have the ability to cling to a surface with his bare hands.

But the walls were manageable. He strained his muscles making progress, wincing each time his sword banged against the rock. Now he was over the river, its torrent gushing below. One misstep and he'd be history. Sweat beaded his brow.

His fingertips groped for the next handhold, while his boot aimed for another recess in the rock. He slipped and almost lost his balance, but then his foot clamped down and he made his target. His hand reached for the next protrusion.

There, he'd finally made it past the raging water. He aimed at a diagonal again, this time heading downward. His arms and thighs trembled from the exertion. He tightened his mouth, forging on, willing himself to prevail. The weight of his sword dragged on his hip, proving an encumbrance. He ignored it, focusing instead on each handhold he gained, on each time his foot found another ridge.

Far off in the shadows on the opposite side of the river, he touched ground. He crouched silently, observing the surroundings for movement. His arrival seemed to go unnoticed as he stood quite alone. Pausing to rest a moment, he allowed his breathing to slow.

His muscles ached but he couldn't tarry. At a junction where the path took a left turn, he slipped into the line of souls shuffling forward. The person behind had a moribund look on his face and didn't react. They trudged ahead until a vista opened to view.

Across a chasm was a gleaming palace of obsidian and gold that stood upon a mountain. Beneath it, in the abyss, were myriads of souls, toiling endlessly at obscure tasks he couldn't discern. None of them looked happy at their plight. Their shoulders drooped with misery while they labored on. Along with the others in his group, he descended toward them.

Ahead was a warden with a list in his hand, ticking off names and giving out assignments.

Time for Magnor to split off on his own.

He dodged down an alley and wound through a jumble of sad individuals who dug and hammered and chiseled away at who knew what. Flaming torches cast wavering light on the scene, while soot dried his throat. He scooped up a shovel along the way to blend in with the sorry souls and resisted the urge to cough. He didn't care to attract the notice of the overlords.

Around a bend, he hesitated at a roped-off area where ragged beings lingered in the shadows. They appeared uncannily similar to the dead walkers who had attacked him and Erika at the movie studio. Their vacant stares gazed at nothing in particular, as though they needed the spark of animation to move. Their skin, patchy and rotted, sagged over bony frames.

Why had they been sequestered from the others?

Finding the answer wasn't on his agenda. He had one goal to accomplish. Magnor hurried on until he reached the palace.

This called for a frontal assault.

He discarded his shovel and strode directly up to the drawbridge. Here he addressed the guards who blocked his access.

"I wish to see Hel. I've a gift for her. Tell the queen that I am Magnor of the Drift Lords." His voice rang with pride. His new name suited him.

"How did you get here?" one of the guards snarled. Whiskers stood out from his chin like straws.

"I took my own life so that I might speak to her. My news is important. Hurry, or she'll be angry at your delay."

They must not get too many folks demanding to see Hel because they took him at his word. Before he knew it, he'd been ushered into a great hall sculpted from marble.

"Wait here," said the guard who'd led him inside.

A general miasma weighted the place, or maybe it was the gloomy lighting that lowered his spirits. Hah, he almost laughed at the term. That's what they all were in this place.

A movement at the corner of his eye made him swivel. He took an inadvertent step back as a hideous being approached him. Fleshy growths covered her bulbous-nosed face. She wore a gold crown over scraggly raven hair. A corset-like garment tapered to her waistline, where her bottom half faded into shadow.

"I am Hel, Queen of the Shades, ruler of Helheim. Who are you and what do you want?"

He resisted the urge to grimace at the smell of decay that

accompanied her. "I am Magnor of the Drift Lords," he repeated. "I have come for the Book of Odin."

She sneered. "Have you, now? What makes you think I have this precious book?"

"Let us not play games, your majesty. I brought an item to trade." He held up his vial. "A drink of this mead will instill wisdom. I got it from the dwarfs."

"You have the mead of inspiration? Why would they give you such a thing?" she scoffed, raking him over. A spark of interest flared in her expression but was quickly suppressed.

"They didn't. I took it. I'll take the book, too, if necessary, so you might as well trade it for an item of value."

She gave a cackling laugh. "Secrets in that book can harm my father's allies. Why would I aid you, son of Thor? Your relative, Odin, was the god who cast me here. I was innocent of any crime except for being Loki's daughter. Yet the All-Father hurtled me into the realm of darkness, to dwell here forever."

Magnor detected her resentment. "He made you sovereign."

"Of the dead, yes. But soon we'll rise again. When Loki regains his power, he'll call upon us, and we will join him in the final battle." Her smile widened, revealing rotten teeth.

Magnor gave her a scornful glance. "Humans survived Ragnarok, and the seed of the Gods passed down to us to ensure their supremacy. You failed before, and you will fail this time, too. Loki will be sealed in his prison again, and you'll be stuck here for all eternity. You might as well drink this mead. The knowledge you gain might entertain you in your misery."

She floated closer, her body suspended in mid-air. Her eyes gleamed with malevolence. "Give it to me, and I'll see that your suffering is lessened. You may serve me in the palace instead of joining the multitudes outside."

He compressed his lips. "Do not underestimate my intent. Give me the Book of Odin." He spied a glass dome on a pedestal. "Is that it, inside the case over there?"

"Do not move, Drift Lord. You've met my ghost fighters."

She gestured to a bunch of figures emerging from the gloom. Their robotic movements mimicked puppets. "One word from me, and they will send your soul to Niflhel, where you will suffer unimaginable torments."

"Oh, like this place is any better? If it's where good people go after death, they're not so blessed."

"You see what you expect to see, Drift Lord. Now give me the mead and forget about your earthly concerns. They will no longer matter when the dead rise to life."

"Is that what your father has promised you? That you'll all live again and inhabit the upper realms? Didn't he tell you of his plan to destroy the multiverse and everyone in it?"

Her nostrils flared. "You underestimate my power. I have my own plans in the event Loki fails. The Soul Stealer works to increase my army. When we are strong enough, we will prevail."

Unsure what Hel's words meant, Magnor didn't care. He had a task to complete. His gaze swept the glass case that might hold his target. Hel seemed so secure in her dominion that she may not have instituted additional security measures beyond the dome.

Reaching inside his jeans pocket, he groped for the horn given to him by Imogene. She'd said it would sound a warning when his true enemy was near. But what would happen if he blew the instrument?

He'd soon find out.

He whipped the horn from his pocket and put the narrow part to his lips. His mouth closed around the cool nub. He sucked in a large breath of air through his nose. Hel's pockmarked face took on a look of alarm as he blew out in one mighty burst.

An ear-piercing note blasted forth. Even as he shut his inner eardrums, the glass case shattered.

The noise woke the wraiths, who lifted their heads in unison. Hel snapped her fingers and pointed at him. They limbered up and aimed in his direction.

He lunged toward the sacred book exposed on the pedestal, grabbed it, and turned to face the onslaught.

"Now, Erika," he hollered, hoping she'd be there for him.

Chapter Twenty-Eight

Erika raced through her house without finding Magnor anywhere. Her heart galloped while panic threatened to overwhelm her. Where did he go?

She could have sworn he'd return here, even with the threat from the Trolleks outside. He wouldn't rejoin his team, not without the sacred book. Sure, he might sulk a bit over her, but soon he'd realize they needed each other.

And, oh Lord, she didn't like the emptiness that yawned ahead without him. She'd grown accustomed to his comforting strength and gentle touch. If only she'd told him the truth from the beginning. He was the first man who truly appreciated her and she'd let him down. Tears pricked her eyes. She'd make it up to him somehow when she found him.

She'd vectored directly inside her house, keeping away from the windows as she searched each room. His backpack lay where he'd left it on a kitchen counter. She scooped it up during her search. Her stomach roiled and ice filled her veins at the possibility he'd gone. She didn't even know how to contact his team.

The other possibility scared her even more. He might have taken the poison pill, intent on sticking to his mission despite her absence. Afraid of what she'd find, she rummaged through his knapsack. The gifts from Imogene were gone—the horn, too.

Inside her home office, the screen saver swirled on her computer. She dropped into the seat and scraped the mouse along its pad. A website popped into view. So Magnor had been here! He'd looked up Norse legends, Hel in particular.

Erika scanned the page before clicking on a link for Odin. Among his other talents, the All-Father could banish souls into the earth. He also had the power to open funerary mounds and take spirits from the underworld to bring them back to life.

Wait, how had he accomplished this? She squinted at the monitor as she read further. The Norse god had imparted some sort of magical breath. Was it possible she'd inherited a measure of this ability?

According to Imogene, she'd find the means to revive her husband among the Fae. But even though fairies didn't fit into Norse mythology, her figurines might still provide a clue.

Crossing over to her pottery studio would expose her to any Trolleks patrolling the premises. Magnor must have used his invisibility shield to bypass them. Or maybe they'd left. Erika didn't hear the buzzing sound she usually got in their presence.

She peeked out the rear door from her kitchen. Not seeing anyone nearby, she slipped outside and hurried around to her studio. Her purse flapped against her side along with Magnor's backpack as she trod across the soft ground.

She pushed open the unlocked door, her pulse jumping when she noticed the lights blazing inside.

A quick scan absorbed the drying racks, the counters, the long table where she taught children's classes, the potter's wheel, and the kiln.

At first glance, everything seemed to be in order, but something wasn't right. She could tell from the smell of dust that the air had been disturbed.

And then she saw the pair of boots on the floor sticking out from behind a counter.

Her heart leapt into her throat. *Oh. My. God.*

She slammed the door shut behind her and rushed ahead with a cry of dismay. Magnor lay stretched out on the ground, the container Imogene had given him spilled from his open palm. Erika fell to her knees. His eyes were partially closed, his face as gray as granite and just as still.

"Magnor, wake up." She pushed him but he didn't respond.

Should she try CPR? No, that wouldn't help if he'd ingested poison. She needed an antidote. Could the answer be here, among her finished porcelain fairies?

She scoured the contents of her studio, but her whimsical designs didn't offer any solutions. Their delicate faces stared back at her, as imaginary as Tinkerbell. At least that fairytale heroine could fly.

The germ of an idea sprang into Erika's mind. She locked the door while thinking about it. What had she just read on the computer? Something about a breath that could give life.

Night had descended, but if a beam of sunlight could cut the gloom, it would have illuminated the dust motes suspended in the air.

She inhaled deeply. The particles filled her nostrils, tickling her nose and making her want to sneeze. But they also filled her heart with hope.

Therein lay her salvation. The truth did lie among the fairies. Precisely, in fairy dust.

With her special power, she had control over the earth and all that derived from it.

Her chest swelled with the realization that the means to revive Magnor came from within herself. She had only to believe strongly enough and focus her ability. Could she do it?

She'd have to try.

After sucking in two deep breaths to inflate her lungs, she crouched by Magnor's side again. Her fingers smoothed away the lock of dark hair that had fallen across his forehead. Then she trailed her forefinger along his cheek to the beard that darkened his jaw.

Would his soul fly to Valhalla if she failed? So it was in the Norse stories for fallen warriors. But she wouldn't give up on him yet. He had to live.

She couldn't imagine her life without him.

Bending forward, she hovered over his face, her mouth

nearly touching his. His lips were parted. Tempted to touch him with a kiss, she instead took another deep breath. Then she squeezed her eyes shut and blew softly into his mouth.

In her mind's eye, she pictured the dust swirling into his throat. The particles sparkled like magical fairy dust as she imbued them with her power. Riding this dust was the wind of life, the breath of respiration.

She envisioned this breath twisting down his trachea and entering his lungs, where it revitalized each cell. And from there, it would get absorbed into his bloodstream and circulate throughout his body. His metabolism would restart like a rebooted computer.

Her temples throbbed, her pulse pounding from the effort expended. She'd done her best.

Opening her eyes, she gasped in dismay. Magnor lay unmoving, still as death.

She'd failed. Now they would never recover the Book of Odin and the means to destroy the Trolleks.

She had doomed her world to catastrophe. And she'd lost the one man with whom she wanted to stay until the end of time.

Too shattered to go on, she covered her face with her hands.

A muted cough made her glance up. Was it her imagination, or had Magnor's nose twitched?

When he took a short, choking breath, she cried out in joy. Her spirits soaring, she shook him and called his name.

"Magnor, can you hear me? Wake up."

His eyes popped open, and he stared at her in bewilderment.

"Oh, thank the Lord. You're alive." Leaning over, she hugged him.

"You did it." His voice held a note of wonder. "You brought me back."

She kissed him, rejoicing in his revival. "That was my job, remember?" Moisture tipped her lashes as contrition filled her. "I'm so sorry. Please forgive me for not telling you about my trust fund sooner. I was afraid to lose you."

He struggled to a sitting position. "No, it is I who begs your forgiveness. I should have given you a chance to explain."

When he opened his arms, she settled onto his lap and embraced him. They clung together, tightly bound. As his mouth inched close to hover over hers, she lifted her face. His lips descended on hers in a desperate, hungry kiss. She matched his moves, unable to tear away, wanting to keep the world at bay so they could have a few moments together.

A hard object jabbed her leg. Was that his arousal, or his sword? A glance downward showed the corner of a book sticking from his pocket.

"Is that what I think it is?" She broke off and stood, smoothing down her clothes.

"Yes, I got the artifact, and you retrieved me just in time. How did you figure out what to do?" Magnor scrambled to his feet.

"I'll tell you later." She picked up his backpack off the floor where she'd dropped it along with her handbag. "Let's go back to the house and talk. I want to hear all about your experience."

Relaxing in her living room, she listened while Magnor related his tale. Any thoughts of a more intimate reunion fled when a banging noise sounded on the front door. At the same time, Erika's ears buzzed.

"We have company."

Magnor leapt up from his chair. "Take us to my team using your transport device. We must give Nira this book to translate."

The banging turned into a series of crashes as if someone were applying an axe to the door. Why hadn't the Trolleks vectored directly inside her house? She glanced at the sculptures displayed on her shelves. Perhaps they shielded her.

Shield Maiden.

The thought came unbidden into her mind. Or had she heard it spoken? No one else was present in the room with them, so why did she feel as if they weren't alone?

Wait, wasn't shield maiden was another name for a

Valkyrie, the warrior women who guided dead soldiers to Odin's hall at Valhalla?

Perhaps one of their kind had selected Magnor, to take him there if he didn't survive his quest. Or maybe the opposite was true. A Valkyrie, like a guardian angel, was protecting them.

Does it matter? Get us out of here.

As Magnor instructed, she gripped his arm and focused on their destination.

When they arrived, it wasn't to any familiar location. They stood in a tropical jungle with raucous bird cries and crickets singing a chorus as stars twinkled in the night sky. Thick foliage surrounded them while a spicy scent permeated the moist air.

"Where are we? This doesn't look like Florida. That's where I meant to bring us."

"You were thinking of my team so we must have come here for a reason." Magnor took out his PIP and did a few quick calculations. "We're on a Pacific island with imminent volcanic activity. I'm reading body heat signatures up ahead about five klicks away."

A tremor shook the ground, startling them both.

"What's that?" She glanced around, but it was difficult for her to make out shapes in the dark.

"This area is volatile. We should move on. I'll check in with my team to make sure they are here."

"Join us as fast as you can," Zohar's terse voice said in response to his hail.

They made slow progress through the jungle. Sharp tapered leaves slashed at them, and sticky webs clung to their skin.

Erika shuddered to think what creatures might live in this steamy place, ready to drop onto her head. At least she'd had the foresight to change into sneakers back home. She hoped the dead leaves underfoot didn't hide any snakes.

In the lead, Magnor pushed aside overhanging branches and vines. A screeching noise came from above, making her wonder if monkeys inhabited the trees.

She rubbed her aching forehead. If only she could sleep for a few more hours, she'd feel better. Those catnaps she'd taken had helped, but they didn't lessen her overall fatigue. Unfortunately, time was of the essence. Enemy troops would be gathering for battle, and warriors didn't have the luxury of rest.

Did that include her, now? Had she graduated to warrior status with the rest of her legendary sisters?

She supposed so. People could fight with skills other than combat. Pride straightened her spine. She'd do whatever it took to fulfill her part in the prophecy.

Magnor's eyes glowed, his night vision active as he led the way. She yielded to his sense of direction and the compass on his PIP.

The ground shook again as though the ancient gods were angry at their intrusion. Or was it Loki preparing to launch Ragnarok with a catastrophic eruption?

They kept on for what seemed like hours, but her watch said only ninety minutes had passed. She yelped at a sudden howl coming from the vegetation. Hopefully, they wouldn't meet any of the larger wildlife.

Several feet further, Magnor halted so abruptly that she bumped into him.

"There, up ahead. Do you see it?" His deep voice resonated in the dark.

She could barely make out a structure among the shadows. A low whistle sounded.

Magnor whistled back.

Zohar emerged from the jungle, a grin splitting his face. The two men clasped each other's shoulders in greeting.

"You made it! Welcome to the temple. This is the island where Nira and I landed after we fell through the mirror." Zohar saw Erika's questioning glance. "That's a story for later."

"I thought we were regrouping on Togura Island?" Magnor said.

"This turns out to be the site where we must chant the rune

to banish Loki. Unlike last time, we are better prepared to face any hostile natives. No one has shown up so far."

"I have the book." Magnor withdrew the ancient text and handed it to his commanding officer. "Nira will need to translate the language. It looks runic in origin."

"The ladies are inside. We are fortunate that part of this temple is still standing with its walls and roof. Erika, it is good to see you again."

"Thanks. You, too." Sparing a glance at the pillars that dotted the grounds and the offerings of fresh fruit in an altar-like alcove, Erika darted ahead and climbed the stairs to the temple's gaping entrance.

Inside, electric lights were strung overhead to provide illumination. Wires led to a mobile generator that hummed in the background. The interior wasn't immune to the ravages of time. Vines intruded into cracks and crevices, while piles of rubble dotted the floor.

A couple of the guys huddled around a laptop, studying the screen, while the women conferred over a collection of documents laid out on a marble slab. Yaron's lady wasn't there. Perhaps she'd stepped outside or into another chamber.

"Erika, you're finally here." Nira welcomed her with a smile and a wave. "Come on over."

Zohar handed Nira the book. "Here, see if you can find mention of the weapon. We don't have much time."

After exchanging news, Nira suggested Erika get some rest. She was happy to comply and found some bedding set up in a corner. Allowing the others to worry about their next move, she stretched out and shut her eyes.

Her thoughts drifted to Magnor and his tender touch. That happy notion brought a smile to her lips and eased her into a dreamless sleep.

****

"Guys, I've got it. Come and take a look," Nira cried.

The men hurried over. Magnor assumed a place at his captain's side.

"What have you learned?" Zohar asked, his face eager.

She pointed to the book spread out on the marble slab that served as a table. "This verse claims the light of day turns Trolleks into stone."

"That's unlikely, since they live among us in broad daylight. Even Jak'Tar has cycles like ours."

"I believe it means that a certain frequency of light can adversely affect them." Nira crooked her finger at Kaj, their engineer. "Explain about the spectrum."

Kaj plowed his fingers through his unruly hair. "The visible spectrum is the light we can see. The electromagnetic spectrum includes near infrared, medium range wavelengths, and a longer infrared range. These are not visible to us."

"Like ultraviolet light?" Magnor said for clarification.

"Right. That has a shorter wavelength compared to visible light. Some insects, like bees, can see it."

Zohar rounded on Nira. "How does this help us? Are we to flash a light in a Trollek's eyes to subdue him? That makes no sense."

"I'm not sure yet, but I feel we're on the right track."

Turning back to the book, she compressed her lips, while Magnor glanced in the corner where Erika rested. She needed sleep, so he resisted the urge to check on her.

His gaze swung toward the temple's open entry. If they were all inside, who was standing watch? Had Zohar set a guard, or had he been too distracted? They were vulnerable here, all gathered in one place.

"Tell me," Zohar said to him aside from the others, "how did you acquire the book? What happened since we last saw you?"

Magnor related their adventures. Then Zohar took a turn filling him in on the team's progress.

Finally, Magnor glanced toward the entrance again. Unease clawed at him. "Shall I take a look outside, sire? Or did you post guards?" Perhaps Zohar had deployed their allies for that duty.

"Go ahead. I set a perimeter alarm but getting a visual is a good idea."

"Hey, I've found something," Nira called before Magnor headed away. "I thought the book binding felt too rigid. This object was hidden inside the spine." She held up a crystal rod in her hand. "I believe this is the weapon we were meant to find."

The crystal's polished facets reflected light in rainbow colors. Red, green and blue beams shot across the room, dancing on the walls.

"What is it?" Zohar said with a perplexed frown.

Kaj's face lit with excitement. "It's a prism that disperses white light into different frequencies. We see them as bands of color, but in actuality, there are no such definite boundaries. The color spectrum is continuous."

Yaron veered their way and plucked the prism from Nira's fingers. "I can explain. Human retinas contain two types of cells, rods and cones. Rods function at night, while cones support daytime vision along with color perception.

"Three types of cones exist. Each one contains pigments activated when they absorb light. We perceive discrete bands of color as a result of these pigments because their responsiveness varies. For example, one pigment may be receptive to short wavelengths, another to medium ones, and the third to longer ranges."

"Can you speak more plainly?" Zohar shared an exasperated glance with Magnor. Combat strategy was more their thing than science.

"The Trolleks might be hypersensitive to a certain frequency, as Nira said earlier."

"If true, how does that work for us?"

Kaj stole the prism from the medic. "We have to adapt the idea on a larger scale. I'll need to tap into the global satellite system. I'm guessing the prism's harmonic resonance in combination with its refractory properties will do the job."

"Harmonic resonance? Do you mean sound?"

"That's correct. You know how the Trolleks dislike loud noises? Imagine the piercing note you get when you tap a crystal glass. Now magnify it."

"Can you access the satellite feed from here?"

"Aye, but the setup will only work after sunrise."

"What about Hel's army of dead walkers?" Magnor asked the engineer. "Do we have an anti-magnetic shield in case they show up?"

"I didn't finish it," Kaj replied, "and now this project takes priority."

"Get back to work." Zohar signaled the others. "Magnor and Dal, you're with me. We'll do sentry duty. Yaron, keep researching your antidote to the confounding spell. Paz, assist the others and contact me when Nira has pinpointed the site for the final ritual."

"Do you think people's minds will clear once we eliminate their puppet masters?" Paz asked with a hopeful lilt.

Yaron responded. "Chemical changes are responsible for the mental compliance. We need a treatment that blocks this interference. I'm almost finished refining my compound. If it works, we'll require a means of dispersal."

They split up. Magnor accompanied his team leader and their demolitions expert out a side opening that might have once held a door.

His muscles tensed. A pregnant silence alerted him that they weren't alone. He'd grown up surrounded by woods and knew the signs.

Zohar sniffed the environs. "Cors particles. Trolleks are vectoring in." The perimeter alarm sounded at the same instant that he drew his T-6 phase pistol.

Eager for battle, Magnor unsheathed his sword.

Chapter Twenty-Nine

Trolleks advanced from the jungle, mean looks on their ugly faces, axes and clubs in their hands. Some of them wore disruptors at their sides, likely the officers. Magnor debated using his invisibility shield to sneak around and attack them from behind, but their numbers were too great. As he, Zohar, and Dal stood their ground, more emerged from the foliage.

They lined up in battle formation but then inexplicably split into two rows. He saw why in another minute.

Down the center sauntered their self-proclaimed liege, their former chief scientist, Algie Morar. The blonde's glacial blue eyes lit upon her enemy.

"Prince Zohar, your cause is hopeless. Surrender now, and we can avoid bloodshed. We'll allow you and your paltry team to leave this planet."

"By what means?" Zohar squared his shoulders. "Not that I believe you," he muttered under his breath.

"You have a shuttle. Obtain orbit and call home for pickup. Oh, but I'll be keeping the ladies. They're valuable to me."

"No deal." Zohar stepped forward. "Do you truly think Loki would let your kind live when he unleashes his full power? He intends to kill everyone. Not a single dimension will remain unscathed if he succeeds in widening the dimensional drift."

He aimed his weapon at the Trollek queen. "How does he plan to do it since we sealed the rifts, eh? He cannot rely on a buildup of cors particles at the event horizon anymore."

Magnor glanced at him askance. The captain knew what

Loki had planned, so why question her? Ah, his prince must be stalling for time. He stole a look at the horizon. Was it his imagination, or could he distinguish a variation in the shades of gray?

Algie chuckled as the mountain rumbled and shook the ground. "When this volcano erupts, it'll set off a chain reaction underground. Fissures will expand and race outward. The seismic shock wave will vaporize this planet, crack open the space-time continuum, and free Loki from his prison."

"And you? You'll be killed when the Earth explodes."

"Loki promised to send us back to our dimension at the instant he's freed. He said he'd limit the destruction to protect us. We'll bring the women along. They can provide the genetic material we need to save our species. My original plan might still work with modifications."

"How do you think your king will react to your taking charge?"

She shrugged. "I'll deal with that when the time comes."

Zohar jabbed his forefinger at her. "Loki's actions will set off a shock wave, true. But it will reverberate throughout the multiverse and wipe every dimension from existence. He means to rule over the ensuing chaos. Your world will not escape his wrath."

"Liar. We are chosen to survive. You, on the other hand, are useless to us. This is your last chance to lay down your weapons and to peacefully retreat to your shuttle."

"Do not listen to her false promises," a female voice said from behind.

Magnor spun around to view a consortium of people who'd arrived. Edith, the rune caster. Sylvia, the girl who'd assisted Erika at their Vegas wedding. Dikibie, the old man with a beard. And Imogene, former prisoner of the dwarfs. The Gatekeepers had come to their aid.

A whupping noise sounded in the background. Helicopters churned into view, spotlights aimed below searching for landing sites. Kaj must have called for reinforcements from world governments. Zohar had known Loki's minions would oppose them and had probably given Kaj the order upon their arrival.

But the enemy had allies of their own. Hel didn't let her demonic father down. As Magnor watched, dozens of dead walkers shimmied from the ground, their skeletal hands holding pitchforks, shovels, and sledgehammers.

And then suddenly the lines blended. Magnor swung his sword, slashing at one beast's throat and stabbing another one's vitals on the backswing. From the corner of his vision, he saw Smitty the dwarf running out to join them from behind the temple. A force of angry dwarfs brandishing gold daggers swarmed alongside him, as did a contingent of Grotes led by Ribald.

The sides engaged, while more friends and enemies joined the battle. Uniformed soldiers, disgorged from the helicopters, charged into the fray.

Magnor's momentary distraction cost him a gash on his forearm. With a growl of rage, he hacked at the ghost fighters aiming to maim him so they could suck the iron from his blood.

His sword thrusts pushed them back but then a couple of Trolleks came at him. He'd meant to guard Zohar, engaged in fighting the monstrous wolf, Fenrir, who had bounded from the jungle. Meanwhile, the mountain rumbled and spewed steam into the lightening sky.

A club struck him on the side of his head, and he staggered back. Momentarily stunned, he didn't duck in time when a Trollek sped forward in a blur of speed and knocked him to the ground. His teeth rattled, and his senses reeled. He'd dropped his sword. He scrabbled for it in the dirt, dodging as the beast tried to jab him with a shock stick.

He swung his feet behind the Trollek's ankles and yanked him off balance. When the beast crashed to the ground, Magnor rolled atop him. At the same time, he pulled a knife from the Trollek's belt and drove it into his foe's armpit, a vulnerable spot for their species. He twisted the blade, pulled it out, and stabbed it next into taut thigh muscle.

As the beast writhed in agony, he leapt up to fight off another one stalking him from behind. A series of kicks kept the Trollek at bay until Magnor was able to dive for his sword. He came up with a lunge into the beast's gut.

So far, their allies had managed to keep the Trolleks from accessing the temple, but soon they'd tire in the face of such overwhelming numbers. Hel's supply of dead walkers was unending, but he had an idea. In the underworld, they'd used a bridge to cross the river.

What if they needed that for more reasons than avoiding the fast current? Could the walking dead have an aversion to water?

On the one hand, his team needed the sunlight. On the other, they could use a rain cloud.

What would the two produce together?

A rainbow.

The proverbial light bulb exploded in his head. He had to tell Zohar.

Fighting his way over, he downed a couple of more Trolleks until he reached his prince's side. Zohar was holding his own, a bevy of bodies lying at his feet. The wolf had vanished. Had he been recalled by his demonic father?

"As soon as the sun comes up, we need it to rain." Magnor wielded his sword against another onslaught.

"What? We need the sunlight to hit the satellites. Kaj will have tilted the array in that direction."

"Yes, but the rain may dispel Hel's creatures and produce the prism effect. We only need it locally. The satellites will cover the rest of the globe."

"Go inside. Tell Yaron to send the shuttle to seed the atmosphere. That should work."

Magnor turned to follow orders but Algie, who'd been fighting a cluster of dwarfs, threw them off and charged him. With a snarl of rage, she swiped at his eyes with her sharp fingernails.

Ducking sideways, he slashed at her with his sword. She dodged the blow. He twirled, aiming for an upper thrust, but she was too fast. She sped behind him in a blur and drew her disruptor. He jumped aside as the beam sizzled through the air. He'd evaded it by a hairsbreadth, but a squeal told him someone else had taken the hit.

A flash of brightness in the distance drew everyone's attention. An arch of fiery lava had erupted from the volcano, ending in a string of fire. It wouldn't be long before the entire top blew off. Ash floated in the air like gray snowflakes, visible now as the sky brightened.

Zohar pushed him aside to engage Algie in combat, allowing Magnor a window in which to sprint up the steps and inside the temple. Nira huddled over the Book of Odin, while Kaj worked on the portable computer. Paz stood guard, his phase weapon aimed at the entrance.

"Lord Magnor, how goes the battle?" Paz said, his face grim. "I should join you."

Magnor waved a hand. "You're needed here. Stay and protect the women. Our allies have enlarged our ranks. Kaj, listen to me." He explained his theories.

"You're right. That may work." Kaj altered his settings. "I've signaled the shuttle, and I've set the trajectory of the satellites. My job here is done." He shoved back his chair and stood, collecting his weapon. "Now I can fight the enemy with you, brother."

"Dawn has broken. The sky is lightening. It won't be long now before our plan goes into motion." Magnor turned toward the exit, but Lianne's soft voice stopped him.

"Seeding the clouds isn't necessary. My power involves water. I can bring the rain here faster."

He spun around. Dal's woman looked sweetly innocent with her long, wavy hair and flowing dress, but Magnor knew she would possess an inner strength like the other Earth women in the prophecy. He had no doubt she could accomplish what she said.

"Zohar's orders stand. None of you women is to leave this shelter. If you can manage from here, do so. Otherwise, we'll carry out our plan as arranged." The sounds of men grunting, weapons clashing, and the mountain rumbling drew him outside.

Lifting his bloodied sword, he engaged the enemy. With combatants all around, he couldn't spot Zohar, but he saw Dal lying on the ground. He hacked and thrust his way over, crouching for a quick feel at the fallen man's neck. Relief washed through him. Dal had taken disruptor fire, but he lived.

As the sinewy warrior groaned, Magnor jumped up to fight a cluster of dead walkers thirsting for blood. Their numbers kept coming. He saw Zohar, who fended off two Trolleks, kicking at them and dodging their blows.

Allied troops from the world's armed forces battled Hel's ghost fighters, but as soon as they hacked the head off one, two more shimmied from the ground.

Magnor lunged at a Trollek who'd cut down a dwarf. He had just taken care of the fellow when a phase beam sizzled past his ear. He whirled around. Dal had shot an enemy soldier who'd swung an axe at him from behind.

Yaron, who'd come outside to fight alongside his brethren, hastened to the fallen warrior's side. He hauled Dal toward the temple entrance. Magnor and the other Drift Lords fought their way free to join him.

Zohar's mouth thinned, his expression somber. Sweat ran in rivulets down his face. Blood smudged his belted black tunic.

"Nira, how are you ladies progressing?" he hollered toward the interior.

Nira appeared in the open doorway. "We're ready. I know where we have to go, but we need a clear path." She gazed beyond them and paled. "Oh, no, is that Edith? She's been hurt." Nira dashed forward before they could stop her.

Magnor sensed movement in the periphery of his vision and ducked, avoiding a blow from a spiked club. As he fought another agile beast brandishing a shock stick, a herd of Trolleks darted past and inside the temple.

He parried his assailants' attack and sprinted after the troops. They'd rushed Paz, who battled them in close combat.

The women, including Erika, had grabbed whatever tools were handy and joined the fight. Alarm mingled with pride as he watched Erika swing a canteen and bash a Trollek on the head. The beast stumbled back but then came at her again with a snarl.

Yaron's woman interceded. He hadn't seen her among their group earlier, but she fought fiercely holding a round shield and short sword that she knew how to wield.

Lianne had retreated to a corner. Her arms raised, she muttered like an ancient priestess.

As the first rays of sunlight pierced the interior, Magnor tuned out the grunts of pain, clash of weapons, and howls of rage. He focused on the sweet sound of rain splashing down, splattering onto the ground and through the holes in the roof.

Had that been Lianne's doing? A smile played about her mouth as their glances met.

Wanting to know what was happening outside, he crossed to the entrance and stood under its arch. His gaze lifted to the sky where rain clouds dumped their moisture.

Along with the rain came a sulfuric smell as droplets mixed with ash. He retreated to shelter as the acidic rain poured down, turning the ground into mud. When it hit the dead walkers, the rain sizzled. With a unified shriek, Hel's soldiers crumpled where they stood and dissolved into dust. Rivulets of water washed the remnants away.

Algie approached, shoving Zohar ahead of her at the point of a disruptor. "Fighting us is useless. We still outnumber your forces. Surrender now, or we'll raze your hiding place to the ground along with everyone in it."

"You're the one whose reign is ending," Zohar replied.

Magnor spied the prism that Kaj had fastened to the top of a column. The crystal protruded through a gap in the roof. As a sunbeam hit its apex, a burst of brilliant colors radiated throughout the room and into the sky.

Algie stood transfixed, staring at the prism. An eerie glow enveloped her. Her mouth opened, but she didn't have the chance to cry out before her skin turned the color of alabaster and hardened into stone.

Then a single musical note pierced the air. The ear-splitting sound continued as the Drift Lords and their women covered their ears.

The newly formed stone cracked like brittle candy. This same fate happened to the other Trolleks inside the ruined temple.

One by one, the beasts turned solid and cracked into pieces that blew away on the wind.

The singular note dissipated.

Magnor plunged outside, where the same effect had occurred throughout the jungle. Kaj's satellite network must have reproduced the phenomenon around the world. A breeze rustled the tree branches and swept away the rain. The clouds cleared as sunlight broke through.

His teammates joined him. Together, they stood on the steps in awestruck silence.

Another tremor shook the earth, and the crater coughed globs of molten rock into the air. Magnor's peripheral vision picked up movement, and he whipped around, thrusting his sword just as Fenrir, the wolf, pounced at Zohar.

His blade plunged into the monster's flesh. With an agonized cry, the creature tumbled to the ground.

Magnor dismounted the stairs, withdrew his weapon and wiped it clean on the animal's fur. Pride swelled his chest. He'd saved his future king as he'd been hired to do.

"Good work." Zohar slapped his shoulder. "Let's get our gear and move out, people, before anything else surprises us."

As his team hustled to obey, Zohar conferred with their friends. Magnor overheard him telling them to return home and assess the results. The Trolleks should be gone across the globe.

"What about the souls turned by those creatures?" asked an army colonel.

Yaron stepped forward. "Once our new cruiser arrives, I can synthesize the compound I've refined as an antidote. In the meantime, spread the word that a pandemic virus is affecting people. This rumor will account for any erratic behavior by confounded individuals."

Nira bustled toward them, tear tracks marring her cheeks. "The earthquakes are getting worse. We need to reach the mountain, or Loki might still win."

"How is Edith?" At Nira's sad shake of her head, Zohar patted her arm. "I am sorry. She will be missed." He turned to the assembled fighters, his resonant tone commanding attention. "Our loyal friends, we thank you for your assistance this day. You joined us in battle as promised, and we have triumphed because of you. We can carry on from here but know that you have our eternal gratitude."

Sylvia sidled up to Magnor and pointed to his gold wedding band. "Remember your amulets, Drift Lords. They will protect you from the demon's power."

"We regret Edith's death," Zohar told her.

"She did her duty. Now complete your destiny without further delay, Captain."

"Do you wish us to bury her?"

"No, use the setting on that weapon of yours. She'd want it that way."

Zohar vaporized the body while they all stood around. The Gatekeepers muttered a prayer in a strange tongue as Nira sniffled. Then after a final farewell, their guardians walked into the jungle and vanished from view.

By the time his team had packed their equipment and shouldered their backpacks, their allies had gone.

Magnor searched for Erika in the commotion, relieved to find her in Lianne's company. Needing her close in the aftermath of battle, he strode in her direction.

"Ah, Magnor, there you are. I was telling Lianne that Dal will be fine, but he can't stay here to rest. We have to bring him along. Nira specifically said the incantation requires all twelve of us."

"I can manage." Dal's gruff voice made their heads turn. His pallor attested to the effort it had taken him to rise. "Yaron used a tissue regenerator where the disruptor got me. I can keep up."

Lianne hurried over, putting an arm around his waist for support. "Are you sure? I know you act tough, but this is one time when you're going to accept help."

Zohar gathered everyone into a circle. "Where do we go from here?" he addressed Nira.

The redhead waited until she had their full attention. "When Zohar and I first landed on this island, it held green-covered mountains. We didn't realize this range had volcanic origins. The other side of the island probably shows more evidence of former blasts. That's where we're going."

"What if we don't make it there in time?" Zohar asked.

Nira regarded him as a teacher to her student. "Two types of eruptions can occur. One is a benign flow of lava, like a slow-moving stream. The other is a huge blowout. When magma rises but its access to the surface is blocked by rock, internal pressure builds up. Eventually, this magma bursts through the mountaintop in a violent explosion.

"So we can expect a concussive wave?"

"In a way. The eruption propels ash, cinders, and molten rock into the air so fast that it causes a sonic boom. The debris cloud mushrooms upward and spreads. But the fallout from this cloud is much worse."

"Wasn't Mount Vesuvius at Pompeii this type of disaster?" Erika asked in a squeaky tone.

"That's right." Nira surveyed each one of them in turn. "The fallout will contain pumice stones riddled with holes and superheated rocks that can pile as high as nine feet. These will bombard the earth, but that's not the only danger. When the cloud collapses, it'll create a pyroclastic surge that shoots out sideways and spreads for miles. Picture a dark cloud with superheated temperatures and filled with choking ash racing at you like a tsunami."

"Good Lord," someone in their group murmured.

"I'm not done." Nira jabbed a finger in the air. "The ash and debris will mix with moisture in the air, causing thunderstorms along with mudflows known as lahars. This planet will perish from fire and floods and choking clouds of ash. The shock wave will not only crack open Loki's prison, but it'll widen the dimensional drift as he wanted all along."

Magnor gave a low curse. "And you believe we can stop him?"

"The words we chant together will counter his power and force him back to his prison. As for the eruption, if we can turn it from a massive explosion to a lava flow toward the sea, we'll relieve the pressure in a benign manner."

The earth shuddered, and a column inside the temple crashed to the ground. They jumped aside as a fissure opened, issuing forth noxious vapors into the air.

Zohar gestured to his team. "Time to move, people."

****

Erika clutched Magnor's arm as another tremor shook the earth. Visions of fiery plumes, choking ash, and scalding rocks made her heart race with dread. She'd been fascinated by Pompeii and the sequence of events that had buried the ancient city. Was the whole of humanity doomed to a similar fate?

She didn't want to die without telling Magnor how she felt about him.

He gave her a reassuring smile as they began their trek through the jungle toward the volcano.

"Listen, we didn't get to finish our talk back at my house." She glanced around to see if they could be overheard, but the other Drift Lords were busy with their own concerns.

"We've been occupied. We have eliminated the Trolleks on

this side of the rift, and now we know how to deal with them if they ever breach the barrier again. But our battle isn't over."

"I know." This may not be the best time to air her feelings, but she couldn't let things go unsaid between them. "Look, I apologize again for not telling you about my trust fund. I really do want to give our marriage a chance. If it makes you feel better, I'll refuse my inheritance."

She'd thought about it long and hard, and that was the only offer she could make that would show him how she felt. Maybe they'd be short on money for a while, but she could apply for a scholarship to the local college and earn her education degree that way. And she still had her pottery studio.

What did she need a gift shop for, anyway? To give her an excuse to travel and buy interesting objects around the world? She sucked in a breath, realizing that had been part of her dream all along. She'd felt confined, stuck in a rut. Expanding her business and furthering her education were a way out. They were also a means to earn her family's respect, but she'd had their affection all along without realizing it.

Nor would marriage tie her down. Magnor could take her places she'd never thought to visit. With him, she could travel the stars.

He completed her and made her feel cherished. She'd be lost if he abandoned her after all they'd experienced together. Erika clung to his arm as though the physical contact would convince him to remain.

"You would give up your family's money for me?" A muscle in his jaw twitched as he gave her a sideways glance.

"If you'd decide to stay as a result, yes, I would."

"I see." His lips compressed, and he maintained his forward pace.

Maybe she'd been wrong about him. Maybe he didn't really care about her at all. His mission was what mattered, and she'd merely been a tool to that end. As soon as they vanquished Loki, he'd be free to leave.

Except, his people had cast him out, and he had nowhere to go. She could create a home for him here and be a loving wife.

Dear Lord, did she love him? Was that why her gut churned and her pulse beat an erratic rhythm in her throat?

"This isn't the time or place to discuss our future," he said without meeting her eyes. "Your safety is paramount. Promise me you will stay out of harm's way."

Her stomach sank. The man only wanted her to play her role in the prophecy. Then he'd tell her to take a hike.

Pride made her give a cool response.

"Sure, husband, I promise not to be a bother." She doubted he knew the meaning of her crossed fingers behind her back.

Chapter Thirty

Magnor felt bad about his curt reply, but he couldn't lose his focus. Nor did he want to worry about Erika in the heat of battle. If this meant turning her away so she'd be safe when the time came, so be it. Yet it broke his heart to see the hurt and disappointment on her face at his cold answers.

Had she been sincere when she'd offered to refuse her inheritance for his sake?

Hope swelled in his chest. Her presence brightened his life. Her bravery and resilience made him proud. He wanted to shout to the heavens how much he needed her.

With her by his side, he no longer felt adrift. He could make a new home here and get a job in security. He'd study their justice system and pursue the goals that had become evident to him in Hel's domain.

Magnor purposefully avoided looking in Erika's direction, or he'd come undone and confess his dreams for the future.

How ironic that they were the only married couple among their group, and yet they knew each other the least. Assuming they survived the coming ordeal, he would admit his plans to her later.

They followed a dry riverbed, muddy from the rain. After hiking for miles, they began to climb the mountainous slope. Dense vegetation inhibited their progress. Ash coated their hair, gray flakes that mixed with moisture in the humid air to make a slimy sludge.

It took them hours to trek uphill toward the volcano. By

then, the afternoon sun had dimmed behind a veil of ash. Finally, the dense jungle gave way to a cindered plain that stretched several miles across. Purple orchids on green stalks dotted the black soil along with the occasional fern, the only splashes of color on this bleak site.

They crunched over the flat surface, sooty grit covering them along with the ash that clogged their nostrils. Magnor wished they'd thought to bring filtration masks, but his team had limited supplies. By the time their warship arrived, it would be too late.

He glanced at Erika, whose red curls had become whitened from the ash fall. Like the other women, her face was pinched but she didn't complain. He knew Zohar wasn't pleased about their presence under these dangerous conditions, but they were essential to fulfilling the prophecy.

"Let's stop here and rest a minute." Zohar raised his hand to call a halt to their group.

They separated into couples and found rocky outcroppings on which to perch. A brief repast of water and nutrient bars refreshed them, but the recent battle and the climb had left them weary. No one seemed in a hurry to move until another tremor shook the ground with a spurt of fiery lava beyond.

"Let's finish this, people." Zohar unwound his legs and stood. The rest followed suit.

Magnor helped Erika to rise, his hand lingering on her arm. Their gazes locked.

"We'll be fine," he said in a reassuring tone.

He wished to ease the anxiety in her eyes, but his heart felt heavy. Loki was awakening to his power. He could sense it in the ominous glow that lit the distant ridge and in the hot wind that howled across the cinders.

On the plain's distant edge, globs of molten rock tossed into the air along with noxious gas clouds. The volcano belched, spouting forth a black plume. He tasted sandy grit on his tongue. With a last glance into Erika's troubled green eyes, he let her go and drove forward to the battle ahead.

****

Erika's limbs weighted with fatigue as she trudged along, careful to avoid the charcoal-sized rocks that flew like miniature bombs through the air. Her eyes stung, and her lungs burned. She supposed it didn't matter if they choked on the ash particles obscuring the air. Soon they might be dead anyway.

Nira said they had to get within sight of the demon before they could work their spell. From the way things were going, very likely he'd spit lava at them and they'd be incinerated before the words left their lips.

A vent issued a thick gaseous cloud ahead. She held her breath and shut her eyes until they'd pushed past it.

No one spoke in the hour or so it took to cross the plain. Her dry throat craved another drink, but she dared not stop.

Beyond the far rim was a drop into the crater. A cliff rose on the opposite side, shaped by a former blast. Erika's heart lodged in her throat at the sight of the fiery pit below. It glowed like an eye into hell. Bubbles of lava popped and dissolved, leaving strings of fire in their wakes. Rumbling booms rolled across the ledge where Erika and their team huddled.

"We have to get closer." Nira pointed to a spot below that Erika could barely see through the clouds of swirling steam.

Her pulse raced and her stomach spasmed. Descend into a volcano? Surely, they would perish!

Nonetheless, she gamely followed Magnor and the others as they scooted over black cinders, crossed more ridges, and dodged piles of rock. Acidic gas bit into her nose and made her eyes water. The air smelled of sulfur.

A roar hit her ears as the volcano exhaled. With each puff, it superheated the air. Her ears popped from changing pressures. Dark silhouettes of bats flew overhead. They must be drawn to the lava glow, she thought with a grimace.

They climbed down a ridge, careful to avoid the edge that plummeted to the crater. Pumpkin-sized globs of molten material leapt into the air. Fiery filaments strung off from them, cooling in the updraft and creating glassy threads carried by the wind.

She remarked about the varied colors inside the cone. "It's beautiful in an awesome sort of way."

"Sulfur coats the rocks and gives it that yellowish tint," Yaron explained. "Those other sections are bright orange due to iron, while manganese near the vents causes the dark green. Other sections have been bleached white by chlorine gas."

Careful not to dislodge any loose boulders, Erika soldiered on. The incessant wind and crumbly surface made their path more treacherous. Gusts so strong they could knock one over whipped by. They crossed a narrow ledge within a few feet of a sheer drop. Dark clouds swirled past, while sometimes the fog was so thick it obscured the trail.

Step-down ledges led lower. She could barely breathe, gasping in pants of air and wishing this nightmare would end. Then again, she could always give herself the breath of life if her throat clogged on the grit. Magnor hadn't asked again how she'd revived him, nor had she offered the information. They'd had other priorities.

A reddish glow from the pit below lit the rock face as they descended. Watching their footing, they climbed over rubble and avoided a fiery splash from a bubbling pool. Waves of hot, pressurized wind battered them as it blew past.

Finally, Zohar called a halt at a ledge overlooking the lava lake.

She peered at the cracked layer of crust that covered the crater's surface. Orange-red splatters burst into the air from molten rock that escaped confinement from below. When the full force of magma reached the surface, it would burst forth, incinerating everything in the vicinity.

As they regrouped, a high note pierced the air. Magnor shot a startled glance at Erika and then patted his pocket. He reached inside, bringing out the horn given to him by Imogene and holding it out for the others to see.

"Imogene, the Gatekeeper, gave this to me," he said after the horn silenced. "She said it would sound a warning when our true enemy was near."

Erika swung her gaze to the expanding lava lake. A face formed in the bubbling pool, a monstrous face with slanted eyes of fire and a slash for a mouth.

Nira gestured for the team to gather close. "Here, we can see Loki now. Form a circle."

Loki gave a roar of rage so loud Erika had to cover her ears. Fingers of lava emerged from the lake and shot bolts of energy at them.

The sizzling beams swerved around the tightly-knit group.

The gold medallion hanging from Zohar's neck gleamed brightly amid the reddish-orange glow of their surroundings. So did Paz's arm bracelet, Magnor's gold wedding ring, and similar items worn by the other Drift Lords.

Zohar addressed his team, speaking loudly to be heard over the background noise. "These amulets are protecting us as the Gatekeepers said they would. Nira, tell us what we must do to dispel the demon back to his prison."

Loki snarled and thrashed, spewing noxious fumes into the air in a flare of fire and smoke. He hurtled more bolts their way, along with molten rocks. His glistening red face twisted with fury. The ground shook violently as he tried to dislodge them from their perch. If the ledge crumpled, they'd fall to their doom.

"Everyone, join hands and repeat these words with me." Nira grasped Zohar's hand on one side and Paz's on the other.

"Silence is a treasure beyond words. From mountain, to plain, to sea, shall silence reign and discord be forever tamed." She followed with some words in a foreign tongue which they all intoned.

Loki flung blobs of lava their way. When the molten rocks curved around them, he bellowed his rage. Part of their ledge broke away and tumbled down the cliff, the chunks bouncing off the rock face until they crashed below.

"Odin, our All-Father, empower us with your wisdom and imbue us with Thor's strength so that we might enforce your sentence upon Loki, who cruelly caused the death of your beloved son, Balder."

A howl echoed across the great chasm, and Loki arose like a fiery demon from the pit. His open mouth spewed flame and his hollow eyes glowed with incandescent fury. He looked like Satan incarnate.

Erika heard his voice in her head.

"You puny humans will not stop me. You are nothing. I hold the power of the gods."

Nira raised her defiant face to regard him. "You were born of the frost giants, Loki. Don't you realize what fire does to ice? You'll melt into your own pool of evil."

"I use this form only to exact revenge on your forebears. When I am whole, I will tear apart the multiverse and their place in it."

"No, you won't." Another piece of their ledge cracked off and plunged down the cliffside. "Erika, use your power to secure our foothold while we chant the next verse," Nira directed her.

Clinging to Magnor's hand, Erika summoned her inner strength to bind together the molecules of black soil, ash, and cinder beneath their feet. The other women, awakened to their purpose, bolstered their defense.

Jen could manipulate fabrics. As she concentrated, strips tore off the hems of their clothing. They used this material to fashion masks over their noses and mouths to keep the ash from their lungs.

Maggie, who was Kaj's girlfriend, could work with metal. She extracted mineral ores from the rocks and designed them into spikes which she hurled at Loki.

Yaron's partner had power over fire. She deflected any balls of flame spiraling their way that weren't spawned by the demon. The men's amulets deflected his fiery missiles.

Lianne called forth water from the sea until a great spout

hooked over the ridge. She poured it onto the plain and into the crater where it gushed into the fire pit. Steam billowed into the air, while Loki screamed and railed at their defiance.

All the while, they chanted the ancient words Nira had interpreted from the runes.

A fissure split the crust, but instead of a massive explosion blasting into the stratosphere, lava oozed out in a widening stream that Yaron's woman directed toward the sea.

With an anguished cry, Loki reverted to his true form, a frost giant. Cracks appeared on his frozen skin. As they continued to chant, he collapsed into an expanding pool of fire.

Ripples spread outward from where he submerged. A wave of energy burst into the air and flung sideways in all directions.

"Now, Yaron," his girlfriend hollered.

Yaron stepped outside their circle, holding up something that almost looked like a dreamcatcher. What was he doing?

Erika's attention returned to the demon as Loki emitted a final, desperate howl. His horrified face sank below the surface, until nothing of his presence remained.

Quiet descended over the crater. The wind lessened. The fiery pops and sizzles decreased. The rumbling abated as the earth settled. Lava gushed down the cliff and out to sea, immolating everything in its path, but without the explosive cataclysm they'd expected.

The Drift Lords and their women broke apart, tore off their makeshift masks, and stared in wonder at nature's power.

Erika clutched Magnor's hand, stunned by the sudden silence. The phrase they'd chanted replayed in her mind.

Silence is a treasure beyond words.

Chapter Thirty-One

Back at the safe house in Florida, the team settled in the dining room for a debriefing before taking a much-needed break. Paz had summoned the shuttle to the cinder plain for pick up, and Erika had been glad to slump in her seat and close her eyes. Now she forced herself to full alertness at the table for their conference. Time for rest would come soon enough.

She cast a curious glance at Yaron. He hadn't explained his actions at the time of Loki's demise, and she wondered if it had anything to with the secret he, Kaj, and Dal were keeping from Zohar. That notion troubled her, but she'd discuss it with Magnor later.

"Seismic readings confirm that the volcano has stabilized." Kaj displayed a holographic image of the globe in the center where all could see. "The tectonic plates are settling, and the danger of more quakes has passed. The dimensional drift is within normal range."

"Thank the Creator." Zohar rubbed his stubbled jaw. "With the star cruiser arriving this week, Yaron can synthesize his antidote to the confounding spell. If this solution works, we can deploy it worldwide. Then I must return to Karrell. I shall expect you all to attend our wedding, directly following my coronation as emperor."

He smiled proudly at Nira, who gave him a silly grin in response.

"After we're married," the mythologist said with a twinkle in her eyes, "I'll come back to complete my doctorate degree. I've proposed setting up an Institute for Cultural Studies on Karrell. It can help foster understanding and tolerance among the different peoples in Zohar's empire."

Erika's heart squeezed. If only things were that simple for her and Magnor. They had yet to have a frank discussion about their relationship.

"Jen and I are staying here," Paz announced, kissing the fingertips of the svelte fashion designer at his side. "I've sent in my resignation to SattCom Networks. I'll work on my prototype for the nexus space relay until Jen's lease expires on her Manhattan apartment. Then we'll consider where to move." He beamed at her, his smile full of affection.

"Lord Magnor, what about you and Erika?" Zohar asked. "Your duties as Drift Lord don't apply during times of peace. Remember, though, that we meet at the Academy once a year for a review and training session."

Magnor stiffened, his eyes on his captain. "Sire, if you plan to expand enrollment, you'll need instructors. Perhaps I can—"

"Thank you, but no. Rule number one of the League is that your life is your own when our services are not required." His somber glance encompassed the others. "Up until now, our special ability to detect cors particles forced our participation. Our founders vowed that when off duty, we'd be free to follow normal pursuits. I'll hire instructors in the required disciplines for our new recruits."

Magnor's mouth tightened. "Then I'll go home with Erika, if she'll have me. I thought I would look for a job in security or maybe pursue a career in the justice system."

"That sounds like a plan." Erika's voice cracked. This was the first she'd heard of his thoughts for the future. It sounded as though he really meant to stay.

He gave her an oblique glance. "Are you sure? Because if you don't want—"

She touched his lips. "Of course, I want you to come home with me, husband." She flashed her diamond wedding ring for the others to see. "You're mine, and I'm not letting you get away."

"Kaj, Dal and Yaron, what will you do once you're dismissed from duty?" he asked them. "You still haven't told me how you all got together again and where you met your ladies."

Erika tickled his arm. He could probe into their business later. All she wanted was to get her caped warrior home alone. Besides, she had a feeling those three weren't done with their fight. She didn't want them to drag Magnor into it.

"Save it for next time," she said with a seductive smile. "I want to share my future plans with you." Scraping back her chair, she stood. "Come, I'll show you what I mean."

****

Erika turned off the shower spigot and stepped out for a quick towel dry. Then she reached for the outfit she'd bought for this occasion. Finally, she and Magnor had some privacy. She'd used her vector device to whisk them home to Arizona.

Magnor had dove into the shower while she phoned her parents to let them know she was okay. Then it had been her turn. She donned the silky fabric, fluffed her curly hair, and opened the door. Her feet padded on the carpet.

Magnor waited in the bedroom clad only in his briefs. He whirled at her approach, and his jaw dropped.

She wore a red teddy that barely covered her bosom and ended just below the juncture at her thighs. Magnor scanned her with a predatory gleam, like a wolf facing its prey.

Ugh, that brought to mind the image of Fenrir. Not a good analogy.

"What is this?" he said, his voice thick.

"This is my way of showing you how much I want you." She sauntered toward him, her hips swaying.

He took the bait and wrapped his arms around her. "Do you really wish me to stay?"

Erika's body fired at their points of contact. She wanted to rub herself up and down his hard form, take him inside her, and show him how much she cared.

"Yes, I want you to live here with me."

"Why is that?"

"Because..." Erika struggled to force the words out.

She wondered what was in his heart. Did he care enough to make their marriage real, to stick with her regardless of the hurdles they faced in the future?

Did he love her? Maybe her confession would spur his own.

His hand roamed to her breast, gently caressing her through the silken fabric of her teddy. She moaned when he stroked her with his thumb, the words almost spilling from her lips. Low in her belly, a kernel of need kindled into a spark.

"I want you to stay because I love you." Moisture tipped her lashes. There, she'd said it.

He drew in a sharp breath then pulled her closer to nuzzle her hair. "You are my beloved, now and for eternity. Do you accept me as I am?"

His words sounded familiar. Hadn't he said something similar before?

"I do. And do you promise the same for me? You'll stay with me through the good and the bad, through sickness and through health as in our vows?"

"Yes, my glorious bride." He muttered some words in a foreign tongue. "By this pledge, we are bound as one according to the customs of my people. I will make my place here. You are my home now."

"Oh, my dear lord." She kissed him passionately as her hands splayed across the broad planes of his back.

Setting her away at arm's length, he grinned down at her. "I'll share my last secret with you, wife. You've helped me restore my honor, and so you're earned the privilege of learning my name. My first name is Vil."

"Vil." She rolled it on her tongue and smiled at him through her tears. "Well, I have news for you, Vil. Your name is likely to be carried through to future generations."

His puzzled glance turned to one of joy as comprehension dawned. "You carry my babe?"

"It's possible. That time of the month is late, if you know what I mean."

He whooped and lifted her in the air. When she'd settled down, she raised her face toward him.

"I love you, Drift Lord."

"And I love you, my *knesta*." He kissed her hair, her eyelids, and her mouth. Then he nudged her toward the bed.

He might have come from the stars, but as Erika's body descended upon the mattress, she knew his soul was bound to earth with hers.

Their breaths mingled as they entwined their limbs and gave way to passionate abandon. No outside sounds intruded on their lovemaking.

The blessed silence was a treasure beyond words.

THE END

Author's Note

Initially, I'd meant for the Drift Lords saga to be a six-book series. But as I wrote the stories, I realized they needed to be told in chronological order. It turned out that Kaj, Yaron and Dal's stories ran parallel to books two and three in the first set. While the team might have defeated Loki by the end of this trilogy, another threat has emerged that hints at things to come. If you want these stories to be written, please write to me and leave reviews on the first three books to support this series. Meanwhile, I hope you'll check out my other scifi/fantasy romances such as the Light-Years series beginning with *Circle of Light*.

****

For updates on my new releases, giveaways, special offers and events, join my reader list at https://nancyjcohen.com/newsletter. Free Book Sampler for new subscribers.

Thank you for taking the time to read my book. If you enjoyed the story, please consider writing a review at your favorite online bookstore. Your recommendations are critically important in helping new readers find my work.

Rules of the Multiverse

Just as the Earth has tectonic plates, dimensional plates exist on a cosmic energy level. These fuel an electromagnetic grid that intersects at twelve distinct geographic areas. These points, known as Vile Vortices, are sites of anomalous activity. Twelve such locations exist around the world. The Bermuda Triangle is one of them. Rifts occur at these sites. The lines connecting these points are termed ley lines.

The dimensional plates are usually in alignment except for occasional drift. When the plates grind against each other, the resultant pressure forces open a door between dimensions. Normally, the event horizon at this natural rift produces a substance called cors particles. When their mass reaches a critical level, the resultant pressure forces the rifts to close.

The Trolleks have devised a means to force open the rifts and keep them from shutting down. With the portals remaining open, the accumulation of cors particles will breach the point of no return. The dimensional drift will widen, causing a massive shock wave that will destroy everything in existence. In the meantime, the Trolleks have invaded Earth with the goal of enslaving mankind.

Trollek males are super strong. They move with unusual speed and agility. Females lure victims with their beauty and compelling scent. All Trolleks secrete a chemical substance that directly alters the human brain. They transmit it through touch, via their palm. The confounded person follows orders from the Trollek who touched them. Confounding is irreversible and eventually causes amnesia or madness.

The Drift Lords polarize themselves against the Trollek mind touch. Each day after bathing, they shock themselves with a painful pulse emitter. Coating themselves with a permeable oil helps to mitigate the discomfort. The effects last twenty-four hours. They also use a nose numbing spray to ward off the alluring scent of a Trollek female. But the best method of protection is the immunity transferred by physical contact with their destined mate.

Their team is responsible for monitoring the time-space continuum and maintaining its integrity. They can detect cors emissions through their heightened sense of smell. This means they can tell when a Trollek does a vector shift or opens a portal. They cannot pinpoint the location. For this purpose, they use a device to track cors particles.

In *Warrior Prince*, they learn the Trolleks are shielding the cors particle emissions. The team must turn off the jammer in order to locate the main portal plus any other breeches the Trolleks have initiated. Then they must shut down the portals to stop the Trollek troops from coming through these rifts and invading our planet. As for the Trolleks who would be left stranded here, legend says there's a weapon that can defeat the enemy.

Glossary

ACTUATORS: Engine parts.

AESIR: The warrior gods in Norse mythology.

ALAMIR: A battle during the border dispute with the Morano Confederation.

ANRIAT: A planet with an unsavory underworld of criminals and desperadoes.

ASGARD: The celestial abode of the Aesir gods.

BERMUDA TRIANGLE: Also called the Devil's Triangle, this area in the Atlantic Ocean ranges from Bermuda to Puerto Rico to Miami. It is the site of anomalies where ships and planes disappear, and radios and compasses stop working.

BOGGER: Derogatory Trollek term for a female.

BORATUS WORMS: Creatures that bore into nerve ganglia.

CARONA: Karrellian term of endearment.

CAVENDII TWO: A military base of the Star Empire under command of Colonel Yaloom.

CORS PARTICLES: Matter produced at the event horizon of a dimensional rift.

DAZLITE: A thumb-sized pocket light.

DISRUPTOR: A hand weapon with two settings—stun and kill. Disrupts neural pathways. Used by planetary patrols and local military units for crowd control. May be assigned as a secondary weapon to ground troops, more often to officers. Class One military use restricted armament. Blue beam.

DOKTER: Trollek word for doctor.

DONIK: Curse word equivalent to bastard.

DONJON: Tower.

DRAGON'S TRIANGLE: Also called the Devil's Sea, this is an area in the Pacific basin southeast of Japan between Iwo Jima and Marcus Island that is the site of anomalies where ships and planes disappear, and radios and compasses stop working.

DRIFT LORD: A warrior who has the special ability to sniff cors particles and who is trained to fight Trollek incursions.

DRIFT WORLD: An adult role-playing theme park in Orlando, FL. "A place where your fantasy job becomes reality. Whatever part you want to play, it's yours for a day."

DROTT: Trollek military form of address for superior officer.

DWARFS: Short-statured men who live underground. They have pale faces and long beards. Skilled metalworkers and goldsmiths who craft magical items for the gods. Greedy fellows, they can make themselves invisible. Weakness: Their power is woven into their hair.

DYTHIUM CHARGES: Explosive compound.

EDDA: An epic of Germanic origin.

ELVES: Nocturnal beings that live in wooded areas. They enjoy dancing and gambling, but people who dance with them must be wary.

EMP GRENADE: A grenade that emits an electromagnetic pulse of a high intensity, short duration burst of electromagnetic energy.

EVENT HORIZON: Rift caused when dimensional plates grind against each other.

FAFNIR: A giant disguised as a dragon to guard his treasure.

FARARRA: A pleasure planet with resorts, emporiums, eateries, and entertainment complexes.

FENRIR: A son of Loki and a fire giant disguised as a wolf. He killed Odin at Ragnarok.

FOUNTAIN OF WISDOM: A source of water under the roots of the giant World Tree. Guarded by the god, Mimir.

GATEKEEPERS: Allies of the Drift Lords, these shapeshifters help protect humanity during Trollek incursions on Earth.

GIANT: According to Norse mythology, giants were the first living creatures. They have the gift of disguise. Two types: Fire Giants and Frost Giants.

GJOLL: A river in the underworld that souls must cross to reach Helheim.

GLITTER BUG: A lightning bug type insect on Paz's home world.

GRAND MARSHAL: Governor of Trollek towns. Addressed as "Your Eminence".

GRIMSHAW: Lord Magnor's name for his sword.

HAGRET: A bird with outstretched wings.

HAS'PUTE: A Karrellian curse word.

HEL: Goddess ruler of Helheim and Loki's daughter.

HELHEIM: The realm of the dead ruled by the goddess, Hel.

HERIS: Form of address for a Trollek landowner, second in rank to a Grand Marshal.

HYPERSPACE: Faster than speed of light travel via a distortion of the space-time continuum.

IMMOBILIZER: Stun weapon used by Star Empire military units in covert ops. Class Two restricted armament.

JADLOK: Elven liege of the lake's region.

JAK'TAR: The Trollek home world.

JAWANI: A standard universal language.

JORG: King of the Trolleks.

JORGONAUTS: Followers of the Trollek ruler, King Jorg.

KABAK: Trollek who commands a confounded human.

KAG: Man who likes boys.

KARRELL: Home world of Zohar Thorald and training ground for the Drift Lords.

KASH: A Trollek dice game.

KEWA STONES: Diamonds.

KIMMLEBUSH: A curse word in Dwarf language.

KLICK: A kilometer or approximately .6213 miles.

KNESTA: "Beloved" in Lord Magnor's tongue; a term of endearment.

LASER CARBINE: RAD-4 Rifle with enhanced infrared scanner; used by military troops.

LAVA BOMB: Explosive device, similar to a grenade.

LEERA: A term of endearment in Paz's native language.

LIEMA: A long-necked animal that moves with grace, native to Paz's home world.

LEY LINES: An energy grid intersects Earth at twelve distinct geographic points called Vile Vortices. Ley lines are the lines connecting these points of the electromagnetic field.

LEYTNANT: Officer in Trollek military force.

LOKI: Loki is a mischievous trickster and shapeshifter who was banished to an underground prison by the Norse gods. He is a malevolent being bent on revenge and galactic domination.

LOXOTAN: A painkiller.

LYTHIX SERUM: Truth serum used by the Trolleks.

MALNATIUM: A volatile but powerful energy producing compound.

MAUG: A curse word used as an adjective; a derogatory term.

MENIG: Lowest enlisted rank in Trollek military force.

MIDGARD: The middle land occupied by mankind in Norse mythology.

MIMIR: God who guards the Fountain of Wisdom.

MIMIR'S WELL: The Fountain of Wisdom guarded by the god, Mimir. This water supplies one of the roots of the great World Tree.

MIN DROTT: Trollek form of address for superior officer.

MINGLING: Sexual intimacy.

MJOLLNIR: Thor's magic hammer, forged by the dwarves. When thrown, it returns like a boomerang.

MODGUD: Giantess guardian of the bridge over the river Gjoll leading to Helheim.

MORABI NERVE JAB: A hand chop to a sensitive bundle of nerves.

MORANO CONFEDERATION: An alliance bordering the Star Empire.

MORATA: Paz's home world, a desert planet in the Zood System.

NEUTRINO: A small elementary particle that carries no electric charge.

NIDHOG: Dragon who gnaws on a root of the World Tree and guards the spring Hvergelmir.

NID RUNE: A curse.

NIFLHEL: A lower level of Helheim where the evil dead suffer endless torment.

NORNS: Three Goddesses of Fate who guard the Urd Well.

ODIN: Ruler of the Norse gods.

ORIGINALS: Early sentient beings who inhabited Earth.

PAMADORE: A type of poultry consumed on Karrell.

PFRELL: Flying creatures with sharp talons and spear-like beaks; a hunter species native to the Trollek world.

PHASE GUN: Type of energy weapon. The Drift Lords carry Monix T-6 laser pistols. Three settings—stun, kill, vaporize. Spare power packs (miniature energy cells) are carried in utility belt pouches. Older model: T-4, has to be reloaded more often.

PHASE RIFLE: Long-range version of above. Powered by portable energy converter.

PIP: Portable Intel Platform; handheld data unit with sensors and scanning capability. This device also has a levitator beam to move heavy objects.

POLARIZE: The means by which Drift Lords protect themselves from the Trollek spell.

PURPURA BLOSSOMS: A sweet- scented flower on Karrell.

RAGEESH: Honorary form of address for the Crown Prince of the Star Empire.

RAGNAROK: End of the world and destruction of the multiverse.

RIFF: Karrellian term for lowlife or thug.

SCREEN (verb): To hide from sight.

SHAPESHIFTER: Beings who can alter their form.

SHELL SHEDDER: Old-fashioned projectile weapons favored by the Trolleks. Drift Lords' lightweight clothing armor protects against these projectiles.

SHIRAJO MANOR: Trollek stronghold on Togura Island.

SHOCK STICK: Rod-like punishment device used by the Trolleks for slave control. It delivers a painful electric shock.

SIRE: Honorary form of address for royalty on Karrell.
SIRA: Honorary form of address for noble ladies on Karrell.
SKAP: Slang term for a Viden.
SLOGG: Trollek word for slave.
SMARK: A curse word in Paz's native tongue.
SNIPELING: A reptilian creature that lives in rock crevices. Poisonous venom.
SONIC GRENADE: Weapon used by Star Empire troops. It causes a blast of sonic waves.
SPATIAL SHIFT: Instantaneous transport from one place to another.
STAR EMPIRE: An alliance of sentient planets ruled by a hereditary Emperor.
TEECAHT: A derogatory name for a Trollek woman who steps out of bounds.
TENT TEN: Site of Trollek medical experiments on humans.
THOR: Warrior god of Norse legend who carries Mjollnir, a magic hammer.
THOR'S HAMMER: Thor's magical weapon, Mjollnir, returns to its thrower.
TROLLEK: Intelligent creatures derived from the Originals, the Trolleks revere nature, despise humans for chasing them from their land, and believe in taking by force what suits their needs.
UGRON: A grizzly bear-like creature.
URD WELL: Fountain of Youth protected by the Norns, its spring feeds the root on the World Tree that supports Midgard.
VALHALLA: Odin's hall where dead warriors reside and prepare for Ragnarok.
VALKYRIES: Warrior maidens of the god Odin, these women carry warriors who die in battle to Valhalla. Also called Shield Maidens.
VANIR: Norse gods who were farmers and merchants.
VECTOR: An invisible line on the time-space continuum.
VECTOR SHIFT: See spatial shift.
VEILED: Shielded from view.
VIDENS: Faction of Trolleks who support science instead of conquest as a solution to their problems.

VILE VORTICES: An energy grid beneath the earth's crust intersects the globe at twelve distinct geographic points called Vile Vortices. These are often sites of anomalous activity. Five each of these vortices are at an equal distance above and below the equator. Two are located at the north and south poles.

WAGMIRE: A type of rodent.

WIGONK: A domesticated canine on Karrell.

WONK: Trollek slang term for male appendage.

WORLD TREE: The great ash tree that connects all nine realms of the universe. Also called Yggdrasil.

YMIR: The first Giant in Norse mythology.

About the Author

Nancy J. Cohen writes the Bad Hair Day Mysteries featuring South Florida hairstylist Marla Vail. Titles in this series have been named Best Cozy Mystery by *Suspense Magazine*, won the Readers' Favorite Book Awards and the RONE Award, placed first in the Chanticleer International Book Awards and third in the Arizona Literary Awards.

Her nonfiction titles, *Writing the Cozy Mystery* and *A Bad Hair Day Cookbook,* have earned gold medals in the FAPA President's Book Awards and the Royal Palm Literary Awards, First Place in the IAN Book of the Year Awards and the *Topshelf Magazine* Book Awards. *Writing the Cozy Mystery* was also an Agatha Award Finalist.

Nancy's imaginative romances have proven popular with fans as well. These books have won the HOLT Medallion and Best Book in Romantic SciFi/Fantasy at *The Romance Reviews*.

A featured speaker at libraries, conferences, and community events, Nancy is listed in *Contemporary Authors, Poets & Writers*, and *Who's Who in U.S. Writers, Editors, & Poets*. She is a past president of Florida Romance Writers and the Florida Chapter of Mystery Writers of America. When not busy writing, Nancy enjoys reading, fine dining, cruising, and visiting Disney World.

Follow Nancy Online

Website – https://nancyjcohen.com
Blog – https://nancyjcohen.com/blog
Twitter – https://www.twitter.com/nancyjcohen
Facebook – https://www.facebook.com/NancyJCohenAuthor
LinkedIn – https://www.linkedin.com/in/nancyjcohen
Goodreads – https://www.goodreads.com/nancyjcohen
Pinterest – https://pinterest.com/njcohen/
Instagram – https://instagram.com/nancyjcohen
BookBub – https://www.bookbub.com/authors/nancy-j-cohen

Books by Nancy J. Cohen

The Bad Hair Day Mysteries
Permed to Death
Hair Raiser
Murder by Manicure
Body Wave
Highlights to Heaven
Died Blonde
Dead Roots
Perish by Pedicure
Killer Knots
Shear Murder
Hanging by a Hair
Peril by Ponytail
Haunted Hair Nights (Novella)
Facials Can Be Fatal
Hair Brained
Hairball Hijinks (Short Story)
Trimmed to Death
Easter Hair Hunt
Styled for Murder
Star Tangled Murder

The Drift Lords Series
Warrior Prince
Warrior Rogue
Warrior Lord

Nancy J. Cohen

Science Fiction Romances
Keeper of the Rings
Silver Serenade

The Light-Years Series
Circle of Light
Moonlight Rhapsody
Starlight Child

Nonfiction
Writing the Cozy Mystery
A Bad Hair Day Cookbook

Order Now at https://nancyjcohen.com/books/

9 781952 886348